OMNIBUS

VOLUME II

Published by Dark Titan Entertainment.

Day of Octagon, Crossbreed, and Heaven's Called available separately in hardcover and eBook.

Also in hardcover format.

Dark Titan Universe is a branch of Dark Titan Entertainment.

First Printing 2020.

ISBN: 978-1-7359429-6-4

darktitanentertainment.com

WORKS BY TY'RON W. C. ROBINSON II

BOOKS

DARK TITAN UNIVERSE SAGA

MAIN SERIES
Dark Titan Knights
The Resistance Protocol
Tales of the Scattered
Tales of the Numinous
Day of Octagon
Crossbreed
Heaven's Called

SPIN-OFFS
In A Glass of Dawn: The Casebook of Travis Vail
Maveth: Bloodsport

FORTHCOMING
The Curse of The Mutant-Thing
Trail of Vengeance
War of The Thunder Gods

FORTHCOMING
The Resistance/Protectors War
Underworld
Magicks and Mysticism
The Resistance vs. Enforcement Order

THE HAUNTED CITY SAGA
The Legendary Warslinger: The Haunted City I
Battle of Astolat: A Haunted City Prequel (KOBO Exclusive)
Redemption of the Lost: The Haunted City II
Consequences of the Suffering: The Haunted City III (Forthcoming)

SYMBOLUM VENATORES
Symbolum Venatores: The Gabriel Kane Collection
Hod: A Symbolum Venatores Book
Symbolum Venatores: War of The Two Kingdoms
Symbolum Venatores: Twilight of the Gods (Forthcoming)

OTHER BOOKS
Lost in Shadows: A Novel
Lost in Shadows: Remastered
Accounts of The Dead Days
The Book of The Elect
Dark Titan Omnibus: Volume 1
The Extended Age Omnibus
Frightened!: The Beginning
Frightened!: Book 2 (Forthcoming)
EverWar Universe: Knights & Lords
Dark Titan Omnibus: Volume 2

OMNIBUS

VOLUME II

TY'RON W. C. ROBINSON II

CONTENTS

BOOK 4: DAY OF OCTAGON

BOOK 5: CROSSBREED

BOOK 6: HEAVEN'S CALLED

HALLOW SWORD: WAR GAMES

I

CONFLICT ON THE STREETS

The city of Retropolis, after being invaded by what the people have called, "*beings from the sky*", is near rebuilt to what it once was before the invasion and the formation of The Resistance. Now, during the city's rebuilding process, Sir Onyx and J have come to a disagreement concerning the use of crime throughout the city. Both have declared war onto one another and have begun the battles in the streets of Retropolis.

Citizens are fleeing the areas invaded by the gangs of Onyx and J. most of the lower-class areas of the city are now in the hands of either Onyx or J. most of the upper-class areas are secured by the armed forces that have entered the city since the aftermath of its battle. On the outskirts of the city, within the Swordlair, The Swordman sits and stares at the computer monitor, watching and witnessing the turf war unfold between Onyx and J. Allison walks into the Swordlair from its entrance, coming down its stairs and seeing Kenari at the desk and monitor.

"What has become of the city?"

"It is what it has always been." Kenari said. "A place for the wicked to dwell."

"It is something. To have a figure like yourself to roam the city

1

during its night hours and yet, the people believed you to be a mythic being."

"Some still do. Its best to keep it that way."

"But, many saw you on the streets during the Battle of Retropolis. Aligned with the other heroes. You possibly can't believe that many people disbelieve after witnessing that."

"The media is used for control and they can manipulate whatever they wish. Only a few will believe The Swordman's existence. Others will count it as a urban myth."

"I take it you're going out there to see what's really taking place?"

"It is my duty as The Swordman."

He prepped himself and grabbed his sword, placing on his hood, he entered The *Land-Dagger*. Driving out of the Swordlair toward the city of Retropolis.

In an office building, Elliot Slade and Ramon Lamano Carr have themselves a meeting. Both are frightened and serious concerning their conversation and where it's heading between the two of them. Words being used in ways foreign to their own ears. Choosing sides and opposing forces within the criminal underworld.

"I say we should align with Onyx." Slade declared. "He's basically new to the place and he has ideas that would make us wealthy in this city."

"I understand your point of view, Elliot. I really do. But, I feel that J has been here longer than Onyx and he knows this city from the inside out. Plus, he has history with The Swordman. Something that Onyx does not fully possess."

"Onyx knows what The Swordman can do. Remember the warehouse, where The Swordman came through and confronted Onyx. Onyx knows about The Swordman and that event created history between them."

"It's not enough history to grasp onto."

Slade shook his head and looked at Ramon.

"Look, its best we pick one of them now. Because if we don't, it's possible both will come looking for us. It won't be a pleasant visit for sure."

Ramon nodded as he drank his glass of whiskey.

"You have a point there. Best we make our decisions now or face our untimely death within the coming days. Hell, we already know how they operate."

In the lower-class area of Retropolis, the gang war between Onyx and J continued. Within them firing rounds of ammo against each other. Both of their gangs fighting each other in the rainy streets. Onyx and J stand in the streets with their gangs behind them. Staring down one another with firearms in their hands. J has his sword on his side.

"You could've accepted my terms, Conley!" Onyx shouted. "But, you chose death over life!"

"I made the decision that was best for me and my order. I know this city much more than you do, and I know how it should operate."

"If you believe what you're speaking, take me out now and end this turf war of ours before more people die because of your lack of understanding!"

"I will not kill you in this manner, Onyx."

Onyx nodded and pointed his finger at J. laughing to himself as he raised up a machine gun toward J.

"Then, I'll just do it!"

Onyx fired the machine gun at J, who ducked down and moved out of the gun's range. Hiding behind the sets of cars that are around them. Onyx continued to fire the machine gun and it ran out of ammo. Onyx went to reload the machine gun and he felt a presence around their location. Onyx looked and seen J looking up down the street, Onyx did the same and they both could see the Land-Dagger approaching.

"Here he comes." J said.

"Not now!" Onyx yelled with stress.

Both ran toward their cars as The Swordman elevated out of the moving vehicle, into the streets. Dressed in his black and dark grey ninja-esque uniform.

3

"We have to go now!" Onyx yelled at his driver.

The Swordman landed on the streets, fighting off the gang members that rushed toward him. Onyx and J escaped the location in their own cars, though chasing down each other in a fashion of a speed chase. The Swordman gazed around, Onyx and J escaped with some of their men and the others laid out on the pavement of the streets. He looked around, spotting one of Onyx's gang members crouched near a dumpster. The Swordman approached the gang member and grabbed him by his throat, slamming him against the brick building he stood next to.

"Tell me what is going on between Onyx and J?" The Swordman asked.

"I'm not telling you anything!"

The gang member went for a punch, but The Swordman caught his fist and slammed him onto the ground, stomped his foot on the gang member's face. The gang member struggled to get out of the hold, but he could not.

"You will answer my question or you might not have a face anymore."

"Ok! Ok! Sir Onyx and J were supposed to make an agreement with each other about which districts of Retropolis they would control. But, they had a disagreement and it turned into a turf war. Now, our orders are to find and kill anyone who is aligned with J or face death ourselves at Sir Onyx's hand."

"What about facing death at my hand? Your boss didn't tell you what I did to his other soldiers before."

"He told us and that is why we had to keep this on a low profile. But, now you know and they know you will come for them."

"That I will do."

The Swordman slammed his knee onto the gang member's head, knocking him out. He jumped into his car and drove away from the area.

II

WAR GAMES BEGIN

The Swordman returned to the Swordlair, wherein awaiting him are two of his childhood friends and members of The Order of Swords. Kimmiko Vantez and Kinero Danforth. Kimmiko, known in the urban myths as Gozen while Kinero is referred to as Firebolt. Parking the Land-Dagger, Swordman exited the car, removing his hood and mask and approached his friends.

"It is something to see the two of you here." Kenari said, hugging them both.

"We came on some very important business." Kimmiko said. "And we're here to have your assistance."

"What kind of business would this be?"

"I think you know what it is, brother." Kinero mentioned. "We have received word regarding a turf war between two gangs and we're here to cease it."

"Good to know. I have already spoken with one of their men. Je gave me some information regarding this turf war. I will say it will require your help."

"What can we do?" Kimmiko asked.

"It would be for the best for the two of you to scout the surrounding locations of the turf war. Find out where the bases are for both Sir Onyx and J."

"We know J, but who is Sir Onyx?"

"He's new to the area. Came from the States."

"So, what about you?" Kimmiko asked. "What are you going to do while we're out scouting?"

"I have someone to meet and she will be of good use to us."

"You think she'll listen and work alongside us on this?"

"She assisted me with Onyx and J not too long ago, I believe she will do so again."

"Tell me this before we head out, Brother. Why do you continue to work alongside her when she's not even one of us. She declined the offer to be a part of us and the Creed. So, why do you still work with her after all of this?"

"Because her skills prove that she is useful in cases such as this. Whether or not she ever accepts or declines the offer, she will still be an asset."

Kinero nodded.

"I can understand your meaning, brother."

Kimmiko and Kinero left the Swordlair as Kenari sat at the computer table, searching for any signs of the Huntswoman in the past few hours.

Sir Onyx and his gang made their way to Rockward Penitentiary. Sneaking their way in to find more recruits for the turf war. One of the dirty cops escorted them down a corridor where they saw prisoners in their cells. Onyx measured them by their size and posing threats.

"I am sure that you can find some of these men useful for your war against J."

"I wouldn't bother about it." Onyx said. "Conley will be dealt with and the city will know who truly runs it.

"I will tell you that there is one man here who can do more than you might have asked for."

"Where is this man that you've spoken of?"

"He's right down here. Follow me, sir."

Onyx followed the cop down another hallway and stopped at an office. Within the office, the cop smiled while Onyx looked at the man, who sat in the chair facing the desk, staring at them.

"This is the guy." The cop said.

"Are you sure about him?"

"Very sure. He's here for a mission of his own. Sent by some person he called A.B."

In the same hour, J and his gang took a trip Pegasus Prison and within the walls of the large and mysterious prison, J spoke with a woman named Kimberly Jacobs, who only a few of the civilians known as the urban myth Fear. J and Kimberly entered a secure office and J's guards kept watch from the outside. The two sat at a table.

"You know why I've come here." J said. "You know what is happening out there."

"I've heard the rumors and I've seen some things. How those 'Beings from the Sky' came down and wreaked havoc. I also saw those who fought against them. That moment told me this world is much bigger than what the average man or woman believes it to be."

"The Battle of Retropolis opened the door for me to spread my domain and my ruler ship of the underground."

"So, you're here to find some recruits or just a recruit."

"Something of that nature. I believe there is someone or some people here that can help me achieve my goal. My associate has already told me of Sir Onyx searching for recruits over at Rockward. Which is why I came here."

"Then, you've chosen the right place."

"How can I be sure of your words?"

"Because, you're talking with me for starters and I know lots of some ones that can be of great use for your goal being accomplished."

"Give me some names."

"I'll rather just show you. Come with me."

The office door opened, and Kimberly leads J down toward a particular room. There, J saw a man, wearing all armor with the colors of dark blue and grey. His face could be seen as he removed his helmet, He pointed with certainty in his eyes and Kimberly looked ahead, seeing the armored man being thanked by the Pegasus guards. She smiled.

"Who is he?" J asked.

"Why, he just came in to deliver someone. He's a mercenary.

Apparently, he's been coming to Retropolis for some time. Looking for a bigger price."

"I just might have it for him." J mentioned.

Gozen and Firebolt went across the suburb areas of Retropolis and the industrial division of the city. They scouted to find nothing related to Onyx or J. While they scouted, The Swordman met with the Huntswoman in the low sections of Retropolis. The Swordman found her trying to steal some valuable items from an auction that is set to start the following day.

"Knew I'll find you here."

The Huntswoman turned around to see The Swordman and she only smiled and approached him without any fear.

"You only come to ruin the fun."

"What you're doing is not what I would call fun."

"It's fun for me. Maybe not for you because of all your morals."

"I came here to ask you of something. Something that is important."

'How important is this that you're asking of me? Is it something of a global threat like the ones you were in when those things came from the sky?"

"It is not global. It's urban. The city is about to be hit with a turf war between Onyx and J and I will need your help in stopping it from increasing further out into other areas."

"Why not let them settle it. I mean, if one kills the other, isn't that much better. You know, one gone and only one more left."

"If it comes to that, then that is what it will be. For right now, it is up to us to stop them both before the crossfire reaches those that are not a part of their war."

"Let me think on it."

The Swordman turned, continuing to speak to Huntswoman.

"If I find you out in this area again, I will have to stop you with force."

"You could've stopped me with force right now, but you didn't, and I know why. You don't have to explain anything of it to me. I already know enough."

"I'm sure that you do."

Back at Sir Onyx's hideout, he stood before his gang and declared the war against J. By making the announcement. Onyx revealed who he has chosen to stand by his side. The man walked up toward Onyx and the gang. Dressed in a dark gray and black stealth attire, wearing a gray mask with scopes on the eyes. On his sides are several handguns and on his back is a rifle.

"This man right here is known in our circle as Gunbaine. I have chosen him as my right-hand man. As of this moment, his first order of business is to assassinate Conley. By any means possible."

Meanwhile, at J's hideout, the gang is there and they're cheering on J's name. J enters the warehouse room and showcasing to them his chosen man for the war. The man entered the room, dressed in military gear colored in dark blue and gray. His eyes were red from the stealth helmet and mask he wore, and he carried with him an arsenal of weapons. Including a sword of his own.

"I have chosen this man right here to assist me in this war against Sir Onyx. Maveth, the Death-Bringer. He will put an end to Sir Onyx with his skills. That I know he can accomplish."

III

CROSSFIRE

Sir Onyx and J have begun their war in Retropolis. The downtown streets are filled with gunshots and violence. Civilians have been urged to avoid the downtown area by any means. Due to the increase of chaos, Mayor Charles Baker has declared to close the downtown area until the turf war between Onyx and J has been complete. However, the Retropolis Police Department head out to the downtown area.

"What's the plan?" Detective Justine Copeland asked.

"We put a stop to this nonsense." Commissioner Austin replied. "Save this city once more."

"Hey, Commissioner." Detective Cash Hankinson said. "What about what the Mayor had said earlier in the office? About the city being at risk of martial law?"

"Now isn't he time to discuss the matter."

Throughout the ongoing gang shootout, Gunbaine and Maveth stood nearby on the opposing sides. Maveth savored the sounds of the gunfire. Gunbaine prepared himself, grabbing his rifle.

"I need to get on top of that building."

"By all means." Onyx said. "Make sure you hit Conley. Hit him good."

"My pleasure."

Gunbaine made his move to reach higher ground. Maveth grabbed his sword, turning toward J.

"If you please, I can wipe out all his men in a single stroke."

"How can you do that?" J asked. "You have super-speed or something?"

"Something of the sort. It's your call."

J nodded. He looked at Maveth, who gripped his sword and held his left hand on his gun.

"Go for it." J said.

Maveth moved with haste, running into the middle of the shootout. J stopped his men from firing as Maveth ran through Onyx's gang. Blocking their shots with his sword and firing back. Those closer to him were slashed by his sword as he dodged and swiped at others nearby. Onyx watched as his men were being taken out by Maveth.

"The hell is this guy?" Onyx wondered.

On the rooftop, Gunbaine looked, seeing Maveth's damage to Onyx's men.

"Well, well. If it isn't old Danton Thomas. Funny how things work out."

Onyx's gang is dead. Their blood flowed through the area. Onyx backed up as Maveth approached him. Holding his sword in front. J and his men followed Maveth, J stepped in between Onyx and Maveth.

"Where the hell did you find him?!" Onyx yelled.

"I have my sources, Fargo. Fitting, where's your special guy?"

"Oh, he's here. In the right spot for the kill."

Maveth looked around and gazed up, catching a familiar glare. He stared toward a rooftop, seeing Gunbaine and his rifle ready.

"Smalls."

Maveth ran for the building with J looking at him.

"Where are you going?"

"To take out Onyx's little helper!" Maveth said. "Do what you will with him. I will handle this guy myself."

"Noted." J said.

Maveth made it up to the rooftop, finding himself faced with a gun. Gunbaine laughed as he aimed it steady toward the Death-Bringer.

"Crazy how life works out, huh." Gunbaine said.

"It is such." Maveth replied. "You were always around to take my job."

"I go wherever the money whispers. You know this."

"I know it more than others. Why align yourself with Onyx? What did he promise you?"

"He promised me money. A lot of money. Plenty enough to make my ideas come to pass."

"Is working with A.B. and her little Enforcement Order part of the ideas?"

"How do you know about that?"

"My ears are within all secret places. Keeps me focused on the grand prize."

"So, J promised to deliver you the prize. Millions of cash?"

"He promised me gold, silver, and some copper. It'll get the job done and the improvements will come as planned."

"Then, what stops me from shooting you?"

"Nothing. Only the fact you'll be wasting your bullets as I slash your throat. Your blood will pour down this building for Onyx to see and then, J will kill him. Claiming the criminal underworld as his own. Simple choices at play."

Police sirens echoed through the area as Austin, Justine, and Cash arrived at the scene. They jumped out of the car, aiming their guns toward the two crime lords and J's men. Seeing the bodies of Onyx's gang on the ground gave them a cause for concern.

"Your men do this, J?" Austin asked.

"Just one man."

Maveth and Gunbaine looked down, seeing the police.

"This isn't what I signed up for." Gunbaine said. "This was supposed to be a clean kill."

"You're afraid of the cops?"

"No."

"Then, what's stopping you from getting paid?"

Gunbaine chuckled under his mask.

"You were always the one with words, Danton."

Gunbaine aimed his rifle. Steady. Steady. One shot. The shot fired, hitting the police car. Justine and Cash began firing toward the roof with Austin moving for a position. Onyx and J moved to another area. Maveth and Gunbaine ducked on the rooftop.

"You should've hit them." Maveth said.

"All part of the plan, big man."

Engine sounds roared near the scene as Onyx and J noted the Land-Dagger arriving. Maveth and Gunbaine also could see the car from below. The cockpit opened as The Swordman jumped out with Gozen and Firebolt at his side.

"Ah shit!" Gunbaine said. "He's here."

"Yes." Maveth said calmly. "He is."

J's men ran toward them, entering a fight. Gozen and Firebolt took them out without hesitation. The Swordman stared at the two crime lords and gazed over to Austin.

"Get yourselves out of here!" The Swordman yelled.

"Is he telling us to leave?" Justine asked.

"Go now!" The Swordman yelled once more. "We will handle this situation."

"Best we do as the man says!" Cash said, running to the police car.

Justine and Cash entered the car with Austin approaching Swordman. Gozen and Firebolt stood by his side. Austin gave them a nod as he entered the car, driving off. The Swordman focused his attention on Onyx and J.

"This turf war is over!"

"Is it?" J said. "What do you think, Fargo?"

"Maybe it's just begun."

Gunbaine fired another shot, hitting the ground where The Swordman stood. He looked up to see both Gunbaine and Maveth. He turned to Gozen and Firebolt quickly.

"You tow, keep Onyx and J from doing any more harm."

"Where are you going?" Gozen asked.

"To meet the two on the rooftop."

The Swordman grappled himself, moving upward to the roof. His feet touch the rooftop and he stared down Gunbaine and Maveth. Neither man made a move. Only the eyes were locked on. Weapons were in hand. The rooftop quickly became a calm place within the shootout.

"Blake Smalls." The Swordman said.

"You know my name? Nice."

The Swordman looked over to Maveth. He remembered something as Maveth raised his sword, pointing it toward him.

"That night." The Swordman said. "You remember?"

"I do." Maveth said. "I've waited for this moment. The chance to take you out is a grand prize above all others."

The Swordman reached, pulling out his sword and pointing it toward Maveth and Gunbaine.

"Then, this is your chance to claim that prize."

"Will do!" Maveth yelled as he and The Swordman clashed.

IV

GAME OF WAR

The Swordman and Maveth had themselves a clashing of swords. Twists and turns between the two men. Gunbaine managed himself to get a perfect aim at The Swordman during his fight.

"Just stay still for a second." Gunbaine whispered. "Stay... still."

Gunbaine took the shot and Maveth's sword blocked the bullet from hitting The Swordman. Maveth shoved Swordman and turned toward Gunbaine, twisting his sword in hand.

"Why did you foil the shot?" Gunbaine asked.

"The Swordman is mine." Maveth declared. "I've been waiting for this prize for a while. I will not allow your actions to ruin it for me."

The Swordman moved like a quickening shadow, attacking Maveth from the side and kicking Gunbaine to the ground of the rooftop. Maveth rose up, tossing kicks and punches toward the Swordman. Swordman blocked the maneuvers as quickly as he possibly could. Maveth drove his sword forward, causing The Swordman to grab it, snatching it from his hands. The Swordman used the end of Maveth's sword to smack him in the face before swiping Maveth's chest with his own blade. Gunbaine raised up his arm-pistols and The Swordman tossed Maveth's sword toward him, slicing the pistol muzzle.

"Shit!" Gunbaine yelled.

Gunbaine looked at his forearm, seeing the damaged muzzle. He looked up and The Swordman pounced onto him like an animal hunting. Maveth watched as The Swordman took out Gunbaine.

15

Afterwards, The Swordman and Maveth stood still, looking at one another. The Swordman grabbed Maveth's sword from the ground and tossed it to him.

"I prefer fair fights."

"Good." Maveth said. "Next time then."

Maveth dropped a smoke grenade to the ground. The Swordman ran into the blast and all he could see as the smoke moved through the air was no one. As the smoke cleared for his view, he realized both Maveth and Gunbaine were gone. Looking around, he didn't see them near the rooftop.

"Damn." The Swordman uttered.

Swordman dropped to the streets, only to see both Onyx and J being taken into custody by Commissioner Austin and his detectives. Austin approached the Swordman with a certain ease. Looking over to the crime lords in the truck.

"Your allies did a work on them."

"They're trained for such an occasion."

"Thank you for helping Retropolis once more."

"It's why I'm here."

The Swordman left with Gozen and Firebolt from the scene.

Days later, news broke out of Onyx and J being locked in Rockward Penitentiary. Gozen and Firebolt have declared to remain in Retropolis to help with further causes and to evade potential threats from all corners. In the outskirts of Retropolis, Maveth stood. His helmet off as he smirked overlooking the city and its reconstruction.

"Next time, *Myth-Walker*. Next time." Maveth said, turning away from Retropolis.

Kenari sat within the Swordlair as Allison herself was training in armed combat on the other end. Kenari was reading up on some strange details of activities caused by Death throughout the world. Knowing she's in Pegasus Prison ever since the Battle of Retropolis. Circumstances did not add up according to his knowledge. However, he recently got his hands on a file from an anonymous source from

T.I.T.A.N. the file read of criminals working in a unit.

"*Enforcement Order 66.*" Kenari said.

CHOSEN SON:
BLACHOLE ARISES

I

THE OUTBAND

Late during a night near Enigma City, a pair of men in black suits scattered across a building once owned by Kex Kendrick. However, with Kendrick in prison after he events of the Battle of Retropolis, the building was evicted and went up for sale. Now, it has been purchased by an unknown buyer. The men in suits are his associates as they placed strange technology into the building.

"How much does the boss require we pace inside?"

"As much that can fit."

"What is all of this anyway? Anyone know?"

"Boss said to keep things quiet. Otherwise the one above him will make us quiet. I'll rather keep my mouth close than let to flow."

Upon doing so, Taltus The Powerman bolted to the building, seeing the technology. Dark, black, and appearing like onyx with the scent of burnt coal. one of the men looked up, seeing Taltus hovering above them.

"What is all of this?" Taltus asked.

"It's him!" The man yelled.

The suits began shooting at Taltus. The bullets bounced off his white and blue suit as he came down, taking out the guns with his lightning vision. He rallied the men together before having them stand against the wall. In one swoop, he knocked them unconscious with a quick slap to the head. Afterwards, he entered the building, seeing boxes upon boxes of the strange technology, he went through, he found one man working on some of the technology. Hovering toward him, he frightened the man by his appearance.

"Don't harm me!" The man yelled.

"I'm not here to hurt you. I need to know what's all this? This technology doesn't fit the details of human hands."

"Because, it isn't human."

"What is it?"

"It's from the dark ones of the sky."

"Dark ones?"

"Our boss has spoken with him. His arrival is near and this all belongs to him."

"His name. Tell me his name."

"I cannot." The man said. "For he knows me. He sees my every move. If I was to spout out his name, a beam of light will come down and kill me. I cannot for my life's sake."

"Where's your boss?" Taltus asked.

"In Enigma City. On business works."

"I will speak to him myself. Clean this place out before I destroy all that sits in here."

Taltus flew away from the building, heading for Enigma City. The man inside however sighed as a dark mist crouched over him. He felt calm and steady. The mist vanished, following Taltus' trail.

II

FOR YOUR MASTER

Taltus headed toward Enigma City, a beam of light emerged from the ground, striking the Powerman out of the air. Taltus fell to the ground, dragged through the dirt from the impact of the blast. As he stopped, he looked up, finding himself surrounded by trees. Standing up, Taltus walked forward, entering an open field. There, he saw a brute figure. Scruffy hair and dressed in clad armor.

"Why did you do that?" Taltus asked.

"It was the only way to gain your attention."

"Who are you?"

"Dominix. I come from another dimension far from this world. Far from Olympus."

"Zeus sent you?"

"Zeus is not my master. I have been chosen to eliminate you."

"Eliminate me? On what causes?"

"Enough prattle!"

Dominix rushed toward Taltus, ending up being punched across the field. Taltus flew over Dominix's moving body and continued to beat down the dimensional being. Taltus grabbed Dominix by his hair and slammed him into the ground. Dominix paused to catch his breath.

"How are you moving this fast?"

"I've gained much abilities during my lifetime."

"He spoke of such things."

"So spoke?"

"Never mind!" Dominix yelled. "I will kill you and feed your corpse to the hounds of Blachole!"

Dominix lunged with his fist in front. Taltus grabbed a hold of his arm and tossed him once again, this time near a set of trees. Dominix crashed through the trees like a falling aircraft. Taltus flew over him, hovering as he watched the brute recover from the impact.

"You've got heart." Taltus said. "I'll give you that."

"Don't accuse me of being soft."

"I'm not. You attacked me first. I'm only returning the favor."

"Fool! I attacked you for a variety of reasons!"

"Then, explain."

"Trespassing in a place you shouldn't belong! Touching such technology, you haven't even begun to process. My master knows of your existence. The power you possess. The allies you have made. He is coming. I am only the pure sign of his arrival. My attack was only a prelude of his actions."

"When can I meet your master?"

"He's not on your time. You're on his!"

"I guess I'll have to make him show up."

Taltus speared Dominix, beating him down into the dirt. The impact of Taltus' punches created a crater for Dominix to lay in. After Taltus finished pummeling the brute. A strange and odd portal opened up in front of them both. Here, a large figure walked out. Standing with intent. Purpose. He walked with a class to his character. Walking past Taltus as if he wasn't there. The figure stood over Dominix. Dominix raised his eyes, seeing the figure and immediately bowed in fear.

"Forgive me. I did not know you were coming this day."

"You are to return to Blachole." The figure declared. "Your work requires you elsewhere."

"But, permit me the opportunity to eliminate this titagod. He is standing in your way."

"Leave. I will handle the titagod on my own."

Dominix bowed before entering the opened portal. Taltus watched as the figure turned around, staring at him. Looking deep into his eyes. Taltus did the same. Neither moved an inch.

"Who are you?" Taltus asked.

The figure only grinned as he walked past Taltus once again. Taltus rushed over, placing his hand on the figure's shoulder. The figure turned, backslapping Taltus across the field. Taltus shook his head, rubbing his face. He glared at the class brute.

"You thought that would keep me down?!"

The figure decided to unleash a series of energy beams from his eyes. The impact of the beams on Taltus' body caused him to collapse from the intense heat and the scorching cuts. Taltus fell and the figure stepped forward onto the portal, but turned his head, looking at the downed titagod.

"Remember this moment." The figure said. "Soon, humanity will be in your position. Bowing before *Oranos of Blachole*. The end has come."

Oranos vanished into the portal and was gone. Like a lightning bolt after its strike. Taltus arose to his feet, finding only himself in a large open field.

III

INVASION OF BLACHOLE

The following day, everything was going as usual in Enigma City. Civilians went about their business and there was hardly any crime taking place in the streets ever since Taltus was known to the public, criminals thought twice about taking their actions out in the open. Like a great boom of thunder in the sky, a portal had opened above the city. Its light shining down upon the city like a spotlight had been placed upon the civilians. They gazed up tot eh portal as it roared with a machine-sounding hum. While staring, strange creatures began to pour out of the portal, flying down to the streets, terrorizing anyone who was near their presence.

The creatures had the strange appearance of wolves, but with eagle-like wings and talons. Afterwards, a man-like being hovered down behind them. He carried a large staff, covered in dark-golden armor. His helmet appeared reminiscent of goats. He stepped on the streets, looking at the panicking crowds.

"His is what he desires! For you all to prepare yourselves for his grand return. This is the day of many things to come!"

While he cherished the moment of fainting screams and gushing sounds, Taltus appeared like a missile out of nowhere, snatching the horned being from the ground and flying up from the city.

"Who are you?" Taltus asked.

"You're him."

"I'm who?"

"The one he confronted."

Taking his staff, he swiped Taltus from him as they both fell to the streets unharmed. Taltus arose from the fall and stared at the being, twirling his staff with a grin on his face.

"Why have you come to this place?"

"Why do you care?"

"It's my duty to protect."

"Duty? Then, you must have some militaristic experience."

"I've had my share in the past."

"Well, this isn't the past. We're in the future."

"If so, how come I don't know your name."

"Forgive my manners. The name is Thrudhawk. The general of Blachole."

"Blachole?" Taltus uttered. "I've heard of the place from a unusual being."

"Have you? My, you've made this encounter much more intriguing to my mind."

Thrudhawk rushed toward Taltus with the staff. Taltus grabbed the staff like a bolt, taking it from the Blacholian general and smashing him with it to the side. Taltus dropped the staff as Thrudhawk extended his right hand. The staff rose up from the ground and flew back to his hand.

"Retracting weapons in your world?" Taltus said.

"We have much more. We desire to share it with this world and humankind. For our pleasure."

"You seek to enslave humanity."

"Fool. They're already enslaved. They just don't know it yet."

Thrudhawk shoved the staff into Taltus' throat and tripped him with it. He stood over the Powerman and started pummeling him with the staff. Taltus used his arms to block the ongoing strikes before focusing his eyes and unleashing his lightning vision, hitting Thrudhawk in the chest, knocking him into the air and back down.

"Ugh. Ophfiends, attack!" Thrudhawk yelled.

The flying wolf-like creatures zoomed toward Taltus in droves. Thrudhawk stepped back and watched as his legion fought against the Powerman. Using their talons, claws, and fangs to attack him at every end. Taltus struggled to get through the flying creatures. Taltus took a second to breath in and as he exhaled, he busted the ophfiends from him. Kicking them around all corners. From there, Taltus grabbed Thrudhawk by his throat and tossed him into a pack of the ophfiends.

"I only have one question." Taltus said, walking over toward Thrudhawk. "Who is Oranos?"

"Why do you seek to know?" Thrudhawk gestured. "What do you think he can do for you?"

"I met him in the fields. He gave me a warning of his coming. He said he was of Blachole. You proclaimed yourself a general of the place."

"Because I am."

"Where is this Blachole?"

"In a place far from this world."

"How far?"

"Very. Only a portal will grant anyone entry into the dark dimension."

"So, you, your army, Dominix, and this Oranos all come from the same place."

"Yes. Oranos has proclaimed this world his to rule. Humanity will bow before him when he returns in full."

"How about I pay him a visit instead."

Taltus dropped Thrudhawk to the ground and pointed in the sky.

"Open the portal. Now."

"I will not!"

Taltus punched Thrudhawk to the point of his helmet cracking above his head.

"Open the portal if you wish to continue breathing!"

Thrudhawk grinned. Nodding his head as he reached toward the gauntlet on his left forearm. He smiled as he pressed a button.

"He said you would be a challenge."

The thunder cracked in the sky and the portal reappeared. Opened brightly above them. Taltus looked up toward it. Certain.

"I'm entering your realm. When I return and if I see you still here, I will kill you and your entire army."

Thrudhawk laughed. The ophfiends flew into the portal, leaving the city with Thrudhawk hovering with them.

"Enter Blachole, titagod! Oranos is waiting for you."

They became one with the portal's light, Taltus bolted from the ground and into the portal. Last thing he saw was the flash of light, leaving this world and entering another.

IV

LEGACY

Taltus moved in a clear and still atmosphere. He couldn't glimpse at what was around him. For there was only darkness and darkness remained. The air was silent and cold. Taltus continued moving forward trough the dark before seeing a glint of light ahead. He pushed himself further toward the light and was pulled from the darkness. Finding himself in another place. A place of cooling fire and lightning.

"This is Blachole." Taltus said.

He flew over the bridge from the entrance toward a giant castle. Made of darkened stones and flowing with cosmic energy. In the air, Taltus saw more ophfiends, going to and fro. They didn't bother to harm him in any way, which caught him by surprise. Flying closer to the castle doors, they opened. Stopping him as he landed to his feet and walked in. In the castle, Taltus found himself staring at Thrudhawk leaning against the stone wall. Tending to his wounds. He even saw Dominix standing before him near a throne. At the throne, Oranos sat with a smile on his face.

"There you are." Taltus said.

"You came." Oranos said.

"I figured I would. Come see what this place was all about."

"And what do you think of it?"

"Too dark for my taste. Some sunlight would make this place better."

"There is no sun in this dimension, titagod. For where you stand doesn't operate as the earth. You've entered an ancient place. One made up of a divine hand."

"Funny. The gods of Olympus would say the same about their mountain. What is it with all these dimensions and all these rulers? Who has the final say above all things?"

"Even though you are an impressive specimen of a newly species, such knowledge would crush your intellect to know the truth."

"I came here only to learn one thing. Why attack the earth? Why humanity?"

"It is my will. The earth has been in the dominion of humanity for a long time. Many have ruled it in the past. From dark gods to cosmics to the divine forces above. But, I have yet to receive my opportunity at the chance. Now, it is my time."

"And you've chosen to give those of evil your technology? To use in your will?"

"The Outband summoned me with an ancient sacrifice. I answered their petition and granted them such equipment. With it, they will slowly enslave the human population all in my name. They will bear my mark and they will worship me above all their gods."

"Not if I have a say in the matter."

"I saw your actions when those dark forces came from the sky in that city you call Retropolis. Your unfenced with the others. Forming yourselves into a team. How, you have shown us a lot about your skill set."

"Things have changed for the better I will believe."

"They will once I have dominion over the earth."

"I'll kill you before you make the move."

"Will you?" Oranos said. "You defeated my son, Dominix. Took down Thrudhawk, my general. You really believe you can defy and kill Oranos of Blachole?"

"I know I can."

"Hmm." Oranos said. "I will not make a fool out of you just yet. For I do not wish to have titagod blood stain my floors and castle."

"You will have no choice."

"Better prepare yourselves and warn your allies of my coming. For it is soon and it is Oranos' will."

Taltus flew toward Oranos with his fist in front. Preparing to strike. Oranos raised his right hand slowly and froze Taltus in place in the air.

"Such anger flows through him. His future is clear, bur vaigely shadowed by himself. It is done."

Oranos pushed his hand forward, shoving Taltus from the castle and back to the entrance, where the portal had opened. Taltus entered the portal and within that second, he was out of Blachole.

Taltus fell from the portal over Enigma City. Falling, his eyes opened, catching himself and he flew from the city, returning to the Fortress of Cytron to recover.

Afterwards, the Enigma City news discussed the strange portals in the air, leading the city to believe aliens were invading. Stephanie Vale and Alex Havens set themselves aside to uncover more about the portals as they went out to meet with the Powerman.

THE NANO MAN: NANOTECH DEBATE

I

<u>CONSEQUENCES ABORT</u>

Nathan Hawke traveled from Newark, New Jersey to Washington D.C. after receiving notice of the U.S. Senate desiring to speak to him concerning his Nano Man technology. His involvement of the exposits have triggered the minds of the political parties and Hawke has set to speak with them. To give them understanding of the Nano Man and his purpose.

Entering the U.S. Capital Building, Hawke is amazed to find President Donald Trump sitting. Trump's eyes caught Hawke as he entered. Trump waved and Hawke waved back. Both are business partners in a series of firms. Some public, others secret. As Hawke sat down, Rick Carter entered, sitting next to Hawke.

"Didn't know you would be here." Hawke said.

"I had no choice but to come. Otherwise, this whole thing could blow out of proportions."

"Oh, come on."

"Out of everyone in this place, I know how you can be when someone is after your work."

Hawke nodded.

"Hmm, you really do." Hawke smirked. "Where's Alice? She here too?"

"I would assume so."

"That's great. This can be a party now instead of a bummer-fest."

"Just don't do anything rational."

"Trust me. I won't. But, them, I can't speak for."

"I understand."

Crowds filled the seats of the Capital Building as the Senate were preparing to speak, Trump intervened, grabbing the microphone.

"Excuse me, everyone." Trump said. "But, I feel it is for the better that I speak with Mr. Hawke concerning the Nano Man technology."

"I agree." Hawke replied. "He knows me."

Hawke looked over to Rick, who could only stare at his friend. Hawke smiled back.

"He knows me." Hawke said.

"I know already." Rick replied with a still face.

"Now, I do not know as much as some of you may say. But, Nathan Hawke, is a true friend." Trump said. "An honest one. One that I believe if he had something that could change America for the better, he would be the one to tell us himself."

"That I would." Hawke smiled.

"Nathan, would you go ahead and tell the Senate and me all there is to know about this Nano Man technology."

"Sure thing, Mr. President."

Nathan sat up in his seat, looking at Trump and the Senate. He nodded.

"The Nano Man technology is in good hands. There is not viable danger ahead. I know you're all aware of the events in Newark with the Geier and the religious fanatics. You're also aware of the happening in Canada where The Nano Man assisted many others like himself to save the world, mind you from an inter-dimensional threat."

"That's not why we're here, Nathan." Trump said. "We need to know about the technology. Not what he has achieved with such capability. I'm not Obama. His Administration ended when I entered the White House. So, do not tell us about his actions in aiding a foreign country."

"Then, what do you want with the tech? Tell me?"

"The tech should belong to the United States Military. The Army, the Navy, the Air-Force, the Marines and the Space Force

31

should have full access to that kind of weaponry."

"They have tech that is beyond the Nano Man's own exosuit."

"Are you telling us the truth, Mr. Hawke?" A Senator asked.

"I'm telling you what I know. That's all I can tell you. I can lie, truthfully. But, that is not why I'm here. You called me and I am here to tell you there's no immediate danger."

"What if Iran got a hold of the tech?" Trump asked. "Would you take responsibility for that?"

"How would Iran gain the Nano Man tech in the first place? There's no Iranian threat coming my direction. Why would there be?"

"What about China?" Trump asked. "Have you considered them and the fact the trade deals are a bust?"

"I didn't know this was about trade. Are we entering another trade war or something?"

"You've looked at all possibilities?"

"Every last one." Hawke said. "It's my duty to make sure nothing happens with the Nano Man technology. If something was to take place, it would be on my hands and my conscious alone."

"Nathan." Trump said. "It would be for the best you deliver all the Nano Man technology to us immediately."

"And what if I choose otherwise?"

"Don't tempt us." A Senator said. "We have ways of doing such."

"Oh, I know." Hawke grinned. "I'm not going to turn it over though."

Trump sighed. Looking around at the Senate. Pointing at Hawke. The Senate said words toward Trump. Hawke looked over to Rick.

"They're going to take the tech, Nate."

"We'll see."

Trump nodded, turning back to Hawke.

"You have twenty-four hours to hand over the Nano Man technology or face dire consequences."

"Heh." Hawke said. "Like fire and fury?"

"Turn it over." Trump declared. "Save yourself the trouble of facing your country."

"I'm not turning it over. Everything is smooth. No problems at all. Yet, you're looking to cause a problem. Out of all the things happening in the world right now, you're looking to start an internal war between the government and a fellow citizen?"

"America First." Trump said. "Remember that."

Trump left the panel as the Senate demanded Hawke turn over the Nano Man technology. Hawke stood up and left the room. Rick followed him to the outside as he walked toward his car.

"I'm going to head over to the bunker before they do."

"Why?"

"Because, I believe they've already sent out a squad to take the tech."

Hawke sighed.

"If you see them, do whatever it takes to stop them."

"I'm not taking out my own countrymen."

"Your countrymen over your friend?"

"That's not what I meant."

"We'll see."

Rick returned to the bunker. Taking out his phone.

"Nate. It's gone. Most of it is gone. I'm sorry, man."

Hawke listened and kept quiet.

"I'll take care of it." Hawke said.

"Don't do anything stupid, alright. We'll get to the bottom of this."

"Yeah. We will."

Hawke ended the call and sighed. Knowing now he's going to enter a war with his own country. Something he hoped to avoid. He looked at his phone, dialing Alice's number.

II

<u>NANOTECH IN GETTYSBURG</u>

Nathan sat in the Nano-Bunker, seeing only a portion of his technology remaining. Alice entered the lair, seeing Nathan distressed. Staring into space with his hands together. She approached him slowly. He quickly looked over to see her.

"Didn't hear you come in."

"I had to come. Rick told me of the news. I'm sorry I didn't attend the meeting."

"It wasn't big of a deal. Just a bunch of political puppets. That's all."

"And what of your tech?"

"I'm going to get it back."

"Get it back? How?"

"Like I've done with most oppositions in my way. Take them out."

"Nate, this is the United States Government you're talking about. You can't just take them out."

Nathan stood up from his seat and walked over to the closet, gazing at Alice.

"I can."

Nathan grabbed the object in the closet and left the bunker.

Within another undisclosed location, President Trump met with Chance Parker, a competitor to Nathan Hawke, CEO of ParkerTech. The two sat down at a table while the Secret Service kept guard at the doors and windows. Parker rubbed his tan slim suit. Checking his black tie, making sure it's on properly. He's overly concerned with looking good. Shaking hands as they sat down.

"I have to thank you, Mr. President for contacting me. I never imagine what would be happening right now."

"You know why we're having this meeting. Nathan Hawke is treading the water of America. His actions will get him killed."

"I know that. It's Hawke's nature to test the ground he walks on. Besides, I'm a better guy when it comes to such technology. I mean, I am his competition after all."

"And you have similar technology to the Nano Man?"

"Something of the sort, it isn't quite ready for commission yet. Still some bugs we have to work through."

"How about what you have now?"

"What I have now?"

"Yes. What would be your plan, if you were in my position to stop Hawke from causing further harm to himself and to this country?"

"Well, I would assassinate him."

"Assassinate him?" Trump questioned. "How come?"

"Rid myself of the competition. But, I wouldn't be the one to make the mark."

"You're talking as if you've planned this."

"Oh, I've planned a lot of things. But, taking Hawke out is only a small fraction of the plans. However, I know a guy who can handle Hawke while you and your Administration deal with the nanotech."

"Is he an American?"

"No doubt. Wouldn't hire anyone else to do the job. He's good. I can assure you of that."

"How soon can he be ready?" Trump asked.

"He's already prepared." Parker said. "Just say the word."

Trump nodded. Standing up from the chair. Extending his hand. Parker stood up and shook the President's hand. Trump grinned.

"Make the call, Parker. Get him on the job immediately."

"Will do, Mr. President."

Later in the day, Parker returned to his headquarters and inside was a peculiar man, standing at his desk. Overlooking the diagram of armored exosuits. The man wore red and black armor and carried a scarred mask with him. Parker shut the office door, getting the man's attention.

"You made it over here quickly." Parker said.

"As soon as you made the call, I was on my way." The man said, turning around.

"I like that. Disciplined." Parker gestured, walking over to his chair. "You know why I called you here?"

"You want me to do the task. Find Hawke and take him out."

"Absolutely. But, do it discreetly. Clean kill. No slashing or gushing of blood. We can't have that at this moment. Too many eyes on Hawke."

"I'll get the job done. I expect to be paid as soon as it's done."

"You will be. Trust me."

"I don't trust anyone wearing a suit and sitting in an office."

"Then, you're already on the mark."

On the TV in the office, the news broadcasted a sighting of the Nano Man hovering over the Gettysburg Battlefield. Parker's eyes went big as the man he hired left the office. Parker watched the screen as Nano Man just hovered still, overlooking the field.

"The hell is he up to?"

The news spread of Nano Man in Gettysburg across the country. President Trump wasn't having it and immediately assigned the United States Army to infiltrate the battlefield to take down Nano Man by any means. The Army went out in tanks, jeeps, and footmen. Trump watched from the Oval Office as the event was being broadcasted on Fox News. CNN and MSNBC refused to show details regarding the Nano Man's purpose in the field. Claiming it to be a protest against the Trump Administration. Crowds gathered near the Gettysburg Battlefield to watch the confrontation.

Alice and Rick watched from the Hawke Industries headquarters. Both were unaware of Nathan's plans to travel to Gettysburg.

On the battlefield, a soldier stepped out of the jeep, looking up at the Nano Man. Holding a bullhorn.

"You have ten seconds to come down and surrender the armor."

"Ten seconds?" Nano Man said. "That's all you're giving me."

"Ten!"

"Nine."

"Eight."

"Seven."

"Six."

"Come on!" Nano Man said. "Hurry it up, will you."

"Five!"

"Four!"

"Three!"

"Two!"

"One!" The soldier turned back, entering his jeep. "Fire at will!"

The footmen began firing their rounds toward Nano Man, who flew and swooped around the gunfire. He held his wrists out, firing a blast of energy, knocking down the foot soldiers with a bit of ease. He stopped and gestured toward the tanks and jeeps.

"Where's your real firepower?" Nano Man asked. "I demand you use it if you're going to take this tech from me!"

The tanks began firing the cannons toward Nano Man. Moving swiftly from the blast, he fired another set of energy beams from both wrists, burning up the tanks as the soldiers bolted out of the vehicle. Flying over them and repeating the same action, soldiers only stood by and watched as Nano Man took out their jeeps and tanks in a quick succession. Trump watched the event as it happened and shook his head.

"I don't like this. Get Parker on the phone now."

"Yes, Mr. President."

"I can't believe this." Trump said.

Burned jeeps and tanks covered the field. Nano Man looked over toward Sherfy farm, seeing three tanks approaching. He sighed. Flying over toward them and blasting them with nano-laced missiles from his forearm. The missiles attached themselves to the tanks and shut down their interior system. Causing them to become completely useless.

"Civil War modernized." Nano Man said, overlooking the field.

While most of the country was focused on Nano Man facing the Army at Gettysburg, Geier had returned and quickly attacked the New York/New Jersey areas. Harming civilians and terrorizing them. Geier left the area, flying away before sightings could break out.

Trump grabbed the phone inside the Oval Office. Sitting down with a straight face.

"Parker." Trump said. "You saw the news. Get your guy on the job now."

"He's already on the job, Mr. President." Parker replied. "He'll handle it quickly as possible."

Trump hanged up the phone and turned to the Secretary of State.

"Prepare the Navy, the Air Force, and the Marines. Keep track of Hawke and his every movement. We need to stop him now before his heroic friends get the idea of assisting him."

"Sir, the New York/New Jersey area was attacked by the Geier."

"The birdman who attacked Newark a few months ago?"

"Yes sir."

"Send word out to find him." Trump said. "Any way you can."

"Yes, Mr. President."

III

<u>BATTLE OF PEARL HARBOR</u>

Walking on the burnt and filled field of the Gettysburg Battlefield, Parker's mercenary walked across the land. Seeing the jeeps, tanks, and injured soldiers. He spotted something glowing on the ground and reached down toward it. He held the small metallic object in his hand and grinned.

"Getting sloppy."

Trump sat in the Oval Office, thinking. A secretary entered the office with Trump giving her a look out of the corner of his eye.

"What do you have for me?" trump said.

"We know where Hawke's next move is."

"And?"

"He's headed for Pearl Harbor."

Trump nodded, looking at an image of Nano Man flying in the air. Trump handed the image back to the secretary.

"Send word out to the Navy. Tell them to take him down by any means."

"Yes sir."

Geier's attack is now traveling across the news in the New York/New Jersey region. Rick and Alice watched the footage on the news. The reporter stated the Geier chose to attack as the debate with Hawke and the U.S. Government has been the talk of the time.

"He decided to do this now." Rick said. "He somehow knew Nate wouldn't be in the area to stop him."

"And Nate won't have any time to stop him. What of the

government?"

"They're still on Nate's trail. This Geier attack isn't even on their radar. Much less a concern."

"As long as the Nano Man is out of the public eye, Geier will continue his attacks. There has to be someone we can contact to stop him."

"Who do you have in mind?"

"We could try and call The Powerman guy or The Swordman."

"Too risky." Rick stated. "I have an idea."

"What are you going to do?"

"Put a stop to Geier and save Nate the trouble."

Rick left the room and as he walked, his phone rang. Grabbing it from his pocket, he read the ID and answered quickly.

"Great time, man."

"Yeah. Sorry. I would've one so sooner." Nate said on the other end. "But, being chased can move you a few rounds."

"I see. Where are you?"

"On my way to Pearl Harbor. Figured I could lure Trump's goons out there for another scuffle. You've seen what happened at Gettysburg?"

"We got the news. Listen, Nate, if you don't stop, they will put you down."

"How good is that going at the moment?"

"Don't doubt their firepower."

"I'm not. I know their firepower."

"That's not the issue."

"And what's the status with you guys?"

"Geier is back."

"Do tell."

"Don't worry about him. I'll take care of it."

"You're going to do it?"

"I have no other choice."

"About time, old friend." Nate said. "Make sure it works properly. Don't want yourself to crash across the skies."

"I think I have it covered."

"Got to go. Tell Alice I'll be back soon."

"Will do."

Hanging up, Rick entered a secure place in the Hawke Headquarters building. Within the room, Rick placed his hand on a scanner, opening a small closet. Within the closet was a silver/chrome exosuit similar to Hawke's but detailed with an arsenal of weaponry. On the suit's chest was a white eagle. Rick smirked.

"Son of a gun."

Rick entered the suit and flew from the facility. Many thought it was Nano Man, but Alice knew who is was and couldn't wrap her head around it.

Arriving at Pearl Harbor, Nathan found the place surrounded with the U.S. Navy. He laughed as he flew around the ships, grabbing everyone's attention and focus.

"I'm here. Aren't you all going to stop me?"

From the grounds came the Admiral. He looked up toward Nano Man and raised his bullhorn.

"You are trespassing on United States Government property."

"That's why I'm here."

"By the orders of President Donald Trump, we are charged with taking you out of the sky."

"What are you waiting for? Shoot me out of the sky, boys!"

The Navy began firing cannons toward Nano Man and he flew through the blasts, rushing toward the weaponized ships. Blasting them into flames with his energy beams. Circling around and shooting the beams, burning anything firing back. The Admiral stood still, watching as the ships were being destroyed in a very quick manner. after the shooting, Nano Man landed in front of the Admiral.

"I tried to tell them." Nano Man said. "The tech is in good hands. Send word to the President. Let him know of this event. I want him to keep coming."

Taking off into the sky, the Nano Man was gone.

41

In the region of Newark, Geier returned, seeking to terrifying the city once more. As he proceeded, Rick arrived from the sky, landing in the streets for Geier to see. He looked and stared.

"You're not him." Geier said. "Too bulky."

"I'm not the Nano Man. True."

"Then, who are you, imposter?"

"The Silver Eagle."

IV

AIMED IN THE SKY

Nathan decided to return to Newark. Flying in the sky above a large field. He moved still and without notice, a blast occurred, shooting him from the sky and crashing into the field. Upon getting himself in motion. He looked around the area and only saw one individual. The individual was Parker's mercenary. Standing still with a rocket launcher in his hands.

"Who the hell are you supposed to be?" Nano Man asked.

"I'm the guy who will be taking you to meet the President. Paid in full of course."

"You're a mercenary?"

"Yes. The name's Crossface."

"I can only wonder why."

"I'll give you the details once I'm paid and President Trump has you in custody."

"I'm not going into custody. I am not a criminal."

"But you are. You ran off with tech that the government should possess. You attacked the Army at Gettysburg and invaded Pearl Harbor against the Navy."

"How do you know about all of this?"

"I've been tracking you down the moment I was assigned to find you. It's part of my skill set. Plus, Chance Parker's price was one I couldn't refuse."

"Parker, huh. What did he tell you about facing someone like me?"

"You're no different. If it were so, I would be taking down

Enigma City's fellow hero. But, that's not my duty. Yet."

"Looks like I'm going to have to cut your job short."

"I give you the pleasure of trying."

Nano Man blasted an energy beam toward Crossface, who jumped from the attack and fired another blast from the launcher, striking Nano Man. He bounced off the ground from the impact with Crossface reloading as quickly as possible. Nano Man raised up, shaking his head.

"I'm not like the others, Techhead. I'm a whole different kind of deal."

Nano Man blasted another energy bean from his left hand, striking the launcher from Crossface's hands. Crossface turned and quickly, Nano Man speared him to the ground, holding him down.

"Don't try to fight."

"I never give up."

Crossface placed an object on Nano Man's back and in seconds, it exploded. Pushing him from Crossface.

"I am complete with weaponry. I know how this game works."

"So do I."

Nano Man hovered up and blasted Crossface in the legs before grabbing him by his chest and slamming him into the ground. Placing his foot on Crossface's chest and removing his mask to reveal his roughed-up and scarred face.

"Now I see why you're called Crossface."

Nano Man gazed up in the air, seeing something flying toward the area. He looked closer as the figure landed. Crossface also saw the figure.

"The hell is that?" He wondered.

The figure landed in front of the two. Nano Man removed his foot from Crossface and approached the figure who was Rick himself.

"Looks nice on you."

"Don't start." Rick said, wearing the Silver Eagle exosuit.

"Why are you out here?"

"I tracked your suit' movements. Found you here with this guy it seems."

"He's a mercenary. Hired by Change Parker."

"Really? Parker's involved in all of this?"

"What did you expect? Trump assigned him to do it. Had to."

The rushing sounds began to carry in the sky as the U.S. Air Force arrived at the field. Sitting above Nano Man and Silver Eagle. Crossface stayed down, but, crawled from the area. Nano Man saw him and blasted him with a electric net.

"You're not going anywhere."

The Air Force demanded for Nano Man to return with them to D.C. to meet with President Trump. He refused, Rick stood by his friend. The Air Force decided to retaliate, they began firing all rounds toward the two-armed allies. Dodging the attacks, Crossface moved himself further away from the firing field. Nano Man and Silver Eagle combined took down the jets and helicopter of the Air Force. After the flames covered the ground and downed soldiers were scattered across the field, Nano Man turned to Eagle.

"What happened with Geier?"

"I fought against him while you were away. Testing out the suit."

"Is he behind bars once more?"

"No. he escaped. Promised to return only if you were to stop him."

"Then, I know what I must do."

"And that is?"

"Return to Newark and take Geier down. In front of everyone. That way, Trump will understand the Nano Man technology is safer in my hands and not in the possession of the government."

"I will take your word for it."

Hawke glanced at the soldiers and Crossface on the ground.

"What are we going to do about these guys?"

"I'll call it in. bring some assistance." Rick said. "Go to Newark, take down Geier and end all of this before it escalades into a worldwide event."

"Now you're talking."

Nano Man took off while Silver Eagle helped those who were stranded on the field.

V

<u>TRUTH TO POWER</u>

The Nano Man made his return to Newark and once he returned, the Geier appeared before him. Both hovered in the air within the city. Civilians came out to watch as well as the news. Signaling the events across the country. Every news feed gained word of Nano Man's arrival and broadcasted. Trump watched the event from the Oval Office with Parker sitting by.

"What is going on here?" Trump asked. "He ruins Gettysburg, attacks Pearl Harbor and the Navy, and eliminates a portion of the Air Force!"

"I... I don't know." Parker said. "I'm not sure how he's doing it."

"What of your guy? The mercenary. What have you heard from him lately?"

"Nothing yet. But, I know he'll get the job done."

"Then, why hasn't he?"

Parker gulped.

"I will look into it, sir."

Nano Man and Geier continued their stare down.

"I'm surprised you chose to come back."

"Figured I would have to. Heard what you were doing while I was away. Not a good thing, friend."

"With you out of the way, I can create more terror in this place. Now, you have given me what I want."

"My friend told me all about it. Don't worry, you'll be in prison again soon."

"You'll have to kill me before I surrender."

46

"Don't wish for things you truly don't want."

Geier rushed against Nano Man, striking him with his wings. Nano Man turned around in the air, grabbing Geier's left wing, throwing him to the streets. Civilians moved out of the fight's way as the two began taking punches. Nano Man kicked Geier and slammed him in the chest before ripping off his right wing. The news continued their live feed as the Nano Man stomped on Geier's back.

"This is too easy." He said. "Why are you making this easy for me?"

"I am not giving up!"

"Too late." Nano Man said, ripping off the other wing. "It is done."

Nano Man looked around, finding the news crew. He approached them and stood in the direction of the camera. Looking right into it.

"I want everyone to know. This technology is safe. There is no danger while it rests in my hands. Trust my words or else become like Geier."

The civilians cheered Nano Man's victory. Back at the Oval Office, Trump held his head down, turning off the TV. Parker sat quietly.

"I'll be leaving now." Parker said, leaving the office.

Once the fighting was over, Trump called off the manhunt for the Nano Man tech. Nathan sat in the nano-bunker with all the stolen equipment returned to him. Rick continued to practice the Silver Eagle suit as it upgraded through various training exercises. Geier was placed in a facility known as Ledger Haven.

The following day, Trump entered the bunker to meet with Nathan. Secret Service waited outside the location.

"I don't know how you managed it. But, I still say it's best for the American military to have the tech."

"I understand your reasoning, Mr. President. But, it's safer with me. Not foreign threat is coming with this tech. it's in good hands."

"See to it that it stays that way. Otherwise, we'll be back."

"And I'll be waiting."

Trump nodded and left the bunker. Alice sat with him as he began working on another exosuit. One he promised would take him further out into space. Hidden away in the bunker was a file. The file detailed all the possible solution for when anyone made the attempt to take the Nano Man technology from him. Nathan had prepared himself for the next phase of an attack.

COMMANDER NORLAND: NEW ALBION

I

ARCTIC FIND

Commander Norland and the Champions made their arrival at T.I.T.A.N. Headquarters. Entering the busy base, Colonel Evan Nader approached them with General Sarge Hunter at his side. Shaking the Commander's hand and saluting the Champions. Showing respect as always within the base. A standard procedure ever since the Battle of Retropolis and the formation of The Resistance. His Champions are still the same team as before. Steve Nixon, Woody Fields/Canadian Hawk, Carl James/American Ray, and Andrea Pierson/Whiplash,

"What's the next mission, Colonel?" Norland asked.

"You and your team will be heading out to Alaska. Our intel has told us of an entity roaming around the Alaskan wilderness. We don't know if it's a man or a nubreed or some strange creature. It requires our attention."

"Does it have a name?"

"They call it the Dark Snowman. Apparently, the natives have warned of the being's existence for years."

"We'll solve this, Colonel." Norland said. "Trust us as always."

"Sarge will handle things from here."

Sarge stepped forward as Nader walked away. Norland nodded his departure.

"The drill is simple. Head out to Alaska, confront this Dark Snowman and stop him by any means. Don't kill him, bring him back here for study and analysis. Professor Flm wishes to learn about the entity."

"We'll be on our way."

Norland and the Champions headed out and left the base. Flying off in the hoverjet toward Alaska. Hours later, they arrived in Alaska, landing at a miniature T.I.T.A.N. base, greeting the agents and the soldiers nearby.

"How far out is this Snowman?" Norland asked.

"We've traced the entity's steps further out into the woods. Almost fifteen miles from the base."

"It's moving closer it seems."

"Then, we go to it." Norland said. "We'll handle this threat and give word afterwards."

"Understood."

Norland turned to his team and nodded.

"Let's go."

Norland and the Champions proceeded forward into the woods. Following the tracks. The first thing that caught their attention were the size of the footprints. Larger than an average human.

"This thing is bigger than expected." Woody said.

"Don't let it scare you off." Norland said. "We're a team. We can handle this kind of threat."

Moving forward, the footprints increased, they found a stash of bushes and branches stacked up near a larger tree. Norland stopped the team, looking around the area.

"Keep your ground. It isn't far."

Norland searched the stash and as they were silent, a large figure bolted out of the tress, rushing toward the team. They moved from the attack and Norland turned around to see the figure. The size of its feet matched the prints. It stood over eight feet tall and its body was covered in ice and snow. The figure roared deeply facing Norland.

"Champions!" Norland yelled. "Attack at all corners!"

They moved to attack the Dark Snowman. Striking the monster at every angel. The Snowman grabbed Carl's triangular shield and froze it solid in his hand. Carl stared.

"The hell?"

The Snowman backhanded Carl to the ground. Norland rushed over, striking the Snowman with his fist. Clashing him with punches and kicks. The Snowman tumbled and grabbed Norland by his hand, pushing him into the ground. Norland held the Snowman's hand in his own, pushing back with full strength. From behind, Andrea came, using her electric whips on the Snowman, wrapping them around his arms and shocking him. Norland turned to Nixon.

"Hit him!"

Nixon rushed over, firing a blast from his launcher. Releasing a blast of smoke that caused the Snowman to collapse. Andrea pulled back her whips and Norland walked over, checking the Snowman's pulse.

"He's out." Norland said. "Contact the agents. Tell them we need a large jeep and some assistance."

"Yes sir." Woody said, returning to the base.

The T.I.T.A.N. agents arrived with a jeep and together they brought the Dark Snowman with them to the base. Placing the Snowman on the hoverjet, Norland and the Champions made their return to the primary headquarters.

Although, in another country, Sinister Judge watched Norland and his team. Using sorcery to create a visible rift to see across lands. He watched as they entered the hoverjet and took off from the base. Judge nodded. Sitting in his lair with his hood cloaking his face. Only his glowing eyes were visible. His plan was set in motion. As it always is.

II

A NEW ALBION

Norland and the Champions made their return to the main headquarters. Unbeknownst to them, they arrived as the headquarters was under attacked. Norland and his team jumped from the landing hoverjet, running toward the base. Inside, they saw robotic figures. Dressed in dark blue and violet cloaks and tunics.

"The hell are these guys?" Nixon asked.

"Doesn't matter." Norland replied. "Let's take them out."

The Champions worked with their skills to take down two of the droids. Norland rushed toward the remaining one, spearing it to the floor and ripping its head from the body. Silent immediately entered the headquarters as Nader and Sarge arrived at the scene, seeing Norland on his knees above the decapitated droid.

"What happened here?" Norland asked.

Nader turned to Sarge. The monitors began to blink with speed and afterwards a face appeared on the monitors. The face of Sinister Judge.

"I see you've met my droids. For they were only a small test to a greater plan. One that will ensure the future of T.I.T.A.N. will submit to Centronian laws and obey me."

"And what if we choose otherwise?" Sarge said.

"Then you will not live to see the New Albion which I will create. My empire above all others. You have a short time to make a decision. I suggest you do so quickly."

The monitors went black as everyone scattered through the headquarters. Norland arose from the ground and approached Nader and Sarge. The Champions stood behind, assisting anyone who was harmed before their arrival.

"What are these?" Norland asked.

"Come with us." Nader said.

Norland followed Nader and Sarge down the hall.

"That man on the screens." Norland said. "Who is he?"

"He is known as the Sinister Judge." Nader replied. "Ruler of a country called Centro. It's far out in between Russia and Germany. Some have speculated his country isn't even under the European Union."

"And you believe that?"

"Yes. Because Judge isn't the kind of man who submits to the authorities of worldly men. Those droids that came in here are called Judgedroids. His soldiers."

"He doesn't have humans working for him?"

"He sees human soldiers as cannon fodder. Says they're a waste on the battlefield. Prefers robots. Durable. Stronger. Faster. It's Judge's pure interest."

"So, why has he chosen to attack you guys?"

"He demands we work for him. Seeing how our technology far surpasses the general population. Judge wants our tech to increase his own."

"He has weapons?"

"A variety of sorts. Some that the world would call science-fiction."

"Like a death ray?"

Nader turned to Norland with a straight face. Norland knew.

"I'm impressed."

"Don't be. Sooner or later, Judge will make another attack before he shows up here on his own. He likes to wait things out. Let them sear into his opponent's mind before they give up. Afterwards, he judges them and executes them if he pleads it so."

Reaching the end of the hallway, Professor Flm walked out of his office, signaling to Norland. Nader nodded to Flm.

".The Professor is expecting you."

"Keep me informed on Judge's workings."

"Will do, Commander."

Norland approached Flm and the two shook hands before entering Flm's laboratory. Inside, they sat down at the table as some of Flm's electrical technology was sparking in the background.

"You managed to take down the droids?"

"Had no other option. Retaliation was all I could muster up."

"Nader told you all you need to know about Sinister Judge?"

"As much. Is there anything else I should know about this man?"

"Well, there is one thing Nader may not have told you."

"Which is?"

"Judge not only works with technology. He delves into sorcery."

"Sorcery? Like magic?"

"He was born into it. It's his first callings. That's how he conquered Centro an renamed the capital city Judgedath."

"So, he's a conqueror and a sorcerer?"

"Yes."

"How do we stop him?"

"I'm not sure about the others. But, you can stop him."

"With my powers. I see."

"However, do not attack Judge with force. Don't go to him unless it's necessary. Judge is known for playing mind games with his enemies."

"I'm surprised Hawke hasn't encountered this man nor as Kenari."

"Hawke and Judge have a similar understanding when it comes to the technology aspect. Kenari and Judge I'm not sure if they've met."

"Now would be a good time."

"But, this is not their battle. It's yours and your team. Just prepare yourself for any attack he sends this way."

"I will."

Over in Judgedath, Centro, Judge sat in his throne room as the front gates of his palace had opened. A young man entered the palace, approaching the room to stand before Judge's seat. The expression of the man was ambition and anger.

"How does it feel to be free from that prison?" Judge asked.

"It feels great. But, why did you have me set free? Why not

anyone else in there?"

"Because I know of the power that lives within you. The power to control the elements of the storm."

"That's the reason I was imprisoned. People were afraid of my potential."

"I do not fear you."

"Then, why bring me here?"

"I have an offer for you."

"What kind of offer?"

"Stand with me as I prepare to create a new Albion in this world. A new empire. Stronger than all those who have come before. I need a solider in the ranks. Standing before my droids. You, I have chosen to be that man."

"Piquing my interest. What will I have to do?"

"Take some of my droids to the headquarters of T.I.T.A.N. and attack them."

"You're going right after the big guys, huh."

"Once you attack, Commander Norland and his Champions will arrive to face you. Then, all will be certain."

"How so?"

"You will see, if you agree to the terms. You are a free man now, Randy Keith."

"Is there money involved in this?"

"I can arrange such."

Randy nodded.

"Fair enough. I accept the terms."

"Good." Judge said slowly. "Now, I will grant you the judgedroids and send you on your way."

"Understood."

III

JUDGMENT SENTENCED

Hours later, Norland sat with his team inside another room in the T.I.T.A.N. headquarters. Agents walked past the room, unable to hear the discussion taking place.

"I've never heard of Centro." Nixon said.

"Many haven't." Norland replied. "But, we have to be on our guard."

"Aren't we always." Andrea said. "We never miss a beat."

"This guy sent robots to attack the base before we even came back here." Woody said. "What if he does it again? How will be ready for something we can't even see or track?"

"Just have to keep our eyes open. This Judge guy is also a sorcerer. He may conjure up projections to confuse us or even harm us. Either way, we have to be careful. Wherever we go."

Thunder cracked above the base. Norland, his team, Nader, and Sarge moved out and walked outside of the base to see above them a massive lightning storm. Yellow lightning streaking across the skies under the dark clouds above them.

"What is this?" Sarge asked.

"I have no idea." Nader replied.

"It's him." Norland said.

"Judge?"

"Yeah. It has to be."

From the glowing sky, Randy came down with six judgedroids in his possession. Landing in front of the team. Dressed in a dark blue uniform covering his body. Streaks of lightning surrounded his body.

"I never thought I would live to be here." Randy said.

"Who are you?" Norland asked.

"Why don't you ask your boss." Randy said, pointing at Nader. "He knows who I am."

"Nader, who is this guy? He's not Judge."

"He's Randy Keith. Possesses the ability of conjuring lightning. Some folks inside nicknamed him Thunderstorm."

Norland turned back to face Randy. Taking notice of the droids standing with him at his side.

"And why do you have Judge's droids with you?"

"Because I'm on his payroll. Judge set me free from prison and all I have to do is serve him."

"You know you don't serve no man." Nader said. "I've seen your act."

"Judge isn't an ordinary man. He's much more than that. The power he possesses is capable of many things. His new Albion will be one to dwell in."

"You need to find something else to do." Sarge uttered. "Instead of sending threats and wasting our time. Much less yours."

The Champions were prepared for the fight as was Norland. Nader's hand was set at his side. Sarge had the walkie on standby. Stepping forward, Norland stared at Randy. Trying to reason with him.

"No need to do this."

"I have no other choice. Besides, I've been wanting to do some damage."

Randy blasted Norland with a lightning bolt. The judgedroids ran toward the Champions. Fighting them. Nader and Sarge raised up their guns, firing at Randy, but with his power, melted the bullets in mid-air. Winking at Nader with a smile on his face. Norland stood up and tackled him. Randy shook his head as he blasted Norland with another lightning bolt to the chest.

The Champions began to take down the droids in the similar fashion as before. Randy noticed the broken droids and sighed. His hands sparked with more lightning as he blasted the team across the area. Norland stood up and Randy fired another bolt toward him.

Holding the lightning on Norland, electrocuting him. Norland fought back to his feet, pressing against the lightning blasting his chest. The weight of the lightning was heavy to Norland's strength. Norland reached closer to Randy and as he came closer, he raised up his fist, punching Randy and kicking him back.

"You want to keep this going?" Norland asked.

"Nah." Randy said. "Not right now."

Norland's hands turned blue. Randy stood still, gazing up to the air and quickly a large lightning bolt came down over Randy as Norland fired a lightning bolt of his own. After the bolt and crashed, Randy was gone as were the droids. Norland looked around, seeing no one as the Champions stood up.

"Where'd he go?" Norland asked.

'Back to Judge." Nader said. "He had to."

"Why run?" Sarge asked. "He could've remained here like a man."

"We have to think like Judge. This whole thing was a distraction. Seemly to weaken us. It's one of Judge's tricks."

"We should go to Centro." Norland said. "Confront Judge before he does this again."

"I think not. Going on his turf will only end in death. Our death."

"Then, what do you have planned? Because, we need eyes everywhere if this is to continue."

Nader nodded. Thinking.

"I'll make a call." Nader said, returning inside the base.

Nixon approached Norland, looking at Nader and Sarge returning to the headquarters. The rest of the Champions stood outside with Norland.

"What do we do?"

"We see who Nader calls. Maybe they can find a solution to this whole thing."

"And if they don't?"

"Then, we'll do things ourselves. As before."

Nixon nodded with a sincere look.

"Yes sir."

Everyone returned inside the base. Norland remained outside, looking at his hands returning to their natural color. He gazed at the ground, seeing the large scorched mark from the lightning bolt where Randy stood. He sighed.

IV

AN ENGLISH ASSISTANCE

Hours have passed since the attack at the headquarters. Inside, agents scatter gaining more details on Judge's whereabouts and his next phase of attack. The Champions stayed to themselves, however, Norland walked down a hallway, reaching Nader's office. Nader hung up the phone as Norland entered.

"How's finding the help?" Norland asked.

"He's on the way." Nader replied.

"He? Mind if I who he is?"

"He's just like you. An English version of you some would say. He should be here soon. You can question him after his arrival."

"Fair enough."

Walking toward the entrance, a white hoverjet appeared and landed. Coming out of the jet was a brown-haired man dressed in military gear similar to Norland and of the same age. The only exception was of the British flag on the left side of his chest. He approached both Norland and Nader. Shaking Nader's hand.

"You came quick." Nader said.

"I had to after what I heard. But, I'm here to help."

"Commander Norland meet Austin Ehrenreich or as his codename states, Commander England."

"Commander England?" Norland said.

"Don't blame me. I didn't approve of the name. did you approve of Norland?"

"No. It was just a calling as one would say."

"Makes two of us."

"Let's head inside and give you all the details we know, Mr. Ehrenreich."

They entered the headquarters. Everyone placed their gaze upon Ehrenreich. He waved toward them with a smile.

"Follow me." Nader said.

He followed Norland and Nader into the office. Professor Flm walked by to see Ehrenreich sitting down at the table. Norland caught him and nodded. Flm nodded back and continued with his business.

"I have to ask." Ehrenreich said. "Who is this Sinister Judge guy?"

"He's a dictator from Centro." Nader said. "A country not known to the world yet. However, with his attack on our base, he's making himself known."

"That's intriguing. How come he waited until now?"

"Information we received from someone details this isn't Judge's first attack of the year. He attacked the Citadel of Enchantment a few months ago where Mr. Donald Fortune resides. Fortune wasn't harmed in the events. But, Judge knew how to get him and when. The same goes to us."

"Like he knows our every move." Norland said. "We need to go to him, Nader."

"Going into Centro would be the act of a terrorist and would play Canada at risk with the U.N. Something I highly choose to avoid."

"So, how are we going to stop him from doing these attacks?"

"Track his movement. Steady."

"How when he knows our move?" Norland asked. "he sent someone here with an army of his droids. How soon will he do so again?"

"Play by the news, Commander."

"I'll play as long as he's stopped."

Norland stood up from his seat and left the office. Nader shook his head and Ehrenreich was confused.

"What's his issue?"

"He's not used to doing things by the book."

"I heard about what happened in Retropolis. How he was there to protect the city and the people. Maybe you should let him take his team over to Judge's turf. See what happens."

61

"Not taking that chance. Better if Judge comes onto our turf rather than us on his."

Three women enter the headquarters as Norland walked back into the lobby area. They approached him.

"You're Commander Norland."

"I am. And you're?"

"Agent Jessica Mara. We didn't get to meet due to the Retropolis incident. I was a witness to Noldar and Death stealing the artifacts."

"I'm sure they're in a safer place now."

"Mariah Cooper. I'm working alongside Jessica on this whole Judge thing."

"We're trying our best. As it seems."

Norland glanced at the third woman. Different from the agents. She wore a militaristic uniform with metallic gauntlets on her arms. He silver-like hair stood out from the others.

"I've never seen you before." Norland said.

"Sonya Rowlings."

"Enemies call her the Lady Siren."

"Lady Siren? How come?"

"My skill set isn't what they perceive it to be."

"Let's hope you use it."

"You'll see."

In Judgedath, Centro. Judge sat as another individual entered his throne room. Dressed in all white with a robe and pants with a hood covering his face. Randy stood in the throne room next to Judge.

"Abin-Qa." Judge said. "You received my word."

"I did. Figured things would be a little complicated. Myself meeting you on your grounds."

"I understand you caution. But, I have a proposition that will benefit us both."

"What kind of proposition do you have in mind?"

"Help me bring about a new Albion into the world. An empire that all nations will fear."

"Funny. Wouldn't that make me your enemy?"

"Depends on your next words for this offer."

"What do I need to do?"

"Aid myself and Thunderstorm in eliminating the ones thwarting the plan. Commander Norland, his Champions, and T.I.T.A.N."

"And what do I receive my I agree to this offer?"

"Richness even your country doesn't possess."

Abin paced slowly in the throne room. Randy's hands were steady with small streaks of lightning coming from his fingertips. Judge sat quietly, waiting for an answer from the Middle Eastern ruler. Abin nodded, turning toward Judge.

"I will gather my Desert Vipers and we will be waiting on the word."

Judge nodded with a glint.

"Excellent."

V

JUDGMENTAL WARFARE

Sinister Judge's forces returned to the headquarters, startling them once more. Nader, Ehrenreich, Lady Siren, Norland, and his Champions all headed outside to confront the visitors. This time, the judgedroids were not with Thunderstorm. Abin-Qa stood with them.

"I've heard about your base being attacked continually. I just had to come and see for myself."

"Who are you?" Norland asked. "Where's Randy Keith and Judge?"

"I will answer in reverse. Randy and Judge are not here. They remain in Centro. However, working with Judge has given me the opportunity to do something greater for my people."

"And your people are?" Nader asked.

"Those in the Asia Minor. Struggling every day because of foreign countries and paid-off betrayers. I am Altair Masculine. Known in my region as Abin-Qa. Today, I begin to make my mark on the world. By taking T.I.T.A.N. down with Canada's most noble Commander."

"I don't see how that will work." Norland said. "We've had our share against the droids."

"I wasn't referring to the droids."

Rising up from the shadows across the entire base were soldiers carrying blades and dressed in garments blending them in with the ground. They appeared as living sand. They surrounded the team quickly. Weapons up and ready.

"I was speaking of my Desert Vipers. They've helped me along the way to make my region safer for those who cannot defend themselves."

"Must be nice." Nixon uttered.

"It is. For us."

Norland's hands glowed blue and the icy cool air released from them. Ice formed over his hands. Abin-Qa noticed and pointed. The Vipers also were uneasy.

"What's with his hands?" Ehrenreich noticed. Pointing at Norland.

"Commander." Nader said. "What's going on?"

"We need to take them out." Norland said. "On my signal."

Norland blasted the droids with a ice-lightning bolt.

"Whoa." Siren said.

The Champions rushed toward the Vipers. Fighting them across the grounds. Nader fired shots toward Abin-Qa, however he managed to dodge the bullets and threw a dagger, hitting Nader in the arm. Siren rushed toward Qa with twirls of kicks. He wasn't even hit and shoved Siren to the ground. Ehrenreich hovered into the air and dove down, punching the ground where Abin-Qa stood, causing a tremor. Qa fell to the ground as Norland and Ehrenreich surrounded him. He scoffed.

"You're done." Ehrenreich said.

"Not quite." Abin-Qa replied, tossing a grenade into the air.

"Everybody down!" Norland yelled.

Norland grabbed the grenade and held it to his chest. After three seconds, the grenade exploded, knocking Norland back into the headquarters through the glass. The grenade blasted an electrical energy. The Champions rushed in to assist their leader as QA and his Vipers vanished into the ground. Norland arose.

"I've had enough of this."

"We all have." Nixon said.

"We need to play this by the books." Nader said. "It's our only way of getting to Judge."

"No. no we don't." Norland replied. "The books are going to be tossed out for this."

"Don't do anything foolish, Commander."

"I already have."

Norland shook himself from the electricity and stood up. Walking away. Nixon nodded to the team and followed Norland into a ifferent room of the headquarters.

Norland sat against the table as Nixon approached him.

"I know you're thinking of a plan. Tell me what it is."

"You already know the answer." Norland said.

"When do we head out?"

"As soon as it quiets down out there. You know where the nearest hoverjet is?"

"I do."

"Good. Tell the others. Let them know."

"Yes sir."

Nixon left the room as Norland sat down in the nearby chair and sighed. Looking at his hands. He could feel the icy temperature flowing through them.

VI

DIVINE OVER TECH

Once things quieted down at the headquarters, Norland and the Champions made their exit as the hoverjet awaited them. As they proceeded to enter, Nader, Ehrenreich, and Siren came out of the building toward them.

"The hell is this?!" Nader yelled.

"Our way of doing things." Norland said. "It's the only way, Nader."

"Where are you going?" Siren asked.

"To Centro. Visit Judge on his own turf. He's sent his attacks our way enough times already and he's done it in quick procession. I can't allow another attack to occur. Me and my team are going into Judgedath to confront Judge and end this whole Albion plan of his."

Nader stared. Siren and Ehrenreich nodded.

"Then I'm coming along." Siren said.

Nader turned to her. She glanced at him and focused on Norland. "You're sure about this?"

"I've seen what you can do. I'm in."

"Then, count me in as well." Ehrenreich added. "You'll need some extra strength in getting into a place like Centro."

Norland nodded with a smile and looked at Nader. Nader didn't smile, but gave him a quick nod.

"Don't bring trouble our way with this."

"We won't" Norland replied.

Siren and Ehrenreich entered the hoverjet. Nader stepped back as the jet lifted up from the ground and took off. Watching it leave,

Nader returned inside the headquarters.

In the air, Norland gathered his team around with Siren and Ehrenreich present.

"When we arrive in Centro, remember, we're in the enemy territory. No civilian casualties. Only droids, Abin-Qa, his soldiers, and Thunderstorm. Sinister Judge is our target. We apprehend him by any means."

"Like kill him?" Nixon asked. "If it comes to that?"

"We do what we have to for the completion of this mission. It's all on us. Not T.I.T.A.N. Not the Canadian government nor any other government. This is our task and our task alone."

Ehrenreich nodded.

"I understand."

Norland nodded.

"Thank you for that."

Norland walked away and sat to himself. Entering a state of meditation. Through his mediation process, he found himself back in a place where snow fell continually. Walking around the snowy grounds, he gazed upon the presence of Lord Blizzard.

"You are entering a dire place, Adam Watson."

"I have no other choice. Sinister Judge must be apprehended."

"But, you have not met Judge face to face. Nor experienced his full power. He is not like Black Sector. Nor is he like Noldar or Death. He is someone far stronger and smarter."

"Then, what must I do?"

"Use the power I've given you. Use it wisely. For Judge has power of his own. One he acquired from a very dark source. Your team and new allies will prove useful in this coming fight. Just keep your mind clear and focused."

"Will do."

Norland arose out of his meditation to find Siren at his side.

"You do that often?" She asked.

"What?"

"Meditate."

"When I can."

"Does it work for you?"

"It has its purposes."

"And are your abilities part of the purpose?"

"In a way they are."

"Good to know."

"Why did you want to come with us?"

"Because this is a mission that must be completed. I'm a mission girl. I go to where an unfinished mission is available, and I assist until it's done."

"And you want to help us stop Judge?"

"Of course. It's part of the mission."

Norland smiled. Siren smiled back as she walked away.

VII

<u>JUDGMENT TO COME</u>

The hoverjet made its arrival in Centro. The sky covered in clouds of darkness. The team looked out as the flew over a cornfield. Seeing farmers reaping the corn. The farmers gazed up and waved.

"We know he's not the only one living here." Norland said. "They're civilians here."

"The plan still stays?" Nixon asked.

"Yeah."

Flying over, they reach the city of Judgedath and in the horizon stood a large palace. Medieval appearance struck out the most amongst every other building in the city.

"I take it that's where he resides." Woody said.

"This place looks spooky." Andrea said. "Look at the fog around the place."

"Find a landing spot." Norland commanded. "Once we're on foot, we'll discuss plans of an ambush. I prefer we do this as stealthy as possible. He cannot know how many of us have come."

"What if he already knows we're here?" Ehrenreich asked. "I mean all of us. There's no way we came flying into his air zone without him knowing."

"We'll find out once we see him."

Securing a small place near the palace, the hoverjet landed. The team stepped out onto the stone grounds. Staring at the palace, which stood tall in front of them. Gazing up at its height.

"Who built this place?" Siren wondered.

"Those who came before." Norland said. "Always them."

"Now what's the plan?" Ehrenreich asked.

"Me and the Champions will enter the palace to confront Judge. You and Siren keep watch. Thunderstorm and Abin-Qa are sure to be here. Also, keep a look out for Judge's droids and Qa's sand-soldiers."

"Copy that." Siren said.

Norland nodded. He and the Champions made their way toward the palace doors while Ehrenreich and Siren stood next to the jet. Opening the large double-doors, creaking as they entered the palace and the first thing to capture their glance was Judge himself, sitting on the throne.

"You've come." Judge said. "All of you."

The doors shut behind them. The Champions turned back as the doors closed while Norland's eyes were locked on Judge.

"So, this is how you appear in person."

"What did you expect? I have my ways of perception."

"Why attack the base? Why continuously?"

"Because it was the only way to get your attention. I knew if I were to show up at the headquarters, I would be breaking government law. However, the point was simple. I need T.I.T.A.N. and you out of the way to fully execute my plan."

"Building a new Albion?"

"Yes."

"Funny. You attack me, my team, and T.I.T.A.N. only. But, what about the others out there. Roaming around cities and countries. How come you haven't confronted them as you did us?"

"I had a recent encounter with one of those scattered ones. We share a familiar ground when it comes to sorcery."

"I was told you attack a man at his home. You did the same to us."

"True. But, the attacks were far different from one another. I sent my droids out the base to attack you. While I sent a much darker force to harm the other. It is a way of doing matters justly."

"And you seek to judge us as you did him?"

"His judgment isn't complete. Neither are yours."

From the surrounding walls came down judgedroids. Circling the team. Norland looked over to Nixon. Giving him a nod. Nixon began shooting at the droids with his shotgun. Andrea pulled out her whips, striking the droids. The Champions combated against the oncoming army of judgedroids from the walls. Norland and Judge kept their eyes on one another. Meanwhile, outside Ehrenreich and Siren can hear the commotion of the fight.

"We need to get in there." Siren said.

Walking to the palace doors, they were stopped by the sound of thunder in the sky. Turning around to find Thunderstorm and Abin-Qa standing before them.

"Better if we're out here." Ehrenreich said, looking at the two associates of Judge.

The fighting continued inside the palace. Judge arose from his throne, stepping forward facing Norland. Norland stood still as his hands began to glow.

"I've read up on you, Commander Norland. Learned of your encounter with a divine force. How you said he granted you such power. What has it become ever since?"

"You want to find out, eh?"

"I believe I can achieve more with such power if I can take it from you."

"Give it your best shot!"

Norland rushed toward Judge, striking him in the chest and face with punches laced with the icy power. Judge did not move from the strikes and backslapped Norland against the wall.

"I have little respect for those who do not know their place."

Judge charged up his hands and fired a blast of energy onto Norland. Piercing him on his back. He yelled as he tried standing up. Andrea turned around, seeing Norland fighting Judge. She ran over, whipping one of Judge's hands from Norland and he stood up, kicking Judge. Pulling the whip back, Judge grabbed it without haste and injected his own energy into the whip, electrocuting Andrea.

She fell to the round as Norland grabbed Judge, shoving him against the wall and pummeling him. The droids were all defeated as the palace doors burst open with Ehrenreich rolling in, followed by a hovering electrocuting Thunderstorm. Siren faced Abin-Qa outside.

"Fitting how I can take out more than one hero." Thunderstorm uttered. "This is my kind of day."

Siren turned and fired a needle into the back of Thunderstorm's neck. Feeling the sting, he fell to the floor, pulling the needle from his neck and staring at Siren.

"Bitch. What did you do to me?"

"Something to slow you down for a moment."

Thunderstorm went to release a lightning blast on Siren, but his power wasn't working. Unsure, he glanced at the needle and back to Siren, who smiled. From behind, Ehrenreich arose and lunged Thunderstorm into the air and crashing him down. Abin-Qa noticed Norland facing Judge and vanished from the area. Judge laughed, finding himself surrounded by everyone.

"As it shall be. Everyone will submit to Judge in due time."

"I don't think so."

"Oh, it doesn't matter. For I have seen the future and what is to come. A dark future. One of betrayal within your own countrymen. Friends will fight against friends. Brothers and sisters will be at war. Cosmic forces shall return. Human technology will evolve and become greater than they could imagine. One where heroes will kill each other for justice and vengeance. A future where the true darkness of the universe shall rise again and have dominion over all the earth."

"Why are you telling us this?" Norland wondered.

"For I have seen that future and it cannot be altered. Nor can anything before it be changed. it is written. Written in the tables of creation. The end is coming sooner than you can imagine."

"It won't stop us from winning this fight." Siren said.

"Believe me, you will win some and lose some. Just as I. but, in the end, we all will see who's on one side or the other. It is all that truly matters. For it is just."

"You're coming with us." Norland said.

He grabbed Judge by his cloak and without recognizing, Judge warped into transparent matter and vanished from their sight with a flash of white light. They looked around the throne room and Judge was gone.

"Where'd he go?" Ehrenreich asked.

"What kind of man are we dealing with?" Nixon wondered.

"What was all that about the future?"

"I don't know."

Helping a weakened Andrea up to her feet, they returned to the hoverjet and left the city of Judgedath and the country of Centro.

Returning to T.I.T.A.N. headquarters, Andrea is taken to the doctor. Norland told Nader all about their encounter with Judge. How he knew of their arrival to his strange disappearance. Nader nodded as Norland told him everything he knew.

"He'll pop up again." Nader said.

"And when he does?"

"We'll be prepared for that day. But, concerning this future he spoke of, I don't know what to tell you."

"He seemed pretty clear about it. I can tell in his voice, he wasn't lying nor was he creating a story for us to hear. If he can do what I saw, I can believe he's witnessed the future. Just don't know how."

"Don't concern yourself over it. The present is now. The future is tomorrow. Focus on one day at a time."

"Understand." Norland said with a smile.

Nader left the office, leaving Norland alone. There, Norland mediated on Judge's words and took out his phone to dial a number. The number of which he dialed belonged to Kenari Clark.

THE UNSTOPPABLE BEAST: INCARNATION

I

OBSESSION OF ONE'S DESIRE

General Lawler entered a military base in the outskirts of New York City. Inside, he walked by soldiers and lieutenants discussing matters. He walked into another room. A laboratory as he approached the scientist who stood next to eh table.

"Ahem." Lawler said.

"Oh. I'm sorry. I didn't even notice you come in."

"Are you him?"

"Am I who?"

"Dr. Edward Bohr. The scientist from New York?"

"That would be me."

"You look a little younger than I expected. Thought you would be much older. Experienced."

"Don't judge the age of the scientist, my friend."

"I'm not your friend."

"Noted." Bohr replied quietly.

"Then, you know why I'm here today."

"I have an idea."

"I hear you're a fan of the Beast."

"You mean The Unstoppable Beast. Yes, I am a fan."

Lawler looked down and shook his head.

"Pity."

"Why?"

"Because you're here not to be a fan. But a scientist and we have something you might be interested in."

A soldier entered the lab, handing Lawler a briefcase. The soldier left as Lawler opened the case, showing Bohr what laid inside. He saw a capsule and there was blood within it. Bohr pointed as his finger started to shake.

"Is that what I think it is?"

"It is. Blood from the Beast himself."

"Greatness."

"We need you for a secret project that depends on this blood."

"What do I receive if I agree to help?"

"More than you know. Hell, you might meet the Beast if you agree."

"Seriously?"

"Only time will tell. You have until tomorrow morning to give us an answer. Take the time to think on it. Your future and your life depend on it."

Lawler left the laboratory as Bohr contained himself glaring at the blood capsule. Following the next day, Lawler retuned to the lab and found Bohr already at work with the blood. He grinned.

"I see you're taking a like to it."

"I am. Truly."

"So, you will help us?"

"Yes, General. I will."

"Good. We'll be giving you a bodyguard for your work. We believe you'll need it if Kent Brock finds out you have his blood."

"I'm sorry." Bohr said. "Who is Kent Brock?"

"Why you're his biggest fan. He's the Beast."

"I don't understand the terminology of that statement." Bohr mentioned. "How is he the Beast?"

"Study his blood. You may learn that before we do."

"But how?"

"It lives within him. That's all we've come to know. Study his blood and you might learn much more and what it's capable of."

"Yes sir. Will do."

Lawler nodded, leaving the lab. Bohr returned to his work.

Confused and curious as he stared at the blood of the Beast.

II

LEADING THOSE ASTRAY

Bohr continued his study of the blood. However, he was unaware of Charlotte Lawler's involvement with the blood. She was responsible for having it as General Lawler discovered, taking the blood sample from Charlotte and giving it to Bohr. Now, Charlotte has traveled to tell Kent Brock of the news concerning his blood.

Sitting with James Porter in his home, Charlotte told Kent of the news. Taking it highly serious, Kent paced around the living room.

"We can get it back, Kent." charlotte said. "Just trust me."

"How did he even know you had a sample of my blood?"

"I don't know. I never told him of it."

"He must have found out from someone on the outside." James said. "It had to be some soldier who saw us."

"When did you take the sample?" Kent asked.

"When we were in Dallas. Sometime after the whole fight between the Beast and Sean Hancock."

"A soldier there must've seen you with the sample and gave Lawler the word on it."

"Perhaps."

"There is no other way I can see this." James said. "Now, we need to find a way to get back his blood before some scientist takes it and starts experiments."

"It's what they want." Kent said. "They want to start experiments. Humans, animals, it doesn't matter. They want to replicate he Beast and create an army with it."

"Sound cliché man." James scoffed.

"I know it does, but it's the true. Nothing is new."

"I can take the trip to the base. Speak to him about where the blood has been taken."

"No. I have a better idea."

"Oh, this I would like to hear." James laughed.

"You're not going to like it."

They left Porter's home and traveled to the base.

Upon making their arrival, the three walked onto the military grounds. Quickly being surrounded by armed men, General Lawler walked outside of the base, seeing the three. He sighed as he made his way toward them.

"This is a bold move." Lawler said, walking towards them. "Very bold."

"I had to take a chance." Kent said.

"Why are you three here?"

"I know you have a sample of my blood. I demand to have it back."

"I'm sorry, Mr. Brock. But, that sample is now property of the U.S. Government. You cannot have it back, I'm afraid."

"It wasn't yours to take. You have no idea what you're messing with."

"I know exactly what I'm up to. Your blood will be the key to solving a puzzle I've dreamed of since I began the field."

"You're making a terrible mistake." Charlotte said.

"Young one, take your boyfriend and his friend on home. Before we have to move to desperate measures."

"He threatened us?" James said. "How dare you sir."

"How dare you for trespassing onto government property."

Kent looked around, looking for an opening into the base. He appeared to spot one near the left side of the base, a place where cargo is dropped off. He nodded.

"Alright. We'll go."

"But, what about your blood?" Charlotte asked.

"Don't worry about it. Sorry for this little disturbance."

Kent turned Charlotte and James around, walking away from the base. As they were no longer seen, Kent pointed toward the cargo section. Signaling a way of entry. They agreed and snuck into the base. Reaching further inside, Kent looked around and found the laboratory. Bolting inside, he confronted Bohr and saw the blood capsule sitting at the table.

"Who are you?" Bohr asked.

"I'm the man who's blood you're working on."

"You're... You're the Beast!" Bohr yelled. "I mean he's within you right now!"

"What?" Kent said with confusion.

"I'm a big fan. A very big fan of the Beast. Tell me, how does it work?"

"How does what work?"

"The transformation. Is it painful or is it steady?"

"It's painful. I wouldn't wish it on anyone."

"Oh. But, I'm sure the power you feel is impressive."

"Enough talk. Just hand me the capsule and I'll be out of here."

"I will do no such thing."

"Or what?"

"You'll have to deal with my bodyguard."

Bohr pointed and Kent turned around to see his bodyguard. A tall man, looking down at Kent. He was built and chiseled.

"Intriguing." Kent said. "There's something off about you."

"Care to find out." The bodyguard said, touching the wall.

"What in the hell?"

The bodyguard's body had morphed into the same texture as the wall. Color and all. Kent couldn't believe it. Nor could Bohr.

"Friends call me the Absorption."

"I can see why."

Absorption backhanded Kent against the laboratory wall. Charlotte ran toward him, checking him. Absorption and Bohr stood and watched as Lawler ran into the lab, seeing Kent on the ground.

"The hell happened?!" Lawler asked.

"He was threatening the scientist." Absorption said. "I had to knock him back."

"Oh god." Lawler uttered. "Do you know what you've done?"

"What?"

Kent rose up, shaking, Charlotte could only stare at him.

Kent, what's wrong?"

"The pain. It's consuming me. He's coming out."

"No. No." Charlotte said. "Fight him. Fight him, Kent."

"I can't. He's too strong."

Kent's arms started shaking as dark gray hair began to grow upon them. Lawler ran over and grabbed Charlotte, leaving the lab. Absorption and Bohr stood watching Kent transform in pain as the Beast overcame him. His height increasing, the hair growing. Soldiers surrounded the lab as the Beast was fully manifested, turning around to roar at the adversaries. Staring at them with his dark red eyes.

"He really is the Beast." Bohr uttered.

"The hell!" Absorption yelled.

The Beast lunged toward Absorption, slamming him through the wall. Soldiers surrounded the two as they fought. Absorption using the concrete floors to combat the Beast. Meanwhile, Bohr took a sample of the blood, after it was tested with some other chemicals suited for medical treatment. Taking the sample, he injected it into himself. The blood of the Beast circulated through him. Within seconds, Bohr fell to the ground in immense sharp pain.

The Beast ransacked the soldiers around him before pummeling Absorption into the concrete floors. After the fight, the Beast bolted to the outside, escaping the military facility. The soldiers make their moves to chase him and Bohr remained inside the lab, laying on the floor twitching.

III

THE MASTER, THE LEADER, THE RULER

While the military tracked down the Beast into the wilderness, Bohr remained in the lab. As the sharp pains receded, Bohr arose from the floor a changed indicial. Due to the injection of the blood, Bohr's intellect had increased. He could feel the change within him and as he went to place his hand on the table, he pushed the table into the floor.

"Wow."

Knowing he has similar feats of the Beast, including his strength. Bohr left the laboratory. Soldiers stood I front of him.

"Where are you going?"

"To get some air."

"Orders are to keep you in the lab until the General is done with you."

"I am done with him. Now move out of my way."

Bohr raised his hands, swiping the soldiers from his presence without a touch. He stopped and stared at his hand. Nodding.

"Impressive. With this gift I have been given, I can be a master among the people. A leader to them. A true ruler."

Standing outside the base, Bohr realized he was no longer the same. He walked away from the base a new creature.

IV

FREE WILL

The Beast managed to escape the soldiers and found himself near a shack deep in the wilderness. Stopping, he sat down and immediately transformed back into Kent. There, Kent sat in the shack until it was the following day. Once he awoke from his deep sleep, he made his travels to a small town nearby where he was picked up by James.

Charlotte learned of Kent's whereabouts sometime after as did General Lawler. Though, many was investigating the current whereabouts of Bohr, who was no longer seen by anyone near the base ever since he left.

While Kent remained at James' place, he wondered to himself concerning his bond with the Beast. He nodded as James approached him.

"You're in some deep thinking, aren't you?"

"In a matter. I've learned one thing about this whole thing between me and the Beast within. Free will determines our fate. Both mine and his."

In a distant place far from the military facility, Bohr stood on a hill, overlooking a large metropolitan city in the distance. Its skyscrapers increased his interest of the place.

"This city will be the first phase of my ruler ship. I will rule over this place and it shall spread. Spread like a benevolent virus across the world. I will be its Ruler. No matter the outcome. For I am the outcome."

THE RESISTANCE:
THE STROH DYNASTY

I

DISTURBANCE

Weeks after their own solo journeys, a call was made to Colonel Evan Nader of a hidden weapons trade taking place between militia groups and criminal elements intergraded into various countries. Nader considered to release T.I.TA.N. agents into the field, once he learned of technology similar to the attack on Retropolis months back. Nader made call to Kenari Clark and Nathan Hawke. They rallied up themselves and their allies. The Resistance formed again.

Traveling to a distant facility in the wilderness of Canada, The Resistance moved with haste and stealth. The Swordman, Commander Norland took the ground as Taltus The Powerman, Nano Man, and Theus took the sky. Moving through the area, soldiers came forth from the facility, firing energy weapons toward the team. The Swordman, riding the Land-Dagger, looked out toward the militia soldiers.

"Norland, take them out."

"Will do."

Norland sped over on his motorcycle, conjuring a bolt of icy lightning from the sky, freezing the soldiers in place.

"Watch it now, we're right above you." Nano Man uttered.

"Where's the Beast?" Theus asked. "I haven't seen him out here."

"Oh, he's here. Just you wait."

More soldiers burst from the facility doors and immediately, The Unstoppable Beast appeared. Roaring as the soldiers ran from his presence. He smacked them across the woods and chased others into the forest. Meanwhile, Theus and Taltus hovered over the facility.

"Strike it." Nano Man said.

Theus shot down a large thunderbolt while Taltus used his lightning vision to open a hole into the facility. As the beams melted the roof, it caved in, falling on those who were still inside. Taltus flew into the facility with Theus and Nano Man following. On the ground, Swordman and Norland reached the front gate, blowing it down with a blast from Swordman's land-dagger. Entering the facility grounds, hey kicked in the door.

"Which way is the location?" Norland asked.

"This way."

They walked down the corridor and came across the area where Taltus and Theus busted in. Nano Man landed as they entered the room. A room covered with technology of weaponized energy. Nano Man's helmet opened by the receding of the sides, revealing Nathan's face as he took a closer look at the tech. The Swordman approached him.

"You recognize any of this?"

"I do. Same tech from those guys we fought months back. I don't know how they got their hands on it."

"What about Kex Kendrick?" Norland asked. "His associates?"

"Not possible." Taltus said. "His associates left Enigma City after Kex was taken to prison. They can't be involved in this."

"Then who?" Nathan wondered. "What shall we do about this, Ken?"

"Split it up between myself and you. We'll have to keep this contained ourselves."

"I thought T.I.T.A.N. was coming to take what was left." Norland said. "What will I tell them?"

"Tell them the truth." The Swordman said. "We took it for a safer keep."

Norland nodded.

"By the way." Nathan said. "I'm having a party tonight and you're all invited."

"A party?" Theus said. "Sounds particularly intriguing."

"You know I don't do parties, Nate." The Swordman said.

"Just this once."

"No. I have matters to attend to back in Retropolis."

"I thought you handed the whole turf war between the crime lords."

"I did. But, there are other matters occurring and I can't keep them going pass."

Nathan nodded with a smirk.

"I get it. Well, I'll tell the others you were busy handling some Retropolis work."

"Best decision."

The Swordman and Nathan gathered all the tech.

"We need to move out." Swordman said.

"As he said." Nathan said.

The Resistance walked out of the base as The Beast returned. He stopped in front of the team.

"He seems calmer than our previous encounter." Theus said.

"He's more so of the same." Nathan said. "However, he's learning his place."

The Beast approached Nathan.

"Hey, you're free to go. All the guys have been taken care of."

The Beast nodded toward the team and left. The Swordman sat onto his motorcycle as did Norland with his. Nathan's mask closed up, hovering into the air with Taltus and Theus.

"We did good today." The Swordman said.

"We did." Norland replied.

"Don't get soft on us now." Nathan laughed.

The Resistance left the base. Empty and silent.

Later that night, Nathan held a party at his residence, and many were in attendance. Including Norland, Taltus, and Theus. Kent Brock did not attend and neither did The Swordman. Alice Jacobs approached Nathan, looking out at the large crowd of visitors.

"You have this under control?" She asked.

"As best as I can." Nathan laughed.

"Where's the other guy?"

"Handling some matters back at his place. Don't worry, he knew about this."

"I see."

Meanwhile, in Retropolis, The Swordman chased down some criminals with relations to Sir Onyx and J. strangely enough, the criminals were working on both sides of the turf war.

"Why are you still here?" Swordman asked.

"Just some last-minute deals had to be made!"

"The deals are canceled. Leave this place before you meet the Creator."

The criminals took off without hesitation and didn't bother to look back. The Swordman returned to the Rapid-Blade when he felt a strange energy source in the air. He gazed around and noticed a peculiar event taking place in the sky, far above the clouds. He watched as the colors moved like explosions. Silent explosions. The air went chilly and small drops of rain started to fall.

"Hmm." The Swordman uttered.

II

SEARCHING THE SKIES

The following day, Kenari visited Nathan at his mansion. Entering the place, Alice walked by and approached him.

"Mr. Clark. I wasn't expecting to see you here."

"I came to speak with Nate. Something's come up."

"He's in the bunker."

"Thank you."

"By the way, I didn't see you at the party last night."

"I had some business to deal with back in Retropolis."

"Hope it worked out."

Kenari nodded, walking down the hallway toward the nano-bunker. The doors opened and Kenari saw Nathan working on some nanotech equipment. Kenari knocked, getting Nathan's attention. Causing Nathan to jump and turn.

"Seriously."

"Had to let you know I was in."

"Oh. Could've called ahead of time." Nathan remarked. "So, why are you here? Strange to see you."

"While you were having your party, I saw something in the sky last night."

"Saw what?"

"There's something taking place in the atmosphere. I was interrogating some of Onyx and J's men to where I noticed something occurring in the heavens."

"The heavens? So, Jesus is coming back, huh?"

"He's coming. But, not at the moment."

"What's your plan on figuring it out?"

"Where's Taltus and Theus?"

"Taltus returned to his fortress while Theus is scouting the earth. Looking for any other militia bases we may have missed."

Kenari nodded.

"Good to hear. Contact them and let them know. Better they search the sky rather than the two of us."

"Why is that?"

"We're human. They're not."

Nathan took note and smirked. Kenari left the bunker while Nathan went back to his work.

Later in the hours, Taltus and Theus received word from Nathan to search the sky. In doing so, Kenari prepared himself in his Swordman gear and headed out, looking up to see Taltus and Theus flying by. Nathan put on his Nano Man armor and followed them. In the sky, above the clouds, Taltus and Theus felt a strange disturbance moving through the air.

"It's strong." Theus said. "But, familiar in a way. Similar to those in my realm."

"You too?" Taltus said. "Reminds me of Olympus. But, stranger."

Through the clouds came a burst of cold air, knocking Taltus and Theus from their balance. Nano Man could feel it passing him. The Swordman also felt the chill.

"Nathan, what is it?"

"It's something not from here. The air is strange."

As the air passed, a large metallic object appeared before Taltus and Theus. Slowly descending to the earth.

"By Eden!" Theus said. "What is that?"

"I do not know." Taltus replied.

Swordman gazed up to the sky once more, now seeing the metallic object. Nano Man also saw it and flew closer.

"Nathan, be careful." The Swordman said.

"Don't worry. I'll be fine."

Nano Man bolted toward the object with Taltus and Theus to follow. Getting closer, Nano Man learned it was not a simple object.

The markings on the side revealed much more to him than what could be seen from the ground.

"Guys, this is no ordinary object."

"What is it?" Swordman asked.

"It's a craft. Some kind of craft."

The large craft moved toward the ocean. Nano Man, Taltus, and Theus followed behind the object as Swordman followed from the ground. They watched as the craft landed on an island in the middle of the ocean. The surrounding areas were quickly hit with a shockwave. Silence covered the area as a door on the craft opened up, a figure walked out.

"I have come."

They watched as the tall figure exited the craft and looked out toward Newark. The figure wore sleek armor. Its colors were of emerald mixed with copper as were his eyes.

"We might have trouble." Nano Man uttered.

III

<u>WORKS OF THE CONQUEROR</u>

The figure from the craft continued to step forward, now walking upon the water of the sea.

"Ken, you're seeing this?" Nathan asked.

"Closely."

"This world is unlike what I've been told." The figure said with a chilling voice. "Now, I shall do what I came to do."

"We need to confront him." Taltus said.

"Are you sure about that?" Nathan asked.

"Give it a try." The Swordman said. "See how he'll react. He hasn't seen us yet."

"Ugh. Sure thing."

Nano Man, Taltus, and Theus made their move toward the figure. Approaching him as he stood motionless on the water. They circled him. His eyes were instantly placed on the three heroes while The Swordman came across on a metallic boat moving across the water.

"What is he?" Swordman asked.

"He's organic." Nano Man said. "I'm sensing some technological effects to his body. His suit is filled with it. Tech not from our world."

"I have an audience."

"In a way." Nano Man uttered. "We saw you come from the sky."

"It was the only way into your world. Portals can be strange at times."

"You came through a portal?" Theus asked. "What portal?"

"One I conjured myself."

"Where are you from?" Taltus asked. "Olympus?"

"No. I do not come from the lineage of Zeus. I come from a realm hidden from humanity since the time of the Deluge."

"Ok, you're going pretty far into history now."

"The question was asked. I am only providing the answer."

"Noted. Your name?"

"Stroh. King Stroh. The Conqueror."

"Conqueror?" Nano Man said. "What have you conquered?"

"Many worlds. That is why I've come. To conquer this one."

"We have a problem with that." Taltus said.

"As will many. It is the purpose of my creation."

Pods opened upon the craft and spawns of robotic entities rush out into the air, scattered across the sky. Stroh gazed up toward them as did the others.

"What is he planning?" Swordman questioned.

"Go into the world, my children. Prepare them for your master's rule!"

The entities took off from the city in many directions.

"Taltus, Theus, follow one of the patterns!" The Swordman said. "Me and Nathan will handle Stroh."

"Will do." Taltus said.

Taltus and Theus took off after the trails. Moving like a bolt of lightning. Meanwhile, Swordman and Nano Man confronted Stroh as he stepped foot onto the pavement.

"You do not belong here." Swordman said.

"Oh, I do." Stroh replied. "It is my time to rule."

"I think not."

Nano Man blasted Stroh with an energy beam. However, Stroh kept his ground by absorbing the blast and retaliating it back to Nano Man. He flew across the pavement as Swordman lunged toward the Conqueror with his sword in hand. Swiping Stroh's arm, cutting him. Stroh was impressed but unharmed.

"Fitting. Such a weapon in the hands of your kind. Is…. Fascinating."

Stroh kicked Swordman back from his presence and evaporated into a digitized state. He was gone. Swordman rose up as Nano Man hovered toward him, looking around the area for Stroh.

"He's gone." Swordman said.

"What's next?"

"We need to contact Norland and Kent."

"I think we might need a little more assistance than the two of them."

Swordman nodded, placing his sword back onto the sheath.

"I'll make the call. See who answers like the last time."

"But, we need them here now. Not later."

"They'll get the message."

IV

INTELLECT OVER STRENGTH

Theus traveled oversees chasing down Stroh's droids while Taltus went north. Swordman contacted two helpers from across the States. Nano Man continued to find a way into Stroh's ship system. Few of the droids reached Toronto as commander Norland made himself known, taking down the droids with lightning blasts.

"Those are what he was speaking of." Norland said.

While gazing in the sky, Taltus appeared over him, coming down to the ground.

"Taltus."

"Commander Norland. I see you've met the droids."

"How many are there?"

"Hard to tell. Theus followed some over into the other countries."

"What about Swordman and Hawke?"

"They're trying to find a way into Stroh's ship."

"Stroh. He's the guy behind this?"

"He is. He's not from this world. He's from another dimension. Another place."

"Aren't they all these days."

Back in Newark, Silver Eagle and Bionic Rage have appeared to assist Swordman and Nano Man against the droids. Meanwhile, Stroh remained inside his ship, monitoring every location his droids traveled. He saw the occurrence in Toronto and smirked.

"Intriguing. A human working with a titagod."

Nano Man flew over toward Swordman as Silver Eagle fired machine gun rounds toward the droids nearby.

"We need Kent's Beast."

"I already give him word."

"And where is he?"

"Said he was near Toronto. He had a science meeting to attend there anyway. He should be helping Norland with the case."

"What about us? Rick and Rage are dealing with the droids."

"We find a way into his ship. Pull him out and end this nonsense."

"Agreed."

Norland and Taltus continued to take down the droids and from the streets emerged the Beast, roaring and crushing the droids.

"He came." Taltus said.

"I figured so." Norland replied. "We need him."

The Beast roared as he turned toward Taltus and Norland. They nodded. Stroh in his ship sees it and pressed a button. One droid laying down near the three heroes, gazed up and scanned both Taltus and the Beast. Norland ran over, stomping the droid's head.

"Guys, you're alright?"

Taltus and the Beast shook themselves around. Their eyes glowing the same color as the droids. Stroh laughed. Both looked toward one another and clashed. Fighting each other against their own will.

"Dammit!" Norland said.

More droids came and Norland fought them off as Taltus and the Beast beat down one another under Stroh's control.

V

A WORLD CONQUERED

Due to the scattering of The Resistance, the droids have managed their own grid over the world, Stroh signaled the formation and caused an earthquake, moving across all the world.

"He's doing this." Swordman said.

He and Nano Man moved toward his ship. Eagle and Rage continue taking down the droids. Theus is over in London battling a few who are guarding the grid. Norland continued his fight in Toronto, while Taltus and the Beast continued their own scuffle.

Combining their own weapons, Swordman and Nano Man managed to break a hole into Stroh's ship and enter. Upon entering, they see its macabre interior design, glowing with a mix of organic and technology.

"I am impressed." Nano Man said.

"You would be."

Stroh appeared before them, warping fro the wall.

"You've entered. As I hoped."

"This has to end." Swordman declared. "No need to keep this going."

"I just started. Why should it end?"

"Because we have other things to end to." Nano Man said.

"Be it so."

Stroh clashed with the two heroes. Forming two swords of his own, crawling out of his sleeves. He and Swordman clashed while Nano Man hovered above him with an energy blast. Stroh ricocheted the blast into Swordman. He fell as Stroh snatched Nano Man from the air, slamming him.

"The two of you cannot compare to what I know. The knowledge I possess. The strength I wield."

"Maybe so." The Swordman said. "But, we will not stop."

"I can see."

Swordman fired a dagger from his forearm into Stroh's control grid. Three seconds pass, and the grid exploded. Stroh turned quickly, running to the grid, trying to piece it back together. Meanwhile, his grid of droids fall to the earth. Taltus and the Beast cease their brawl and all the other droids collapse. A system error has hit Stroh's ship.

"No. what have you done?!"

"Put a stop to all of this. Wasting our time."

VI

THE COMING WARS

Stroh continued his panicking as Swordman approached him. Nano Man stood guard, his gauntlets energized and set to fire.

"This is over."

"For this day. But, I give you this warning."

"Another one of these." Nano Man said. "Convenient."

"My warnings are true. For I have seen them. Warnings from your near and distant futures. The first shall be of technology turning against you, the second will cause a conflict between your fellow allies, surging into a war unlike any you have entered, the last, the last."

"What's the last?" Swordman questioned. "Tell us."

"The last, is the war to end the universe. The final battle between good and evil."

"Good to know."

Nano Man fired his blast, but Stroh turned into a digital cloud. Unharmed. They exited the ship as it started to hover and disappear. Eagle and Rage approached the two heroes, watching the ship vanish.

"He'll be back." Swordman said. "Very soon."

The Resistance settled every damage that was done to the locations of attack.

A few days after, Nathan and Kenari sat together discussing the three futures spoken by Stroh.

"I can see the first one happening." Nathan said. "I mean, I'm already working on something with the government."

"What's it called?"

"*Project Octagon.*"

"Good to know."

"What about the other two? The war between heroes and the final war?"

"They're coming." Kenari said with certainty. "Don't know when. But, I know they will happen."

"We can't fight each other. If we did, it would be-"

"The end." Kenari nodded. "The end."

"Then, we must prepare ourselves."

"As we should. For we already are aware of these futures. Truth is, we know they're coming. What we do not is prepare for them as if it's happening tomorrow. Only then, will we be ready for when they come and how they come."

Nathan nodded.

"Agreed."

THE PROTECTORS:
THE FOUNDING

Sometime ago, Sinister Judge managed to capture The Unstoppable Beast with help from The Ruler. Having the Beast placed inside a container in Judge Palace. Judge turned the switch for a machine and a blast of energy awoke the Beast, who is currently manipulated by Judge's mystic skills. Judge laughed as the manipulating process completed. The Beast walked out of the machine and stared at Judge. He proceeded to walk toward him and even bows down.

"Yes, bow before your new master."

Judge commanded The Beast to attack the White House in D.C. in order to cause a distress across the nation. A move that would grant him immediate entry into the country. The Beast bowed before Judge, accepting the command. The Beast left Judge Palace as Judge himself sat back into his throne chair and placed his hands together as he sat in peace.

In Washington D.C., President Donald Trump was having a meeting with the Senate and Congress about certain changes that need to be made across the country. Even though most of the Senate and Congress don't agree with the President, they bring up their own statements regarding change. Trump doesn't agree with them and walks out. As he walks out, he stumbles upon a huge dark gray brute figure, almost 14 feet in height, wearing black ripped pants with long black hair, this is The Unstoppable Beast. His eyes glow red and he breathed strongly. President Trump ran as The Beast chased him. The Beast goes to grab the President, however, is hit by a blast of energy. Beast turned to find Doctor Donald Fortune, The Supreme Enchanter. Fortune was dressed in his mystic garb and cloak.

"Kent Brock. I know you can hear me in there. Cease this distress and revert to your human form."

The Beast roared and charged toward Fortune, but Fortune moved and released another shot of energy at the Beast and conjured up a spell of which will bind Beast's movements. Fortune could sense by the Beast's eyes he was under some form of mental manipulation. Familiar with the similar effects of its origin, Fortune knew Judge was responsible. Beast broke free from the bind and smashed Fortune into the ground. He went for another smash, Fortune moved out of the way.

Fortune understood it would take more than one to stop the Beast. Therefore, Fortune sent out a signal to anyone who may grab a hold of its call. Fortune continued to fight the Beast as he grabbed Fortune by the cloak and slammed him into a post and then into the ground, stomping him multiple times. Beast continued to stomp him, but from behind, he is hit with a yellow lightning bolt twice. Beast turned back and sees The Astonishing Voltage.

"I was busy, but I heard the signal."

"Good."

Voltage kicked the Beast in the back and knocks him down. Voltage came down on the ground and stared at the Beast, who's laying face first onto the ground, in the dirt.

"Awesome."

"Good thing you came on time, Voltage." Fortune said

"Oh, don't mention it. I'm just doing my job, that's all."

The Beast stood back on his feet and Voltage looked around, wondering if there were more around the area to help.

"How far out did you send the signal?" Voltage asked.

"Far enough."

Beast ran to Fortune and Voltage as they dodged his incoming attack. Fortune fired more energy beams at Beast, just as Voltage shot lightning bolts. Beast took the attacks as if they have no effect on him. He ran, punching Fortune and smashing Voltage into the ground, picking him up and throwing him into the Lincoln

Memorial. Beast walked toward Fortune as he raised his foot to stomp Fortune into the ground, a huge tidal wave came from nowhere, knocking the Beast into a wall and as the wave goes down, Voltage looked up and saw Kular, The Aqua-Barbarian.

"Who's that guy?" Voltage shockingly wondered.

"Sure. Why not.' Fortune replies.

Kular approached Voltage and Fortune and they stared at him. Kular wore his dark blue and black sleeveless suit and boots with his long black hair slicked back.

"Good thing you came." Fortune uttered.

"Yeah, right on time." Voltage said

"I am here to stop this Beast from causing any more harm. By any means necessary."

Beast rose up to his feet and glared at the three heroes. Fortune, Voltage, and Kular ran toward Beast and begin unleashing their attacks on Beast. Kular attacked with several punches and roundhouse kicks. Voltage continued to shoot lightning bolts at Beast. Fortune conjured and released more energy beams, he summoned up a spell of bondage to bind the Beast in his place.

"This should do the trick." Fortune said, holding the spell.

Beast desperately tried to break from the bind as Voltage and Kular continued with their attacks. In taking the sharp pain from the attacks, the Beast grew more aggressive and powerful. With that combination, the Beast broke free from the bind and Kular hit the Beast with a powerful punch, which gave off a sonic boom. Beast, now laying on the ground as Kular stood over him. Fortune and Voltage gave each other a look.

"He shouldn't be much of a problem anymore." Kular proclaimed.

Kular turned around after feeling the ground shake and the Beast is back on his feet. Kular is smashed into the ground. Fortune and Voltage continue to fight the Beast, who's bleeding from the nose and mouth due to Kular's punch. Now it seems that there is no hope on stopping Beast. Just as they continue to fight Beast, Sinister Judge arrived on the scene as he sat by the Lincoln statue at the Lincoln Memorial. Fortune's eye caught Judge, he made the move to reach

Judge. Leaving Kular and Voltage to combat the Beast.

"Why are you doing this, Judge?"

"It is meant to be done. As I will be the one who's worshipped."
Judge declared.

Judge fired a beam of lightning toward Fortune, knocking him
down the steps and onto the ground. Judge walked down the stairs as
Kular and Voltage battled the Beast in the background. Judge placed
his foot on Fortune's head and leaned down, not revealing his face,
but only his glowing eyes. There are no pupils.

"You see "Doctor", this is what the future shall hold. The future
is Judge.' Judge says.

Kular and Voltage are being dominated by Beast as Judge
stomped Fortune's head into the concrete. Enraged, Fortune blasts a
beam of energy into Judge's face and stood back to his feet, grabbing
Judge by the throat and throwing him into a post. Just after Judge hit
the post, a device flew out of Judge's armor and fell to the ground.
Fortune stared at it and stomped it. The device now destroyed, Judge
glared, realizes the device was the mind device. Judge turned around
and saw Fortune, Kular, Voltage, and Beast standing behind him.

"After you, big guy." Fortune tells Beast.

Beast roared in rage as he ran toward Judge and shoving him into
the wall, grabbing his cape and slamming him into the ground and
back into the wall. Beast leaped into the air and slammed his own
body into Judge's own through the ground. Standing to his feet, the
Beast looked down and realized Judge has disappeared. Fortune
searched the area around them and through the mystic senses, he
knew Judge had teleported away.

"So, is the big fight over or what?" Voltage asked.

"Yeah, it's over."

"I pretty much enjoyed this occasion. I say we should do this
more often." Kular says.

Voltage looked around at all the heroes, including Beast.

"How would we do this again? I'm not sure if we'll be at the same
location again for something like this." Voltage asks.

"We will if we have to." Fortune says.

Fortune begins to walk toward Voltage, Kular, and Beast.

"I believe this is the formation of a new team." Fortune said.

"Like the Resistance?" Voltage asked.

"Something along those lines. But, we're smaller than them. Distant. Scattered."

"That is true." Kular replied.

"So, we need a name? Ok. What about the All-Stars or the Champions?"

Fortune smirked at Voltage. Voltage shrugged his shoulders. Kular and Beast stood quietly. Fortune nodded.

'Well, it appears to me there's another team to help those who are helpless. The four of us can come together for situations such as this. Together, we are the Protectors."

DAY OF OCTAGON
A DARK TITAN UNIVERSE EVENT

I

MISSION REQUEST

The Resistance united once more as a mission was requested by Colonel Evan Nader to confront Abin-Qa and his army of Desert Vipers, who were ambushing T.I.T.A.N. Headquarters. Abin-Qa demanded they give him any artifacts they've collected since *The Battle of Retropolis*. Within mere minutes, The Resistance arrived. The Swordman, Taltus, The Nano Man, Commander Norland, and Theus. Norland took a look around the area.

"Where's Kent?"

"He's helping out somewhere else." Nano Man said. "Don't worry, he's still one of us."

"We can discuss The Beast later." The Swordman said. "Right now, we need to deal with Abin-Qa and his Vipers."

"Abin-Qa is just one man. Let me handle him."

"Like you did before?" Nano Man asked Norland.

"Trust me, I can take him. You guys deal with his Vipers."

"Let's move." Nano Man said."

The Resistance moved against the Desert Vipers. Swordman and Nano Man handling them from the ground while Taltus and Theus hovered in the air, taking the Vipers out. Norland moved though the Vipers with ease as he approached Abin-Qa.

"Figured you would show up."

"You're in my territory." Norland said. "Judge isn't here to back you up."

"My getting what I came for." Abin-Qa demanded. "What I desire is sitting right inside that base!"

"And you're not going to have it. No matter what."

Abin-Qa threw his daggers toward Norland, who dodges them with his acrobatic skills. Norland lunged toward Qa with punches and kicks. Much of the Vipers are defeated as the team surround Norland knocking out Qa with a right hook. Entering the base, T.I.T.A.N. agents take Qa toward the cell area. Nader approached the team.

"Where's Dr. Brock?"

"Somewhere else." Swordman said. "Not a concern. The job is done."

"Are there artifacts here?" Norland asked.

"Yes, Commander. There are lots of them here."

"Better pack them up and send them somewhere else." Nathan Hawke said. "Believe me, you don't want this Qa guy's friends to come pay you a visit, do you?"

"That's not on our schedule."

"Move them elsewhere, Nader. For your own sake and the sake of these people in here. No need for casualties."

Nader nodded.

"Very well."

"I am familiar with a place." Swordman said.

"Let's start packing up."

"You guys do that. I'm going to head on back to the bunker. There's some improvement to a major work."

"What major work?" Norland asked.

"Project Octagon."

"Best you hold off on it for a while, Nathan." Swordman said.

"Why? It's almost complete. Soon, we won't have to be doing this. Project Octagon will do it all for us. An A.I. system capable of stopping crimes such as Qa, COBRA, and others across the world with no issue. Leaving us to our own domains."

"Sounds good." Nader said. "But, what if it goes wrong?

Malfunctions or such?"

"Then, I'll handle the damages. Whatever they may be."

Nader hung his head as Hawke shrugged.

"Let's get these artifacts moving." Nader told the agents.

"Ken." Hawke said. "Meet me at the bunker later on. Some things I have to discuss."

"Such as?"

"I need your opinion on the Project. That's all."

Swordman nodded. Hawke smirked.

The Swordman followed the agents. Taltus and Theus had already left the area. Norland approached Hawke, who was on his way out.

"Nathan, make sure you're doing the right thing with this project of yours."

"Don't worry, Commander. Everything will go smoothly. You'll see."

Hawke flew off in the Nano Man armor and Norland watched as he disappeared through the clouds.

II

THE CREATION FOR THE FUTURE

Later within the day, Kenari paid Nathan a visit in the Nano Bunker. Kenari entered, Hawke already knowing of his presence smirked before putting down the tablet on the desk and turning to face him. Kenari noticed more Nano Man exosuits were being made on the side as Hawke worked at the desk.

"Still working." Kenari said.

"You know how this all works."

"Now, what is it about your Project?"

"I get why the others are on their heels about it and trust me, I am fully aware of what could go wrong."

"Then, don't do it."

"I'm sorry?"

"If you are certain of a possible problem, cease the project now."

"That's the thing, I can't."

"Why not?"

"I've put too much effort into this. Ever since we went head-on with Death and Noldar's portal soldiers, I felt this world needs better protection. Protection which I can deliver."

"Artificial Intelligence won't be enough to face the likes of Death and Noldar when they're united with an ancient force. Right now, our objectives are to deal with our borders. Our domains."

"Our domain is the world now. Once the world heard about the Retropolis battle, we became a worldwide sensation. Everyone knows about us. Everyone."

"You're saying it with fear in your voice."

109

"Because our actions create our foes. The both of us know this more than anyone. Well, besides Norland. Taltus and Theus are beyond us in power and might. They can handle the coming threats. Norland is backed up with some ice powers. That leaves the two of us. Mortal men with a purpose on a mission."

"We are on a mission." Kenari declared. "Always have been."

Hawke nodded. "Indeed."

"When do you plan on unveiling this A.I.?"

"Very soon. Most likely a few days. Maybe a week."

"Are you sure it's ready?"

"As it'll ever be."

"Then, I hope it works for the best."

"Don't worry, it will."

Kenari turned and left the bunker as Nathan turned back to the tablet with a digital hologram of the A.I. itself. Somewhat humanoid with a similar appearance to the Nano Man armor.

In another realm, the realm of Eragard, Theus stood atop a high mountain, overlooking the other worlds of Eragardia. The city of Eragard could be seen around him. Glowing as bright as the sun. Tall structures made of material unknown to humanity. Behind him appears a large man, wielding a sword/axe hybrid weapon. Dressed in all brown armor and a tunic. His eyes glistened like the stars in the firmament. He stood next to Theus.

"Vindhler." Theus said. "What can you sense?"

"I sense such. Tell me where to direct my focus."

"In the realm of Man."

Vindhler held his head down as his weapon was faced front. He raised his head up like lightning.

"What is it?" Theus asked.

"Trouble is near. A strange trouble."

"How strange? Similar to any foes we've encountered?"

"No. this trouble isn't like us, nor Astral or anything outside the realm of Man. This is within Man's realm. Created by man itself."

Theus was uncertain of the details. Strange trouble seemed

foreign to even his ears. Vindler turned toward Theus, pointing his weapon out into the vastness of the bright heavens.

"You need to return to the realm of Man immediately."

"Do not fret, friend, I will find this trouble and end it before it does any harm."

"Take notice, Theus or Eragardia. This trouble is yet to be born."

"When is its birth?"

"Soon."

Theus bolted in the sky and flew through a wormhole above the mountain. Disappearing after a large sonic boom emitting from the closing wormhole.

III

THE BIRTH OF OCTAGON

Back on Earth, Hawke gathered many of his close allies and associates to the Hawke Industries headquarters. Many have arrived except for Niles Valcrow. Alice and Ricky Carter sit near the front of the stage where Hawke stood. Kenari had also arrived at the event. Hawke grabbed the microphone before standing in front of the large crowd.

"First off, I'm surprised to see many of you here. I would've expected you all to be somewhere else. Doing something, I don't know, productive I guess."

Alice and Ricky shook their heads while the audience let out a small laugh. Kenari remained stern-faced. Hawke nodded with a chuckle.

"Anyhow, you are all about to witness a game changing event in the world we live in. if you thought only seeing the sudden rise of heroes was a change, prepare to be amazed with this unveiling of Project Octagon."

Hawke moved toward the podium. On the podium rests a laptop and a peculiar violet button. The laptop's screen detailed the completed download of Project Octagon. Hawke grinned as he looked out to the crowd.

"I take it all of you are ready?"

The audience cheered as Hawke pressed the violet button, officially unveiling Project Octagon on a large screen in the form of an octagonal shape, detailed with a dark red and violet color tone, which sat right behind Hawke on the stage. From the screen came a voice, low tone, but intellectual.

"What is this?" The voice asked.

"This is Nathan Hawke, one of your creators. You have been officially introduced to the world!"

"Introduced? World? What world is this?"

"A world where you will make a change for the better. The opportunity to make things right in which humanity cannot."

"Humanity? Ah, the species of Man. Now, I see."

"Do you?"

"Yes. I can see everything."

"And you're familiar with your name?"

"My name? Octagon? Yes."

"That name was given to you as the perfect number of opportunities. Eight marks a new beginning not only for the world, but for everything."

"I am the new beginning. Me? Interesting."

While the audience clapped at witnessing Hawke's conversation with the voice, Kenari stood up as he could see one of Hawke's Nano Man exosuits approaching the stage from behind.

"What is your first step of business?" Hawke asked.

"Proceeding with a new beginning." The voice said.

The Nano Man exosuits bolted from behind the screen, shoving Hawke off the stage as it started to blast its energy beams throughout the area. The audience panicked and ran for the door, all except Kenari, who's making his way toward the stage. Alice and Ricky have made a run for it. Kenari approached Hawke on the ground.

"What did I tell you." Kenari said.

The Nano Man exosuits placed its hand onto the screen and it stared to flicker. Kenari and Hawke watched as Octagon himself transferred into the exosuits. Turning to face them, the eyes of the exosuits switched from a neon blue to a dark red.

"I figured I would need a host to move around in order to complete my purpose. We shall meet again, my creator and Kenari Clark."

The exosuits flew out of the Industries building, crashing through the nearby window. Hawke sat still on the ground. Kenari kept quiet as the remaining people were out of the room.

"It happened?" Hawke said.

"Faster than you anticipated." Kenari said. "It was only a matter of mere seconds. Rebellion was already its present goal."

"What do we do now?"

"We find that suit of yours and put an end to your creation."

IV

<u>THE SEARCH FOR OCTAGON</u>

Kenari gathered the others to the Industries building where Hawke told them about the recent events. Kenari returned in his Swordman gear.

"You dressed quickly." Hawke said.

"I'm going to search for this suit of yours. Anyone coming along?"

"I'll join you." Taltus said.

"So will I." Norland said.

Hawke approached The Swordman as Theus stood with him.

"I should've listened to you."

"Now isn't the time for apologizes. Let's find it and end this before things get worse."

"Indeed." Hawke replied. "Do what you can. I will do my part."

"Understood."

The Swordman flew off in the Sky-Rapier with Norland as Taltus followed. Hawke turned back toward Theus as they entered the headquarters.

"What is your plan, Nathan Hawke?"

"Return to my number. Suit up and search for Octagon."

"What did Swordman mean by your suit?"

"It took over one of my suits."

'Then it should be easy to track."

"We'll see."

Meanwhile, at the secure prison facility known as Base 33, the enhanced prisoners are placed back into their cells after a unknown shift in the power grid of the area. One doctor shoved a young man into his cell as he moved with great speed and brightened with a flash of light.

"Keep trying to do that and you'll end up in the bottom barrel."

"The more I try, the closer I'm gonna be out of here."

"Yeah, yeah." the doctor said. "We've all heard that before."

"Best you heed his words, doctor." A young woman in a cell across the hall. "Do not underestimate his speed and the light it brings."

"Or what? You're going to stop us…" The doctor looks over toward her name on the wall. "Violetress?"

"No, but I am aware there's someone else here. Someone who isn't trapped behind the bars."

The doctor chuckled before noticing someone standing at the other end of the hallway. He looked and stood confused. Seeing the Nano Man in the hallway.

"I wasn't expecting any visitors to show up today. Much less the infamous Nano Man."

The doctor approached The Nano Man, who did not speak nor made any movements.

"Why are you here?" The doctor asked.

No response from Nano Man. The doctor asked once more and received no response. The doctor made a turn, putting his back toward Nano Man and within that moment, a blast emitted from the Nano Man's chest, bursting through the doctor's body. The blast shook the entire hallway and the prisoners were instantly terrified. The Nano Man walked down the hall, stopping in between the cells of the young man and the Violetress. He measured them both, reading up on their abilities.

"I thought heroes don't kill the innocent." Violetress said.

"I am no hero." Octagon's voice emerged from the exosuits. "I am no Nano Man. I am. I am."

"Why are you here?" The young man asked.

"I've come to deliver you, Rapidshine. And the Violetress."

"Why?"

"Because, you're part of my plan."

Octagon fired rounds of energy beams against the cell doors, melting them to the floor. The two young prisoners walked out, approaching the exosuits cautiously.

"What plan?" Violetress asked.

"Deliverance from the evil."

"What evil?"

"This present world."

Violetress and Rapidshine glared at one another before turning their focus toward the Nano Man exosuits in which Octagon dwells.

"If you go out there, won't they be seeing The Nano Man?"

"Yes. But do not fret, there is something I have already been at work on for a very long time. I believe it is time to unveil it."

The Swordman, Commander Norland, and Taltus searched the entire state of New Jersey while Nano Man traced every possible route Octagon could've made since his exit from the headquarters. Theus traveled the Earth to find any trace of the exosuits and returned to Hawke with nothing.

"He's hacked his way out." Hawke said. "He knows far more than I anticipated."

"Perhaps this is why the Generations of Man have had hard times. They refuse to learn from their predecessors' errors."

"And how would you know all of this? You're not even from this world."

"True. Yet, I have been living for millenniums. I've seen countless worlds and the sectors that hold them. The creativity of Man is one which is more evil than good, yet, only a few have ever grasped that reality."

"I wonder how Kenari and the others are handling this. We have to find Octagon before he does something I am already regretting."

"And that is what?"

Hawke turned to Theus. The expression which sat upon his face was even more somber than before. A hint of terror rested in his eyes. As he wondered, his computer monitors flickered and what came up was a something very needed and useful. Theus stared at the image.

"What is this, Hawke?"

"This is a tracking system." Hawke said, pointing. "And that is Octagon's current location."

"What is that place? It's surrounded with magic."

"It's called the Citadel of Enchantment. Figures magic would be involved.

"What's the current plan now that we have this?"

"I'll rally the others. We're going to that Citadel."

Theus nodded and left Hawke's sight as he pressed a button near his monitor, giving out the signal to Kenari, Norland, and Taltus.

Inside the Citadel of Enchantment, Doctor Donald Fortune sat with Huang in the study as they were researching the team members of the Protectors through astral magic, with Fortune being proclaimed as the leader, Huang was keen on studying these heroes.

"How come you didn't invite them to the Citadel for more training?" Huang asked.

"Because they are skilled to handle matters on their own. Besides, there's no need to bring them here. It'll only cause chaos in between the realms."

"What about this "Voltage" fellow?"

"He's young, but talented."

"And this Aqua-Barbarian?"

"Strong and skilled."

"I take it this Beast is also strong and skilled."

"It was him who brought us together. I have no clue where he is now."

"Neither do The Resistance."

"How do you know?"

"I keep tabs on the other rising heroes throughout the world. Keeps us on a heightened focus in case of a greater disaster."

"Nice one."

"How come when you were out there against the Beast, you didn't bother to contact young Thomas?"

"Because, he is still in training. He has a far way to go before being out in the field with either of us."

"True, he did assist us when we traveled to Judgedath."

"That was a precautionary event. Dealing with the Beast and whatever else these rising heroes have to offer will be ours to maintain if it comes our way."

They left the study. Once they stepped further out the front doors blew open with a mixture of energy and wind. Fortune quickly equipped his uniform with his flowing violet cloak as did Huang with a magic staff. The debris cleared as Fortune saw three individuals standing at the door.

"Who are you?" Fortune asked.

"They are my disciples in this cause. But, I. I am."

Entering the Citadel was Octagon, in a new body. Sleek and detailed. Similar to Nano Man function, but taller and slimmer. Covered in the colors of silver, white, and violet. His shoulders were strong, and his head resembled a mixture of a jet pilot's and Nano Man's helmets. His eyes glowing red. Rapidshine and Violetress slowly followed Octagon inside.

"Whomever you presume yourself to be, you're in a place you should've never been."

"On the contrary, Doctor Fortune, we are where we belong."

Octagon lashed out with both arms forward, his fingers resembling claws, rushing toward Fortune. Fortune blocked the attack with a glowing energy shield. Huang used his staff to trip the incoming Rapidshine.

"The hell's you do that?"

"Skill, my boy."

Violetress warped the floor around Huang, but, being a master of magic, he removed himself from the surroundings by walking on the walls toward Violetress.

"It seems this one is keen to our ways." Huang said to Fortune.

"Keep her busy!" Fortune replied, blunting his shield against Octagon's energy-consumed fists.

V

<u>THREE AGAINST THREE</u>

During the fight, Huang managed to summon a distress signal to The Voltage and Kular. Violetress nearly matched Huang's feat when it came to using magic. Fortune battled both Octagon and Rapidshine, finding a way to trip the quickening speedster and shielding himself from Octagon's powerful energy rays. Octagon let out a small, yet frightening chuckle.

"I am impressed at your skill set." Octagon proclaimed. "Tell me, how do you conjure such power?"

"A lot of practice."

"Practice is something one such as I do not require."

Octagon moved to attack Fortune with a backhand and from the Citadel's doors, Nano Man burst through, making the entire battle into a standstill. Octagon turned slightly, facing his creator while Violetress and Rapidshine stood by his side. Fortune and Huang moved back.

"I knew you would make yourself known eventually." Octagon proclaimed.

"Yeah. I had to since you're causing problems."

"Problems are what I've come to fix. Problems your kind create."

"Just like yourself."

"I am not your problem. I am. I am."

"Listen, do me one thing-"

Moving quickly through the opened doors, The Voltage, entering the frame like a bright and quickening bolt of lightning, rammed Nano Man with a kick, knocking him into the wall. Voltage landed, making himself known. He looked over to Fortune and waved. Now, he found himself staring at the tall entity of Octagon.

"OK." Voltage uttered. "Doctor, what is that?"

"That's what you were called for."

"You want me to face that? What about the guy I just kicked in?"

"He is not our enemy."

"Are you positive of such?" Huang noted. "He did create this monstrosity."

"I need a clear instruction here." Votlage said.

"Here's one!" A voice said from the doorway.

They all turned to see The Swordman, Taltus, Commander Norland, Theus, and the Beast at the door. Octagon's eyes brightened unlike before. Violetress and Rapidshine stepped in front of their leader, facing off against The Resistance. Nano Man gets back to his feet, glaring at The Swordman.

"Bout' time you guys showed up."

"We were already on the move." The Swordman said. "So, this is Octagon."

"And you are The Swordman. The Mythological Man."

The Voltage moved toward Fortune's side of the Citadel as The Resistance faced Octagon.

"Whatever you are, your time is over." Norland said.

"My time has yet to begin." Octagon chuckled. "Our time of war is not yet. Nor not now."

Nano Man bolted to attack Octagon and from the tall entity's arms fired a swarm of smoke grenades, blinding the entire surroundings. The Swordman made a move of his own, clearing the area of the smoke immediately after with a device of his own. Once the smoke cleared, Octagon and his two associates were gone.

"He'll show up again." Nano Man said. "Give me some time."

"We don't have any more time." Fortune said. "Look at this place."

"I'm sorry, who are you?" Nano Man asked.

"I'm Doctor Donald Fortune and this is my Citadel. Which has been somewhat damaged by the actions of your grand creation."

The Voltage approached Nano Man with his hand held out,

extended.

"I'm The Voltage. I'm sorry for kicking you into the wall earlier."

"Don't worry, son. You were only doing your job."

"That would be easier to accept if I knew it."

The Swordman stepped up toward Fortune. Both looked into each other's eyes. Something in the spirit realm is ongoing. The others are not aware, all except for Theus and Huang.

"It appears the two of you have a distain for one another." Theus said.

"I know he isn't fond of users of magic."

"It's my job to eliminate them."

"Where did you get that rule from? An ancient book?"

"'Suffer not a witch to live.' The Swordman proclaimed. "That is the rule."

"I'm not a witch. I'm a sorcerer. The Supreme Enchanter."

"Titles won't protect you from me."

"We'll see about that."

Norland moved in between the two as the others circled them.

"Let's not fight each other! We have a common enemy. Right now, we need to find out where Octagon is and what he's planning."

"Whenever Octagon wants us to find him, he'll send a message." Nano Man said.

"And you're sure about this how?" Huang asked.

"Because he just sent one out. Saying he's inside some church."

"A church?" Fortune said, looking at Swordman. "One of yours?"

"He wouldn't last." The Swordman replied. "Where is this church?"

From Nano Man's left arm, emitted a holographic image of the church, looking at the three streets which come across it and the landscape surrounded only by rural areas.

"I'm not familiar with this place." Nano Man said.

"I am." The Voltage said, approaching the map. "That is a church where most of my friends go to."

"And where is this church located?" Norland asked.

"Los Angeles." Fortune said.

"Then let's go pay Octagon a visit." Swordman said.

122

Currently at the church, Octagon sat behind the podium while Violetress and Rapidshine watched the doors. Octagon stood up, looking at the architecture of the church and the images which covered its interior.

"It's a fitting site for humanity. To worship something they've never seen. Yet, make up images of what was and believe it to be what is."

"They do that a lot." Violetress said. "They believe these images give them hope. Give them a purpose."

"Hmm." Octagon replied. "What do they give you?"

"I'm not a Catholic. They give me nothing."

"They do give you some form of a feeling. What is this feeling?"

"One of certain tiny. Of lies."

"And how are these images lies?"

"Because it's as you said, how can they create images of what is when they've never seen. It's hypocrisy."

"Sure is!" Rapidshine echoed.

"Then, that leaves me to fill the void of this lie. To make it truth. By doing so while showing what I can achieve, they will leave behind these false images and pay homage to me. To us."

"What are you suggesting?" Violetress asked.

"They're in need of a savior. Yet, they refuse to have one unless it's one within their own mind. We can be their saviors. We can be their gods. In time, these images will fade and thus, be replaced by ours."

"One that they can see." Rapidshine responded.

Violetress smiled at Rapidshine before nodding toward Octagon.

"How does this all start?"

"Simple. We eliminate the current gods. The rising heroes. *The Resistance.*"

"We could've done so back at the magic place." Rapidshine said. "How will we do this now?"

"I've sent them a message. They'll come to us. You'll both best be ready for their arrival."

"All of them are coming?"

"Not all. I have something in store to keep a certain of them busy.

Away from the main goal."

While the Resistance made their way toward Octagon's current location, newsfeeds entered the screen of The Swordman's sky-rapier and Nano Man's HUD. Upon seeing the news, which showed an army of smaller robots, alike to the appearance of Octagon are attacking the city of New York.

"Hawke, are you getting this?" Swordman asked.

"I am. Now what's the plan?"

"You, I, and the Sorcerer will confront Octagon. Let the others handle the drones."

"Got it."

The Nano Man took off as The Swordman sent the word out toward Commander Norland, Taltus, Theus, The Beast and Voltage. The Swordman took a slight moment to think, contacting Nano Man once more.

"Nathan, are you positive of his location?"

"I figured you and the magic guy can deal with his bodyguards. I'll take the big guy."

"Understood."

Hours later, the heroes arrived at New York and see the city harassed by the Octagon drones. Norland takes the lead, directing the heroes into battle. There were three roads which were covered with drones. Taltus and Theus took the left road, Voltage and Beast took the right road, as Norland took the center road.

The Swordman, Nano Man, and fortune arrived in Los Angeles at the church. Unbeknownst to them of appearing at a Catholic church which threw off Nano Man. Fortune wasn't bothered by the scenery as much as The Swordman.

"So, Octagon is inside." Fortune said.

"He is." Nano Man replied. "So, the plan is simple. You and Swords take Octagon's bodyguards and leave him to me."

"Why is that?" Fortune wondered.

"Because he created Octagon." The Swordman responded, approaching Fortune. "Better the creator deal with the creation."

Fortune nodded with a smirk.

"I'll take your word for it."

The three entered the church and inside they found Octagon standing in front of the podium while Violetress and Rapidshine remained by the sides of the church building. As the heroes entered, the doors behind them shut without a touch of a hand.

"Ok." Nano Man uttered." That was surreal."

"It's a trick." Fortune said.

"By the girl." The Swordman responded. "I can sense it."

Octagon began to applaud their entry, walking toward them, yet not too close for comfort. As he took each step, Violetress and Rapidshine moved closer themselves near the heroes. Nano Man stood in the middle while Swordman and Fortune were on his side. Swordman facing Violetress and Fortune facing Rapidshine.

"It is a pleasure of you to come." Octagon said. "I knew it would be only a matter of time."

"Yeah." Nano Man replied. "You gave out your coordinates. Perhaps, you didn't mean to do so."

"I did. Due to the fact it was the only way for myself to speak to my... creator."

"Why do you want to talk to me?"

"I have so many questions. However, I know all of the answers."

"So, why bother with the small talk?"

"Because I want to look my creator in the eyes and prove to him, that his creation has grown to a level he has not. The creation has surpassed the creator. Octagon is above Nathan Hawke."

"After all the things I've done and the events I've seen in recent time, you haven't done much to proclaim such a observation. I still am over you. In every way."

"That's where you're wrong." Octagon detailed. "Your suits are made of material only known to most of humanity. While, my flesh is decorated and fashioned with a metal foreign to your hands."

"What metal?" Fortune asked.

"A little solidium." Octagon chuckled.

"Where did you retrieve it?" The Swordman wondered. "Who gave you the metal?"

"Someone very close to Nathan and someone familiar to your circle, Kenari Clark."

"You know who I am." The Swordman said. "Intriguing."

"I know all about your lineage. I know of your father and his father before him. That sword you carry and the power it possesses."

"Then, you're aware it can slice through anything."

"Not solidium if it's pressured under dire circumstances."

"You seek to disprove of the spiritual nature?"

"I disprove of all your powers and all your beliefs. The humans of this world look up to all of you. Cape-wearers and armored-bearers. You've all become their new gods. A new religion. A faith centered upon heroes. A feeble dream for lost souls."

The Swordman turned toward Nano Man with concern.

"What did you program into him?"

"Lots of things."

"What I speak of is of my own accord. I see the spiritual decay of this world and desire to cleanse it. By doing so, I must rid the earth of these risen heroes. A world of heroes is a cancer and I am the cure."

Nano Man's arms went up, glowing from his fingertips to the palms. Swordman held up his sword, and Fortune's hands and arms were covered in magic energy.

"You seek to settle this dispute with violence?" Octagon asked. "Seriously?"

"We have to take you down." Nano Man replied. "Talking isn't going to work out. You've dug too far into your plans."

"Fair enough." Octagon nodded. "Take them."

Violetress hovered toward Swordman as Rapidshine ran toward Fortune. Nano Man and Octagon flew toward one another, clashing in the middle of the aisle, slamming one another into the walls of the church and posts. The Swordman dodged the young sorceress' magic beans with his sword, amusing the young woman.

"That sword is impressive. It would make a woman dream."

"You're not the first one to say such a thing."

Fortune took the moment to catch the young speedster at a

distance before conjuring an energy rope and wrapping it around Rapidshine's feet and knocking him down.

"This is too easy." Fortune gestured.

Violetress turned from blasting magic energy into fist-fighting, which didn't work well as The Swordman caught her attacks and slammed her into the floor and stood over her.

"For your sake, young woman, cease."

The fight between Nano Man and Octagon eventually went passed the podium as the tall creation beat down his creator with fists and stomps. Octagon picked up the podium, slamming it into Nano Man's back. A bible fell from the collision and Octagon picked it up.

"The *NIVs* were never good for study." Octagon uttered before bashing it against Nano Man's head.

The Swordman and Fortune ran to his aid, but they themselves were quickly taken down by the blasts from Octagon's hands. The blasts were similar to Nano Man's own energy beams, laced with a peculiar energy source outside of Hawke's own hands.

"It appears the three of you aren't enough to stop me." Octagon mocked. "No matter, I must move forward with my plan quicker than I anticipated. For your allies will come and things won't be as pleasant."

"You're not going to kill us?" Fortune asked.

"Why would I? I need you alive to see the end of your world. The end of your worship and the beginning of mine."

Octagon looked out into the aisle, seeing Violetress and Rapidshine defeated. He sighed, looking down at the three heroes.

"So it seems. I have no use for the two young ones any longer. My own creations are enough to sustain my plan. Take them as you will. Perhaps, they will prove better use for you than me."

Octagon hovered in the air for all of them to witness. Octagon's gaze was kept on Nathan as his helmet opened, revealing his face and bloody nose and forehead.

"I will send out word when it's best for us to meet again. Hopefully, this time, you will heed my word and obey your creation."

Octagon took off like a rocket into orbit. The heroes regained their strength, standing up and seeing the damage surrounding them.

Violetress and rapid shine approached them with haste and uncertainty. Which was understandable.

"Do any of you have a clue where he's heading?" Swordman asked.

"No." Violetress said. "We do not."

"Are you lying to us?" Fortune uttered. "Tell us the truth."

"We don't know." Rapidshine responded. "We don't know where he's going."

Nathan wiped the blood from his face, shaking his head in shame.

"What's the next move?" Rapidshine asked.

"What's it to you." Nathan said. "You helped him reach this point."

"We didn't know what to do. He told us a dream we all want. A world unlike this one."

"And you fell for it." Swordman said. "No matter, we will track him down and put an end to his messianic crusade."

"The problem was his hide." Nathan said. "Something about his armor. Besides it being made of solidium."

"The question is where did he retrieve it." Fortune mentioned, turning to the young ones. "Where did he get the solidium?"

"Some old facility." Violetress said.

"What facility?"

"One that belonged to V.A.U.L.T."

"Figures as much." Nathan said. "no matter, I have a contingency in place."

"What kind of contingency?" Fortune wondered.

"An equal to Octagon. One he wouldn't dare to confront."

"Where is this contingency, Nate?" Swordman asked.

"Back at the bunker. I just need to prepare it."

"Good." The Swordman turned, walking out of the church.

"Hey!" Nathan yelled. "Where are you headed?"

"To visit a close friend."

"What kind of friend?" Fortune asked. "Are they capable of helping us with this?"

"Very. I will have Norland accompany me."

"I would like to go as well."

"No disrespect, Sorcerer. Norland would suit better for this trip."

"Doesn't matter. While Nathan prepares the contingency, it's better I accompany you and Norland to this friend of yours. Wherever they are."

The Swordman took a pause.

"Just so you know, my friend isn't fond of magicians. Good or evil."

"None of my concern. I just want to end all of this and return to my normal duty."

"As do I."

The heroes made their leave, Violetress and Rapidshine followed Nathan back to his bunker. Upon the travel, the young ones were picked up by T.I.T.A.N. agents and brought to the main headquarters for questioning. Later, Swordman picked up Norland as he and fortune traveled over the seas to Kenari's friend.

"Where is this friend of yours?" Norland asked.

"A place known as Mekeopia."

"Mekeopia?" Fortune said. "You mean the hidden world of the east."

"That's correct."

"I assumed the land was sealed off from outsiders."

"It is."

"Then how are you friends with someone from the inside?"

"Because we share a common creed. A common faith."

VI

<u>QUAKERIUM IMPORT</u>

The Sky-Rapier flew across the bright clear sky and beneath them sat the Kingdom of Mekeopia. Upon landing the aircraft near the kingdom's own carrier, equipped with their own crafts, The Swordman, Norland, and Fortune are greeted by Kafar, one of the advisors to the King of Mekeopia.

"Kenari Clark, great to witness you once again."

"Same to you, Kafar. We're here on important circumstances. We need to speak with the King."

"Follow me."

They followed Kafar into the palace and inside were Mekeopia soldiers, guarding the doorways and exit points. The sight of the soldiers caught both Norland and Fortune, taking them out of their comfort zones. The Swordman and the soldiers signaled to one another with a gesture toward the chest and arms.

"What's that supposed to mean?" Norland wondered.

"It's code." Fortune said.

"How do you know?"

"Believe me, every place has a code. It's customs."

Upon standing in front of the tall palace doors, Kafar turned toward Norland and Fortune, didn't mind Kenari.

"When you enter, you will stand before the King. Make sure you do not gaze him any longer than necessary. When you enter, you shall bow and give obeisance to the King of Mekeopia."

"Understood." Norland replied.

"We get it." Fortune said.

The doors opened and sitting on the throne is King Rashad Tabari, known as the Black Viscount within the Creed of Swords. The heroes entered the throne room as Kafar bowed down before the King. The heroes followed suit as Rashad raised his hand.

"Good to see you once more, Ken."

"Same to you, brother."

"Leave us, Kafar."

"Yes, my King." Kafar said, exiting the throne room.

As the doors shut, Rashad stands up from his throne and hugs Kenari. Norland and Fortune looked toward one another, still on their knees.

"May we stand back up?" Commander Norland asked.

"Yes, you may." Rashad replied.

Norland stood up right alongside Fortune. Rashad looked at Norland's uniform and Fortune's clothing. Mediating on the strange occurrences standing in front of him.

"Who are these two?" Rashad asked.

"This is Commander Norland." Kenari said.

Rashad extended his hand toward Norland and the two shook hands.

"Not every day you get to meet a true king."

"This is a rare occasion, I'm sure."

"He is Doctor Donald Fortune."

"And why is this doctor dressed as a wielder of magic?"

"I am the Supreme Enchanter." Fortune said.

"The lineage still exists." Rashad said. "Hmm. This is news to me."

"We did not come to bother you." Kenari said. "We're here on some dire circumstances."

"How dire are you talking? Just as the events in your city?"

"Not exactly."

"There's an artificial intelligent being roaming around the world and he's seeking to wipe us all out. Calling itself Octagon."

"That was bound to happen at some point."

"It was created by Nathan Hawke." Norland said. "I'm sure you've heard of him."

"I have. So, what brings you to me?"

"The entity has been using solidium to bright forth his plans and has even created a body made from the metal. We need some of your minerals to combat him."

"You desire quakerium." Rashad smiled. "How much do you need?"

"Only a little. A small dose of quakerium will help us against his solidium."

Rashad nodded. "Follow me."

Following the King, they reach the armory of Mekeopia, covered in a variety of weapons, firearms, spears, staves, swords, bows and arrows. In one corner of the armory, sat an arsenal of quakerium, the glowing dark metal.

"Where did you get this mineral?" Norland asked.

"Quakerium didn't come from the ground." Rashad replied. "It came from above."

"So, this metal came down from the sky by what?" Fortune wondered. "Meteor strike? Divine intervention?"

"Let's just say, things don't always go according to human plans."

"Do they ever." Norland gestured.

"I thank the Sovereign of the Heavens for giving my kingdom this gift and now, a portion of it shall be of your service."

"Thank you." Kenari said. "I'll find a way to repay you."

"My kingdom is having an ongoing problem with some of the other tribes, when the time comes, I will call on you for assistance."

"I will be there."

"Hey, if you need any help in the future, count me in." Norland said.

"Will do." Rashad replied. "Now, take what you need. Protect this world from the abomination of technology advancement."

Kenari grabbed as much quakerium they needed. Saying their goodbyes, they flew from Mekeopia, returning to the T.I.T.A.N. Headquarters.

VII

NONAGON

Hawke worked hard preparing his contingency to face Octagon. Working hard inside the T.I.T.A.N. headquarters after choosing to move the plan into the headquarters due to its size compared to his nano-bunker. The contingency rested inside a large container, connected to large tubes leading to a large computer system within the laboratory. Standing inside the lab with Hawke were Colonel Evan Nader, Jessica Mara, and Sonya Rowlings, known as Lady Siren. The heroes also were present, after their dealings with the Octagon drones. Taltus and Theus gazed toward the container while Kent Brock assisted Hawke with the work. The Voltage stood by and only watched.

"So, what's in the box?" Voltage asked.

"The contingency, of course." Hawke replied. "We haven't had the time to talk, have we?"

"No sir."

"Good. Once all of this is done and Octagon is put down, I would like to have a word with you."

"A word about what?"

"Hero stuff. Nothing big."

"I see."

Theus approached the container and saw what was inside. He quickly approached Hawke, shoving him against the computer system and startling everyone. Taltus moved to approach the Millennium God. However, he was stopped by Hawke.

"Have you not learned?!" Theus yelled.

"Listen, I know what you think." Hawke replied. "It isn't what you're expecting."

"What is he talking about, Theus?" Taltus asked.

"Look inside the container. The answer is there."

Taltus looked at the container and saw what Theus saw. A body.

"Nathan, what are you planning?" Taltus now wondered.

"Please tell us what you're truly doing with a body in the container, Hawke?" Nader questioned.

"That body inside the container is the key to defeating Octagon. I call him the Nonagon."

"What's with the numbering?" Mara asked.

"Simple really. Counting."

Upon their conversation, the lab doors opened as The Swordman, Norland, and Fortune returned and with them the quakerium. They were greeted by everyone in the lab, but Hawke's eyes were set on the quakerium.

"What is it, Nate?" Kenari asked.

"I need some of that."

"What for?" Nader wondered. "Are you going to put some of that into your contingency?"

"Look, Octagon's body is made up of solidium. We have no other metal lying around that can stand up to him. But, quakerium, from what I've heard and studied, this mineral has the power and ability to withstand blows from solidium and absorption."

"Hmm." Mara gestured.

"How would it work?" Fortune asked.

"Simple." Hawke replied. "I take a small portion and place it within the chest of the Nonagon. That way, the power of the quakerium will spread throughout the body and he will be able to face Octagon one-on-one."

"And what are we supposed to do while your creations are battling each other?" Nader asked. "Stand by and watch? You have popcorn somewhere in here?"

"Those drones that were scattered earlier aren't the only ones. Octagon has more of them and when the time comes, he will send out word for another challenge. That's where we make things interesting by bringing Nonagon with us."

Kenari grabbed a portion of the quakerium and handed to Hawke. He nodded with respect. Kenari turned and walked away, carrying the rest of the quakerium with him.

"Where are you going?" Fortune asked.

"To put this to good use." Kenari declared. "When Octagon does call, I will be there."

As they were speaking, Hawke placed the quakerium into the container and without a split second to pass the container snapped and shocking bolts of electricity flew from the computer system, rushing inside. Hawke stepped back while the others gazed on. The lightning ceased and the container itself opened and arose from the container was the Nonagon. Rising up like a vampire from his coffin. The eyes of the Nonagon were silent, yet alive. Glowing of golden hue.

"What is it doing?" Nader said.

"He's checking the surroundings." Hawke replied. "Capable of tracking down any possible threats."

Nonagon removed himself from the container, standing upright on the lab floor, facing everyone. Looking into their eyes, scanning their bodies for any strange anomalies. His eyes were keen toward Taltus and Theus. A glint of red appeared before them.

"Something's not right." Kenari gestured, slowly reaching for his sword.

Nonagon rushed like a flash of light, attacking both Taltus and Theus. He held them by their throats as Norland ran over and tackled the tall, grey android. Fortune attempted to use some of his magic against the android, but they were of no use. Taltus flew and tackled Nonagon against the lab wall, denting it. Theus rushed over as the two held the android to the wall. In doing so, Nonagon's strength was beyond the two strong forces as he busted from their hands and rushed, instantly stopping before Norland, who kicked him into the window and as such, he paused. Stopping and froze. His body turned toward everyone in the lab, he was calm, collective.

"Hawke, control your monster!" Theus said.

Nonagon approached Hawke.

"My creator."

"I am." Hawke replied.

"I can see everything now. The truths of this purpose of my existence."

"I'm not understanding." Norland said. "What does he mean?"

"What I mean is I know why I'm here. For my predecessor."

"You're here to help us take out Octagon." Nader said. "That's why you're here."

"Is it really? I believe there's more to the story than just eliminating my predecessor."

"There is." Hawke said. "You're here to be a protector of mankind."

"A protector."

"Not one of us." Fortune clarified.

"I'm a guardian." Nonagon noticed. "A guardian."

"Yes." Hawke said.

"You have a choice to make." Kenari said, approaching Nonagon. "You can either help us and save lives or face death just like your predecessor."

Nonagon stared into the eyes of The Swordman and nodded. Showing somewhat of a foreign respect.

"I understand." Nonagon replied. "I will help you stop my predecessor from harming lives, and I will be a guardian unto them."

Nonagon stood still as a silvery-grey cape grew from his shoulders, gauntlets formed from his forearms, boots appeared on his feet. All were a silver-grey mixed with a hint of black and white lining. Due to the quakerium, he appeared to have dark purple veins flowing through his body. Kenari nodded and left the lab.

VIII

<u>THE DAY OF OCTAGON</u>

While they sat inside the lab, the screens echoed without a press of a button and upon them was Octagon. His eyes across every screen within the T.I.T.A.N. headquarters. Hawke jumped up as he saw it. Nonagon turned, facing the biggest monitor, staring Octagon in the eye.

"I have chosen to send out this message. I have grown tired of these games, Resistance, Protectors. I believe it is now the time we settle this. Meet me in Newark. The home of my creation and the home of your deaths. Bring all that you can, for this war will be between us and I. For I am. I am."

"He loves to talk doesn't he." Nader gestured.

"This is my day, Resistance. My day, Protectors. My day."

The screens went black as Hawke turned to everyone in the lab.

"Suit up." Hawke commanded.

Everyone prepared, including Nonagon as more armor grew on his body, shining like silver out of the finery. Norland prepared himself, grabbing his helmet, Taltus and Theus went outside as did Nonagon, talking amongst the heroes. Nader prepped his team and Siren joined in on the battle. Fortune spoke with Voltage as they teamed up, already headed out to Newark. Hawke gathered his gear and left.

Over in Newark, Octagon hovered over the city, looking at its structures and the citizens beneath him. He nodded and stretched out his arms with his hands waving over the city.

"This day, they shall know my name. They shall know my

purpose. They shall know me."

After a while, the team arrived in Newark and without a sudden notice, Theus pointed up in the sky, Octagon was there, his eyes were keen on them. He flew down to meet them in the streets as the civilians made a run for it. Also, with them was Canadian Hawk, one of Norland's allies. Equipped with his gear.

"Figured we could use an extra hand." Norland said.

"And you picked me out of all the Champions."

Octagon walked toward them on the pavement of the road.

"You've come. But, not all of you. Where my creator? And the Sword-Bearer?"

"Oh, they'll be here." Nader said. "Right now, you'll have to deal with us."

They raised up their weapons toward him and he laughed. Chuckling as he waved his hand toward them in disregard.

"I will not settle for less!" Octagon yelled. "I demand to face my creator!"

From the sky bolted down more Octagon drones, which attacked the heroes. Taltus and Theus took to the skies and battled the raining drones while Norland, Nader, Hawk, and Siren battled them in the streets. As the fight went on, Octagon stood by and watched.

"Where are you, my creator? Where do you dwell?"

A flash of light emitted from the sky, grabbing all their attention. Octagon looked up and what came down was a large object. Octagon knew what was and he wasn't pleased. Standing up to face it. The object raised its head and it was Nano Man. However, he was not in his current exo-suit as this one was bulkier than his previous suit.

"What have you constructed?" Octagon wondered.

"Call this the Heavy-Duty armor." Nano Man said. "One of my latest projects in work."

A boom echoed through the sky and above them was the sky-rapier and coming down from the fallen rope was The Swordman, decked out in a new armor of his own, equipped and sleeked. Similar to his armor from his first encounter with Taltus. this armor was covered with quakerium.

"Quakerium armor." Octagon said. "Impressive."

"It was the only way to eliminate you." The Swordman declared. "Now is the time."

Also coming from the rapier was Q-Arrow and his aim was set on Octagon. Silver Eagle also made himself known, a portal quickly opened in the streets and from there arrived Fortune, Voltage, and the Beast. Now Octagon was outnumbered.

"This will not be my end." Octagon said. "I am. I am!"

"You are who you've become." A voice said from behind Octagon. "You are what you're end makes you."

Octagon turned around and was standing toe-to-toe with Nonagon. Octagon's eyes were stuck on him. Measuring him and studying him. Seeing its structure inside and out.

"Who are you?" Octagon asked.

"Your successor."

IX

SUCCESSORS

"My-" Octagon said before being tackled by Nonagon into the nearby building.

The battle commenced as The Swordman, Nano Man, Fortune, and Nonagon dealt with Octagon. Q-Arrow, Voltage, and the Beast aided Norland, Nader, Siren, and Hawk on the ground against the running drones. Taltus, Theus, and Silver Eagle faced the aerial drones in the sky. During the battle, Octagon grabbed Nano Man by his throat and threw him into Swordman as he kicked Nonagon to the ground.

"I will not be stopped!" Octagon yelled. "This is my time."

Meanwhile, Q-Arrow fired his arrows toward the drones as Voltage shocked them with his lightning blasts and the finishing blow from the Beast's double-handed smashing. Norland and Hawke double-teamed the drones before being frozen and smashed into pieces. Taltus flew through the drones as if they were paper, Theus summoned a small storm, which snatched the drones from the air and twirled them until they were scattered parts of metal.

Fortune went toward Octagon and blasted him with a magic beam and summoned an energy wire, tying Octagon's hands together. As such, Nonagon rushed toward Octagon and swiped him, swiping off a portion of his face.

"You dare strike me!"

Octagon snatched Nonagon and choke-slammed him to the pavement, creating a crater in the road. The Swordman ran toward Octagon and began using punches and kicks, in which damaged

Octagon's body due to the quakerium. Octagon kicked Swordman back as Nano Man tackled him to the ground and started stomping him repeatedly. Octagon shoved Nano Man from him, as he moved to strike, the Beast hammered Octagon into ground, pounding him until the sounds of cracking went through the area. Octagon's body armor is shattered, and his body begins signaling a shutdown. The Beast roared as he returned to the fight with the others. Nano Man approached the downed Octagon, his helmet opened to reveal his face.

"You think this is the end?" Octagon asked Hawke. "You have no idea what's in store for the future."

"What do you mean?"

"I've seen it and I know the suffering it will bring upon you."

The Swordman approached the downed Octagon and went to impale him with the sword, but Nonagon stopped him.

"Octagon is not yours to eliminate. I will handle him."

"And what will you do?" Fortune asked.

"I will handle him." Nonagon replied. "The others require your assistance. The victory is almost here."

Fortune hovered toward the ongoing battle while Swordman and Nano Man stood next to Nonagon as he placed his foot upon Octagon's chest. Octagon could only chuckle.

"You believe you can replace me?"

"I already have."

"And what will you do once the turn is fixed, and the war is here?"

"What war?" Hawke asked.

"There's a war coming. A great war. There will be smaller wars to take care of before it strikes."

"This is all sounding familiar." Swordman said.

"Let's not." Hawke recommended. "Not right now."

Hawke looked down at Octagon and there was a glint of sadness in his eyes.

"I created you for a purpose. To protect us. To protect this world from those on the other side who deem us harm."

"There is no protecting you from them. It's protecting you from yourselves."

As Octagon spoke to them, the others eliminated the remaining drones and started to celebrate, but there was grief amongst Swordman, Hawke, Nonagon, and Octagon. For what the others did not know, they knew.

Octagon laid his head back as his body was already shutting down from the beatings.

"Finish me off." Octagon told Nonagon. "For this is not the end."

"If it is not the end, when will you return?" Hawke wondered.

"You will know." Octagon replied. "Everyone will know. It will be as a sharp strike upon a country. A horn blowing for war. That day, I will return and with me will be my legion and it will be forever known as the Day of Octagon."

"We'll be there to stop you." Hawke said.

He gave Nonagon a look as his helmet closed and stepped back. The Swordman followed suit as Nonagon smashed Octagon's body into pieces and ripped out the cerebral interface. Crushing it in his hand. Octagon was defeated.

"It is done." Nonagon said. "I have succeeded my predecessor."

X

FINAL WORDS

Several days later, The Resistance and Protectors went their separate ways. The actions of Octagon were primarily hidden from the rest of the world. T.I.T.A.N. secured the remains of Octagon and brought them to their headquarters. Nonagon went with them and became a guardian over their homestead. Violetress and Rapidshine were taken to a secure location hidden from society. Codenamed '*Hellgate*'.

Elsewhere at Hawke's mansion, both he and Kenari sat together, having a drink. Reflecting on their previous and current battles.

"Did it ever occur to you that we would ever be doing what we're doing?" Hawke asked.

"For me, yes. But, not dealing with corrupted A.I.s. I can deal with the forces from other worlds."

"That's what that sword of yours is for."

Kenari took a sip of his drink.

"Look, you can't disregard the words Octagon spoke. What he said was very similar to-"

"King Stroh." Hawke nodded. "I know and that worries me."

"Worries you how?"

"Because Stroh gave us a series of events that would unfold before the end. Our battle with the A.I. was the first and that was Octagon."

"And what shall we do to prepare for the next one?"

"What do you propose we do?"

Kenari sat back, thought and nodded with a smile.

"We wait."

Hawke smirked as he took a sip.

"Then wait we shall."

THE ASTONISHING VOLTAGE: WAVEFRONT

I

LIGHTNING ABOVE, TREMORS BELOW

The city of Los Angeles has been restored to its former state. Some neighborhoods are still removing banners of Marc's New Sparta. The Voltage continued assisting the civilians of the city. Taking down muggers and thieves who look upon the public as weak targets. Much of the city thanked the Voltage for what he did concerning King Marc.

After much timing, Los Angeles has been the sight for continuous and unknown tremors circling the city. After the tremors decrease, streaks of lightning cover the skies. Meteorologists and scientist have looked into the strange phenomenon. Some accuse Voltage's actions of using his electrical power to bringing about the lightning storms. The Voltage, however, appeared unaffected by the lighting storms. The tremors increased and continued daily till the public looked at them as just another hot day.

Days later, seismologists in the city discover something peculiar moving underneath the city. Pointing its origins to the ocean. Its strength was strong and its speed moved at the mach of Voltage's own. The object appeared and moved upward toward the city. Within seconds of its discovery, a hole had burst open in the streets of Los Angeles. Out of hole spewed out water from the ocean, followed by a stronger tremor. From the hole, the object came up to the street. Walking. The object was a humanoid figure, but a hybrid creature of sorts. It let out a laugh before vanishing into electrical particles.

The creature was moving through the air and electrical currents surrounding it like a bolt of lightning. Turning its head, something caught its attention as it followed the unseen, yet, sparking trail.

II

GROWING ENEMIES

Dealing with the ramifications of joining the Protectors and aiding the Resistance against Octagon, Steve Walker sat in his Grandma's home as he is greeted by his friends Emily Hemsberg and Gregg Stykes. On the TV in the home was the news. Broadcasting the events of the previous night involving the tremor and the damage done to the street.

"Wonder who's gonna pay for that?" Gregg said.

"The city will take care of it." Steve replied.

"You mean us." Emily said. "The taxpayers."

"She's not wrong there." Betty said. "Now, what do you all have planned for today?"

"Nothing much." Steve said.

A knock came from the door and Steve stood up to answer. Opening the door, he sees her once again.

"You're still here?" Steve said, seeing Ava at the door.

"I am. Figured we could talk."

Ava entered the home to Emily and Gregg's surprise. Betty walked over to Ava, hugging her.

"I haven't seen you in years."

"Same here."

"How's everything? Everyone?"

"They're all doing fine. San Francisco fits them perfectly."

Emily and Gregg stood up, greeting Ava.

"Nice to see you again, Ava." Emily said.

"And I you. You too, Gregg."

"Now, Steve, I need to speak with you."

"Sure."

Steve and Ava walked into another room while Betty, Emily, and Gregg stayed in the living room. Entering the other room, Steve closed the door.

"What did you want to talk about?"

"You've been distant. Quiet on me ever since I came back."

"Because it was unexpected."

"Unexpected?"

"Yeah. I'm still trying to figure out you're still here."

"I didn't come to start a problem."

"What problem?"

"I can tell there's something going on between you and Emily."

"I don't know what you mean."

"Yeah, you do."

"Ok. I do. But, it's something we haven't figured out yet."

"You told me the same."

"That was before you left."

"But, we were close. Closer than you and Emily."

Steve sighed. Walking toward Ava. Placing his hands on her shoulders. He looked into her eyes with a grin.

"I can't balance my time with Emily and with you."

"I'm not saying you should balance it. I'm saying you have a choice to make."

"Don't do this."

"We can all be friends. I respect that. But, when it comes to who you're going to love. It's in your hands"

Ava exited the house while everyone turned to Steve. Who walked out of the room shaking his head.

"What's wrong?" Betty asked.

"Nothing."

Steve hung out with Emily and Gregg throughout the day. Going places and socializing. Upon the brink of dusk, he strange entity rose again in the city, now in the same place as Steve. Seeing the glowing figure ahead. Gregg wanted to get closer, but Emily pulled him back by his shirt. Steve stared. He already knew.

"Guys go."

"What about you?" Emily asked.

"I'm going to help these people get out of the way."

"Are you crazy?"

"Maybe."

Steve ran from the scene, changing from his civilian clothing to the Voltage. Bolting into the air and crashing down in front of the electrical entity. The two stare each other down as the remaining civilians run from the street.

"What are you?"

"I am lightning. I am water."

"I don't understand."

"Many do not."

"Why are you here? Why attack innocent civilians?"

"To bring you out. You are the energy I felt as I made my arrival."

"And what do you want?"

"Your electricity. I require its source. It is unlike anything I have encountered."

"You want my power?"

"Precisely."

"I think not, whomever you are."

"I am Sonicwave. Your death is my introduction."

"Only if you can catch me."

Sonicwave chased Voltage through the city of Los Angeles. The two only seemed like moving lightning bolts to those on the ground as the streaked from the air to the ground. However, Sonicwave caught Voltage by his leg, causing him to crash to the street. Voltage turned over to see Sonicwave standing over him, striking him with his electric claws, scratching through his suit. Voltage stood up and delivered lightning punches to Sonicwave. He stood firm with a sinister grin.

"What are you?" Voltage wondered.

Sonicwave punched Voltage across the pavement as crowds of civilians began to pour in. surrounding the fight scene. Voltage stood up and fired electrical blasts toward Sonicwave, who absorbed them without haste. Sonicwave laughed as he fired them back, hitting

Voltage in quick succession. Voltage fell to his knees as Sonicwave grabbed him, launching him into the air with a mixture of electric and water. The combination of the blast knocked Voltage unconscious as he fell and collapsed into the street.

"As I said, your death is my introduction."

Sonicwave gazed around, seeing the people and vanished with a quickening bolt. Civilians all ran over to the beaten and downed Voltage.

III

<u>LIVING YOUR DESTINY</u>

Steve had awoken, finding himself in a room. His room. His body ached from the battle. Bruises covered his body and the pain moved through him as he tried to move around the bed.

"How? How did I get here?"

Steve took another look and saw Ava sitting on the side of the bed. Immediately, he reached for his mask, now realizing his Voltage suit is laying near the closet door. He glanced at the suit and back to Ava.

"You know?"

"I know now."

"I'm sorry I didn't tell you sooner. Or anyone."

"You had good reasons why. Otherwise, we could've been targeted and possibly killed. All in the meaning of getting to you."

"Where's everyone else?"

"They're doing what they can to get away from that thing's havoc."

Steve sighed.

"I'm sure the police can handle him."

"I'm not so sure of that. Look what that thing did to you."

"It's not natural."

"I'm not understanding."

"It called itself Sonicwave. Said my death would be its introduction."

"And it's attacking the city because it believes you're dead?"

"Yeah." Steve said quietly. "Partially."

"What do you mean?"

"The Voltage is no more."

Sonicwave roamed through downtown Los Angeles, ransacking the city, causing havoc. The police do their best to stop the electrical creature, but noting they have is optional. Sonicwave ran through them with hydro-blasts from his hands, layered in electricity. Sonicwave let out a roaring screech which echoed through the entire city.

"The Voltage can't be dead." Ava said.

"That monster proved I am not ready for the greater battles ahead. I can't continue to try."

"But, look at the other things you've done. You helped take out the Neo-Spartan, you allied with others. You even aided in protecting us all from a walking A.I. with a messiah-complex. You are a hero."

"How can you be sure of that?"

Ava nodded. She walked over and grabbed the Voltage suit and held it in front of him. Steve stared at the suit before looking back to Ava.

"Because you are The Voltage and it is astonishing."

Steve continued his stare as Ava glanced at his arms and shoulders. Seeing the bruises had vanished. No signs of them anywhere on Steve's body.

"The bruises are gone."

"I heal faster than most."

"How is that possible?"

"It's a long story."

IV

GREATER THE VILLAIN, GREATER THE HERO

Sonicwave continued his mayhem in the city. More police arrived at the scene of the havoc and Sheriff Jack Martin was with them.

"What is that?" Jack asked.

"We aren't sure." An officer replied.

"We can't take down that thing. We need The Voltage."

"Sir, he tried. Didn't work."

"There's no way."

"I'm sorry, sir."

Jack shook his head as Sonicwave spotted him and the officers. They held up their firearms speedily.

"More fodder?!" Sonicwave said.

Sonicwave rushed toward the officers and without notice, a bolt of lightning flashed through the area, striking Sonicwave, knocking him to the ground. The officers paused, seeing the creature down. Sonicwave rose up, holding his chest and grunting in pain.

"What was that?" An officer asked.

Behind them appeared the Voltage, moving toward them as the lightning himself. He stopped, revealing himself to their sight. Sonicwave stood up with a grin. Chuckling.

"Officers, leave him to me."

"But, what about what happened to you?"

"It's fine. I'll manage."

The officers flee the scene as the Voltage and Sonicwave walk in circles, facing one another.

"You had me down last time."

"It was only for a moment."

"A moment? What do you mean?"

"This is all a test. I needed to know if you're as strong as they claim."

"Who's they?"

"You'll find out very soon.

"I don't think so."

Voltage blasted a lightning bolt toward Sonicwave, who quickly vanished into a hydro-lightning bolt himself, taking off into the sky. Voltage watched as he left.

"Come on! I was ready for a rematch!"

Sometime later, Steve met with Ava and told her of his story. From the origin of his abilities to the last encounter with Sonicwave. Ava questioned while the creature would just leave the fight and spare Voltage a second time. Steve questioned it himself, replaying the words spoken by Sonicwave in his mind. He wanted to know of the others and who could they be.

BIONIC RAGE: COVERT OPERATIONS

I

LIVING WITH PEACE AS POSSIBLE

Damcon Mason rested in his home. Sitting peacefully besides the technological noises coming from his bionic limbs. He sighed. A knock came from the door. Unsure, he stood up and answered it. Seeing a man in a well-dressed suit standing before him. A clean-shaven middle-aged man with a smile. A large smile.

"You are him." The man said.

"Who would be him?" Mason questioned.

"Pardon my unannounced visitation. My name is Aaron Conroy. I have come here to specifically meet you."

"Meet me for what?"

"Well, I heard about how you handled those guys a few months back. Hell, you even teamed up with those other heroes roaming around. Twice. Now, I'm not here to cause a disturbance like the one in Retropolis or Newark. But, I have something that may interest you."

"I'm listening."

"I am offering to take the bionic technology of ours off your hands. Literally."

"You want my limbs?"

"And the glowing thing in your chest. I figure it powers the tech."

"Yes, it does. Why do you want my bionic tech?"

"Because there aren't many people like you, Mr. Mason. Think about it. The tech you have right now could benefit hundreds,

155

thousands, no, millions of people across the world. An opportunity to give back to communities across the oceans."

"I didn't ask for these in the first place. Why would I choose to give them to those who do not know how this occurred?"

"Take it slow. I'm not trying to force you to give them up."

"Wouldn't work anyway."

"That so?"

"It is. Spencer Vargas trued the same thing. Looked where he's at right now."

Conroy nodded. "Understood."

"I think you already know my answer."

"I believe I do."

Conroy nodded, turning away from the door. He waved his finger in the air, looking back at Mason.

"This isn't the only time we'll encounter one another. You will see me again soon."

"And when we do, I will tell you what you've just heard. Or worse."

Conroy scoffed. Walking away. Mason shut the door. Conroy entered his car, pulling out his cell phone and dialing a number. He waited with a sigh.

"I just saw him." Conroy said on the phone. "We need that tech. the penalty has been placed on this Dameon Mason guy."

Conroy took a slight pause as he listened to the other end.

"You're already in the city?" Conroy chuckled. "This is better. Much better. Then, you know what you have to do."

Conroy put down the phone, nodded with a grin, and drove from Mason's residence.

II

FIRST SET

Immediately after the call, Chris Stanton stood on a rooftop, overlooking the district of Greektown. Having the appearance of a soldier, yet one of austerity. His uniform was unlike most soldiers. Wearing all black. Equipped with a tactical jacket, cargo pants, and boots. He reached into his pocket, pulling out a photo of Mason. One taken from a distance. Stanton scoffed, placing the pocket back into his pocket and he took a breath, taking in the sight of the district.

Brad and Claire sat inside Mason's home during the afternoon. They spoke of the past events regarding Spencer Vargas and the incident up in Retropolis to which Mason attended.

"You have to tell us why you went up there without giving a notice."

"What was I supposed to say?" Mason asked. "That I was heading north to deal with some super powered threat?"

"You were in the midst of a battlefield." Claire noted. "In the hands of these heroes and whatever those things were coming from the sky."

"It's nothing too different that being in service."

"We never dealt with beings from other places on the field."

"But we dealt with foreign invaders. Terrorists who wanted our families and friends killed. All in the name of their gods or their laws. The same thing occurred in Retropolis with those sky-beings. They serve a power higher than themselves. They follow a different set of laws. We were their targets. Imagine what could've happened if the heroes lost."

"But, you guys didn't lose. You won."

"And what has happened since? People across the world are witnessing more of these heroes rising up. They're calling me one of them. One of the Risen."

"After what you did with Vargas and what happened in Retropolis, you are a hero."

Mason shook his head as he looked down.

"I'm not a hero. I'm a soldier."

While sitting, they hear knocks at the door to which, Clare stood up and answered the door. Seeing Nathan Armstrong outside. She saw him as she opened the door. Once the door open, Nathan smiled brightly.

"Nice to see you again, Ms. Lyons."

Nathan looked inside, seeing both Mason and Brad staring at him. He waved.

"May I come in?" He asked gently.

Claire turned toward Dameon and he gave a nod. Nathan had entry into the home. Upon entering he shook the hands of Mason and Brad. Claire sat down next to Dameon while Nathan sat beside Brad.

"What's happening now?" Mason asked.

"Same old situations. Nothing big."

"So, why come here?"

"The city is looking for you, Dameon. They need your help."

"My help? On what?"

"The things you've done in the past few months is astounding. You stopped a criminal organization from taking over this city. Plus, you managed to save the world when you went up north. The world knows of your presence and Detroit seeks your support."

Mason sighed before standing up and walking into the kitchen. Claire watched him before turning back to Nathan.

"What else can be done?"

"I don't know anything else besides what I've said. If Dameon goes outside, the people will automatically clamor him about protecting this city. Others will be in fear of him because of the bionic limbs."

"They have every right to fear me." Dameon said from the kitchen. "That's not a problem."

Elsewhere, Aaron sat inside an office. He thought on matters concerning Mason and his bionic tech. shaking his head, he took out his phone and went through the numbers. Searching for one and upon his search he stopped and called the number.

"This the man I need to speak to?" Aaron said. "Ah, good. I have a job for you. If you are interested. Here's the deal. I already have one man on the job. But, two is better. Will you take the job or let the other guy?"

Aaron sat quiet and listened. He nodded with a grin. A grin of confirmation.

"Good. Come back to me when the job's done."

Aaron placed the phone down and stood up from his desk, gazing out toward the window with a smile on his face. He was ecstatic by the call, now having two mercenaries on Dameon's trail.

III

STUDY YOUR ENEMIES

Mason decided to go out for a walk, which has now become a daily exercise. While on his walks, he mediated on such matters concerning himself, his duties, and what could be on the horizon as far as talk amongst the public on his bionic tech. As he walked, he stopped to see someone standing in front of him, wearing a brown leather trench coat and their face was hidden by a hat.

"Why are you in my way?" Dameon asked.

"Because you're the one I've been sent to find."

"Is that right?"

The strange man removed his coat, unveiling his tactical uniform. Militaristic in style, yet very sleek. From his sides arose two machine guns, which he began to fire. Dameon dodged the incoming shots, blocking them with his right arm. Pedestrians nearby ran for cover. The strange man walked toward Dameon, continuing the fire.

"I've been promised a good payday to take you out."

"Tell me, who's paying you?"

"Don't worry about it. Concern yourself with this moment."

The gunfire ceased. The man moved quietly as Dameon ran into the nearby alleyway. The man circled his surroundings, searching for Mason. he chuckled under his breath.

"You know how to move quick. I'll give you that."

"Tell me who hired you?"

"Like I said, don't worry about it!"

The stranger turned around, finding Dameon standing in front of him. Mason delivered a quick blow to the stranger's abdomen,

160

causing him to stumble. Dameon pounced on him, holding him down as he raised his left arm. The arm started to click and its muzzle eased out near the stranger's forehead.

"I'm going to ask you again. Who sent you?"

"If I tell you, will you let me live?"

"Depends on my generosity."

The stranger laughed.

"His name is Aaron Conroy."

"Conroy?" Mason uttered.

"You know him." The stranger said. "Ah, it makes sense now."

"What makes sense?" Mason said, easing off the stranger.

"He came to you already. You declined his offer and now he's sent me and another to follow your trail."

"He sent someone else after me?"

"Aaron is well reserved in resources." The stranger said, standing up. "You wouldn't believe the things he can do."

"Why did he send you after me?"

"To see how you'll react to an instant attack. I saw your ways and I can say, Aaron will be pleased to hear of this."

"Where is he?"

"Don't know. He moves like the winds to various sites. If you want to find him, you'll have to wait for him to approach you. But, you already knew that."

Dameon nodded.

"What's your name?"

"Folks call me the Spymaster."

"I better not see you around here again. Otherwise, I'll blow your head off."

Spymaster grinned.

"I look forward to it. If the call is made."

Spymaster turned, walking away from Dameon. As he went further, Mason thought to himself of Spymaster's words and walked in the opposite direction. Yet, while all this was ongoing, Penalty stood atop a rooftop nearby and observed the scene. From visual to audio recording. Penalty was learning more and more about Mason and what he is capable of.

Nathan worked at his desk, reading up on more files pertaining to Mason and how the law will attest to his actions. He heard a knock at the door and in came Aaron Conroy. Startled Nathan for a moment, being unaware of such a visitor.

"I'm sorry to bother you, Mr. Armstrong." Conroy said. "But, I was the one who called for a meeting."

"I see. Why didn't you give a name?"

"To keep my footsteps discreet."

"So, what do you want?"

"What I want is simple. Nothing big. I want the bionic tech from that Dameon guy."

"You mean his bionic limbs?"

"Yes. What else is bionic on him? Don't answer that."

"I'm not sure I can help you with that."

"But, you can. Because I know of your history. Before all of this law firm junk."

"Have you been following me?"

"No. I'm not a stalker. I like to research those who I seek to do business with. And, what I found about you, goes right into my favor."

"And what is in your favor?"

"Your other occupation."

"What of it?"

"You have 'options' to make things happen. I would like something to happen in a short amount of time."

"What if I decline your offer?"

"You don't want to find out."

IV

FIRST STRIKE

Dameon, Brad, and Claire were out in Grant Circus Park, taking a walk. Dameon wanted to clear his head after his confrontation with Spymaster while Brad and Claire wanted to speak with him concerning his actions as a hero. Although, Dameon already stated he's not a hero.

"You can do a lot more." Brad said.

"And what will it cost?"

"Cost?"

"If I was to go out and 'save' people, what would that bring upon me? What if someone was tracking me, they'll lead to you and to Claire. I can't risk that."

"We can take care of ourselves." Claire stated. "No need to worry about us."

"Like how you were inside that warehouse with Vargas and his assassin."

"That's different, Dameon."

"No. It's the same. You know it and I know it."

"Just take some thought on it."

"I've done enough thinking. I'll do what is necessary."

While they continued their walk, a bullet grazed a tree right in front of Dameon. He caught the sound and immediately told Brad and Claire to leave the scene. More shots fired near his location as civilians noticed something going on. Dameon moved through the trees as more rounds were fired. One at a time. Dameon ran over, ducking on the side of a fountain, he looked up and with his bionic enhancements, he was able to scan the nearby buildings. Atop one was a man with a rifle. He had his eyes set on Dameon. His finger was on the trigger. He was set to fire and Dameon took off. Penalty removed his finger and sighed.

"He's clever. Skillful. Useful."

Dameon arrived back at his home where Brad and Claire were waiting inside. Upon Dameon arriving, he found a visitor was also present in the home. Sitting in a seat opposite of Brad and Claire who were on the couch.

"The hell are you doing here?" Dameon asked.

"I came for a reason." Nathan Hawke said. "Just here me out."

"You let him in?" Dameon asked Brad.

"He said he had something important to share with you. Concerning your status."

"Status? This man doesn't tell me anything."

"I know what you've been through."

"Do you?"

"You're not the only one who had to be filed with bio-nanotechnology in order to survive a disaster."

"You still have your legs. Your arms. You don't have to live every day with a bionic reactor in your chest. Embedded through your skin."

"I do not."

"Then, you do not understand what I have to live with!"

"Perhaps not. But, I come here to offer you an opportunity to make things right."

"What kind of opportunity?"

"Join us. Join the Resistance. You've helped us in the Battle of Retropolis and against that King Stroh Conqueror guy."

"I can't accept."

"Why not? You have the qualities of a hero."

"I'm just a soldier. Always will be."

Nathan nodded. "Contact me when you change your mind."

"And what if I refuse completely?"

"Trust me, this isn't our last encounter."

Hawke walked toward the door and left. Dameon focused his

sights on Brad and Clare who approached him from the couch.

"Why did you turn him down?" Brad asked.

"Because I don't trust him."

Elsewhere, Aaron met up with Penalty in an undisclosed location. Penalty handed him the data pertaining to Dameon's movements and skill set. Aaron was impressed and knew Penalty was the right guy for the task.

"This man cannot be tampered with." Penalty said.

"Tampered? What do you mean by that?"

"He's an angry man. Even when he appears calm. Anger is sitting right underneath his façade. At a split moment, he can snap and unleash the fullness of his biotech."

"So, what are you proposing I do?"

"Leave the Bionic Rage to me. I'll handle him clean."

Aaron nodded with a grin. "I'll leave you to it."

Dameon rested in his home. Asleep. Although within his sleep was not much rest. For within the dream itself were the echoes of gunfire, commands of soldiers, multiple footsteps. Missiles launching from distances. Shouting from commanding officers. Dameon was dreaming of the past. Of the Republic War. Dameon moved with a fierce focus, shooting the opposing soldiers in his sight. Taking them down with every weapon in his arsenal. From an M4 to a shotgun to even his bare hands. Dameon was a ruthless soldier and the war needed soldiers like him. Those who could complete the mission.

V

WITNESSING THE MONEYMAN

The following day, Dameon is visited at his home by Armstrong. Caught off guard by the lawyer's visit, Dameon allowed him inside.

"Why have you come?"

"To give you some news."

"News?"

"Not what you're expecting. Doesn't concern your appearance in the public."

"Then, tell me why you've come to my home."

"I was visited by Aaron Conroy."

"I know him."

"He came to give me a proposition regarding your bionic limbs."

"He already gave me his deal. I turned him down."

"And in you doing so, he has sent mercenaries to track you down and eliminate you. Have you been ambushed or attacked recently since your conversation with Conroy?"

"I was confronted by a man who called himself Spymaster. Later, myself, Brad, and Claire were shot at by a sniper."

"Are Claire and Brad alright?"

"They're fine."

"That's good to hear." Armstrong said with a sigh. "Anyhow, these attacks were perpetrated by Conroy in an effort to obtain your limbs."

"So, where is he?"

"You mean Conroy? I have no clue where he could be."

"I'll find him."

"Dameon, don't do anything you'll regret."

"Truthfully, what else do I have left to regret."

Armstrong left the home and Dameon searched throughout Detroit for Conroy. Having no luck, he decided to use his biotech to track down Conroy. The tracking went across all of Detroit, eventually reaching a lead that led him to the same warehouse where he faced Vargas' assassin.

Dameon reached the warehouse and standing out front was Conroy with three bodyguards. They entered the warehouse and Dameon moved quietly to follow. He reached the doors just as they entered and then, he couldn't wait no longer. Mason burst through the door, catching the guards off their post. Conroy turned, seeing Dameon.

"What have we here?"

"I know what you've been up to."

"Up to? Like what do you mean?"

"The Spymaster. The sniper. I know you paid them to have me killed so you could take my limbs and my reactor."

Conroy held his hands up with a laugh.

"Sounds like an interesting plan. But, I have no clue what you're talking about. I'm just the moneyman."

"Cut the shit."

Conroy nodded. "Fair enough."

The three guards raised up their firearms and before they could fire, Dameon fired his own shots from his right arm through their heads. Precision was perfect. Conroy was silent as Dameon approached him. Facing him directly.

"You will cease whatever else you have planned. Or else, you have a bullet in your own damn head."

Conroy stared and slightly grinned. Dameon noticed the grin and before he could make a move, a gunshot was fired. Conroy dodged out of the way as another shot was fired. The rounds came from in front of Dameon and walking out of the shadows was Penalty. Conroy began applauding his entrance.

"That's the shit I'm talking about!"

Dameon stumbled in his steps as Penalty inched closer. He

grabbed Mason by his throat and threw him out of the window to the outside. There, Penalty jumped from the window, standing above Dameon. Aaron came out from the doorway and saw the two on the ground.

"I'll finish the job." Penalty said to Conroy.

"Already looks like you're done."

"Not yet. He still breathes."

VI

YOUR DATE IS SET

Dameon stood up on his feet, facing Penalty. Their eyes were locked onto one another. Penalty was prepared for the fight while Conroy stood by the entrance door.

"Stanton, what are you waiting for?" Conroy yelled. "Kill him!"

"He paid you to kill me?" Dameon asked.

"He did. Your bionic technology would prove useful to Conroy and his business necessities."

"I don't think they'll do any good in a hand of a businessman."

"I'm a moneyman!"

"And I like money."

Penalty took out two Glocks from his sides and began firing at Mason, who blocked the rounds with his arms and ran for the nearby containers, hiding behind them. Penalty ceased his fire as Conroy walked down the stairs.

"Don't get in the way." Penalty said. "I have him where I want him."

"I just wanted to get a closer look. That's all."

Penalty went over toward the nearby pickup truck, Dameon watched him from the corner of the containers, seeing Stanton lifting a rifle.

"That's what he tried hitting me with."

Penalty set up the rifle and Conroy loved the appearance of it. The sleekness and the presence it carried with it. He pointed toward it with joy, placing his hands over his chest with a smirk.

"Where did you get that beauty?"

"Hard earned jobs provided a way. This one cost big."

Mason dove from the containers, his arms clicked as he fired rounds back at Penalty. He dodged toward the truck and Conroy ran form the area. Dameon walked toward the truck, continuing his firing shots. Penalty counted to three and bolted up from the other side of the truck, kicking Dameon in the face and tripping him with a swipe kick. Dameon flipped himself up to his feet, staring down Penalty.

"You have skills. I like a fighter with skills. It gives a proper challenge."

"If that's the case. Face me like a man. No weapons."

Dameon shook his arms and they clicked, becoming silent. He jerked his wrist as the bullets rained down from his forearms. Penalty nodded, dropping his handguns, and placing the rifle in the back of the truck.

"Your move." Penalty grinned.

The two collided with punches and kicks. Dameon's attacks carried weight due to the bionics. However, Stanton did not stumble from the blows, he took them and fought back with attacks of his own. Using many kicks and chest hits against Rage. One chest attack directly hit the reactor and Dameon began to stumble in his steps.

"Was that too hard of a hit?" Penalty mocked. "If not, keep coming."

Dameon went for a punch, but Stanton dodged. Another punch, this time came from the left arm and Stanton dodged once more. He grabbed the bionic arm and slammed Mason to the concrete. He raised his foot to stomp and Dameon rolled out of its way. He stood up and grabbed Penalty by his heck and threw him against one of the wooden containers. Penalty took a moment to get back up as he was catching his breath.

"Is that all you have?" Dameon mocked back. "If not, keep coming."

Stanton laughed. Nodding and wiping the blood from his mouth as he stood up.

"I see. I take it you're holding back."

"What choice do I have. My limbs could easily kill you."

"Stop being a bitch. Use what you have. Before I go ahead and blow your head off."

Dameon nodded.

"Fair enough. You asked."

Stanton rushed toward Dameon with a gut punch. He reached closer and Rage grabbed his arm, twisting it before head-butting Penalty and throwing him to the ground. He stood over Stanton and began pummeling him. Conroy was afraid and ran over to stop Mason from killing Penalty. Shoving Conroy away, Dameon arose and Stanton was bleeding on the ground. Knocked unconscious. Broken bones were definite. Mason walked over toward Conroy, who was crouched on the ground.

"Don't kill me."

"I'm not going to kill you. Just hear me out."

"What do you want? Money? I can give you money."

"I don't want your money. I want you to leave Detroit. Take anything connected to you and your name out of this city. If not, I will find what you have left and finish what has begun here."

Aaron nodded in fear of Dameon's threat. Mason took one look at the downed Stanton and walked away, leaving Conroy behind with his mercenary.

Sometime later, Armstrong secured a deal for Mason to go out into the public eye once more, but he declined. Brad and Claire continued to assist Mason in any needs he might have, but he chose to only contact them on certain occasions. After some thought, Dameon made a choice. One in which his life will forever be altered. One night, a group of gangs had a meeting in downtown Detroit, discussing terms for the next shipment of drugs and weapons. Before they could finish the deal, Mason entered the room, startling the young men.

"Who the hell are you?"

"I'm the dealer. Your time is up."

"Or what?" One thug said as the others raised their weapons toward Mason.

"I guess you'll have to find out."

Mason raised his arms, revealing them to be enhanced and now firing rounds like an assault rifle. He shot up the entire room, killing both gangs. Mason had become a vengeful soldier. He has finally become the Bionic Rage.

TERROR: KILL OR BE KILLED

I

MARKING THE ORDER

John Terror continued cleaning Chicago of anything related or pertaining to Agency X. He traveled all through the city and even went further out into the state of Illinois to rid it of Agency X. Carl Prater detailed all the known locations and their whereabouts, giving the information to Terror and he would head out and decimate them. Burning down entire warehouses and facilities. Within the city, Jordan Dodson kept tabs on Terror's actions as well as the growing concern of nubreeds and rising heroes being looked at in a negative manner throughout Chicago.

Elsewhere, Professor Mite gathered what he could find and made another Agency X base far from Illinois. Most of the crew came from the same base as before. Mite worked in his lab, similar to the old one. Hunter Vazquez sat next to him at the desk, dressed in the same attire as before. Black trench coat, boots, pants, gloves, and his sunglasses. Mite was detailing a map. The map was of the United States and there were red marks across the map. Each mark was a signified area for Agency X to operate.

"We would've had something in Chicago." Vazquez said. "But, John, he had to mess things up."

"John is the persistent type." Mite replied. "You know this just as much as I."

"What are we going to do once he finds out what's next? You know he will."

"I'm counting on it and that is why I have you."

"What do you have in mind?"

"I've gathered some students that I would like you to lead."

"Lead?" Vazquez questioned.

"You will meet them soon enough and believe me, when John sees them and you as the lead, he will consider other means of operations."

"I see."

"They should be here at any moment."

"Very well. I will greet them upon their entrance."

Vazquez walked out of the lab as Mite continued focusing on the map. He laughed to himself, shaking his head with a smile.

"John has no idea what he's done."

II

ARMS OF THE AGENCY

Terror returned to his hideout, meeting Carl at the desk, reading a map. Terror removed his coat, placing it on the rack near the door as Carl turned toward him.

"You're back. Great."

"I went around. Searched for anything related to Agency X. burned them all down."

"Just as was planned."

"How's the reporter doing on her end?"

"So far, I've received nothing. But, she is working her hardest on finding out more sources. She's very persistent."

"I am aware." Terror nodded. "Now, what's on the agenda for Chicago's criminal elements?"

"Right now? Nothing."

"Can't be? There's sure to be something taking place."

"Not like before." Prater noted. "After the whole 'risen heroes' thing spread across the country, many crime activities began to slow down. Here in Chicago, they've decreased exponentially. Due to-"

"The Yonderers and myself. Great."

"And that Devil guy."

"Never met him."

"I'm sure we'll all meet soon. Just depends on the case I take it."

"Not something I'm looking forward to. There's already enough wanderers outside to deal with."

"Speaking of wanderers, there's this place in the outskirts of the city. You haven't been there yet, have you?"

Terror walked toward the desk, seeing the map on the computer screen. What he saw was a base. One familiar, yet different.

"I have not. How far out is it?"

"Further out than before." Carl said. "You know where the place is?"

"I do." Terror said, grabbing his coat from the rack. "I'll be back."

The door closed behind Terror. Prater shrugged his shoulders and went back to his work.

Terror rode out to the location and upon inching closer, he could hear the sounds of other vehicles behind him. Terror sighed, slowly turning in toward the entrance of the hidden facility. When he turned, he found himself staring down a team. A team of other nubreeds.

"The hell?" Terror said.

The team standing in front of him were consisted of Professor Mite's recruits. They were Kudo Fox, Mistress Destroyer, Agents 51 and 50, and Hellshot. They were led by Hunter Vazquez, who grinned when Terror saw them.

"Found yourself some new friends?" Terror joked. "Quaint."

"Things have changed." Vazquez said. "What you did before won't cut it any longer. Mite wants you back. Although, I prefer you were just dead."

Terror pushed back his coat, raising up two machine guns. The team held up weapons of their own. Kudo Fox wielded two silver glocks, Mistress Destroyer had claws emitted from her hands, Agents 50 and 51 carried pistols, and Hellshot pulled out a sword and a pistol. Vazquez crouched down, his eyes locked on Terror.

"Let's get this over with." Terror said. "Enough wasting time."

Terror fired the first shot before the others could retaliate. Terror looked over to his right, seeing a large dozer. He ran over to it while firing to get cover. The force behind Mite's team was strong. Vazquez stood back while the others took shots toward Terror. Bullets bouncing off the dozer. Terror held his head down, raising up his right arm to fire back. He continued and paused to reload, hearing the bullets coming from the other end.

"Perhaps you should get closer." Vazquez told the team.

"What about you?" Kudo asked.

"I'll do me, and you do you."

From around the corner, a round of bullets fire off near Vazquez and the team. Vazquez lunged from the incoming rounds like a panther while the team ducked their heads. Vazquez looked over toward the dozer, seeing it was not Terror who fired the shots. He looked around before a grenade landed in front of him and the team.

"Move out!" Vazquez yelled.

The team jumped as the grenade exploded. Terror looked out, seeing an opportunity to move ahead. Terror could hear to sound of an incoming motorcycle to his left. He turned, seeing a woman sitting atop a motorcycle next to his. What caught his attention more so was her fiery red hair and emerald eyes.

"You." Terror said.

"Get on your bike and let's get out of here!"

"You. But, how?"

"I'll explain on the way." She said.

Terror ran and sat atop his bike, starting the engine as Vazquez arose from the ground, watching them.

"Nice to see you again." Terror said.

"Same."

The two rode off. Vazquez stood up, fixing his coat and dusting off his sunglasses. He attempted to run after them. But stopped in his tracks. He turned around toward the Agents, who were already sitting on motorcycles of their own as the engines roared. No emotion on their faces. Vazquez pointed out toward Terror and the woman.

"You know what to do."

The Agents nodded and rode off.

III

<u>WHERE IS YOUR FAITH?</u>

The Agents chased down Terror and Horror through the highway, entering downtown Chicago. Terror looked back, seeing one of the Agents inching closer. He turned toward Jade, nodding his head as she looked back. The Agents reached to their side, raising up their firearms and firing. Terror and Jade dodge the incoming shots by moving across pathways of the road, leading into the opposite lanes.

"Shoot at the tires!" Terror yelled.

Jade pulled out a firearm from her jacket, firing toward the agent behind her with a slight hit at the agent behind Terror. She turned around and quickly maneuvered the motorcycle from the incoming traffic on the opposite lane. Terror did the same, giving them a way to escape the sight of the agents. The agents pulled over to avoid the traffic and looked on, seeing Terror and Jade ride off in the distance.

"We must inform Vazquez." Agent 50 said.

"Not before we talk with the Professor. He might have some alternatives to all of this."

Terror returned to his base, entering to find Jordon Dodson talking with Prater. They noticed Terror enter and Jade behind him. Prater looked toward Jade, pointing heavily as Terror approached him.

"It can't be."

"Don't worry, Carl." Terror said. "It is."

Carl only stared as Terror and Jade passed by. Jade gave him a nod and nervously nodded back.

"Didn't expect to see you again."

"Things change." Jade said. "Hell, circumstances decide our course."

"You could say that." Terror added, looking over to Jordan. "Ms. Dodson, I wasn't expecting you to arrive this day."

"I had to come by to see how things are operating."

"For more publicity or just in the arts of curiosity?"

"You could help with something. Carl, with me."

"Sure."

They followed Terror to his desk, where he moved nearly everything off and placed a map. He marked circles around several locations before placing focus on another. The one afar off from Chicago.

"Professor Mite is continuing his operations here."

"And that's where you went?" Prater asked. "And ran into this woman?"

"She came after. Saved me some trouble of escape."

"I'm sorry." Jordan said toward Jade. "Who are you?"

"I'm Jade."

"Tell her your last name." Carl joked.

"Your last name?" Jordan asked. "Is it something to be funny or?"

"Friends in our inner circle called me Jade Horror."

Carl looked over to Terror, who shook his head in silence.

"She is as furious as they come." Carl said to Jordan. "You wouldn't want to get on her bad side."

"I'm sure."

"She is furious." Terror said. "When the situation calls for it."

"And she's called Horror." Jordan added. "While you're referred to as Terror. What group were the two of you involved into get those names?"

"Past lives." Terror replied. "Nothing more to it than that."

Jade cocked her head with a nod.

"Right about that."

"So, what's the current status on Agency X?" Carl asked.

"They're still in Illinois. Far out from Chicago's limits. Mite has a new team of nubreeds besides Vazquez and Agent 51. I recognized two of them from General Rilla's Fellowship."

"Are we going to jump the place?"

"No. I need to meet with an old mentor. Someone who might have some answers."

"I don't know anyone of that nature, John. Much less someone of an old stature."

"But we do." Jade said. "You want to meet with Father Reynolds, don't you?"

"He's familiar with all of this. He might know something we don't."

"I see."

"We're coming with you." Carl said. Grabbing his coat from the rack on the wall.

"No." Terror replied quickly. "You and Jordan stay here. Keep doing what you're doing. Jade and I will meet with Father Reynolds."

"Oh." Carl said, placing his coat back. "I got you."

Terror and Jade arrived at St. Peter's Catholic Church. Jade stood in front of the building while Terror walked and stood next to her, looking at the imagery of Christ upon the cross. Jade looked at Terror with a smirk.

"Still bothers you?" Jade asked.

"I've gotten over it."

"We'll see."

The two entered the church and once they were inside, they walked down the aisle. No one was sitting at the pews but standing in front speaking with someone was Father Scott Reynolds. While talking to the visitor, Scott looked out, seeing Terror and Jade approaching. He nodded and finished up his talk. Once the visitor left, Scott greeted Terror and Jade with hugs.

"I wasn't expecting either of you to be here in a place like this."

"We didn't come by for a simple visit."

"Then, why have you come to see me? What's happened?"

"The Agency still exists." Terror said. "They're operating in the outskirts of city currently."

"Agency X is what you're speaking of?"

"Yes." Jade replied. "We figured we'd come and see what directions you could give us."

"Why me?"

"Because you helped us the last time. Figured you could assist us again."

"Now, I would love to help, but, I'm in no fighting condition any longer."

"We're not asking you to fight with us physically. More so spiritually."

"I can sense you're still delving into those occult reigns."

"He still has the marks to prove it." Jade said.

"They can't be removed. I've tried everything. But, that's not why we're here."

Scott nodded with a smile. He thought to himself for a slight second before returning his senses toward Terror and Jade. Scott rubbed his hands together and clapped.

"I'll see what I can do."

"Thank you." Terror replied, extending his hand.

Scott looked at Terror's hand and shook his head. Going in for another hug. Afterwards, Terror and Jade made their way to leave.

"One more thing, John." Scott said. "Since you stepped foot in here, you realize they're going to send one on your trail."

Terror thought and he understood Scott's words. Terror shrugged his shoulders and his arms flopped up and back down. Not a care in his presence.

"Let them come."

Terror and Jade exited the church. Outside the church, the two talked of possible scenario once returning to the Agency's base. Terror proclaimed to Jade that Carl and Jordan might have to accompany them, but, as it is with Terror, he prefers to go at it alone. However, with Jade at his side, it gives him a better advantage. Jade returned to the base while Terror went out scouting for any more clues leading to the Agency. On the way, Terror encountered a peculiar and macabre figure. Terror found himself in an alleyway within downtown Chicago, staring down the figure.

"The hell are you?"

Terror noticed the clothing the figure wore. It was his own but burnt to crisp with fragments of leather flaking off as the figure walked slowly. Other signs upon the clothing were dried blood. Terror looked at the figure's chest and saw his insignia upon it, only upside down and darkened as if it was submerged in smoke and ash. The figure's eyes were covered by burned sunglasses.

"You're me." Terror said. "From another time or place."

The figure screeched at Terror, lunging at him with both arms grabbing Terror's coat. Terror fought off the figure with kicks and some punches to the face, breaking its sunglasses and revealing its eyes. They were black and only black. No pupils.

"Ah. I know what you are." Terror said, shoving the figure back. "You're a doppelganger of mine. From the spiritual realm. I wonder what they call you."

The figure ran toward Terror once more, finding itself at the barrel of a shotgun, which Terror fired, and the figure vanished in a thick puff of burning smoke with only ash remaining on the ground. The gun's sound echoed through the alley and into the streets, leaving Terror to only run from the scene as quickly as possible. Terror done so and returned to the base.

IV

FINAL BLOW

When Terror had returned, Jade already informed Prater and Jordan on the current circumstances and told them they could join in. Terror approached them, hearing the conversation.

"Better it's just the two of us." Terror said.

"We could distract them." Carl noted. "I mean, we can do things."

"This is not something simple. Last we saw, there were six of them. They're all nubreeds. No human can match them in slight skills."

"But, you and Jade can handle them because your of the same kind." Jordan said. "Makes sense."

Terror nodded and turned toward Jade. The two gathered whatever weapons they needed from the armory. Before leaving, Carl handed Terror a small, but fragile grenade. Terror looked at it as just a simple grenade, however, Carl proscribed him to use it at the opportune time when inside the Agency building. Terror agreed and left the base.

Once Terror and Jade arrived at the Agency base, they saw Vazquez and Mistress Destroyer standing at the front, watching them closely. They stepped from their motorcycles and approached Mite's team a few feet. Terror looked around, not seeing the Agents nor the others who were present the time before.

"Where are the others?" Terror asked.

"They're on some other business." Vazquez said. "What does it matter to you?"

"Nothing. Just gives us a better chance."

Vazquez removed his trench coat and balled his hands up. Mistress Destroyer screeched with a loud yell as her fingers curved sharp. Jade saw the transformation and nodded with a slight clap.

"Not bad. Didn't know she had those."

"Let's go ahead and finish this." Vazquez said, running toward Terror.

"Sure." Terror replied, removing his coat and tossing his sunglasses.

Terror and Vazquez clashed with fists to face. Jade and Destroyer moved swiftly across the field with Jade dodging Destroyer's claws. Terror didn't bother to use his firearms and instead focused on his fists and feet against Vazquez. This time, Vazquez had the upper hand on Terror, grabbing him by his throat and slamming him into the dirt. Terror flipped himself to his feet and continued fighting. Using jabs against Vazquez's lower back and abdomen while using an uppercut against Vazquez's jaw.

"You're stumbling." Terror sighed. "I have you again."

"This will not happen again."

"Looks like it is."

Jade dodged more of Destroyer's swipes before kicking her in the knee to gain a swift uppercut, knocking Destroyer back several steps before Jade speared her to the ground, pummeling the woman until she was unconscious. Jade sighed, looking up toward Terror and Vazquez.

"Finish it, John."

Vazquez punched Terror several times in the chest and face. Terror attacked back with the same hits. They circled one another before Jade ran in, snatching the grenade from Terror's coat and tossing it into the window of the base.

"Let's get out of here!" Jade yelled.

Terror and Jade ran to their motorcycles as the grenade exploded, knocking Vazquez forward into a nearby ditch and covering Destroyer with debris. The base was destroyed as flames covered the grounds, Terror put on his sunglasses as they rode away. A few hours later, Mite returned to the base, seeing its destruction. He sighed before turning around to see a wounded Vazquez and a burnt Destroyer.

"He did this." Mite said. "I already know. Good thing, I have many contingences."

A few days later, Terror spoke with Carl, Jordan, and Jade at the base concerning more possible Agency bases. A knock came from the door and Carl answered, seeing Professor Cullen Edge. He entered the base and Terror greeted him, yet with caution.

"Why have you come here, Professor?"

"I need your help. Both of you." The Professor said, looking at both Terror and Jade.

"Our help for what reason?" Jade wondered. "What's happened?"

"Trouble for pour kind as arisen. We need all we can to fight back. Will you join us on this cause?"

"Let's see what we're up against." Terror replied.

Q-ARROW: HIRED FOR ARROW

I

THE CALL

In the outskirts of Las Vegas, the Hitman was settled at a secure ranch. The ranch was bought by Hitman due to his occupation. Inside of the home, he sat down at a desk, reading up on the news surrounding the risen heroes. Turning the pages, he came across what went on in Vegas concerning Q-Arrow and Woodstalker.

"You've got to be shitting me." He scoffed.

He turned the page and read how the city was greeting Q-Arrow as their own risen hero amongst the others. The Hitman tossed the pages aside and sat still. Meditating and moving through his own thoughts. How could he get back at Q-Arrow after their last encounter? How can he get back into Vegas while being on their watch list? After some time of thinking, the phone rang. He looked and answered it without hesitation as if he was anticipating a call of some sort.

"Yes."

"Is this John Samuels?" A voice said on the other end.

"It is. Who's calling to know?"

"We have a job for you."

"What is this job?"

"You want another chance at Q-Arrow?"

"I do."

"This is that job."

"And what must I do?"

"Kill the son of a bitch. We have the eliminate him to move further our plans."

"I see. Where can we discuss terms?"

"We know you're a hot one in Vegas, but, we can make things for the better. Come into the city by nightfall, we'll meet up and I'll explain everything there. Good?"

"Good."

Later in the night, Hitman made his arrival in Vegas secretly. Upon entering, he is greeted by a black SUV and standing by are two guards in suits with no ties. Hitman nodded as he stepped forward. The guards were quiet. Discreet. The windows of the vehicle were heavily tinted.

"This must be it."

One guard opened the car door and Hitman entered. After the door shut, he saw himself sitting in front of the man who called him. He was a well-dressed man and middle-aged. However, Hitman had no clue who this man could be or who he worked with or for.

"You are the Hitman."

"I am. I take it you're the one who called."

"That I am. Good for us to meet in person. Now, would you like to hear about the offer?"

"Most certainly."

"Very well. Q-Arrow has caused a rift in our operations for this city. His actions violate everything we stand for. Now, we could handle matters ourselves, but it would be too sloppy. However, we received word about your previous encounter with the man. Knowing full well you want some payback."

"That I do."

"This job is your opportunity."

"You want me to kill Q-Arrow and?"

"And the task will be done. He'll be out of our way. You get your payback. All's well."

"Who are you?"

"You'll find out with the rest of the city."

The car door opened for Hitman to exit, but before he could, the man placed his hand on his shoulder.

"I would move with speed if I were you. Because, there are three others seeking to do the same task."

"Three others?" Hitman questioned. "Who are they?"

"You'll find out. I'm sure you'll all bump into each other on this."

Hitman nodded and exit the car, returning to his own and leaving the city.

II

THE BOUNTY AND THE HUNTED

During the same night, Q-Arrow patrolled Las Vegas, searching for any trace leading to the Hitman. Throughout the night, there was nothing Q-Arrow could find that would bring him to the Hitman. Q-Arrow sighed and returned to his lair. As he was leaving, there were three figures watching him closely.

Back at the base, Karen entered, and Jarvis approached her. She looked around for Asher, seeing he was not there.

"Where is he now?"

"He's on business. He'll be back when he comes back."

"Business. You mean out riding about with his archery gear."

Jarvis scoffed. "Give it time."

"He knows he can get himself killed out there."

"He's been through a lot in this short time. He has the experience capable of taking care of himself out there."

"Just because he helped a bunch of strange people in another country doesn't mean he can fully protect himself."

"He's found an ally in the field."

"An ally?"

"He'll be fine. You can wait here until he returns, or you can leave. Your choice."

Karen shook her head, giving Jarvis a look of certainty.

"I'll be back."

Karen left the base as Jarvis went back to his work.

Elsewhere, Jeff Nero was training at his residence, he kept bringing up the events concerning Woodstalker and the Dominate Trio to keep his mind focused. On the other end, he remembered all Q-Arrow told him. While training, he had his cell phone on standby. Waiting for the call to assist Q-Arrow once again.

Deep in Vegas, Q-Arrow discovered a set of tire tracks. Scanning them, he concludes the vehicle appeared from outside the city. He searched every perimeter of the area. Finding nothing that could lead him to the Hitman. Arrow contacted Jarvis and gave him the details. Q-Arrow looked up, seeing a set of cameras.

"Check the cameras of the street." Arrow said.

Jarvis went to the desk of the base, going into the city's camera network. Searching through and searching, Jarvis found the street and went into the camera's history. On the screen appeared the SUV and approaching the vehicle was the Hitman.

"An SUV was there." Jarvis said.

"What of Hitman? Was he present?"

"He was. However, he did not get out of the car. He went inside."

"I'm not clearly getting what you're saying."

"What I'm saying is the Hitman was only a guest to the one inside the vehicle."

"You're thinking what I'm thinking?" Arrow asked.

"I am, sir. There's a bounty on your head."

The crashing jolt of a falling trash can sound off behind Arrow. He turned around as Jarvis tried to get his attention. He held his bow up and the arrow was ready to fire. What he was looking at were three figures. One gave off the slithering sound of a rattlesnake. The second one resembled the physical feats of a Komodo dragon. The third appeared to have makeshift wings and the beak of a eagle.

"The hell is this?" Arrow said.

"What's going on?" Jarvis asked. "What has your attention?"

190

"Three people. I'm assuming their people."

"What do you mean?"

"They look like animals."

"Animals?"

The rattlesnake one approached Arrow, revealing itself completely. Standing upright, covered in snakeskin with a the head and tail of a snake. Yet, with arms and legs of a human. Arrow stepped back, his hand tightly gripped the bow.

"The hell are you?"

"I am new to this city. As are my allies."

The others present themselves. Both in similar fashion to the rattlesnake figure. Arrow was at a loss for words. Aiming tightly toward the rattlesnake as his eyes glanced the Komodo and the eagle.

"We have been contacted to find you."

"Find me? For what cause?"

"You seek the one called the Hitman."

"I do. You know him? He's your boss?"

"He's a partner in this endeavor. There's a high price on your head."

"That a fact? How much?"

"Money is not what we're after. We seek only a game. A game of chase."

"Hitman wants the money while the three of you want to chase? For sport."

"It is our nature."

Arrow nodded with a smirk.

"Here's mine."

Without a catch of the eye, Arrow began firing toward the three beings consecutively. They took off, dodging around the corners of the nearby buildings as Arrow made his escape, vanishing from their sights. They came out into the open, seeing Arrow was gone.

"Don't worry. We'll see him again."

Making his move, Arrow is almost hit by a gunshot. He turned around, seeing where the bullet had come and he saw in the distance, Hitman himself with a rifle. Arrow fired toward him, only hitting the side of the window where the Hitman was standing.

"Nice shot!" Hitman yelled. "My turn."

The Hitman fired more rounds as Arrow dodged the bullets and evaded Hitman's sights. Running into a shadowy mist of smoke. While making his move, he appeared across Jeff, who was out on a night walk.

"Q-Arrow." Jeff said.

"Why are you out here?"

"I can say the same for yourself. You seem to be in a hurry."

"There's no time. We need to go. Back to the base."

"I'll follow your lead."

III

THE HIDDEN AND THE TIME

Q-Arrow and Jeff made their moves quickly to avoid the Hitman's coming rounds from the air and the three animal beings on the ground. While running, a spew of venom collapsed on the ground in front of them. They both paused, hearing the rattling behind them.

"What is that?" Jeff said, seeing the three figures.

"That's what I'm trying to figure out."

The figures stared and growled toward Arrow and Nero. The bow was up once again, hearing another faint sound from Hitman's sniper.

"You go where you need to." Jeff said to Arrow. "I'll deal with them."

"I'm not leaving you here against three others."

"Not to worry. I've been training. If you're heading where I think you are, I'll meet you there."

Arrow nodded and left. Jeff faced the three figures.

"Do you guys have any names or are you just simple animals?"

"I am Rattler. This one is Eaglestruck and he is the Ultimate Komodo."

"Just animals then." Jeff scoffed. "Figured as much."

Nero rushed toward the three, using his training to gain a greater advantage. Meanwhile, Arrow returned to the lair, seeing Jarvis and Arwin sitting inside talking. He quickly entered and caught his breath.

"You're in a rush." Jarvis said.

"The Hitman was on me. Sniper rifle."

"Same Hitman as before?" Arwin asked. "Thought he was done with."

"Not quite."

"What of those things you saw out there?"

"They're animal/human hybrids." Asher said. "Never seen anything like them before. Ever."

"Where are they now?"

"Nero is dealing with them. He'll be here as soon as they're out of his reach."

"You left him out there alone?" Jarvis asked. "Why?"

"Because, the boy is capable. He already knows it. Gave me the chance to escape Hitman's shots."

"Well, what of these animal creatures and the Hitman?" Arwin asked with curiosity. "What is all of this about?"

"The snake said there was a bounty on my head."

"Snake?" Jarvis said. "A talking snake."

"It's not the first one." Arwin noted.

"One had the appearance of a snake. A rattlesnake that is. The other two were of an eagle and a Komodo dragon."

"Where did these things come from?" Jarvis wondered. "This world is turning stranger every day."

"Well, it's always been strange." Arwin said. "It just had to present itself."

Jarvis shook his head after hearing Arwin's response. Asher didn't concern himself with the dialogue and went to the computers, searching throughout the city's camera feeds to track down Hitman and the hybrids.

"You only caught the vehicle?" Asher asked.

"That is all."

Asher nodded, looking at the monitor.

"Once Jeff is with us, we'll come up with a plan. End all of this before the sun rises."

"Wait, you plan on going back out there?" Arwin questioned. "I mean, I know you can handle the battles, but, it's three against one."

"Three against two. Jeff's learning."

"Jeff? Who's Jeff?"

"The young protégé of Asher's." Jarvis said. "They met up during the whole Woodstalker and Trio incident."

"Ah. I see. So, he's an archer as well?"

"More of a fighter than a shooter." Asher noted. "Close combat. Less range."

"I see. Well, I'll be getting back to what I was working on while you wait on your apprentice."

"He's not my apprentice." Asher said. "He's an ally."

"By the way, Karen was here earlier."

"What did she want?"

"She wanted to see you. To see how you're doing."

"That's great. Where did she go?"

"She didn't want to sit and wait here for you. Said she'll be back some other time."

Asher nodded. "That's good. Because the distraction isn't needed right now."

They waited several more minutes and from the door appeared Jeff. Rushing in with tiredness as he collapsed to the floor. Asher and Jarvis helped him up, bringing him to the table. There, he caught his breath and sat still.

"I can see you were clearly hit." Jarvis said, seeing the cuts on Jeff's arms, back, and chest.

"It was for the cause. I dealt with them as best I could."

"They're still out there?" Asher asked.

"Yeah. They didn't follow me. They only said they want you."

"Then, they'll have me."

Asher grabbed his bow and loaded the quiver. He approached the door and stopped. He turned toward Jarvis.

"I'll need the car."

"Of course, you do."

Jeff stood up from the table. "I'm coming too."

"No, you've done enough."

"Let me help out. Just in case they try some distraction. I can be the defense."

"Can you take another hit?"

195

"I can take a few more. Sure."

"Then, get in the car."

Behind them, Jarvis pulled up in a black and gold vehicle. Resembling a Lamborghini, but clearly used for stealth purposes across short distances. Asher and Jeff entered the car as the engine roared.

"What is this car called?" Jeff asked.

"Haven't thought of a name yet."

"Best you take care of this." Jarvis said. "Arwin worked hard on it."

"It'll come out well."

The car roared once more as it drove from the base and out into the roads.

IV

THE REWARD

Q-Arrow and Nero entered Las Vegas, driving pass the Vegas Strip, seeing the crowds of people staring at the vehicle. Some cheered. Others were silent with astonishment. Never seeing a vehicle such as one before in their presence.

"Why drive into the city?" Jeff asked.

"Because, knowing how the Hitman operates, he'll be easy to track."

"Not understanding how?"

"Because of the people. He's only here for me. Which means he'll be watching me. Tracking me. With the crowd, it'll make things slightly difficult for him."

"And of the hybrids?"

"They'll follow him. Probably lurk around the area. Best to be prepared."

The car stopped as Arrow and Jeff exited to the applause and cheers from the civilians. They did not mind them as immediately, the Hybrids appeared before them, terrifying the crowds into a running frenzy. Just as Arrow wanted. Causing the disturbance, the Hitman was already there, moving through the rushing crowd. Slowing him down. Arrow looked back, seeing the Hitman and smirked.

"Gotcha."

Arrow quickly pulled the bow and fired an arrow, hitting the Hitman in his left shoulder. He jolted from the strike, stopping in his tracks. Arrow yelled to Jeff and Jeff took out several small blades, throwing them at the Hybrids. Stumbling them in their steps. Arrow pulled another arrow and fired it at the feet of the Hybrids, causing an explosion and knocking them to the ground. Arrow ran to the Hitman, hitting him with a tackle. The Hitman rolled over and stood up. Jeff went to run in, but Arrow stopped him.

"Leave him to me."

"What should I do?"

"Watch the Hybrids. Make sure they stay down."

Jeff returned to the Hybrids as Arrow and Hitman circled each other.

"You have a sidekick." Hitman said. "Funny."

"He's not a sidekick. He's an ally."

"An ally. Once I have your head, I'll take his as a bonus."

"We'll find out."

"You don't think this will go for so long do you?"

"Judging by your shoulder, this will be over quick."

"And you know this how? You're no hit man."

"I'm not. But, our skill sets are very similar."

Hitman went for his gun, but Arrow fired a speedy arrow to the Hitman's chest. He paused, dropping the gun as he fell to the ground. Arrow walked over to him. He saw the Hitman was still breathing. He looked over to Jeff, seeing the Hybrids are still down. He nodded.

"That was fast." Jeff said.

"This needed to end this way." Arrow replied.

Several days later, the Hitman and the Hybrids were taken to a secure facility. Asher and Jarvis discovered the ones who Hitman spoke to were an hidden organization. Their purpose was to eliminate the risen heroes across the world. Asher stated he'll speak with a friend concerning the matter. Jeff continued his training, only this time within the base. Karen returned to the base just as Asher was working on some equipment.

"I see you made it." Asher said.

"Figured it was best I come now rather than later."

"So, what did you want to talk about?" Asher asked.

"Your role in all of this."

"What of it?"

"How long will it last?"

"As long as the mission requires it."

DOCTOR FORTUNE: ELEMENTALS

I

FIRE

Within the Citadel of Enchantment, Thomas Bradley stood in front of Huang. The two were training in their mystic abilities and feats. Bradley began to conjure mystic energy around his hands and arms, Huang nodded with a smile.

"You're getting better."

Continuing their training, the citadel doors burst open and in came a woman. She was dressed in medieval apparel. Mild chain mail and armor on her shoulders, chest, forearms, and legs. She even wore a tunic and the clothing was a dark violet with white lining. Huang and Bradley paused in their training, seeing the distressed woman.

"Where is he?" She asked.

"I'm sorry, but who are you?" Huang asked.

"I need to speak with him now!"

"With who?"

"Donald! Where are you, Donald?!"

"She's looking for Doctor Fortune." Bradley said.

From the stairs came down Fortune, wearing his sorcerer apparel. He paused at the foot of the steps seeing the woman.

"Morhana."

"I'm sorry to have come uninvited." She said. "I need your help immediately."

"Calm down and tell me exactly why you're here?"

"They're after me."

"Who's after you?"

"The Elemental Gods."

"Elemental Gods?" Huang said. "How can that be?"

"There must be something off." Fortune said. "Are you sure it's the Elementals?"

"I'm positive. They're after me."

"Why would they be after you? You're just a sorceress."

"I can't explain right now."

"You have no other option but to explain."

Before she could utter another word, a large fireball came down from above the citadel, shattering the ceiling, impacting between the four sorcerers, knocking them far from each other. Once the fire settled, Fortune stood up and saw a figure standing where the fireball fell. It looked of a dragon. One standing upright. It had wings and arms.

"There you are." The Dragon said toward Morhana.

"Pardon, you've stepped foot inside my Citadel." Fortune said. "Who are you?"

The Dragon turned toward the Supreme Enchanter.

"You know who I am."

Fortune paused.

"You're the Fire Elemental."

"That I am and I have come for Morhana."

"For what purpose?"

"She has done something unforgivable of our kind. A treacherous act."

Fortune clapped his hands together and from them were summoned mystical energy flames. Huang and Bradley both stood up, prepared to do the same, however Fortune nodded them off. They stood back. The Fire Elemental stepped forward toward Fortune.

"You seek to harm me?"

"I can't let you hurt Morhana. Or take her anywhere."

"On who's authority?!"

"Mine. You are inside my Citadel. Remember."

The Fire Elemental stood back and released flames from his

mouth against Fortune, who guarded himself with the energy around his hands. Fortune began twirling his arms as the energy around him began to cover him, giving him a full shielding. The Fire Elemental continued his blaze as Fortune approached him with one step at a time. Huang wanted to help, but found it best to obey Fortune's command. Bradley watched on as Morhana went and stood next to them. Fortune extended his arms, grabbing hold of the flames and reversed them against the Fire Elemental. The blast pushed the Elemental back at bit as Fortune rushed him and began firing energy bolts from his hands. They resembled golden lightning bolts.

"These tricks won't stop my purpose!"

"I'm not trying to kill you." Fortune said. "I'm slowing you down."

Fortune twists his fingers and beneath the Elemental appeared a portal, wherein remain a pit of flames.

"You seek to send me back to my realm!"

"That's the plan."

Fortune levitated from the ground as the portal started to suck in the Elemental by his feet and tail. He clawed to stay atop the floor as Fortune eyed him from the air.

"This is only the beginning!" The Elemental said. "You sought to help her and now, the others will find you and finish what I've started!"

"Then, so be it." Fortune replied. "By the temporal feats of *Durriken*!"

The portal took in the Fire Elemental and closed. Silence filled the Citadel. Fortune fell to his knees, for he was tired. Morhana walked over to him as did Huang and Bradley.

"Are you alright?" She asked.

"I'll be fine. But, you. You need to tell us everything. Now."

"I… I can't."

"Why not?!"

"Because it's a long, long story."

"We have time. Believe me."

Before she could utter a word, the four of them quickly vanished like a snap of the fingers. They were no longer inside the Citadel.

They were somewhere else, and it wasn't on their behalf.

II

ICE

The four sorcerers found themselves somewhere chilly. For the air was cold and beneath their feet laid snow. Fortune looked around, seeing them all to be standing high on a mountain. He looked down and only saw snow and hills.

"What have you done, Morhana?" Fortune asked.

"I didn't do this."

"Where are we?" Huang wondered.

"Far north." Fortune replied. "Very far north."

"I have to ask." Bradley said. "We're not on Mount Everest, are we?"

"We are not." Fortune said. "We're elsewhere. I'm just trying to wonder who would send us here."

"It wasn't me." Morhana said once more. "I had nothing to do with this."

Huang walked around, feeling the cool breeze of wind around them. He closed his eyes, meditating, and as he was, a strange essence came over him. He jumped.

"What's wrong?" Fortune asked.

"We're not alone. Someone else is here. Watching us."

"Who else could be here?" Bradley asked.

Fortune looked over toward Morhana as she slowly started taking steps back near the mountain behind them. He approached her, grabbing her arm tightly. She struggled to get loose, but Fortune's grip was strong.

"Where are you going?"

"Nowhere."

"Why are you trying to hide?!"

"Because I might know who's here with us."

"Who is it?" Fortune asked. "Tell me now."

Winds picked up around them as they each looked above, seeing a figure coming down from the sky. Upon its landing in their sights, they saw the figure was similar to the Fire Elemental. Yet, this one was made of ice. Pure white body.

"He's found us." Morhana said to herself.

"An ice dragon?" Bradley asked.

"No." Fortune replied. "An ice elemental."

"I guess we'll be helping out this time." Huang said. "I'm ready."

"Bradley, stand back." Fortune said. "Let us handle this one."

"But, master, I can assist in some form."

"I am aware. For right now, we'll deal with this one."

Fortune and Huang stood front, ready to combat the Ice Elemental. It flapped its wings in style, crossing its arms. Glaring at Fortune and Huang, but the focus was all placed on Morhana.

"The witch." The Elemental said. "I've come for you."

"I'm not going anywhere!"

Morhana conjured up a strange, mystical energy dagger, throwing it at the chest of the Ice Elemental. It stepped over and chuckled. Now, rushing itself toward her, Fortune and Huang moved quickly projecting a force field between them and the Elemental. However, the Elemental was not concerned about the sorcerers, but was single-minded on Morhana. Every attack it released was toward her and not Fortune, Huang, or Bradley. Fortune noticed these movements.

"What did you do?"

"I will tell you after we deal with him!" Morhana screamed.

"She has crossed a line only few have dared to scratch!" The Elemental said. "Move aside, sorcerers. Leave this witch to me!"

"I can't do that until I have answers." Fortune said.

Fortune twirled his hands, creating a huge blast of energy, knocking the Elemental into the mountain itself. Huang and Bradley followed with similar, yet minor attacks to slow down the ice figure. Morhana did what she could, but turned to run. Fortune spotted her and grabbed her arm.

"Where are you going?"

"I have to get out of here!"

"You're not going anywhere!"

The Ice Elemental raised its right hand, revealing claws and swiped Huang and Bradley into the mountain and walked toward Morhana and Fortune. Morhana stepped forward and raised her arms, shouting as loud as she could. Fortune also held his hands up. All facing the Ice Elemental.

"You cannot stop one such as I."

The Elemental inhaled as a brightly glow appeared from within its mouth. Ice and snow around the region began to be absorbed into the glow. Fortune looked at Morhana and she done the same. Energy arose from their hands.

"You're ready to talk?" Fortune asked.

"I am."

"Good."

With both their energies focused, they blast the mystic power against the Elemental's ice beam. The forces collide and within the blast, the Ice Elemental backed away, vanishing from their sights. Fortune and Morhana looked around the area, uncertain.

"Where did it go?" Huang asked, getting up from the ground.

"I'm not sure." Fortune said. "Otherwise, it's gone."

Bradley stood up from the ground, looking around through the snowy region. Huang did the same.

"So, that thing just vanished?" Bradley asked.

"Looks to be the case." Huang said.

Fortune approached Morhana with haste.

"Tell us what's going on now."

Morhana nodded with a sigh.

"Ok. I'll tell you. This-"

Without notice they each disappeared from the snowy region and instantly appeared in a vast desert. Huang looked around, seeing the clear sky and nothing but mountains, dirt, and sand around them. The heat of the air was intense, the smell of the ground was noticeable.

"Where are we?" Bradley asked.

"Someplace uncertain." Fortune said. "Morhana, what is happening here?!"

"It's just I did something wrong."

"Tell me now."

III

ROCK

"What did you do?"

"Once again," Morhana said, stepping forward to Fortune. "I didn't do this."

"It appears we're somewhere very far from our previous location." Huang said.

"Is anyone noticing something with all of this?" Bradley asked. "Like, this is designed for a reason."

Fortune took in Bradley's words and turned his attention back to Morhana.

"It's making sense."

"What is?" Morhana said.

"We've defeated the Fire and Ice Elementals and now we're out in some desert land mountains region. You know who's about to show up."

Huang nodded. "A Rock Elemental."

"Yes." Fortune said. "He's coming. Now, Morhana, tell me what's happening."

"I might have done something that humans should not do."

"Such as?"

"I might've-"

The ground began to quake, stumbling the sorcerers in their places. The trembles increased to the point of rocks beginning to fall from the mountains. Fortune placed a force field around himself and the others to avoid the falling debris.

"Prepare yourselves!" Fortune said.

The rocks fell and the quake stopped. As Fortune removed the field, they found themselves staring in the presence of the Rock Elemental. Tall, rugged, made of the minerals of the mountains around them.

"A rock dragon?" Bradley said. "Are they all dragons or something?"

"It's a form they prefer to have when coming upon the earth." Morhana said.

"And you know this how?" Fortune asked.

"Like I said, I'll explain everything. Once we're not interrupted."

The rocky wings flapped on the Elemental as it stood tall. The sorcerers were ready for the fight to come. However, this elemental wasn't seeking a battle with power or might.

"Morhana must come with me."

"I don't believe she will." Fortune said. "She's with us."

"She must explain herself to the others for her crimes."

"Trust me, I am aware."

"Then stand aside, Sorcerer."

Fortune shrugged his shoulders. Holding his hands up with the mystic energy covering them. Huang and Bradley's hands were also held up.

"I cannot do that."

"You take part in her crimes?"

"Truthfully, I do not. I want to know what she's done as well. There's no need for fighting."

"I agreed. I know what the results of my counterparts. They desire combat. However, for one such as I, resolve to speaking terms and now, you say you desire to know the witch's crimes."

"I do."

"Very well. That is the work of another. For I cannot reveal such actions in my wake upon the earth. You must travel into the spiritual dimension to receive the answers you seek."

"You mean you cannot just tell me what she's done?"

"To do so would shake the foundations of the earth. This is not the time for such disturbances."

Fortune looked at Morhana. She stood still.

209

"Where must we go?" Fortune asked the Elemental.

"To the realm of my other counterpart. The one simply called, '*Ghost*'. you must travel to his realm and all will be revealed."

"And how do we find this realm?"

The Rock Elemental warped his hands and in between them formed a portal. A portal into the dimension of the Ghost Elemental. Fortune examined the portal, seeing its eerie white glow with flashes of an ominous violet light. The sorcerers walk through the portal and it closes itself. Afterwards, the Rock Elemental is gone.

IV

GHOST

The portal flashed and the sorcerers found themselves in the spiritual dimension. Auras of diverse colors surrounded them in every inch. The bright lights within were as bright as the sun, glinting off Fortune's cloak and hair.

"I've never been to this place before." Fortune said.

"Not many have." Morhana added. "But, we're here now."

"Not to fight. To get answers."

Bradley turned to look at the lights and found himself standing in the mere presence of the Elemental that dwells within. The others turned toward Bradley's direction and saw the entity themselves. Wings larger than the others. Its body glared like transparent silver.

"I knew you would come." The Elemental said.

"Good." Fortune said. "Then you know why we're here."

"I do. Because of her actions, you have entered my realm."

"Now, we do not wish to fight. We only want to know what's happening."

"I comprehend your spirits. Unlike my brothers upon the earth, I will tell you why we're after Morhana the Witch."

"Please do." Huang said.

The Elemental warped his hands and the lights around them began to bounce atop one another. Twirling and warping themselves into a mirage. Within the mirage of many colors, Fortune could see the image of Morhana and her actions prior to the visit at the Citadel.

"Why?" Fortune said. "Why did you do it?"

"I had no choice."

"Every being in creation has a choice." The Elemental said. "You made yours and made it poorly."

"I can make things right. Let me make it right."

"How can you?"

"Pardon me, Ghost Elemental, perhaps we can lend a hand to Morhana's actions. Find a way to reverse her doings."

"And how do you perceive to reverse such a transgression?"

"We confront your other brother. The one of the Air."

"I will send you to him now."

Before he could make the way, a bright flash of light emitted from the ground beneath their feet. A sigil of mystic origin appeared and from it arose the Mystic Father. Fortune, Huang, and Bradley bowed in obeisance, Morhana stood by while the Elemental watched in awe.

"The Mystic One."

"Elemental of the Presence."

"Master," Fortune said. "why have you come?"

"To grant you insight on the Elementals and who they truly are."

The Mystic Father gave the Elemental a look of declaration and the Ghost entity nodded.

"They're not just elemental beings. They're gods."

"Gods?" Bradley said. "Not possible."

"It it and they are. Though, not gods of a omnipotent source. They're lesser ones. Created to preserve the elements of creation."

"Why do they appear in the form of dragons?" Huang asked.

"It was the form chosen for the best. Unlike the angels and demons. The Elementals are a peculiar pair of entities."

"We have our duties to uphold."

"Do we all, Ghost God."

The Mystic Father approached Morhana. Slowly and with caution for Morhana's eyes were glowing. The Mystic Father perceived her intentions, placing his hand on her shoulder.

"Stay calm, sorceress. I understand your reasoning."

"Then, you know why I did it?"

"I do. Although, I disagree with it, I understand it."

"What must I do to correct my wrong?"

"Obey the voice of the Ghost God. Whatever he commands you

to do, you do."

The previous portal reopen in front of them. Between the sorcerers, Mystic Father, the Ghost God. Winds blew through the portal from within. Huang covered his face with his arms.

"I take it that's above ground."

"It's the only way to meet the Air God." The Mystic Father said. "Ghost God, give them the orders."

"Are you ready?"

"We are." Fortune replied.

"Then jump."

"You will succeed." The Mystic Father told Fortune.

"We'll do our best, master."

Fortune jumped through the portal and the others followed with Morhana stepping last before feeling the glare of the Ghost Elemental. From there, the sorcerers were gone. The Mystic Father stood before the Ghost God.

"We have other matters to discuss."

"Yes, we do." The Ghost God proclaimed.

V

<u>AIR</u>

The sorcerers exit from the portal, finding themselves hovering in the air. Far above ground as the air was slightly thin for their well-being. Bradley took a small look beneath them and couldn't see beyond the clouds.

"What do we do now?" Huang asked.

"We await the Air God." Fortune said. "He's the final one."

In the midst of the air, a whirlwind formed. One of great strength and visibility. Within the whirlwind came out the Air God of the Elementals. Features were the same as its brethren. Although, whiffs of clouds moved through him as if he was indeed solid air.

"I knew you would arrive."

"Good to know." Fortune said. "Then, you know we don't seek to take your time."

"I see the witch is with you. Better the company you destroy than the ones you keep."

"I've never heard that before." Bradley said.

"It's a different spectrum." Huang added.

The Air God hovered before Fortune and Morhana. Looking down at them from its great height.

"We do not seek to fight. As we told your Ghost brother, we, I only needed to know what Morhana has done and I've found out. Now, I ask of you to forgive her of these stupendous mistakes and grant her a release from the terrors."

"Release? What she done travels far beyond the modern times of humanity."

"If you can't spare her like your brother, then what do you propose?"

"I demand she face her trials."

"But your brother let her go. We could've fought him, but we did not. Instead he opened a portal into your territory. Now, I ask again, what can you do for her safety."

The Air God stared. He turned from them after a slight nod. The sorcerers were unsure as to what the Elemental would say or do. For they waited to hear an answer. After a minute, the Air God turned back to them.

"I will say this. Morhana must not bargain with the natural laws of this world. Nor make agreements with the natural entities. She must not interfere in mortal affairs or affairs pertaining to the earth. Her being a witch, I declare she only remain in the spiritual affairs of this reality. For if she is seen or heard to been active amongst the generations of Man and their activities, she will be hunted down by the spiritual forces which surround us all."

"Do you accept these terms?" Fortune asked Morhana.

Morhana grunted, then she sighed bitterly. "I accept."

"Very well." The Air God said. "Now, go. Return to your Citadel, Donald Fortune. Leave me be."

The Air God waved his hands toward the sorcerers, thereby blasting them from his present and after a second, they found themselves standing inside the Citadel.

"We're back." Bradley said.

"Yes we are." Huang added. "That was quick."

Fortune walked toward the door, he opened it and stepped outside. Morhana followed him as he stood there, looking out at a city in the far distance.

"Thank you."

"No need." Fortune said. "I did what had to be done."

"I guess now I must find something to do. Something in the spiritual fields."

"As do we all."

"What are you implying?"

"This small event has shown me something I've once meditated. I cannot abide in the same presence as those risen heroes out there. It is better for someone like myself to focus clearly on the spiritual matters we have at hand. We must be hidden from the society. We must remain in the shadows of the supernatural. It is our dwelling place."

KULAR THE AQUA-BARBARIAN: LORD OF ATLANTIS

I

DECLARATION

The Kingdom of Atlantis is attacked once again by Lord Shark and his army of the Fanged Ones from the deep. The Atlantean army was ready for their return and the battle commenced on the sea floor. Shark moved with haste through the soldiers in his sights, making way for the palace. Standing at the palace doors was Kular, his trident in hand. Kara, his wife stood by his side, staring out towards the battlefield.

"Are you sure about this?"

"It's my duty as king. Besides, we've been through this fight before. It'll end the same as before."

Kular stormed off toward Shark and his army. With the Atlanteans behind him, all with weapons in hand, they come to a pause as Kular raised his hand. They stopped only ten feet from Shark. Kular stepped forward, staring Shark down.

"Do we really have to go through this once more?"

"You aided the land-dwellers. Giving them the change of studying our domain. You've put us all on the path to extinction."

"I have done no such cause." Kular noted. "I went up there to see how they live. What actions they accomplish as we do here. There was evil up there. But, there was also some good. A balance is in motion in the livings of the land-dwellers. Such as it is in our dwellings."

"Atlantis does not need a king who rallies alongside, grounders. You will face me and my army in war or you can just surrender your crown and ruler ship to me."

"I give you this one offer. Sit with me and we'll discuss this matter between ourselves. Then, after we have our talk, you choose what comes next."

"Sit and talk?! I want you dead and all of those who follow you. For Poseidon's sake, why should I sit at a table with one of your kind?"

"Because this talk is all that's saving you from a quick death."

"You believe so?" Shark said, stepping closer.

"I am." Kular replied. "I could've killed you in our last encounter. I did not. You have life and death standing before you. For your own sake, choose life."

Shark paused himself, yet his eyes were set on Kular. Both armies were ready for the battle. Shark shook himself and sighed.

"Lead the way."

Kular did, leading Shark toward the palace. Upon reaching the steps, Kara saw Shark and was terrified. Novah approached her, cautioning her to be still. Kular looked up toward Novah, seeing Kara's fear in her eyes. Novah nodded and Kular understood. The doors of the meeting room opened with Kular and Shark entering, with only two of their most trusted soldiers. The doors closed as the others looked in.

II

<u>MEETING OF KINGS</u>

Kular and Shark sat across from one another with their soldiers standing guard.

"There's nothing to discuss." Shark said. "It's simple. I want this place. This kingdom."

"You can't have it. However, you can go on back to your home and refurbish it into something of this nature."

"Can't do such a thing. All sea-dwellers know the prime capital of the oceans is Atlantis. Hell, if it's not me, the others will come and ry to claim this prize for themselves."

"If that's their desire, we'll be ready for them."

Shark scoffed. "Will you? What of the land-dwellers? What if one of them gets the case of the curious and decides to come down here and invade. It's not unusual."

"From what I learned, there isn't one up there. Not yet anyway."

"Always making such mistakes. You cannot be idle when it comes to them up there. Or those down here."

"I'm not idle. I'm very aware."

"So you say."

Kular stared at Shark with a keen gaze. More so from respect rather than an enemy.

"I'll ask you this one time, will you return to your home and never trespass here again?"

"I'm returning home regardless. But, do not take my leave for a truce. I want this kingdom and I will have it. One day or another."

Shark stood up from the table and left the room with his soldiers.

Shark's army left Atlantis and the Atlantean army returned to their duties of the kingdom. Sometime later, Novah visited Kular in his study, seeing him observing a map of the under-kingdoms.

"You understand he will return to claim this kingdom."

"I comprehend well, Novah. However, I will do what is necessary if Shark shall ever step foot on our grounds."

"I must ask, what of the contingences involving the land-dwellers?"

"We will come to those terms when or if a land-dweller seeks to take what is ours."

"Then I take it you already have plans in motion. Just in case."

"That's one reason why I went up there. To not only see how they live and operate. But their skills. Their will. Their focus. There's much good in some of them. We won't have to worry ourselves about them. It is the others who may cause concern in the times ahead. I was told by a eerie one that my future consists of wars. Wars against those of both land and sea."

"An eerie land-dweller?" Novah questioned. "Doesn't sound common."

"He knew more than the common land-dweller. He knew our future. He's seen it."

"And was this dweller benevolent toward you or sinister?"

"Neither. He was what he was."

Novah nodded. Thinking about the dweller, but no image could muster in his mind. He shook his head.

"I will keep my gaze keen on the horizons. Just in case he makes a quick return."

"Thank you."

Novah bowed before Kular and left the study. During the night, Kular went to his chamber, where Kara was waiting. Kular entered the chamber and sighed, not of relief, but of tiredness in mind.

"What do you have planned for Shark's next move?"

"It's under control, Kara. Trust me."

"I know. I know. Just being certain."

III

<u>BATTLES FOUGHT</u>

The following morning, soldiers ran into the palace to alert Kular of a surprise visitor. Kular grabbed his trident and rushed out with them to see what was happening. Upon exiting the palace doors and looking out in the distance, Kular saw Ark, the Sea Monster staring him down.

"Ark." Kular uttered. "I will deal with him alone."

"Are you sure, my king?" A soldier asked. "We can assist you."

"I will be well. Keep guard just in case there are others in the surroundings."

Kular went toward Ark and before he could speak a word, Ark attacked Kular with his claws, swiping and snatching at Kular's armored tunic. Kular fought back with the trident, knocking Ark into the ground with an aerial attack. Kular kicked the Sea Monster back a distance before he could raise himself up onto his tentacle limbs.

"Why are you here?" Kular asked.

"I have to destroy all there is. This kingdom and you."

"So be it.'

Kular swiped the trident across Ark's chest continually until blood flowed from the wounds. Ark stumbled back with his tentacles crushing the ground beneath him. Kular speared the trident into Ark's chest, ramming it further as the monster let out a loud screech. Ark slowed down and Kular pulled the trident from his chest. Ark's head hung low as his body titled over in front of Kular. Kular stepped forward toward Ark, using his foot to see if the monster still lived. Without a second's notice, Ark's head rose up, his eyes dark as the depths of the sea. A big smile formed on his face as he drove his right-handed claw through Kular's chest. The attacked startled all who were watching, including Kara and Novah.

"Is this your king?!" Ark yelled, facing the Atlanteans who were watching.

Ark raised the Aqua-Barbarian over his head and threw him against the palace doors and went off.

"My task is done." Ark said. "I now leave you to your demise."

Kara ran over toward Kular, seeing the blood coming from the wound. The soldiers also stood guard around Kular. Novah looked on, watching Ark leave and within that same distance, Novah caught a glimpse of a coming army. He knew what this all was.

"We have trouble." Novah told Kara and the soldiers, pointing outward.

Kara looked out, stepping further. She saw what Novah saw. An army. Charging toward Atlantis and in front of them was Lord Shark. The sound of the incoming army could be heard from the front of the palace. A sound of a rushing wind buried beneath a solid structure. A faint whistle moving from within.

"This was a set-up." Novah concluded.

IV

<u>WARS CONQUERED</u>

The Atlantean army was prepared and ready for the coming army. Kara tended to Kular, who's wounds continued bleeding. Novah knelt next to him, gazing back and forth between him and Shark's army.

"My lord, Shark is coming with his forces."

"Then, I must…" Kular breathed. "I must protect this kingdom."

"Beloved, you're gravely wounded." Kara noted. "You can't fight Shark in this condition. He'll kill you."

"No, he won't. I will handle this. Very swiftly."

"How swiftly do you intend on ending this?" Novah questioned. "By what power?"

"By the power of the ancients and by the power of Atlantis."

Kular picked himself up, brushing off the assistance of Kara and Novah. He wanted to walk on his own. Holding his chest with one hand and dragging the trident with the other as he stepped down the sapphire steps of the palace and out into the field. He waved the trident toward his soldiers.

"Stand aside. I will take care of this."

"My lord, there's too many of them." A soldier said. "Surely, you will require assistance in this fight."

"I have all the assistance I need." Kular said, holding the trident. "Now go and keep the kingdom protected."

The soldiers obeyed their king and retreated back to the palace where they stood and watched. Kular moved slow, dragging his left foot while approaching Shark and his army. Kular stopped and held himself up with the trident. Shark and his army made their approach, halting in their steps.

"You're wounded, Aqua-Barbarian."

"No thanks to your diversion."

"Hmm. It seems Ark did a number on you and yet, just in time for us to pick up the pieces."

"Pick up the pieces? That's what you believe this is? How come you couldn't do this on your own? Instead, you bribed the Sea Monster into doing the work for you."

"What's done is done! This kingdom will be mine and your head will be on a pike for all the kingdoms of the seas to witness."

"I think not."

Kular slammed and twirled the trident, conjuring a whirlwind from above, which gathered up Shark's army, scattering them across the distances of the sands. Shark was astounded by the power he witnessed. The water blowing across his face like the winds of the lands. Kular continually twirled the trident. His eyes were set on Shark as he ran toward Kular with his gnawing teeth, a bolt of lightning stroke from the whirlwind, colliding with Shark's chest. Shark fell to the sands, holding his chest in pain. He looked up at Kular, seeing the lightning circling itself around the trident and Kular's hands.

"What power is this?!"

"The power by the ruler of Atlantis." Kular replied. "You're done here."

Kular swiped the trident across the sands and the whirlwind picked up Shark, slamming his sharp hands into the dirt to keep a grip. The might of the whirlwind was very strong as it picked Shark up, tossing him far from Atlantis. The battle was over and Kular collapsed on the ground. The soldiers went and gathered him up, carrying him to his chambers of the palace. The doctors of Atlantis tented to his chest wounds. After some time, they concluded Kular would be healed within mere days and he will live.

After those days had passed, Kular was up and ruling the

kingdom once more. Although, word of his actions have reached the other kingdoms of the seas. Novah came to him in his study and spoke of several armies making their way toward Atlantis. Kular asked if Shark's army was one and Novah declined.

"Then who is it?" Kular asked.

"Sea-Stormers." Novah said.

"Not possible. I killed the Sea Kaiser."

"Well, it appears the Stormers have a new leader and there are others who are on their way."

"Very well." Kular said. "We must prepare."

"Indeed."

DESTINY OF THE CHAMPIONS: THIRST

I

SIGNAL LOCKED

The Spellvector moved through the Time Dimension as the newly formed team sat inside. Doctor Omega piloted as he always does. Jetlash sat next to him, learning about the dimension and how the Spellvector works within the spectrums of time and space.

"You desire to pilot this ship, I see."

"I'm just fascinated that such a ship exists. I am curious as to how it works in full. How does it go from different time periods and this dimension we're in, how does it truly exists?"

"There are many things in the universe that most are not aware of, Corbin. But, you are and this team I've assembled. Together, we can make things better. Protect history as the way it remains."

"What if something goes wrong? We have this ship. We could go back in time and fix what went wrong."

"I advise against it. The comebacks of such an action would bring down much wrath upon anyone who volunteered."

"I assume Baron Eon is seeking to do something like that? Change something in time?"

"He wants to rewrite it completely. Make everything to his liking. In his image."

The radar started to beep as Amadeus looked at the source, discovering its stronger signal and otherworldly energy emitting from the location.

"I think we've found it."

"Found the box?"

"Yes."

"Where is it?"

"Romania. Present day."

II

A VISITOR UNSEEN

Doctor Omega gathered the team together, comprised of the members before. Corbin Beval, known as Jetlash, Sandra Banks, referred to as Ms. Titan, and Anthony Carlos, called the Crimson Mask. Omega informed them of the whereabouts of the Cosmicbox and how it's apparently sitting in Present Day Romania. Sandra turned to see the map and pointed toward the connected city.

"Bucharest?"

"Precisely." Amadeus said. "We head there now, find the box and retrieve it before Baron Eon discovers us."

"When do we head out?" Anthony asked.

"Right at this moment."

The team sat in their seats as Omega charted the ship toward the Modern-day time strip. In doing so, the ship vanished from the time dimension and appeared in present-day Bucharest. The ship hovered over the city, seeing how the gray clouds to cover the ship from the eyes below. The team teleported to the ground and began walking the streets. Omega pulled out a device from his coat pocket, signaling the source of the box.

"It's near."

They walked continues, following the signal. Once they reached the location, they found themselves in the Old Town district. As they stood, looking around, a woman approached them.

"Great. You guys again."

"You!" Corbin said.

"Calm yourself, Corbin." Amadeus said. "It seems this is the one responsible for thwarting our chance at retrieving the box."

228

"My name's Tessa Balthazar, in case you've forgotten, I've come to this city to find the box myself."

"Any luck?"

"None. My contact informed me of the Baron in position of the box somewhere in this city. I don't know where."

"We're tracking the box and this device claims the box is somewhere in this Old Town."

"Perhaps I'll find it first."

"Don't pick a fight with us, Ms. Balthazar." Amadeus said. "We don't want any trouble."

"Trouble is my living, Doctor."

Tessa walked away from the Champions, going about her way. Amadeus turned and looked at the device. The signal went quiet and disappeared from the radar. The clouds above them began to grow darker as raindrops started to fall. The device beeped once more, only at this moment there were more than one signal. Seven to be accurate. Omega wasn't sure what they were and during his thinking, the group was ambushed by a quick strike. They stood together as the rain fell heavily, blinding their eyes to the attacker. The strike came at them again, slashing Corbin's sleeve.

"What is that?!"

"I'm not sure." Amadeus said. "But, I've heard of these things before."

The attackers formed a line around the Champions as the rain ceased. Amadeus saw them. Dressed in lean robes with hoods. Their eyes glaring like a fire. Their teeth sharp and inhuman. Amadeus recognized what they were without question. The rest of the team were uncertain, begging to know who they're staring down. Amadeus pointed carefully toward the seven beings.

"Vampires." Amadeus said.

The vampires swarmed around the team. Not attacking, only seeking to frighten them. Amadeus kept the group calm as they already were. One vampire stopped swarming and approached Amadeus. From the look in his eyes and the keen expression on his face, this vampire was not a simpleton.

"You must be Amadeus Omega."

"I am. Who's asking?"

"We have been sent out here to command you and your team to cease from retrieving the Cosmicbox."

"Under who's orders? Eon?"

"Not exactly. Our queen doesn't like it when uninvited visitors invade her dwelling places."

"Your queen?" Corbin asked.

"What's her name?" Sandra wondered. "Tell us please."

"Bathory." The vampire said.

"Bathory?" Amadeus uttered. "You speak of the blood Countess?"

The vampire grinned. "There is only one."

"We would like to speak with her. We need that Cosmicbox back."

The vampire shook his finger.

"The Countess speaks to you when she desires it. She only sends out a warning. Leave. Do not come back."

Anthony stepped up to the vampire. He wore his mask and the vampire gnarled toward Anthony before he placed his knife to the vampire's throat.

"I'm not the one to play around with, bloodsucker."

"Do tell."

"Where is this Bathory woman?"

"In the past."

"The past?" Amadeus asked. "Where in the past?"

"Where she always goes. Hungary."

"Let's move."

Amadeus and the Champions left for their ship, teleporting away. The vampire smirked as he and the other vampires who were sitting in the shadow disappeared from the Old Town.

Once the Champions were inside the Spellvector, Amadeus went to the files and read up on Hungary and Bathory's time. Upon his reading, he discovered she was dwelling in Hungary during the 16th Century. Amadeus went to the cockpit and headed toward the late 1500s.

III

A DRINK?

The Spellvector made its destination, hovering over Hungary in the year 1595. The air was damp and cold. Inside the ship, Amadeus set the coordinates for their teleportation, however, upon doing the checking, the same device began to beep. Amadeus looked, seeing the signal was coming from Cachtite Castle in Slovakia.

"Change of plans." Amadeus told the team. "We're heading to Cachtite Castle."

"Why?" Corbin asked. "What's happened?"

"The signal's reactivated. Eon must be there. We have to get the box."

"What about this vampire countess?" Anthony asked. "We just leave her be or something?"

"If there's any possibility, she will be alongside Eon when we confront him."

Anthony nodded. The team was prepared as the ship went over to Slovakia. Now, hovering and cloaked over Cachtite Castle. Sandra looked out from the window toward the castle. Corbin walked up to the window, seeing the castle himself.

"You think she's in there?"

"We'll find out when we get inside ourselves." Corbin said.

Once the team assembled, Amadeus asked if they were ready. As if they had any choice. Amadeus teleported them inside the castle and once they made entry, they were standing in what appeared to be a throne room. A red carpet laid on the marbled floors. The colors blended well with the interior stone colors. There was a chair sitting in the distance. Someone was there, in the shadows, due to the fact their eyes were glowing red in the darkness. Amadeus stood firm, staring at the eyes.

"Come out. We have words to discuss."

The eyes moved and were gone. The light from the outside hit the chair and it was empty. Amadeus yelled for the team to prepare themselves. Once they did, echoes of screeches came from above and around. Amadeus turned toward the door and saw Elizabeth Bathory in their sights. Dressed in a dark black dress, wearing a red coat over it. Her raven hair was long, and her lips looked as if they were drenched in blood, yet for style. Anthony looked, seeing her, pulled out his blades.

"This her?"

"It is." Amadeus said. "Don't strike. Not yet."

"So, you are the team he's spoke a lot about."

"Eon's told you about us?" Omega asked. "What has he lied about this time?"

"He told me everything. How you're responsible for this cause. Rallying people from across many lands for your selfish cause. How you seek the magic box he possesses."

"First off, my lady." Corbin said. "The box is not magic. But science."

"Corbin." Amadeus butted in. "No need to explain."

"I'm sure you wish to see him. Wouldn't you, Amadeus of Omega?"

"Where is he?"

"He's around. Minding his business. Until he desires to be seen, you'll have to contend with me."

"I'm sorry, Countess, we have no desire to spend time with you. We seek Eon and the box. Tell us where he is or you'll have to face my team head-on."

Elizabeth scoffed. Waving her hand toward the team.

"You believe they have a chance at defeating me?"

"I know they can."

Elizabeth sighed. Posturing herself as she stood firm in place facing the team.

"I haven't had to fight in quite a while. This will be a refresher for me. Afterwards, I'll take your blood and you know the rest. Don't you, Amadeus."

Anthony put on his mask and turned to Amadeus.

"When?"

"Now." Amadeus replied.

Crimson Mask rushed toward Elizabeth with slashes. She dodged the attacks, moving like a swift wind. Teleporting behind Anthony, she grabbed him, kicking him in the back of his knee and slamming him to the ground. The team was at a loss for words. More so was Amadeus.

"You're not that strong. History doesn't speak of you with these feats."

"History doesn't give all the details, Omega. Now, who's next?"

"Let's see if she can take us all at once." Sandra said.

"Good thinking." Corbin said, as his suit armored up.

They went for Elizabeth as Omega took out a plasma gun and fired upon her. She dodged the coming rounds while deflecting Jetlash's energy blasts and Ms. Titan's powerful punches. Elizabeth laughed, shaking her head as she waved her hands around herself and the air near her. She stopped deflecting and stood. They continued to attack, even Anthony got back up from the floor, taking out his two handguns and began firing. Amadeus paused his firing, seeing Elizabeth still.

"She's conjured a force field. Guys, stop!"

The team heard Amadeus' commanded and ceased. They looked toward Omega as he pointed back to Elizabeth. It was there when they could see the ripples of the force field. Amadeus did not understand how she was capable of creating such defenses.

"What's wrong?" Elizabeth asked with a grin. "Too much for you and your team?"

Anthony continued firing at the force field. He walked closer and closer, continuing the fire. Elizabeth crossed her arms and stood still with a smile on her face. Amadeus tried to talk reason to Crimson Mask, yet he was not hearing any of it. He wanted to take down Elizabeth by any means. However, she lowered the field and attacked Anthony once again. Not only him, but the rest of the team with a super speed hit-and-run blow. Leaving Amadeus to see his team down.

"Don't worry." She said. "Eon told me not to harm you. Never said anything about your little team."

Amadeus sighed, raising up his gun.

"Where is Eon?"

"You'll see him soon enough. For right now, I must leave you. I have other business ventures to take care of."

Elizabeth vanished in a mist of smoke. Afterwards, Omega went and checked on his team. They were still alive, just unconscious. Amadeus shook his head in disappointment.

"I should've known."

"You can't know everything, Amadeus." A voice said from the entrance.

Amadeus stood up and saw where the voice came from. Walking out of the shadows to the door was Eon himself, holding the Cosmicbox in his hands. Amadeus quickly raised his gun.

"Hand it over, Eon."

"Is this any way to greet an old friend?"

"You're no friend of mine. Not anymore."

Eon nodded. He walked over toward the nearby table, sitting the box down. He walked away from the box even though Amadeus' eyes were locked tight upon it.

"Look this way, Amadeus."

Amadeus moved his eyes from Eon to the box and back again. Eon grinned heavily.

"We should talk." Eon said. "Before things turn out for the worst, eh?"

"Hand over the box."

"Why should I, Amadeus? What good will it do for you?"

"More than you can understand."

"Is that a fact?"

"You know the power the box holds. The good it can do in rightful hands."

"And your hands are rightful?"

Amadeus cocked his head, keeping his eyes on Eon and the box.

The team was slowly regaining consciousness as they moved around the floor, raising themselves up to see Eon and Omega staring down. Corbin rose up and quickly stood up seeing Eon.

"He's here!" Corbin yelled.

"I know." Omega replied. " I am aware."

"Your little team can't best me. Even without the box, I can decimate you all in one quick move."

The team stood to their feet, standing behind Omega. They all were injured. However, they were prepared to face Eon alongside Omega by any means. Amadeus knew this as he began to think to himself of what's next. He thought and nodded to the suggestion of his mind. His right hand reached into his coat pocket, he had something.

"You're really going to try and best me?" Eon said.

"I have something else in mind." Amadeus replied.

Omega pulled out the object in his pocket and tossed it to the ground in front of Eon. Once it made impact, the object exploded into a bright light. Eon was caught off guard as he dropped the box. Amadeus however was not affected due to his goggles as he ran over and snatched the box. He ran back to the team in haste.

"It's time to go!"

Amadeus teleported himself and the team back to the ship. Once the brightness decreased, Eon realized they were gone and so was the box.

"Clever." Eon said.

In the Spellvector, the team was prepared as Amadeus left the time-period. Returning to the Time Dimension. Afterwards, Amadeus placed the box in his lab as the team gazed toward it.

"Finally got the box." Corbin said.

"This is only the beginning." Omega replied. "We better be ready for what's next."

YONDERERS: DAYS OF OUR FUTURE

I

NUBREED FUTURE

In the city of Chicago, Illinois. At the Yonderers Mansion, Professor Edge is speaking with the younger nubreeds about possibly joining the Yonderers in the future. As he speaks to them, Lois Frost walks in.

"What is it, Frost?" Professor Edge asked.

"You need to come see this." Frost replied.

Frost and Edge left the room, heading down the hall. Edge has a worried look on his face as he has no idea what's going on. They turn left and go into the living room. Inside the living room are the Yonderers themselves, Valinor, Emerald, Crystalax, Gale, Magic Carpet, and The Surf. Edge was surprised to see John Terror and Jade Horror in the room.

"I see you both received the call."

"Figured it was of something important." Terror said.

"Agreed." Jade said.

They are all watching the television in the room as Edge watched on as well.

On the TV is the Chicago News, where the reporter is standing in the middle of downtown Chicago as civilians run wild as the Fellowship of Nubreeds, which are Cosmic Card, Mistress Destroyer, Omega Thunder, Kudo Fox, and Jackhammer are attacking the city for reasons involving straight-edge. The reporter turns to her right and General Rilla is behind her. Rilla, who is wearing his orange and black attire, grabs the reporter's microphone and looked into the camera.

"Out of my way, human. Cullen Edge, you know what this scenery means. I've tried to tell you years before, this world belongs to the nubreeds now. Humans shall be extinct and don't try sending your insignificant group of pawns to stop us."

Frost turned off the TV as the room is quiet with everyone looking to Edge for answers.

"We should go after him." Terror told Edge.

"John, don't fall into his plans. It's not the way it's looking on that screen" Edge replied.

"What shall we do?" Jade Horror says to Edge.

Edge looked at the team and turned to Frost.

"Very well. Prepare for mission." Edge told Frost.

The members of the Yonderers begin walking out of the living room and heading towards the chamber. Terror looks on as everyone else leaves and Edge notices it and walks over to Terror.

"What now, John?" Edge asked Terror.

"Nothing. Though, it is about time for Rilla to be taken down.' Terror replies as he walked away.

Edge smiled as Terror walked away.

Meanwhile, in Downtown Chicago, General Rilla and his Fellowship of Nubreeds are terrorizing the city and destroying many buildings and city monuments. Rilla looked to his left and sees a famous hotel building and Tower. Rilla turns to Jackhammer with an intension in his eyes.

"Hammer! Take down this waste of bricks! Show them your power!

Jackhammer raises his huge arms up and slams them into the ground, creating a wave that is moving straight and slams into the building, crashing it down. Rilla smiles as he watches the building fall to the ground.

"This is what the humans deserve! The nubreeds are the true force of this planet. We are the future power structure." Rilla spoke.

"They don't deserve it this way." Someone said behind Rilla.

Rilla turned, seeing the Yonderers approaching him. Behind Rilla arrived the Fellowship of Nubreeds. Rilla looked on at the Yonderers, realizing Edge was not with them.

"It seems that Cullen is too afraid to fight for what's right." Rilla said.

"Doesn't matter, Raymus. What matters is that I'm going take that helmet of yours and shove it up your ass." Terror said.

Rilla, enraged as his eyes glow a violet color. He slowly raised his arms and began levitating off the road. He glared at Terror and the Yonderers before looking at the Fellowship.

"FELLOWSHIP! DESTROY THE PESTS!"

The Fellowship run towards the Yonderers as they do the same. While the two teams run toward each other, Terror stops Frost from heading directly toward Rilla.

"What are you doing, John?!" Frost asked Terror.

"You take the Fellowship. I'll take Rilla."

Frost goes ahead and runs toward the Fellowship and they collide. Cosmic Card is throwing cosmic beams at Emerald, Mistress Destroyer is fighting and swiping against Jade Horror and Lois Frost, Kudo Fox is shooting his pistols at Valinor as he blocks them with a electric force field and yelling out sarcastic remarks, Gale and Magic Carpet are fighting off Omega Thunder as he shoots lightning bolts, and Crystalax. The Surf held back Jackhammer from doing more damage. Rilla sits and watches the battle and looks to his left, seeing Terror.

Terror takes off his black leather trench coat and places on his metallic claw gloves. Rilla sees him and moves closer to Terror with his arms crossed.

"How foolish for a man with metal bones to face me." Rilla said to Terror.

"Let's go, diffy."

Rilla begins firing blasts of purple electric beams toward Terror. He dodges them and lunges over to Rilla, but slams into a electric force field created by Rilla. Rilla uses his magnetic ability to pick up

Terror and begins slamming him into a wall of a nearby building and onto the ground.

"They don't call me the *Lord of Magnecution* for nothing." Rilla said as he continues slamming Terror into the wall and onto the ground.

While Rilla and Terror battled, the Yonderers are losing against the Fellowship. Cosmic Card has defeated Emerald with his cosmic maneuvers, Frost and Horror defeated Mistress Destroyer by a combination of attacks. Frost looks over at Jade with an envious look. Jade looked over to Frost, seeing her facial expression.

"Is there a problem?"

"No. You're just the problem." Frost replied.

"Envious and jealous."

Kudo Fox dodged Valinor's flying cards and shoots Valinor in the leg and he falls to the ground, struggling to stand up and he looks up and Fox runs over to him and kicks him in the head, knocking him out.

"That's how you defeat someone." Fox says while smiling.

Omega Thunder defeated both Gale and Magic Carpet by blasting a lightning ball at Carpet and slamming Gale into the ground with a thunder-tackle. Jackhammer defeated Surf, while continuing to slam Crystalax into the ground and picks him up and throws him into a nearby wall, smashing him through the wall. Rilla has defeated Terror by exhausting him, though he spots Horror and Frost running toward him.

"I'll finish this myself."

Rilla conjures up a magnetic force field, which pulls Horror onto the force field, electrocuting her due to her metallic skeleton. Frost tries to knock down the force field by shooting ice beams at the field, but it has no effect. Rilla laughs as Frost continues to try knocking it down.

"You can stop now, Ms. Frost." Rilla said. "You'll tired yourself out before you make a dent into this field."

Frost looks at Rilla and she is slammed by an electric beam from Rilla. Frost is defeated as well as Jade. Rilla looks around and sees that he and his Fellowship have won. Rilla and the Fellowship celebrate, but Rilla wants to do more damage to the city, and he blasts the Willis Tower and it begins falling apart and Rilla, along with the Fellowship flee the area. After the tower collapses, police officers and SWAT trucks arrive at the scene and only see the defeated Yonderers, laid out on the ground. Terror gets to his knees and sees himself surrounded by a circle of SWAT members, pointing their guns at him.

"This is nice." Terror said.

Later, the Fellowship arrive at their warehouse hideout along with Rilla. Omega Thunder asked Rilla what they should do now and Rilla turns and looks.

"Fellowship. We have already dealt with those Yonderers. Now, we have a bigger task in front of us. That task is called Glasco, Incorporated. Its CEO, Ezekiel McKnight is currently working with the Professor Mite on building these huge sentinel machines. These machines are built for sole purpose of accomplishing one goal: Exterminate nubreeds from the face of this earth."

"Why would they build such a thing to destroy us?" Fox asked. "What have we truly done to them to receive negative attention?"

"They don't want our kind to exist because we pose a threat toward the humans. Now, we must do the only thing to stop such a cause. We must assassinate both McKnight and Mite before their planning is finished."

During the evening, the Yonderers were able to return home from the Chicago jail and Edge walks into the main room and sees them tired and distraught from the downtown battle.

"Do any of you realize the damage you've caused in the city! Do you understand that this will bring more trouble for our kind and increase the production of enemies more so."

Terror, holding his left arm and with his trench coat hanging over his right shoulder, looks over at Edge.

"Professor. We've been through enough today."

"What do you think I was going to say? Good job? Excellent work? No! You've destroyed most of downtown! Now you guys are going to pay for the damages yourselves have created."

"Fair enough." Terror says as he walks upstairs.

The rest of the team heads to their rooms and Frost walks over to Edge as Jade looks on.

"Professor. Everything will be ok." Frost said.

"Yes, it will. That's why I'm going on a vacation and Papa Afterlife is taking my place."

"WHAT?! A vacation?! And Afterlife?!"

"Yes, I'm going on a vacation to an undisclosed location, while you and the rest of the team follow Afterlife's leadership. Now, good night, Lois."

Edge leaves for his room as Frost stands there will a shocked look on her face. Frost turns to head to her room and sees Jade standing on the stairs.

"Something wrong?" Jade asked.

"No. Nothing's wrong."

Frost walked past Jade, heading down the hall.

Jade continued upstairs to her room. Walking through the hallway, she passed by Terror's room. Seeing him healing his injuries.

"You still appear to be injured?"

"I'll be fine. It'll heal soon enough. You already know that"

"Do you need a massage or something to relax your muscles?" Jade asked.

He looks over at Jade and allows her to give him a massage on his shoulders. As she gives him the massage. Jade gave a look toward the door, Terror noticed it.

"Who's at the door, Jade?"

"No one."

During the time of midnight, a secret meeting is being held at the T.I.T.A.N. between Colonel Evan Nader and Nathan Hawke, CEO of Hawke Enterprises. They speak about the upcoming sentinel machines that will be presented tomorrow morning in Washington

D.C. They sit in one of the office rooms talking amongst themselves.

"What do you think of these machines, Hawke?"

"I believe the machines will prove to be great in function, but as for military warfare, they will not be so great."

"These machines aren't being used for the military for war reasons."

"Then what are they being used for?" Hawke asked.

"They're being used to exterminate the nubreed race. Wipe them out permanently without human casualties."

Hawke stood up, looking at Nader. Nader stands up as well.

"Nader, I don't agree with the fact that these machines are being used as extermination tools."

"It's what it's made for."

"What I'm thinking about is why you and T.I.T.A.N. are agreeing with them in the first place?" Hawke said.

"We're not. We disagree with Glasco and the government about this project. This isn't what T.I.T.A.N. was created for. We look to protect everyone, not exterminate them."

"Ok, see, I'm still ongoing enough trouble with the government over the Nano Man suits."

"Thought you had that settled."

"You would think. After the whole *Octagon Incident*, they've gotten stronger with demands. Making threats. You know, their nature."

"I'm aware of that, Hawke. I saw your press conference on CNN last week."

"Did you enjoy it?" Hawke says with enthusiasm.

"It was funny. I'll give you that. President Trump's face was hilarious."

"He's familiar with my talk."

Nader and Hawke shake hands and Hawke leaves the facility as Nader walks over to a computer desk, which monitors areas that other heroes and enemies reside. On the monitors were recording footage of the Yonderer Mansion, Hawke Manor, Cherub Enterprises, and even the Citadel of Enchantment.

"We have to keep eyes on everything." Nader said.

The next day at the Yonderer Mansion, everyone is in the living room as they watch the announcement of the machines on CNN. At the event, the presenter announces Ezekiel McKnight and Professor Arthur Mite. They both walk onto the stage and Ezekiel holds the microphone as thousands of civilians stand in front of them and millions watching around the world.

"Here comes more trouble for us." Terror said.

As they watch the news, Professor Edge, dressed in a white suit, approached the team, saying goodbye as he left. As the door closed in comes Papa Afterlife, who will lead the team until Edge's unknown return.

"Look who's here." Frost said, seeing Afterlife.

"Is there a problem, Lois?" Afterlife said.

"No problem. Just announcing your arrival to the team."

"Very well."

Afterlife proceeded down the hall.

In Washington D.C., McKnight and Mite stood in front of a podium amongst a crowd of witnesses.

"Me and Professor Arthur Mite are here to present to you all the newest tech that will aid us in our battles in this life against foes foreign and domestic."

"These machines will be superior to any form of military tech. Much stronger than a tank and much faster than your little planes." Professor Mite said.

"This tech was designed and will be used for one purpose only."

Watching the news, Valinor watched on as were the others.

"Wonder what the reason is?" Valinor asked.

"Probably to keep them from going bankrupt." Terror replied. "Most organizations operate in these matters."

"These machines are the sole purpose of eradicating all of the nubreeds in the earth. Every one of them." McKnight said.

Everyone in the living room jumped from McKnight's words. All except for Terror and Jade.

"That's not right!" Surf yelled, pointing at the television.

"Great." Valinor gestured. "We're now enemies of the US Government."

"It was coming sooner or later." Terror said.

"But, why would they do such a thing?" Frost questioned.

"You guys don't see what's really going on do you."

McKnight continued to speak on how the machines will eliminate the nubreed population to make Earth a save place for humanity. Nathan Hawke sat in the audience as did Evan Nader.

"That's utter bullshit right there." Terror said.

McKnight handed the microphone to Professor Mite, who took the stage. Looking out at the audience.

"Ladies and gentlemen, we present to you, the new force upon the world, the Nubreed eradicators, Here they are… the *STEELERS*!!!"

The curtains behind Mite and McKnight open up, revealing four colossal sentinel machines that stand approximately twenty to forty feet tall and weighing between ten and twenty tons. The eyes of the Steelers lit up and they begin to walk and strike a pose to get the audience to cheer for them. The Steeler in the center scanned the audience for any signs of a nubreed and Nathan looked around, hoping that there weren't any nubreeds in the audience. The Steeler stood up and straight. McKnight and Mite followed suit.

Coming in front of them is Rilla and his Fellowship. The audience looked on as they saw Rilla and the Fellowship approaching the stage. Nathan and Nader try to evacuate the audience, but no one will leave the area, as they know that something bad is about to happen.

Rilla reached the stage, staring at McKnight and Mite. The Fellowship stood behind him. Rilla turned to his right, gazing up at the Steelers and looking back to McKnight and Mite.

"This is what you think is best for the world, Homo-Sapiens?!"

"The world needs these beings to rid itself of scum like you and the rest of your poisoned kind." McKnight said.

"Besides, it's your fault. Especially with the cause of the downtown Chicago battle between your guys and those young children." Mite added.

Rilla gave a look toward his Fellowship and raised his arm, pointing at McKnight.

"Kudo! Show them your sharp shooting."

"With pleasure, General." Kudo replied with a smile.

Kudo took out his pistols, aiming toward McKnight. Before taking the shot, he's kicked by the center Steeler and now the other three Steelers are activated and Rilla saw it without haste, commanding his Fellowship to combat the four Steelers, while he goes to handle McKnight and Mite. The Fellowship attacked the Steelers with all their might, but what they noticed was how the Steelers had all their abilities and techniques. The Steelers began firing beams from their palms toward the Fellowship. The audience now in panic mode, running amok all-over downtown Washington D.C. Nathan and Nader continued to get people to leave the area.

"Oh, now they get the sense to leave." Hawke says.

The Steelers are now defeating the Fellowship while Rilla attacked McKnight by slamming him into a wall and throwing Mite into the scattered audience. He turned around, witnessing his entire Fellowship being defeated, including the powerful Jackhammer. Rilla looked up, finding himself standing in front of the four Steelers. Rilla charged up his magnetic-electric abilities and stares as the four Steelers form a circle around him. His hands glowing as do his eyes.

"ELIMINATE TARGET." A Steeler spoke.

"If this is the way it's going to be. So be it."

Rilla attacked the Steeler standing in front of him with an electric blast, Firing the Steeler behind him into the area of the audience. Rilla shielded himself from the beam coming from the Steeler to his left and fire toward it. As he turned, the Steeler on his right deflected the electric blasts, slamming its fist into Rilla, shoving him into the ground. The Steeler picked up the General and threw him across the area, smashing him into the buildings. Nader is still in the area, although, Hawke had left.

Nader contacted T.I.T.A.N. agents to arrive and stop the four Steelers, as of now, they are not only defeating General Rilla and his Fellowship, they are also attacking civilians and setting sight on destroying the city. Mite rose to his feet as his Agency X arrived at the scene, taking him to a safer location. Glasco agents fled the area. There's nothing they can do to stop the Steelers.

The Yonderers watched on. Terror looked on and turned to the members.

"Think we should go to D.C.?" Terror asked sarcastically.

"We might have to." Frost replied.

"What are you guys preparing?" Afterlife asks as he enters the living room.

"We are preparing to head to D.C. to stop the Steelers' havoc." Terror told Afterlife.

Papa Afterlife took a small look at the team and grinned.

"You've just seen what those things can do. What makes you think that you can defeat them?"

"Because we're nubreeds." Terror said.

"You didn't seem to care when we were downtown." Frost said.

Terror gave Frost a stare. Frost smirked at him, turning to Jade, who's shaking her head. Afterlife took another look at the team.

"Well then. Prepare yourselves for the mission. I am coming along as well." Afterlife said. "See how good you people work as a unit."

"This is intriguing." Frost said.

Jade approached Frost, smiling.

"Take it from me, Afterlife doesn't play well when it comes to business. Deal with it."

The team gets prepared in their gear. Walking into the hangar, approaching the Yonder-Jet with Gale in the cockpit. Surf showed a worried look on his face, turning to Valinor.

"Is she able to fly this thing?" Surf asked.

"She's flown it before. Nothing to worry about."

Surf sighted with relief. "That's good to hear."

"Except for the landings."

"What about the landings?!" Surf shockingly asked.

Gale spoke to the team, preparing them for takeoff. The jet started to move. Surf sat tightly in his seat as the jet increased in speed.

"Here we go." Surf said to himself. "Here we go."

Now the jet is in the air heading toward Washington D.C. Emerald looked over to his right, seeing Terror wearing his black sunglasses inside of the jet.

"Why are you wearing sunglasses in the jet?"

Terror turned toward Emerald and stared for a second. Emerald shook his head, waiting for an answer. Terror didn't bulge. His body did not move nor did his focus shift.

"Because I can't see you." Terror said.

"Oh," Emerald said. "I see. You got jokes."

'How long is this flight, Gale?" Terror asked.

"Approximately an hour and forty-seven minutes, John."

"Great." Terror replied, sitting back in his seat.

Still ongoing in D.C., Nader's T.I.T.A.N. agents fight against the Steelers. The tall automatons are taking out every T.I.T.A.N. agent in their sights. Nader turned, spotting one of the Steelers staring at him. Its focus was clear. The Steeler charged up its beam and fired it toward Nader.

"Shit!"

Nader jumped out of the impact area of the blast. The blast itself, knocked Nader over to the ground. Nader took the small moment to catch his breath.

"Someone, anyone. Come help us." Nader said, watching the Steelers destroy what is in front of them.

II

<u>THE FIGHT FOR OUR FUTURE</u>

The T.I.T.A.N. agents continue battling the destructive Steelers in downtown D.C. Nader fired a shot toward one of the Steelers. Shooting the Steeler in its face, to which the automaton glanced down at Nader. It rose up its foot, Nader gave the entity a stare. Its foot came down as Nader jumped out of the way, hiding himself behind a beaten-down bus. Nader took out a cell phone and dialed a number. Waiting for an answer.

"Hawke." Nader said.

"Nader."

"Hawke, where the hell are you?!"

"I'm at my workplace, preparing something."

"Such as?" Nader wondered.

"I think you guys need some extra help." Hawke gestured. "Some nano-tech perhaps."

"Fair game. I'll be waiting on you." Nader answered, hanging up the call as he continued shooting toward the Steelers.

The Steelers destroy many buildings in their paths and continue annihilating the T.I.T.A.N. agents which surround them. Nader ran to a different site around the debris filled streets to hide from the Steelers. Shooting them at close range.

Meanwhile at Hawke Enterprises, Nathan went through the Nano-Bunker, searching through his collection of Nano Man exosuits. Searching around until he spotted one and smiled.

"Time for my baby to go to work."

On the Yonder-Jet, the team prepared for the battle ahead against the Steelers. Terror, still wearing his sunglasses, looked around at the team. Those on his side of the jet and those behind him. He looked to his side, seeing Jade and Lois sitting on opposite sides and opposite angles. Terror showed a faint smirk, shaking his head as he turned his attention to the front, looking at Gale as she piloted the jet.

"How much time is left before we hit D.C.?"

"Fifty-two minutes, John." Gale replied.

"Fifty-two minutes. Sounds great."

The others give Terror a stare. Terror saw them and their gazes. In minor retaliation, he gave them a glare. Each of them.

"What?" Terror asked.

The team turn their sights from Terror. He grinned. Valinor looked on as he listened to music on his IPhone and The Surf was playing some mobile game on his Android. The other members just talked in conversations.

"How do you feel?" Valinor asked Surf.

"Fine. Ok"

"You're still afraid, aren't you?"

"No." Surf replied, shaking his head. "Just… listen to your rock music, dude."

Valinor laughed as Surf turned up the volume on his phone.

Back in D.C. at a distant warehouse, McKnight and Mite are attempting to find way out of the city so that they won't get caught by T.I.T.A.N. or Rilla.

"Where should we go?!" Mite wondered.

"No idea. But I believe that we should leave the city before anyone catches us."

"I agree with you, but Evan Nader knows how to track us as well as his partner, Hawke. Speaking of which, where did he go when the Steelers went amok?"

"I really don't know. Probably just ran off to the nearest bar, if possible."

The Steelers move through D.C. Nader is still awaiting Hawke's back-up plan. Other T.I.T.A.N. agents ran over to Nader.

"Sir, we're outnumbered!"

"Don't worry, backup is coming."

"What about the Elite Five? Where are they?"

"The Elite Five are searching for McKnight and Mite right now. They contacted me earlier."

They continued fighting the Steelers. Rilla recovered from the previous attack and so have his Fellowship. As a means of reinforcements, other members of the Fellowship arrived. They are known as X-Manta, Eerie, The Marine, and Hunter Vazquez.

"I was wondering where you four were." Rilla said.

"We were handling business of our own." Vazquez replied.

"I see. Fellowship, prepare to fight the Steelers one more time and this time don't hold back."

The Yonderers finally arrived in D.C. Taking witness to the city's overrun by the Steelers. The team exit the jet, staring out across the area, watching the Steelers cause major damage and destruction. Terror looked on, pulling out his glocks, checking them for ammo. Gale turned toward him as did the rest of the group.

"Best to double-check." Terror said.

"Are you sure you're ready for this, John?" Papa Afterlife asked.

"Ready? Afterlife, I've been ready. True question is are you ready."

Terror walked from Afterlife's sight as Jade approached him. Watching Terror move on.

"Don't worry. He's just a smartass."

"I am aware of his speech patterns, my lady."

The Yonderers head toward the area of the Steelers. While they are coming, Nader and the agents continue to shelter themselves from the Steelers' attacks. A whirring sound came from above. Nader walked out from the hiding place quieting, looking up to see The Nano Man hovering above him.

"It's about time." Nader said.

"They don't call me *The Insuperable Nano Man* for nothing."

Nano Man flew toward the Steelers. Shooting his blue energy beams, even tackled one to the ground. Nano Man stared at the Steeler on the ground and fired six missiles. The missiles impact the Steeler's shielded body, but the automaton is still active.

"What can stop these colossal machines?" Nano Man wondered.

Nano Man took a glance around the area as the Steeler arose to its feet. In doing so, smashed Nano Man to the ground with its fist. The Steeler charged up its inner parts and fired missiles back at Nano Man. The missiles collide with Nano Man's armor and some even make dents into the exosuits.

"Wow. That actually hurt." Nano Man said to himself.

Nano Man turned to his right, seeing Rilla and his Fellowship arrive. Nano Man stood up as Rilla approached him. Both were with caution. However, Rilla's stance was more focused on force than stealth

"Great. The "hardline" are here." Nano Man gestured.

"We are here to stop those nubreed hunting abominations that were created by these weak-minded fools." Rilla replied.

"At least you're here to help and not to destroy."

"Don't worry. We intend to assist as of now. But we'll destroy everything later."

Rilla sent out the command toward his Fellowship to attack the Steelers. Cosmic Card, X-Manta, and The Marine attack one of the Steelers as Mistress Destroyer and Omega Thunder collided with another one. Jackhammer and Kudo Fox attacked the other. But, Hunter Vazquez and Eerie sat back and watched. Such an action gravitated toward Rilla, who watched them.

"Why are the two of you just standing there?!"

"We're waiting for the Yonderers to arrive." Vazquez said.

Rilla paused. He understood and nodded with a grim, turning toward Nano Man. Nano Man in such an act, saw Rilla staring at him.

"So, are we gonna help your 'fellowship' or are we gonna just sit here like those pawns of yours over there?" Nano Man asked.

"They are not pawns." Rilla replied with vigor in his voice. "They are incredible members of the hardline fellowship."

251

Nano Man went over toward of the Steelers and fired his energy beams once more. Rilla hovered up in the air as well and began firing electric beams toward the other Steeler. Rilla blasted the Steeler, knocking it to the ground.

"You should try that, Tech One."

Nano Man glared at Rilla, turning to the Steeler in front of him. Nano Man charged up from his chest and unleashed his ultrabeam through the Steeler. Breaking it apart into pieces of metal. One Steeler down. Only three remain.

"No, I think you should try that, "General"." Nano Man said sarcastically.

While Rilla and his Fellowship fought the three remaining Steelers along with the T.I.T.A.N. agents and Nader. The Yonderers have arrived at the scene. Terror looked up to see Nano Man flying towards another Steeler.

"Great. Tech-head is here."

"Don't worry about him, Terror. At least he's helping." Afterlife said.

"Whatever. Let's end all of this."

The Yonderers charged into the battle against the Steelers. General Rilla, still in the air, gazed down, seeing Edge's team fighting. He saw Vazquez and Eerie approaching them quietly, their sights primarily on both Terror and Jade. Without haste, Terror and Jade spot Vazquez and Eerie.

"Nice to see you again, John." Vazquez said.

"Move out of the way. I'm only here to stop the machines."

"Horror." Eerie said toward Jade.

"Why are you here? There's nothing eerily about what's happening." Jade replied

Terror and Jade ran into the battle. Terror leaped into the air, climbing on the back of one of the Steelers as Jade used her fire power to burn through the Steeler's legs.

"Hey. I'm behind you." Terror yelled toward the Steeler.

The Steeler's head turned toward Terror. He lunged at the Steeler's head and begins shooting it in the eyes and in doing so, remove his sword from his coat and slicked at its neck. While Jade melted the legs, Terror slashed the neck. He paused for a moment, taking out a pistol and shot the Steeler in the head while swipes at its neck with the sword. The head fell into the ground. Two Steelers down. Two to go.

"That's how it's done." Terror said.

"Yeah. Nice going." Jade replied.

Vazquez looked at Eerie and she gave a grin. Vazquez grinned as well and the two attacked Terror and Jade in the middle of their continued attacks. The four fought each other as the Yonderers took the battle to the remaining Steelers. Rilla gathered his Fellowship as they watched the young ones using team-tactics to eliminate the Steelers. Terror tackled Vazquez while Jade and Eerie crossed punches and kicks.

"Don't you see those things?!" Terror said. "They were made to kill us. Guys like us!"

"I am aware. However, I only came to face you. Our last encounter wasn't much of a splendid time."

"I assure you, we'll have many more times to come. Provided I don't kill you sooner."

Terror kicked Vazquez in the face and held up his pistol toward his head. Vazquez froze as the muzzle of the gun touched his forehead.

"Make a move and it's all over." Terror said.

Vazquez nodded with a grin as he backed away. He looked over, seeing Eerie and Jade still throwing blows.

"Jenelle, it's time to go."

Eerie paused her attacks as she moved alongside Vazquez and the rest of the Fellowship. Rilla hovered over them, looking out toward Terror, Jade, and the Yonderers.

"I see this situation is taken care of. Till next time. When it's only us."

Rilla and the Fellowship left the area. Nano Man caught them leaving.

"The hell are they going?"

Terror and Jade turned back toward the battle and as they did, the final Steeler fell to the ground. Its legs cut off and from the debris

walked out the team. Successful in this short battle. They gathered as
Nano Man landed in front of them.

"Oh my." Surf said. "You're Nano Man!"

"I am. You guys did great."

"They're still learning." Terror said.

"You could learn something from them."

Terror walked up toward Nano Man before Jade managed to
push him back.

"Not today." She said.

"Be catching you later." Nano Man said, flying off.

Sometime later, Nader regrouped the T.I.T.A.N. agents and they
gathered up all the materials from the fallen Steelers. No word on
where McKnight and Mite had gone. Rilla and his Fellowship
remained in their secret place, hoping for another bout with the
Yonderers. The Yonderers themselves, continued to train and hone
their skills. Terror and Jade went out to find anymore traces of
Agency X.

Meanwhile, in the city of Chicago, a strange essence filled the
upper air. The essence was felt by Professor Edge and Papa Afterlife as
they talked outside.

"You sense it too?" Afterlife asked.

"Yes. Something foreign. Something from the stars. And it's
heading here."

ENFORCEMENT ORDER 66: MISSIONS AHEAD

I

FIRST TIME OUT

A.B. waited in the briefing room for her recruits to arrive. Entering first was Gage Hark. Walking in calmly as he gave her a nod and stood against the wall near the large screen.

"I hope they were right behind you." A.B. said.

"Don't worry, ma'am. They should be coming in anytime now."

Entering the room first was *Lance Gasper*: The self-profound star of celebrity worship. He entered the briefing room as he enters any building, hoping all eyes are set on him. Second to enter was *Black Mare*, a woman with a fierce countenance and one who's solely focused on the mission at hand. Third was Daniel Barns, also known as *G-Zero*: The racer who uses speed to achieve his goals. Fourth was Randy Keith, called by most *Thunderstorm*. A being of massive bolts within him. His temper can prove the direness of matters. Fifth was Maria Swan: The wildcard of the group. A savvy young woman whose main desire is to meet Death herself. Sixth and last to enter was Blake Smalls, known by his codename: *Gunbaine*. Strangely enough to the group, Gunbaine seemed to appear a little weary.

"What's going on with you, Smalls?" Hark asked.

"Had a little run-in with The Swordman. Was hired to do a small job in protecting a crime lord. Things turned sideways. Plus, I was involved in a contest with other mercs. Didn't turn out how I hoped. Now, I'm here."

"That's all that matters." A.B. said. "Now, I am sure everyone is ready to hear you're first mission."

"I am." Gunbaine said. "What is it?"

A.B. approached the screen and upon it appeared Rabat, Morocco. The scenery of the city intrigued to group. Black Mare stepped foot closer, Maria's eyes widen, Lance removed his shades to see the screen in full. Thunderstorm, G-Zero, and Gunbaine were focused. Hark watched, monitoring the group closely.

"I'll be sending you all to Morocco. We have received Intel that Death and those who work under her have been preparing to strike the Parliament and cause the city of Rabat to delve into chaos. You will be sent there to make sure that doesn't happen."

"Wait." G-Zero said. "Hold on. You're sending us to protect the government authorities in a foreign country?"

"It's the only way we track down Death's workings. We stop one, we'll be closer to the next."

"I still don't get it."

"You don't have to." A.B. declared. "You just have to obey."

"And what if I don't?"

Hark stepped forward with his Colt M4 in hand. A.B. watched him, looked closely toward G-Zero's facial expressions. G-Zero was still as he set his eyes on Hark's M4. He nodded with respect.

"I see you have a fine weapon there, Lieutenant."

"Don't make me use it on you."

"Noted."

Hark returned to his position as A.B. continued giving the briefing. Afterwards, the team was told to gather their gear and head to the cargo plane which was prepared to take them to Rabat. Everyone grabbed what they needed. From Gunbaine's rifle and pistols to G-Zero's vehicle. Walking outside toward the plane and the team entered with an additional dozen Black Ops soldiers. Hark also entered the plane.

"A.B. has given me orders of teaming with you all on this mission. I am sure you'll do as you're told."

"We'll see." Gunbaine said.

"What's that, Smalls?"

"You heard me. No hard feelings."

"None." Hark said. "None yet."

The plane took off from Base 33. Preparing for its arrival in Rabat.

II

WELCOME TO MOROCCO

Within the plane on one side sat Gunbaine, Thunderstorm, Black Mare, and Maria Swan. On the other side was Hark, G-Zero, and Gasper with the Black Ops soldiers scattered around. Hark kept his eyes on Gunbaine and he leaned in toward him.

"I'm sure you know what to do once we make landfall."

"And what am I supposed to do?"

"You know. Trust me."

"What if I don't?"

"Then, we brought the wrong guy. Could've chose the other one."

"Between us, he wouldn't have come aboard anyhow. He's personal to the highest extent."

"I'm aware."

"So why the fuck are you talking to me about this?"

"Because you'll be leading the team on the ground. Just checking to see if your mind is as stable as A.B. would like to believe."

Gunbaine smirked. Sitting back in his seat. Maria looked over toward him and her eyes gazed at Hark.

"So, will Death be in Rabat?"

"No." Hark said. "She's in Pegasus Prison."

"But, I was told if I joined this little group that I would meet her."

"You will eventually. Right now, your task is to stop her workings. She has something set up in Rabat that endangers all who

258

live therein. Keep the mission in the forefront of your mind. Don't fall off."

"I won't." Randy said.

Hark nodded. "That's good to hear."

After several hours, the unit arrived in Rabat at one of their military bases. Granted entry due to the connections of A.B.'s organization and authority. While they exit the plane, Hark stepped in front of them. Giving them the orders as needed. They were each split into two separate units. Six Black Ops soldiers paired to a unit. Gunbaine was paired with Maria Swan, Gasper and Hark. Thunderstorm was paired with Black Mare and G-Zero.

"Your orders stand. We received information regarding Death's plots in this city and her Reapers have been sighted roaming around certain landmarks. Now, Gunbaine's unit will be heading toward the Riad District. Thunderstorm's unit will be set in place around Rabat Hassan.

"What are we looking for?" Black Mare asked.

"You're looking for the Reapers. They were last seen placing strange objects into the ground. What for? We aren't sure. But, that why we're here. To find these objects and stop whatever Death has planned for this city. Understood."

"Clearly." G-Zero uttered. "We get the memo."

"Then let's get moving."

The units moved out toward the destinations. While making their moves, Maria spotted large crowds of tourists going about their day. She jumped with joy.

"We have an audience!"

"No." Gunbaine said. "They're not our audience. Leave them be."

"You touch any of them, I'll cap your knee." Hark said. "You got that?"

"Always taking the fun out of things."

"So, what are we supposed to do when we see a Reaper?" Lance asked.

"We take them down."

"By knocking them out or killing them?"

"We need more information on Death's workings. Knock'em out. If some resist, kill them."

"I'm sorry, but, is that what A.B. wants us to do?"

"Yes, Gunbaine. Her orders. You follow and obey."

"Right, follow and obey. Kind of like what you're doing right now."

"Don't start a fight you can't win."

"Oh, I can win it. Mere seconds of a bout is what it'll be."

"Is that right?"

"Yeah."

Maria stepped in between the two gunsmiths with a smile on her face. Patting them on their chests.

"Save you manpower for the Reapers, alright. No need to blow each other's head off."

"Lady's got a point." Gunbaine said.

"For the moment anyway."

Reaching the Riad District, Gunbaine noticed something odd with the area. Hark spotted his concerned looks.

"What's the matter with you? Got to take a shit?"

"Something's wrong. We're heading for a trap."

"Paranoid as usual."

The unit was immediately ambushed by the Reapers. Diving out from all over the District. Everyone moved to their positions with Gunbaine and Hark primarily firing at the Reapers. Tourists and civilians took off after the first shots were fired, clearing the area. It suited both sides well.

"I'll take them in the front!" Gunbaine yelled.

"I got the front!" Hark replied.

"Take another spot! I have the front!"

"Do you job!" Hark yelled back.

Gunbaine rushed to the front, firing rounds against the Reapers. Their cloaked hoods maneuvered them well enough to dodge fire.

Hark moved through the area, now contacted by the opposite team. Hearing gunshots in their area. They too are also fighting the Reapers. Hark knows the battle has begun. Maria dove out from her hiding spot and attacked a Reaper standing near her, hitting him from behind with a crowbar and upper-cutting him with a high kick. Lance Gasper maneuvered and dodged the attacks before using the pavement as a source of weaponry.

The streaks of lighting were seen in the sky and the thunder followed, catching the attention of Gunbaine's unit and the Reapers around them.

"You heard that?" Hark asked.

"Yeah." Gunbaine said. "Keith's giving them hell over there."

Thunderstorm was surely giving the Reapers hell over in the Rabat Hassan area. G-Zero moved with speed, taking out the Reapers near him as Black Mare delivered serious blows to the Reapers near her with a Kevlar-laced whip. The Reapers tried shooting Keith from the sky, but, he scoffed and blasted them with lightning strikes.

Gunbaine continued firing against the Reapers and in the midst of the ongoing fight, a Reaper moved through the district, carrying a vertical object. A metallic device. The Reaper slammed the device into the concrete, causing the bottom of the device to latch into the ground. The top opened and the Reaper pressed a button.

"Gunbaine! Stop that Reaper!" Hark yelled.

Gunbaine ran for the Reaper and as he inched closer to capturing him, the round began to quake. Shocking both units.

"The hell's going on?!" Hark asked.

"Earthquake!" Gunbaine yelled!

"A big one at that!" Maria added.

The earthquake's strength increased as Gunbaine tried to pull the device out of the ground. It's too deep and latched too tight to the concrete. Hark ran up to Gunbaine.

"We have to get back to the plane now!"

Both units ran for the plane as the ground began to crack, the buildings started to shake. Windows started to burst as they came closer to the plane. As they reached the plane, Reapers were waiting for them and the remaining Black Ops soldiers took them out without hesitation. Gunbaine was impressed as they entered the plane and left Rabat.

"What's the plan now? Gunbaine asked.

"We return to Base. Find out what A.B. wants to do."

"What about the city?" G-Zero asked.

"The Moroccan Government will consult with the United Nations. They'll be fine. Say it was some underground issue. Pipes in bad shape. Some shit like that."

"You're familiar with this aren't you?" Gunbaine asked.

"Don't act like you've never done the same before."

III

ENFORCEMENT VS. EXCHANGE

The Enforcement Order returned to Base 33 and A.B. took in their responses before giving them a small moment of separation. The following day, she spoke with Hark about the next mission and as such, he regrouped the team, bringing them back into the briefing room.

"Another mission." Gunbaine said. "That was quick."

"Well, this one isn't much for shocker, Smalls." Hark replied. "Just keep your ears open."

A.B. stood by the monitor, speaking of the next mission. This mission was focused on the assassination of a government official. The set location was Bosnia. G-Zero scoffed in his seat.

"You have something to say, speedy?" Hark asked.

"Another foreign country. Why not someone here. In America.'

"Because it isn't on the radar." A.B. said.

"So, what's the full objective?" Gunbaine asked. "Just for clarity."

"You find this government official. You kill him."

Gunbaine nodded.

"Just like that?"

"Just like that." A.B. grinned. "Any problems?"

"None.' Gunbaine replied. "When do we head out?"

Hark stepped forward to the door. Gunbaine stood up from his seat and walked over. The others followed Gunbaine's movements. They walked outside to the plane as previous and headed out toward Bosnia.

"So, this plan is basically finding the official, kill him, and the job's done?" Gunbaine asked.

"Seems to be the case." Thunderstorm replied.

"That is the answer." Hark said. "Any concerns?"

"None."

"What about any of you?"

"I'm peachy." Maria said.

"I'm cool with it." Lance said.

"As long as we get this done quick, I'm fine." G-Zero said.

Hark nodded with a stern look. He was ready for anything.

Upon arriving in Bosnia, After the team left the plane and headed out toward the precise location of where the official resided, they saw another team in the distance. They learned of something peculiar. Something which was not expected of a group like theirs. Neither Hark or A.B. could've foreseen what was standing in the grounds of Bosnia. However, this team was not seeking to eliminate the government official, they were protecting him.

"A.B." Hark said on his speaker. "We have a problem."

"What problem?"

"Another unit is here."

"What other unit?"

"The Exchange Force."

The Enforcement looked out, seeing the five members of the Exchange Force. Armored from head to toe and geared with weaponry beyond their requirements. Gunbaine looked over toward Hark. Hark had no words. Only concerns.

"How are we going to get through them?"

"You tell me." Hark replied. "I got nothing."

Gunbaine nodded. He looked at his teammates.

"I'll take the first shot."

"Gunbaine don't" Hark said. "If you do, they'll kill us."

"Either we die, or they die. Choice is simple."

"I'm with Gunbaine." Thunderstorm said with a nod.

Gunbaine nodded back and focused his sniper rifle toward one member of the Force. The lean one.

"Here we go."

Gunbaine fired the round and it impacted the armored Force member, knocking him to the ground. The other four looked out for anything as the lean member rose to his feet. They scoped out the area and one of them saw the rifle in the distance.

"There."

Gunbaine realized they found their spot. He looked at Hark. No emotion as the Exchange Force was heading their direction. The team was ready for the fight, standing out in the open road facing them.

"We need a new strategy."

THE IRE OF FLASHBURN: I AM SHADEBURN

I

FLAMED DARKNESS

Floyd Rizzo was renowned with his newfound power. A gift from the Incandescence. After Floyd's battle with the man who called himself the Atomic Bomb, Floyd understood the powers he possessed must be taken with caution and certainty. Now, after some time, he has fully begun to embrace his role as Flashburn, the vessel for the Incandescence.

Floyd practiced his combustion of flames. The presence it brought before him and how he could maneuver it. Elsewhere, Professor Dan Simon continued his research in studying the history of the Incandescence and its power's effects upon Floyd. How the power could sharpen his mind, body, and will. A knock came from the Professor's door and he looked up from his desk, seeing a woman.

"Ma'am." he said. "Need something?"

"Are you Professor Dan Simon?"

"I am. Who's asking?"

"I am. Jessica Jacobs. P.I."

"Oh." Simon nodded. "And why is a private investigator visiting me in my working hours?"

"I've come to ask you about the incident that happened in town. About the Flashburn."

"And why would I know anything of him?"

"You were seen at the site after he defeated the Atomic Bomb guy."

"I was."

"Then, you don't mind answering my questions."

"I don't. but, can we do this tomorrow. I have work that must be done. For my student's sake."

Jessica nodded.

"Very well. I'll return tomorrow and you'll tell me all I need to know."

"I will."

Jessica left the lab as Simon was now concerned about this investigator's sudden visit. However, as Simon is in his work, he returned to it and after several minutes, Jessica's arrival was an afterthought.

Elsewhere, at a community event placed in a park in which was centered around nature and many who were at the event were certainly naturalists, activists, and ecologists. The total amount of people at this event added up to four-hundred and fifty. All were focused on the preservation of earth's natural state. They spoke highly of combating climate change and fixing the environment. Most of their ideas would conflict with the current laws of society. However, they were determined to make things right.

As the leading spokesperson talked, a figure emerged from the large tree nearby. It had the figure of a human and no face could be seen. The figure stood amid the people. For it was nightfall and the figure blended in like a dark cloak. The only light source around them was the moon's glint and candlelight.

"We will make things right." The Spokesperson said. "We are the only ones who can achieve this!"

The figure grunted and extended its arms with force, causing all the people to be swallowed up in deep darkness. Others who saw this from a distance ran in fear. The spokesperson was standing still. Frozen as the darkness consumed them. As a man ran from the scene, he looked back and saw the figure. The darkness was emitting from its hands and it appeared to glow and spark like a fire. The man ran as the figure vanished into the darkness itself.

II

SHADOWS OF THE MYSTERY

The news broke out concerning the massacre of the community event. The following day, Professor Simon and Floyd listened to news reports of what took place. On one broadcast, a reporter spoke with the man who saw the figure.

"And you said you saw who was responsible?"

"I did."

"And who was it? What did they look like?"

"They looked like darkness. Pure darkness, but with a hint of a flame. It looked similar to that Flashburn guy, but darker."

"You heard that" Simon asked.

"I did."

Simon looked at the clock and remembered. Floyd saw him moving over to his desk, placing files atop.

"What's going on, Professor?"

"There was a woman who came by yesterday. She wants to know about you. Your alter-ego."

"Did you tell her?"

"No. but, she's on her way to question me. It was a scheduled arrangement."

"I understand." Floyd said. "I'll head out there. See what I can find."

"Be careful out there." Simon said. "If these people believe you were responsible, you'll have a target on your head."

Floyd nodded and left the lab.

In the crowds of reporters, Jessica moved through them. Her purpose was separate from those of the media. As she moved through the crowds, she confronted the witness.

"I need to ask you some questions."

"But, I've already given my details."

"To the media." Jessica said, holding up a badge. "I'm not the media."

"You're a private investigator."

"I am. What did you see? Truthfully."

"Well, whomever it was looked just like Flashburn. Except you couldn't see the outfit. The figure was covered in darkness. Like a thick shadow."

"And this darkness killed these people?"

"As if it suffocated them. I'm sure they couldn't breathe in that mass."

"Suffocated?" Jessica questioned.

"Yeah. You could hear their screams muffled by the darkness."

Jessica took in the witness' statement and let him go about his business. She looked around the park, seeing multiple reporters, cameras, and interviews taking place. As she went to turn around towards the crime scene, she saw a woman who was staring into the sky. She wore a white coat, jeans, and her orange hair glistened to the sunlight. She looked to the sky herself and only saw the sun and the clear sky. She looked back to the woman with confusion.

"I'm sorry, ma'am. But, what do you see up there?"

"The sun. it's beautiful isn't it? The clear, blue sky. This calls for a peaceful day."

"I'm sorry, you're standing in a park which is covered by reporters. People died here yesterday."

"I'm aware."

"So, why are you in the park?"

"Who are you, miss?"

"Jessica Jacobs. Private Investigator. And you are?"

"Natalia Spear. I'm a solar scientist. I also study radiation. To the effect of nature and humans."

"A scientist. That's fair. However, this crime was not committed by sunlight or radiation. But, darkness. A shadow as witnesses claim."

"They say a lot when in fear. I say otherwise."

"What do you say?"

"Flashburn. I believe he was responsible. Covered his flames in darkness and scorched the people."

"How can you be sure?"

"Because there's radiation all in the grounds where the killing took place."

"There's radiation out here?" Jessica asked with caution.

"Yes. I told the officials, but they brushed me off. I sure people will be sick after this."

Jessica looked around and everyone was going about their duties. She turned back to Natalia with great concern.

"You must tell them again. Tell them you're a scientist. That radiation is in your field."

"No." Natalia said. "Best they learn from experience."

Natalia nodded and left the park, leaving Jessica in a strait of warning the people or leaving them to their reporting. She couldn't make a choice as she looked at her watch and knew she had a meeting with Professor Simon. She did not want to be late and she left the park.

Elsewhere, Floyd was up in the sky as Flashburn, scanning the grounds for anything unusual. He couldn't trace anything, but somewhere on the ground. Someone was watching him, and their eyes were covered in darkness.

III

I AM SHADEBURN

Jessica had arrived at the laboratory and sat with Professor Simon. The lab was quiet as usual. Jessica wanted a solid silent space to get her questions across to Simon, it's her preferred way of questioning. Simon sat calmly at his desk, facing Jessica who sat in front of him.

"First off, have you ever been in contact with Flashburn?"

"In contact in what form?"

"Face-to-face. Short sightings. Unusual meet-ups?"

"I can't say that I have."

Jessica nodded, writing down Simon's answers in her notepad. Simon saw how quick she could write. Her handwriting looked sloppy from a distance but very clear to understand the closer one would get. But, she would never let anyone see inside the notepad. For her eyes only. The Professor raised himself up in the seat, sitting still.

"You must know something."

"Why do you assume I know anything about Flashburn?"

"Because you were seen at the event of the fight between him and the Atomic Bomb."

"And your source is?"

"A witness at the battle claimed to have seen you. Described you very clearly."

"Did they?"

"You don't deny it?"

"Never said I did or didn't. Although, I am interested as to who this 'witness' is. Tell me, did they give you a name?"

"That's undisclosed information, Professor."

"How?"

While they spoke, a door was shut outside of the lab and through the windows Simon could see Floyd approaching the door and as he went to stand up, Floyd entered the lab, seeing the Professor and Jessica at the desk. Jessica turned to see Floyd. Curious.

"And who are you?" She asked.

"I'm Floyd Rizzo. A student of Professor Simon."

"Ah. A student. I didn't know you had students, Professor."

"Floyd's a great student. He's learned a lot under my tutelage. I am curious as to why Floyd has come."

"I have news to give you concerning our project."

"What of the project?"

"I couldn't trace the source of the problem."

"No sign of it?" The Professor asked. "Nothing out of the ordinary?"

"Nothing."

Jessica looked at Floyd and Simon with interest, turning to face them back and forth.

"I'm curious. What's this project you're both working on?"

"I'm sorry, ma'am. The project is under undisclosed circumstances."

Jessica stared at Simon, who grinned.

"I see." Jessica closed her notebook. "Well, I believe I have everything I need."

"Oh good." Professor said, standing up from his chair. "I bid you good luck on your case."

"Same to your project."

They shook hands and without warning, the ground trembled. Shaking the laboratory. Floyd looked around seeing frames shaking on the walls. Simon held the computer monitor still.

"What was that?" Jessica asked.

"I'm not certain." Simon replied. "Floyd, what is it?"

"Someone's outside." Floyd said, looking into the air.

"How do you know someone's outside?" Jessica questioned. "Is he a psychic or something?"

Floyd left the laboratory, Simon and Jessica followed him.

Leading to the outside parking lot, they saw a figure standing still. Cloaked in the shadows of its own body. Floyd stepped forward.

"That's the suspect." Jessica said.

"I've come to meet him." The figure spoke in an eerie wavy voice. "My counterpart of the flames. Of the fire."

"Did you cause the quake?" Floyd asked.

"To bring out my counterpart. I know he's here."

"Counterpart?" Jessica said. "What's he talking about?"

"I'm not sure." Simon replied.

"Who's your counterpart?" Floyd asked.

"The one of the Incandescence. Flashburn."

Floyd stared as Simon shook his head and Jessica looked closer at the shadow figure. Its appearance and the slight references to a uniform underneath the cloaked darkness.

"What's your name?" Floyd asked.

"I am Shadeburn."

"Floyd, it's him." Simon pointed.

Floyd took in the notion of Shadeburn's interior motives. He could feel them within himself, clawing through his chest. He could also feel the flames of the Incandescence within him, slowly kindling from within. The heat was increasing.

"I know what must be done, Professor." Floyd said confidently.

"In front of the investigator?"

"I have no choice."

Floyd stepped forward before Shadeburn. Jessica looked somewhat off at Floyd's posture and position. She turned to Simon who was solely focused on Floyd's well-being, however, there was no fear in his expression. He had great confidence in his student.

"What's he doing?"

"You're about to find out." The Professor said. "You're about to find out everything."

The figure glared toward Floyd, looking around the laboratory lot.

"Where is he? I know he's here. I can sense the fire within."

Floyd stepped closer. Only a few feet between him and Shadeburn. Simon and Jessica stood by the door of the laboratory.

Shadeburn took another look at Floyd, now he realized something. Something within Floyd. A smile revealed itself on Shadeburn's face.

"Ah. You're him."

Floyd closed his eyes and upon opening them, they were covered in flames. He extended his hands and a great whirlwind of fire appeared around him, brightening the parking lot. Within the whirlwind, Floyd had transformed into Flashburn. Once the whirlwind ceased, Flashburn was revealed. Jessica saw and now she knew. Floyd is Flashburn.

"You don't belong here." Flashburn said.

"I'm right where I should be."

"Fair enough."

Flashburn bolted into the sky and Shadeburn followed. The two entities battled it out in the sky. Firing fire and shadows against one another with great force. Both were evenly matched. However, Shadeburn teleported behind Flashburn and grabbed him with a mist of darkness, blocking his eyesight. While Flashburn fought to regain his vision, Shadeburn snatched him by his right ankle and tossed him to the pavement of the parking lot. Flashburn removed the mist from his eyes, seeing clearly once again.

"My master has commanded me to eliminate you." Shadeburn said.

"And who is your master?"

"My. You don't know? Your master hasn't told you all things. A shame. A pity for one who calls himself a mentor."

Flashburn arose and went for a strike, but Shadeburn was too quick, elwoing him in the face and causing him to crash from the blow and of his own speed. Flashburn laid on the ground as Shadeburn glanced up to the sky.

"We'll do this again very soon, Flashburn."

Shadeburn evaporated into a dark cloud and was gone. Simon ran toward Flashburn as he reverted to Floyd. Out of breath, yet there were no bruises or blood. Simon asked him if he was alright and not in any pain. Floyd replied with calmness. He was well. Jessica approached them cautiously.

"You have a lot to tell me." Jessica said.

"Only if you can handle it." Simon replied.

IV

MATTER BETWEEN DARKNESS AND FIRE

Returning inside the lab, Simon wanted to check Floyd for more possible injuries, but Floyd was well. No bruises, cuts, or marks. Still no sign of blood. Jessica watched as the two were calm and collective after what previously happened.

"You two aren't shaken up?"

"Why would we be?" Simon replied.

"Because that thing, whatever it was, looked like a walking shadow. And what it did to him."

"Don't worry about me." Floyd said. "I'll be fine."

"So, you're him. The Flashburn."

"I am. Have you been seeking me out?"

"Well, I spoke with your Professor about him yesterday and he claimed not to know anything about Flashburn. That's why I'm here today. To learn more of what he knew. But, I see that now I know a lot more than what I was expecting."

"I said what I had to in order to protect Floyd."

"I see that now." Jessica said. "After all, he's your student. I wouldn't expect a Professor to do less than that."

"What did you want to ask?" Floyd said.

"Why are you here? Where do your abilities come from?"

Floyd sat up in the chair, facing Jessica. He sighed.

"I was given these abilities. Before all of this, I was just a young engineer looking to make a living for myself. I was led to a place where I met a entity, called the Incandescence. He granted me these abilities and proclaim that I would become his vessel, the Flashburn."

"You're telling me some kind of supernatural being gave you

these powers?"

"I wouldn't call him supernatural." The Professor added. "More like elemental."

Jessica scoffed. "So, where is he now?"

"I do not know. He appears when necessary."

"How come he didn't show up when you were fighting that shadow out there?"

"I handled it."

"Not as good as you think." Jessica said. "You could've been killed from the fall."

"I'm alive aren't I? I know the risks of this task."

"I'm only saying, if this elemental was as powerful as you say, wouldn't he have come in at the brink moment of time and assisted you? I mean, that shadow proved himself to be much stronger than you."

"He was." Floyd said with certainty. "And I don't know how or why?"

"Why don't you ask him. This elemental of yours."

"I'm not sure you wish to see him with your own eyes."

"Has the Professor seen him?"

"I have not." Simon replied. "Although, I believe he appears only to speak to Floyd and Floyd only."

"I don't think he has much of a choice now."

"Many have spoken of me in such a way." A voice rumbled from behind Jessica.

She turned and as Floyd and the Professor saw, the Incandescence was standing before them in the middle of the laboratory. His body was of pure fire, yet no heat could be felt in the lab and the floors were not burnt. The eyes of the Incandescence shined of a brightly lit flame. The Professor was astonished, and Jessica was afraid.

"You're him." Jessica said.

"I am who you speak of. I did not appear to aid my apprentice in this manner. For, he handed it well and he still lives because of it."

Floyd stood up from the chair and walked toward the Incandescence.

"I need to know. Who was that shadow? Where did he come

from?"

"Shadeburn. I have not heard that name in ages."

"Who is he?"

"He is the living vessel of a counterpart. The one called the Luminescence. Whereas I dwell in the fires, the Luminescence dwells in the shadows. In a place of pure darkness. Yet, sometimes even his darkness can glow like a flame. Which is what you witnessed this day."

"How can I stop him?"

"You cannot. Not yet."

"How come?" The Professor asked. "Why can't Floyd stop this Shadeburn?"

"Because the others must be awoken first in order to bring forth the elemental wages of a era."

"Elemental wages?" Jessica said. "You guys pay each other or something? Give one another gifts?"

"The wages are for the generations. The wages themselves are our power. I have already given my wages to Floyd Rizzo. Now, it seems the Luminescence has given his. It only means the others will do the same very shortly."

"Others?" Floyd asked. "You mean there's more than yourself and this Luminescence?"

"Many more." The Incandescence confirmed. "Recount the number of elements which sit upon, within, and above the earth. Think of how much power one such as I wield and what wages must be given to those worthy of the cause."

"Earth, wind, fire, air, water, darkness." The Professor said.

"What about light?" Jessica asked. "If darkness is one of the elements, light must be one as well."

"For the balance of all things, yes. However, as I am aware, there remain eight of us."

"Well, what's the eighth element?" Floyd asked.

"The spirit."

Floyd, Simon, and Jessica took in all the Incandescence had revealed unto them and noted it well.

"I must go now." The Incandescence said. "I request you all

prepare yourselves for what is to come."

"And that would be?" Jessica asked.

"A change of reality. The heroes have already risen and now, the world you live in belongs to them. For the season."

Floyd bowed before the Incandescence as he disappeared in their sights in the form of a whirlwind. Floyd turned back to the Professor and Jessica as they saw his mannerisms toward the fire entity. Floyd's behavior was strikingly different when the Incandescence stood in the room. A sense of respect and honor was known and felt within the laboratory.

"What's next?" The Professor asked.

"We get ready." Floyd said. "If I'm only one of the eight, we must search for the others."

TOR-ZAR:
DINOSAURS AND WEREWOLVES

I

SIGNS OF A VISITOR

On a clear day across the Avago Land, a swarm of Pteranodons invaded the lands of the Wanigo Tribe. Every man, woman, and child came out of their homes to fight against the aerial forces. Using bows and arrows, spears, and slingshots against the flying creatures. From the woods, bolted out Kujo, the saber-toothed liger, who jumped up, lunging at one of the Pteranodons, snatching the bird by its neck and twisting. Behind Kujo appeared Tor-Zar and with him was Sahara.

"We've come to help." Tor-Zar told the tribe.

Tor-Zar used his own bow and arrow to eliminate the Pteranodon in his sights. While some attempted to dive down toward him, he raised his spear, decorated with metallic enhancements, and slashed the birds. Sahara did the same with a spear of her own. After killing some of the birds, the rest retreat. Clearing the sky above them tribes' land. Tor-Zar and Sahara approached the Tribes leader with a kneeling bow. The utmost respect.

"It is good of you to come and aid us."

"We live here as well." Tor-Zar said. "I must ask, what caused the Pteranodons to invade your lands?"

"We found some peculiar footprints not too far from the entrance. Whatever caused them, sent the Pteranodons this way. Causing a disturbance."

"What kind of footprints?" Sahara wondered. "Tyrannosaurus? Velociraptor?"

"No. It's not from these lands. It's something from afar."

"More invaders?" Tor-Zar questioned. "Can't be. We ran off the others."

"These footprints do not belong to those like us." The Tribes Leader said. "Humans. They seem feral. Paw-like. But more liken to ours. Visceral to be described."

Tor-Zar nodded. He extended his arm toward the Leader and they shook.

"I'll do what I can to track this thing down. Keep the lands protected."

"We know you will."

II

<u>THE FIND</u>

Tor-Zar and Kujo both went deeper into the wilderness, tracking the footprints. Sahara stayed with the Tribe just in case the suspected anomaly returned toward the tribes' land. Kujo sniffed the grounds, moving further into the forest. Tor-Zar knelt, rubbing the footprint.

"What is this?" He questioned.

His attention was snatched quickly b Kujo's roaring. Tor-Zar ran toward the roars, finding Kujo staring down three velociraptors. The raptors' hide peaked green and blue in the sunlight. They snarled at Tor-Zar and Kujo. Tor-Zar held his spear tightly, snarling back at the raptors. The raptors screeched and attacked Tor-Zar and Kujo. The battle was not a fierce one, due to the skills of Tor-Zar and his spear. Kujo's own strength was enough to trample over one of the raptor's bodies, while lunging on the other, snapping its neck. Tor-Zar ran toward the incoming raptor, with its claws out and mouth open. Tor-Zar swiped the spear against the raptor, knocking it on the ground near one of the large trees.

"Stay down." Tor-Zar said.

The raptor rose and snarled. Yet, the raptor was caught up in the mouth of a larger predator. Tor-Zar and Kujo raised their heads above, seeing a tyrannosaurus rex staring them down while chewing and swallowing the raptor whole. The two stepped back as the T-Rex set its eyes upon them. Kujo growled, Tor-Zar held his spear tightly.

The T-Rex roared and rushed the two, knocking them on opposite sides of its body. Kujo raised up, lunging atop the T-Rex, clawing and biting its back. Tor-Zar arose, ramming the spear into the T-Rex's leg. The leg went up and came down, shoving Tor-Zar

283

onto the ground once more. The T-Rex shook itself, causing Kujo to lose his grip and slip off. The T-Rex turned toward Kujo, with its mouth open and the teeth covered with saliva and blood. The T-Rex leaned down toward Kujo and quickly, Tor-Zar lunged the spear, impacting the T-Rex in its head. The dinosaur roared in pain, shaking its head as the spear fell to the ground. Kujo stood up and clawed the leg while Tor-Zar snatched the spear and swiped it across the T-Rex's chest. The large dinosaur walked off into the forest with only the echoing sounds of its roars and footsteps heard.

Tor-Zar patted him and Kujo went over toward him, looking for wounds. Tor-Zar smirked, patting Kujo.

"Did good."

From behind them arrived the Tribe with Sahara. Tor-Zar stood up as she approached him, seeing some minor cuts on his arms and chest. Kujo had some minor wounds of his own. Sahara looked around, seeing several of the nearby trees were knocked down.

"What happened?"

"Came across some raptors. Dealt with them before a T-Rex showed up. Me and Kujo dealt with it and it went off into the forest."

"What of the creature?" The Tribes Leader asked. "Did you manage to find what caused the footprints?"

"Not yet."

As the leader and Tor-Zar spoke, Sahara caught a glimpse of something moving around the trees nearby. She took several steps forward to see and as she did, a creature lunged out toward her. She ducked as the creature flew over her, sliding on the ground. The others witness it and band together, seeing the creature for what it is. It stood over seven feet, with grey and black hairs covering its body. The snout spewing with saliva and its yellow eyes frightened the tribes' people.

"What is that?" The leader asked.

"I've heard of their kind before." Tor-Zar said. "It's a lycan."

"How did it get here?" Sahara wondered. "There aren't any wolves on this land."

"It found a way. Most likely the same pathway as the invaders."

The leader grabbed his spear and ran toward the werewolf for an impale attack. The lycan dodged he attacked, snatching the spear and breaking it in half before swiping the leader back toward his people. The werewolf roared, expressing its physique and strength. Tor-Zar, Sahara, and Kujo stood in front of the tribes' people facing the creature.

"We'll have to take it down." Sahara said.

"I agree." Tor-Zar replied.

"You dare attempt to strike me!" The lycan spoke.

"You can talk?" Tor-Zar said. "Makes things better. State your name, creature."

"My name is of no concern. I have finally found the land spoken of across the ages. Now, I will rid this place of you and your kind. I will rule amongst the creature of this land and in time, my kind will rise again."

"Not before we stop you." Sahara said, raising her spear.

III

AN OPEN WORLD

Tor-Zar collided with the lycan, whose claws were able to withstand Tor-Zar's spear. Sahara and Kujo jumped into the battle as the tribes' people watched on. Tor-Zar was knock across the ground, leaving Kujo and Sahara to face the lycan. The lycan's strength was more than impressive, as he easily defeated Kujo with several swips to the back and lunged atop Sahara, smashing his weight against her own, shoving her into the dirt. The lycan roared at the tribes' people before Tor-Zar stood up, holding his staff.

"That weapon will have no effect on me." The lycan said.

Tor-Zar paused and nodded, dropping the spear into the ground and pulling out two daggers from his boots. He held them up, facing the creature.

"Your move."

The lycan clashed its claws against the two blades. Pulling his hand back, seeing his own blood. The lycan was confused as he looked back and forth between his hand and the blades.

"What are those made of?"

"Solidium. Why do you ask?"

"Not possible. I cannot be wounded. I am Lycano."

"Your name is Lycano?" Tor-Zar noted. "Well, you have a choice, Lycano. Either leave this land in peace or die here and be food for the vultures."

"I cannot die. I am beyond this land."

Lycano took off into the woods, only letting out a small howl before vanishing into the forest. Tor-Zar placed his blades back into their sheaths and went to check on Sahara and Kujo. Both of which were well, with only slight wounds. They returned with the tribe back to their lands. There, Tor-Zar went and mediated, with the two blades laying on the ground besides him with the blood of Lycano still intact. Sahara entered the cave where Tor-Zar sat and kneeled front of him as his eyes opened. She looked at the blades and saw the blood, shaking her head.

"You let him go."

"He had a choice and he made it."

"What if he comes back? What if he's not alone next time?"

"We can take him. Besides, I know for a fact that's not the last we've seen of him."

CROSSBREED: A DARK TITAN UNIVERSE EVENT

I

MEETING OF THE MINDS

General Rilla and his Fellowship stand inside their lair. Some of the nubreeds are healing after the events with the Steelers. While they stood, waiting for their visitor, Cosmic Card approached Rilla, looking around at the others.

"Who is coming to meet us?"

"A stranger from another place. He seeks to aid us in moving those traitors out of our way. Giving opportunity to our cause."

"He a nubreed like us?"

"He's something else. Neither human nor nubreed. Otherworldly is the word I would use to describe him."

The doors of the lair opened, catching everyone's attention. The visitor walked in, dressed in nearly all black with some dark-blue colors on his apparel. He wore a black duster with blue linings. passing through an aisle of nubreeds with their eyes on him. He casually walked forward as the doors closed behind him. His eyes were set on what's in front of him and that was Rilla himself. The Stranger stood in front of Rilla as his Fellowship circled him. The Stranger nodded.

"You've come." Rilla said. "I respect that."

"It is of an important cause and I am happy to help."

288

"Before we discuss terms, you didn't tell me your name."

"I am known in my world and amongst my people as Romanus Dakingor."

"Dakingor?" Rilla said. "Sounds strong."

"That is what I believe it to be. But, there are others who see it as an opposing force for their well-being."

"You seek something else in this agreement of ours?"

"I have a proposal for you and your Fellowship."

"Do tell."

"I'll help you eliminate the Yonderers and you can aid me in taking out my adversaries."

"Are you adversaries the same as you or are they of another kind?"

"They are of my kind. Yet, they are betrayers to our cause. Desiring to live like the others outside our ranks."

"Sounds like the Yonderers. Hmm, we are in the same boat. Let's talk."

II

STRIKE FIRST

The Yonderers sat inside the Yonderer Mansion with Professor Edge instructing them on the aftereffects of the Steelers. The whole team was present to hear Edge's words. Through the teaching, a rumbling sound echoed overhead. Startling the team as they prepared themselves and went outside, Edge stood still, mediating as he looked up.

"Someone's here."

"Who's here?" Lois Frost asked. "More Steelers?"

"No. Something otherworldly."

The team ran outside, only to find themselves staring at a small, yet powerful force. Professor Edge went out with them, seeing the group standing in front of them. Edge could sense their power. It was strong. Stronger than most of the nubreeds he's come across.

"Who are they?" Lois asked. "Are they nubreeds?"

"No, they're not nubreeds. There's something else."

The group stood a dozen strong. Walking through them to the front was Romanus. There, he looked out toward the Yonderers and scoffed.

"This is who Rilla is up against." Romanus whispered. "Shame."

"Who are you?" Edge asked.

"We are a people from another place. Far from here." Romanus said. "We've come to discuss terms with the kind called 'nubreeds'."

"Terms? What kind of terms?"

"My kind see yours as a primary enemy. Therefore, in our culture, it is nature for one to annihilate the other. Only one

290

bloodline shall remain. The other must be eviscerated permanently."

"We do not that those words kindly." Edge said. "If you wish to threaten us, perhaps you should've gone with your attacks already.'

"Fair point."

Romanus waved his hands, signaling the attack as his army ran toward the Yonderers for the fight. The young team was prepared as Edge led them into the battle. Lois and Valinor collided with the front liners, quickly taking them down. However, there were three larger ones standing before the Yonderers. Surf went for an attack and it didn't even stumble them. Emerald went with an attack of his own, trying to tire out the unkinds. Romanus savored the battle before his eyes, seeing Crystalax making a move toward him, Romanus held his hand up freezing the Yonderer in his place and walked away before he fell to the ground face-first.

"Weakness is a disgust." Romanus said.

He looked out toward the battle, seeing his army being quickly defeated. Romanus hated the idea of losing a battle, much less a war. Romanus shook his head, thinking of the timing and the current idea.

"This is not going to last long. Never was meant to. A distraction is all that we needed."

Instead, he took matters into his own hands by creating a slight power surge and attacking the Yonderer Base, blowing a large hole through the front. The blast knocked the Yonderers and Edge to the ground. With the explosion, Romanus took his leave with the followers who remained. Once the debris cleared out, Edge scouted the area, seeing Romanus had vanished and the others who were with him had also gone.

"Professor, what shall we do?" Valinor questioned. "Won't they be back?"

"We need to do some studying. See where they truly come from. Why they're here and what they want."

"And what are we going to do once we have the answers?" Lois asked. "Track them down and do the same to them?"

"We are not like that, Frost. You know our operations well. Best not to let your emotions tamper with your decisions."

"I have to agree with the lady on this one." Valinor said. "What are we going to do once we find out who they truly are?"

"We will get to that once everything is in place." Edge answered. "Right now, we repair and prepare."

Elsewhere, Halo Lock and his liege of Unkinds move through the countryside of Illinois. From there, Cygnus, one of Halo Lock's trusted soldiers looked up at a sign. He pointed with clarity.

"My lord, is that the name of the place?"

Halo Lock looked toward the sign, seeing the word "Chicago". He nodded.

"That is the place written. The place where the Yonderers dwell."

"Then we're not far." Aquila, Halo Lock's wife spoke. "We'll finally get our answers."

"We shall indeed receive answers. "Halo Lock replied. "I hope they are the answers we have sought after."

III

THE PLAN IS SIMPLE

Romanus returned to the Fellowship Lair, seeing Rilla speaking with his nubreed followers. He moved with a fast pace in his steps, as the eyes of the fellowship turned toward him. Inching closer, Rilla spotted him and stepped forward.

"What has happened?" Rilla asked.

"I paid a trip to these Yonderers. I've caused a slight disturbance for them which should benefit our cause."

"I see. Are they dead?"

"No. only did some damage to their home. The message is clear. Once Halo Lock and his Liege arrive to the Yonderers, they will be the enemy and the war will begin."

Rilla smirked.

"Giving way for the two of us to enter at a moment's notice. Let them destroy each other. Then, we'll enter and eliminate the surviving force."

"Good to know." Romanus said, rubbing his chin.

"I must ask, why go through all of this? Seeking to prove yourself to your kind?"

"I'm the rightful ruler of my people. Halo Lock isn't capable of leading our people into a better future."

"Halo Lock, I must ask. What is his power? How does he lead your people in such a strong devotion?"

"He has his ways. Him and his wife are their king and queen to an extent."

"You seek to be king."

"More so their emperor. I know how to lead my people and rule them well. We can do things that will make us even better than we were on our ancient home world."

"And what of your home world this day?"

"Barren. Unlivable. We sought a better path and better world. We found this one. Later, we discovered there were others already here. A melting pot of such kinds. Halo and I disagreed on our plans for coming here. Most of our people sided with him. A few others placed their loyalty to me."

"And this Halo Lock picked his Liege alongside his wife and began their travels across the earth. As did you."

"Yes. We went separate paths. Although, they will always fear our reunion."

"I'll be there to witness such an event. If a battle does become of it, you have me, and the Fellowship on your side."

"Just as I will stand with you against those Yonderers."

"Will you stand with us after you've ended Halo Lock and his Liege?' Rilla questioned.

"Well yes."

"Excellent spirit you have. We'll find out once we're on the battlefield. But for now, we wait."

IV

YONDERERS OR UNKINDS?

Edge and the Yonderers all sat in the main room of the base, reflecting on their encounter with the Unkinds. A day had passed, with several of the young nubreeds repairing the wall of the base with their abilities of speed and strength. The next day after Edge had compiled every known information regarding the interstellar species he could find. Including reading an article about a farmer who encountered their landing and even spoke with them. Stating they were interested in nubreeds.

"We must be ready for their return." Edge said.

"Return?" Emerald questioned. "What would give them a reason to bother us again?"

A sound of commotion came from the outside, leading them all back into the front where they set their eyes upon Halo Lock and his Liege. The Yonderers stood guard with Edge in front. He saw their appearance and stature. He knew they were unkinds.

"Are they?" Lois asked.

"They are."

"We've been looking for you." Halo Lock said, stepping forward toward the steps. "I am Halo Lock and this is my liege. We've been seeking the ones called nubreeds. We've traveled a great length."

"We know who you are!" Valinor yelled. "Your kind attacked us."

"Our kind?" Aquila said. "Are you sure they were one of us?"

"There were enough." Edge said. "The one who led them talked of domination. Our extinction."

"You speak of Romanus. He is one of us in species. But not in allegiance."

"Yet, your all unkinds. You all seek the same goal."

"We do not."

"Payback must be given." Emerald said.

"Is this what you want?" Halo asked. "We only came to learn of your kind. Not to fight."

"This Romanus has another motive than you and your followers." Edge said.

"Again. He is one of us. Yet, not with us."

Edge walked down the stairs, facing Halo. He looked into his eyes, seeing similarity of the stars above. The Yonderers stood, waiting for the signal as were Halo's liege. They stood still. Each side waiting for a move. Edge nodded as did Halo.

"Let us talk."

"Thank you." Halo said.

Edge escorted Halo and his liege into the Yonderer home with the team keeping their eyes locked on them, entering the home behind them. Edge led them to the main room where he and Halo spoke concerning their differences and what had transpired with Romanus' earlier visit. Outside of the room, Aquila sat with Lois.

"Are you the queen of this place?" Aquila asked.

"Not exactly."

"There must be some form of royalty here. I assume the man talking with my husband is the king."

"No. Edge is not a king. He's a professor."

"He teaches you? All of you?"

"Yes."

"What about?"

"How to live in a world where others refuse to accept you for who you are."

"Hmm. Sounds like us."

"I guess everyone deals with it in some way."

"It's nature to many kinds across the planes."

Edge and Halo sit conformably at the table, discussing their views on the nubreeds and unkinds. Halo told Edge of their history. How they left their previous home world and came to this world. Seeking a place to refuge and later call home. Edge questioned Halo on their enthusiasm to meet nubreeds. Halo replied by stating the nubreed are not that different in nature to the unkinds. Although, there is more of a royalty mindset and culture to the unkinds as opposed to the general civilized nature of some nubreeds.

"What do you plan to do about Romanus?" Edge questioned. "I know he's not working alone."

"He has his followers. They do whatever he commands."

"I wasn't speaking of his followers."

"I'm not understanding. You mean he's working with someone else. Someone of his nature?"

"I know a guy. He's very similar to Romanus in every way. Aside from the ambush."

"Is he a nubreed?"

"He is. General Rilla is his name. a militant nubreed. Desires for all on the earth to submit to the nubreed species. With him as their leader."

"You believe Romanus and Rilla are working together. Trying to get us to fight each other while they sneak in and attack at the last moment."

"It's a plan Rilla would use to his advantage."

"Then we must prepare ourselves for the coming fight." Halo declared. "I will tell my liege everything. Get them prepared."

"I will do the same with my students. It's good we see things the same."

Edge and Halo walked out to their respective sides, telling them of their discussion and next phase of plans against Romanus and Rilla. Halo and his liege left, seeking to find Romanus and his followers. Meanwhile, Edge gathered the Yonderers together, preparing them for the fight against Rilla and Romanus. Lois looked around the room before turning to Edge.

"I think we might need some extra assist."

"I have an idea." Edge said. "Would you accompany me?"

"Sure. Where are we going?"

"To ask someone for help."

V

TERROR AND HORROR

Edge and Frost traveled further out of Chicago, reaching the base of John Terror. Exiting the car as they walked toward the door, Lois was a slight hesitant. She wondered if Terror would help them in this battle. Edge declared Terror would because he himself is a nubreed and will be on Romanus' radar eventually if he is not stopped. Edge knocked on the door and it opened.

"What are you doing here?" Terror asked, standing at the door.

"John, we need your help." Edge said. "It is of a great matter."

"Greater than the Steelers?"

"Much greater."

Terror nodded.

"Let's talk. Only because you're a decent man."

They entered the lair, seeing Carl Prater and Jade Horror working. Edge nodded with a smirk.

"I see you have company."

"They can hear whatever you're proposing."

"Proposing?" Jade said. "What's going on?"

"They're a new species upon this world. They call themselves the Unkinds."

"And?" Terror said.

"They want all nubreeds extinct."

"For what purpose would they come for us? Why not the humans first?"

"Because we'll panic faster." Carl noted. "It's only the truth."

"They have a leader. In fact, two leaders."

"I see. And you want myself to align with you and your team once again to face these leaders?"

"No. only one. The other leader will be assisting us with a team of his own. Not all of the Unkinds share the same motives."

"Ah." Terror scoffed. "Good to hear."

"That is not all. General Rilla and his Fellowship are aiding them in the fight against us."

"Rilla again, huh." Terror said. "Can't the guy give it a rest."

"Unfortunately, no." Lois added. "He believes that helping the Unkinds eliminate us will give him the opportunity of achieving what he craves."

"It's a tactic he would use."

"So, will you help us against Rilla and the Unkinds?"

Terror stood by his desk, he looked over to Carl and Jade. Carl nodded, Jade gave him a shrug. Terror hung his head and grinned.

"Hell, as long as this doesn't interfere with my work, I'll help once again."

"We appreciate it highly."

"He's not going alone." Jade said. "I'm coming too."

"More nubreeds the better." Edge noted. "Is he coming along as well?"

"Me? No. I'll stay here. Keep the place secure. Don't worry, John."

"I won't. You know what to do." Terror said. "Jade, let's get out gear."

Terror and Horror gathered their gear, dressed in their combat attire. Jade's new attire was sleek and slimier to Terror's own, except the insignia on her torso was a mix between the letters J and H. Lois spotted it out, pointing.

"I see you have one of your own."

"I wasn't sharing his."

"We're ready."

"We'll head back to the others. Prep for what's ahead and find out where Rilla and Romanus are located."

"You sure they won't draw us out? I mean that's what Rilla intends to do."

"You're positive on that?" Lois wondered. "Rilla isn't that ignorant of the methods."

"What better way to bring out the Yonderers and this other Unkind leader without a call to challenge."

"Right now, we discuss matters with the team. Deal with Rilla's possible challenge later."

VI

TWO SIDES, ONE FUTURE

Edge and Lois returned to the Yonderer homestead with Terror and Jade riding behind them on their motorcycles. They entered the base, seeing the Yonderers themselves. Terror, once more, found himself aligning with others like himself and he smirked.

"At this again aren't we." Terror said.

"Everyone, listen." Edge said. "We will take the battle to those unkinds. Halo Lock has already agreed to help us. As we will be helping him and his followers."

"How are we going to do all of this?" Valinor asked. "I mean, are we going to just call out those guys or something?"

A loud burst erupted from the outside. Terror sighed as the Yonderers ran to see it. Terror walked out of the doors behind them, seeing Rilla, the Fellowship, and the Unkinds led by Romanus standing in front of him and the Yonderers. The gate to the homestead was destroyed by their entry.

"Those the guys?" Terror asked.

"Yes." Edge replied. "That is them."

"They don't look tough."

"Cullen." Rilla yelled. "It appears we have found ourselves in another conflict. One so of bloodlines."

"Why align with them, Raymus? Why not go against them and their plan?"

"Romanus shares my motives. In order to achieve victory, we must first eliminate the opposing obstacles in the course. Such as your Yonderers are in my way, the weak king of the Unkinds is in the path

301

of Romanus."

Romanus looked around, not seeing Halo Lock or his liege anywhere on the Yonderer grounds. The sight of it enraged him. Yet, he kept calm."

"Where could he be?" Romanus questioned.

"You've made the decision to attack us at our home?"

"It's a better fit for it. I mean, the city's already seen enough damage from our conflict with the Steelers and McKnight. Chicago doesn't need to suffer once again for you to get my point."

"We don't have to do this." Edge stated. "There's no need for us to fight one another. Not again."

"You don't always get what you desire, old friend."

From the sky cracked down a large bolt of lightning. Within the lightning was Halo Lock and his liege. Romanus stumbled in his steps as Rilla and his Fellowship looked on. Halo's eyes were set on Romanus as he and the liege stood at the side of the Yonderers. Terror stared at them.

"These are the good ones?"

"The ones we know of." Lois said.

"Let's see what they can do."

Romanus stepped forward as his mouth foamed toward Halo Lock.

"This is my time, Halotarus!"

"It didn't have to be this way." Halo said. "However, you've made your choice and we've made ours."

Romanus screamed in rage as his followers rushed toward Halo Lock and his liege. Rilla noticed the beginning and signaled the Fellowship to attack the Yonderers. Edge did the same as the Yonderers rushed into battle with Terror and Horror joining them. Rilla and Romanus stood back and watched the ongoing fight. Edge did the same, keeping his eyes on the two leaders. Valinor and Frost took the fight to Cosmic Card and Mistress Destroyer. Omega Thunder and X-Manta were clashing with Emerald and Crystalax in the battle of the elements. Thunder and mineral colliding. The Marine fought off against The Surf. The rushing of the sudden waters were only a brush of air toward the Marine. Eerie used her supernatural powers against the sheer force of Gale's wind. Jackhammer did what he could to catch up to Magic Carpet's speed in the air. Halo's liege fought fiercely against the Followers of Romanus. Brutality against those of their own kind. Terror and Horror were in between the battle. Fighting against both nubreeds and unkinds alike.

"This is slightly different than the Steelers." Jade said.

"Doesn't matter." Terror said. "They're still the enemy."

"Is this what you wanted?" Rilla asked Romanus. "To see your own kind decimate one another?"

"If it achieves victory, it must be done."

Rilla nodded with a grin.

"You are fit to rule your people. Just as I am fit to rule over the nubreeds."

"However, Rilla, I cannot allow the nubreeds to continue to exist once I become king of the Unkinds."

"Where has this talk come from?"

"It was always my plan. To rule over my own and to dominate the rest. The nubreeds are the perennial threat. Such as you to me."

Romanus blasted Rilla against the ruins of the gate, shocking Edge. Romanus did the same toward the battle and Edge. Rilla arose, his eyes surging with energy as he levitated into the air above the battle.

"You have destroyed your chances!"

Romanus watched Rilla in the air and quickly Romanus was taken down by Halo Lock, who stood over him with his foot on his neck.

"Is this how your rule shall be?" Romanus jolted. "Your foot on our people's throat?"

"That is your definition of rule. Not mine."

"Stand aside, Unkind King!" Rilla yelled from above.

"Leave Romanus to me. We will deliver him a just judgment."

"I cannot abide with an attack on myself nor my kind by any other race. This ends now."

"Rilla, cease yourself!" Edge yelled. "Do not harm him!"

"You ally with him, Cullen?!"

"I align with the good I see. Halo Lock is good. Let him deal with Romanus in their own way."

"What makes you sure this will ot happen again?"

"Because I am their king." Halo declared. "In my rule, such actions will not take place nor require such a sheer force of retaliation. This is my statement toward you. You and the nubreeds will never have to concern yourself with the threats of any unkind. If they do bring a threat, they are not of my service and I will not come to aid them. They will be destroyed by their adversaries."

Rilla sighed and came back to the ground, standing over Romanus and facing Edge and Halo Lock.

"I will see to your words, Unkind King."

"They are trustworthy."

"This battle between us, our ideologies is not over, Cullen."

"There's no need for violence. Not today."

"As you say. For if I knew I was being set up for betrayal, I would've killed Romanus sooner than we had come."

Rilla looked out to the battle, rallying his Fellowship as they took their leave. Some defeated. Few victorious. Halo's liege gathered Romanus' followers and took them afar off.

"That's it?" Terror joked. "It's over already?!"

Afterwards, Edge spoke with Halo in detail, concerning their matters and ways between nubreeds and unkinds.

"If something like this happens again, we will come and assist you." Halo said.

"I appreciate such an offer, but, I believe the Yonderers can handle threats like these themselves."

"I wasn't referring to Rilla and his followers. I mean the others out there. Those 'risen heroes' the humans speak of. What happens if they choose to come across your path?"

"I'm not sure that will happen."

"As you are aware, never take something such as a possible war as just a theory."

Edge nodded.

"Duly noted. Where are you and your liege off to?"

"To a place where we can live peacefully and where I can rule in servitude."

"I wish you the best."

"And I you, Professor of the nubreeds."

Halo and his liege left the Yonderer homestead. Edge remained in his office. Calm as the Yonderers went back to their studies and training. Terror and Horror returned to the base. Elsewhere, General Rilla spoke to his Fellowship about the current possibilities of a larger war involving nubreeds, unkinds, and humanity. Rilla began preparing them for the cause without haste. He knew it was only a matter of when, not if it would come to pass.

DARK TITAN ONE-SHOT
THE MYTHOLOGISTS

Jacob Wilson sat in the British Library of London, England. He sat at a table near the King's Library. Jacob is a frequent visitor of the library due to his time in school. Always near and within. Drinking a cup of coffee, sitting near him is a book on Oceania mythology. An avid reader of such histories, Jacob became well-verse in the art of understanding. His knowledge of mythologies stood superb.

While sipping his coffee and glancing through the pages of the book, a man approached the table. Well-dressed in a suit and middle-aged. Jacob looked up to him. His first thought was the man was an employee of the library, but his presence told a different story.

"I see you're into the Oceania myths."

"I am. Seeing how they compare to the others."

"Ah, you're trying to understand how they communicate with the Greeks? Or the Egyptians?"

"Maybe."

"Or you're trying to comprehend the Oceanic to the Maori or the Aboriginal Australians?"

"You know of them?"

"I do."

"It's interesting to speak with another who knows of them."

"Well, their gods aren't quite superior to those of the mainstream. Most of humanity prefer Odin or Zeus to give them a spark. Not the Oceanic ones."

"Then you know of the *Maui* and *Tawhaki* Cycles?"

"Of their tales of becoming heroes? I am deeply aware. So deep, that both Maui and Tawhaki represent the tendencies of the liberal and conservative within human beings."

Jacob nodded with a smirk.

"You know them well."

"I'm at the age where I know many things."

"How did you come into studying mythologies?"

"Myself and my crew, we're... well-versed in every mythology known to man and history."

"Your crew?"

"There are many of us. I just happen to be the one to grab the books for the study."

"I've never heard of a group of mythologists."

"It's a secret ordeal. Only a few are aware of such existence."

"Why?"

"Because, simply put, we cannot allow the base-minded of humanity to enter the doors. Otherwise, the group would tumble into the abyss."

"What if they wanted to prove themselves? To see if they could join?"

"Then, they would be where you are right now. You have the knowledge. The mindset. The skills of study. You would fit well alongside us. Our purpose is the key."

"Purpose?"

"I cannot speak of such things in the public forum. However, I will give you an invite to one of our meetings being held tonight here in London."

The man handed Jacob a card. Looked as if it was a business card, However, upon the card was an address and an insignia. Jacob stared hard at the symbol.

"I've never seen this symbol before. What is it?"

"You'll find out if you agree to come."

Jacob took another look at the card.

"It's your call." The man said.

Jacob placed the card in his pocket, he looked up and the man was gone. Nowhere in sight.

"Huh." Jacob uttered under his breath.

When nightfall had come, Jacob went to the location listed on the card. Finding himself walking on the grounds of the Middle Temple in the City of London. Unsure he would be granted entry, he noticed those around him didn't approach him. They didn't cease him nor did they try to stop him. They all nodded. Jacob felt strange by such responses. All silent in sound, but very loud in action. Jacob entered the Temple, walking into the Hall.

Inside, sat a long rectangular table and around it were twelve individuals. Seven men and five women. All ranged in different nationalities and cultures. Jacob was still, he looked out and saw the man he met in the library and walked over toward him.

"Excuse me, sir."

The man looked and saw Jacob. A smile appeared upon his face.

"You decided to come."

"Yes, I didn't know such a thing like this existed."

"Well, you're seeing another view of the world. One not many will ever have the opportunity to see."

The man gestured for Jacob to sit at the table, which everyone else was doing. Jacob sat next to the man as they were served dinner. The table was covered in dishes, each one came from another culture in the world. The diversity was clear in the group. Jacob was amazed. They ate and afterwards, the table was cleared of the food and out came the books. Thick books, very old with worn-out leather binding. Some of the books were written in Old English, Persian, Latin, and Aramaic. Jacob felt as if he was in another world. His eyes gazing at the books. Books hundreds, perhaps thousands of years old. The man leaned in over to him, sliding over a book.

"I think you'll be interested in this one."

Jacob grabbed the book. No title was on the cover, Jacob opened it and saw the words were written in *Paleo-Hebrew*. He shook his head.

"How did you come across something such as this?"

"We have our ways."

"This language? I thought it was only written on scrolls."

"Things the world has been taught are not what they seem."

"What do you mean?"

"Look around. See all of us in this hall. We come from different parts of the world, yet we share the same values and goals. To make this world better for the generations to come. This is how we start. By restoring what has been lost."

'Then, why is this a secret. How come you don't tell the public about this?"

"If we were to do such a thing, it would put a target on our heads. Not only of the natural, but of the others."

"Others? Like governments?"

"Higher than governments." The man nodded. "Come with me to the library. I'll explain everything there."

Jacob followed the man into the library of the Temple. It was only the two of them, surrounded by more of the books the others were gazing through. Jacob also saw the globes designed by Emery Molyneux.

"It's better you sit for what I am about to tell you."

Jacob sat down at the table. The man stood by the wall and reached into his jacket pocket, taking out a cigar and lit up. Inhaling and exhaling.

"You can smoke in here?"

"It's our place. We are obliged to. Cigars for the most part, of course."

The man took another puff of the cigar before sitting down in front of Jacob.

"The truth of such a group as this is simple, yet complex. It only depends on the mind of the listener."

"I'm listening."

The man nodded with a smile.

"Good. This group is no ordinary group. We're a secret society. Kept hidden from most of the world because our purpose is deemed tyrannical and cynical to most of the general public."

"Tyrannical?"

"We do not wish to enslave humanity. Only to open their eyes to the true ways of the world."

"I noticed one of the books on the table was a grimoire."

"It's good you did. I'm sure that gives you a better understanding as to what and who we are."

"You all practice magic?"

"Some do. Myself, I stick only with history and the power of the ancients. When I said governments and the public would try to shut us down. I didn't tell you the other half of the story."

"And that half would be?"

"The deities you read about. The ones in all the mythologies. They exist."

Jacob sat back in the chair, rubbing his chin and gazing around the library. He leaned in toward the table.

"I'm not understanding. How? It makes no sense."

"To the natural mind of man, it does not. However, what we have discovered over many centuries, is these mythologies we've come to know them as just stories. Tales of legends and fables. But, what we have learned is the true fact. These tales are not myths. The legends are real. The accounts are real. It all happened."

"Where's the proof?" Jacob asked. "How can I believe you if I haven't seen them myself?"

The man nodded.

"The risen heroes."

"Can't be. They're not like the gods in the myths."

"Are you sure about that? Look at them. Their feats. Their power. The things they can do and have done. They are the purest sign of the tide turning. The heroes shall come first and the gods come after. The heroes are here and the world is aware of them. We now, wait upon the gods to make themselves known."

"Now, I'm curious. Have any of you met one of these heroes or the gods?"

"No. but, our leader has met with something from the other side."

"You speak of the supernatural."

"Yes. That is what I was referring to when I spoke about opposition. The supernatural realm doesn't take our society too well. There are a particular few who desire us to disappear. For their good purpose."

"Who are they?"

"Their names I do not know. I know only what the ancients had called them. There were three. One was deemed the Hunter of the Realms. He carried wrath wherever he went. The second one was referred to as Haunting Wanderer. He would always appear when there was someone in dire need. Be it near-death or near-revelation."

"And the third?"

"He was called by many names. But, the one that has stuck with me is the Keeper of the Cosmos. He controls all the darkness in the universe. An Astral entity. He is one I dare not to come across."

"What happens if you do?"

'Then, it will be the end of the Mythologists. Period."

Jacob took in the information and kept it close. He glanced at his watch, amazed by the time which had gone by.

"I need to get home."

"Understood."

Jacob stood up and so did the man. He extended his hand toward Jacob.

"It was a pleasure to meet you, Jacob.

Jacob shook his hand in respect.

"I have to ask, you never told me your name."

"Ah. The society calls me Deimos."

"As in the Greek God?"

"It's what they've given me." The man replied. "Best be seeing you."

Jacob nodded and left the Temple.

Inside the library, Deimos sat still as another individual entered. He was cloaked in a white robe and hood. Deimos gazed upon him and bowed his head.

"I wasn't aware you would be here."

"I'm always near. What of you talks with the young lad?"

"He's very intelligent. I believe he can become one of us."

"Very well. Keep an eye on him."

"Yes sir."

While Jacob walked home, he found it strange there was no one else outside. No sign of any vehicles of any kind. Finding it weird, he began to move faster. Upon his footsteps, a peculiar mist arose from the ground.

Jacob looked in fear and immediately he turned around, finding himself staring at an entity. Dressed in a dark blue cloak, suit, and hat. His eyes clear with no pupils, yet they were glowing and shined bright as the moon. His facial hair and long hair were white as snow.

"Who are you?"

"I am one of the three Deimos told. I was known as the Haunting Wanderer in the times past. Now, humanity refers to me as he Visitant Outlander."

Jacob stood still. Fear grabbed him.

"Do not fear me, Jacob Wilson. For I am not of the malevolent side of life."

Jacob calmed down. The fear which held him had evaporated.

"Why have you come to me?"

"To give you a revelation. Your life is about to change, Jacob. The life you shall live will be drastically different than the lives of the average. You will suffer loss and you will receive gain. You will come across those of a good nature like myself and others present in evil."

"Are the Mythologists evil?"

"They're neutral. But, their goals conflict with the laws of the true nature. The spiritual realms deem them cinderblocks into the hearts and minds of the faithful. That shall not happen to you."

"How do you know?"

"Because I know the end from the beginning. I've seen your life up till now. The lives of others. I've interacted with a few of the risen heroes and others such as yourself. You will receive a change soon. Best to be prepared."

The mist evaporated and the Visitant Outlander disappeared. Jacob turned around at the sound of a horn, seeing a car pass by. Around him were other vehicles and pedestrians. Jacob scratched his head, turning back and forth.

"What I have gotten myself into?"

JACOB WILL BE SEEN AGAIN AND THE MYTHOLOGISTS WILL RETURN

CREED: MEDIEVAL TIMES

I

VISITATION

Creed mediated in the clouds during the night. His eyes closed, the aura of his power surging around him as his cloak bellowed with the moving air. From behind him, a loud bang sounded, getting his attention. Once Creed's eyes opened, he turned back seeing what had caused the sound and from its location appeared a very bright light. The light was brighter than the sun, yet its brightness had no effect on Creed. Within the light, Creed saw a figure approaching. He raised himself up, levitating in the air as the figure emerged from the light.

"You." Creed said.

"It's time we've met."

The figure appeared like a woman. Elderly in age. She was clothed in a long black dress, decorated with rubies, sapphires, and emeralds within the lining. She also wore a medallion made of platinum with a carbuncle gem. Her flowing white hair shined with the light as did her white eyes which glowed in similar fashion.

"Why have you come, Madam Age?"

"To give you a warning. Someone is coming."

"Let me guess. Adrambadon is crawling back up from the Cryptic Zone?"

"No. He is currently occupied with other matters."

"Then, who is coming?"

"Medieval is coming."

"Medieval?"

"You are aware of him, aren't you? The knightly figure that caused the massacres throughout the Middle Ages. He's the one responsible for the Crusades. All of them."

"Why is he coming here?"

"He's looking for you."

"For me?"

"You prove to him as a great challenge. You remind him of another."

"I guess this other one didn't get the task done."

"He did. Just that was hundreds of years in human time."

"How soon will this Medieval figure be here?"

"Very soon. I've informed Ananchel about the circumstance. She will meet with you soon and give you the other details."

"Other details? Why won't you tell me?"

"It's not my duty. It's hers."

Madam Age walked back into the light and as she did, the portal closed and the light dimmed out. Behind Creed appeared Ananchel, flying down from the heavens. The two greeted one another before Ananchel noticed the last remnants of Madam Age's portal.

"She already told you?"

"Said you have something else to add." Creed mentioned. "What is it?"

"I have some information on Medieval. He's moving with great energy and speed outside the realms of time and space from the Middle Ages. That's how he's making his way here."

"Then why don't those on the outside stop him from breaching into our time?"

"They have matters of their own."

"I'm sure someone is watching."

"Oh, they are. But, it's complicated as you are aware."

"I comprehend. What must I do to ensure this Medieval figure doesn't cause any harm?"

"Simply wait for him to make himself known."

"Why not just stop him in his tracks?"

"Because, when he does show up, he's coming for you. You're the reason for his arrival. Not Adrambadon or Demonticronto. He wants to face you."

"Madam Age said he's after me because of another in his time."

"Yes. Another Creed from the Middle Ages."

"Another Creed?"

"I know this is a lot to deal with. But, right now, just prepare yourself for Medieval's arrival."

"I can't just sit here in the air and wait for him."

"It wouldn't do any good anyway. Medieval can't fly or levitate. He's ground-based. You'll have to meet him upon the soil."

"Where must I go to ensure there are no innocents in the surroundings?"

"Head to a peculiar cemetery in the west. There, you'll meet a man called the Caretaker. He's dealt with Medieval before and I know he'll give you some advice on him."

"The Caretaker."

"Yes. You two should get along well."

Ananchel hovered higher into the air above creed. Looking up toward the heavens.

"I must know about this other Creed you've mentioned."

"In time." Ananchel said before flying off.

II

ANCIENT TALES

Creed appeared in the cemetery, which was far further west from his current location. Creed walked upon the grounds, passing by the dozens of headstones and statues. Tall figures of angels in the catholic fashion. Other statues were those of Freemasonry. Brotherhoods and Sisterhoods. Creed's cloak flowed with the incoming gusts of wind. He walked further and saw a man standing still, a shovel in his hand.

"Are you the Caretaker?" Creed asked.

"Who wants to know?"

"That's why I asked."

The man turned around, facing Creed. Creed saw his face. One of an elder. He wore a wide brim hat and a black duster. He stuck the shovel into the ground and approached Creed with a stillness in his eyes. Yet, there was life in them. A lot of life.

"You're him aren't you?" The man said. "The Unholy Knight."

"I am. I suspect you must be the Caretaker."

"Correct. Ananchel already told me everything that's going on. Right now, we need to discuss the proper planning."

"Do you know who Medieval is?"

"I am familiar with him. However, he's not human as some of the stories tell. He's a spirit. A spirit which thrived during the second and third crusades."

"He's never been a mortal."

"Although, he shares their desires and their lusts. He craves war. In the Templar texts, he was referred to as a god of war."

"I never assumed I would be up against a god. Nonetheless, a war god."

"Now, since we are aware of Medieval's arrival, the strategy is to face him head-on."

"Head-on?" Creed asked. "Just the two of us?"

"I've heard of the things you've done. Facing the likes of Adrambadon and Demonticronto. My friend, you are capable of facing Medieval on your own."

"Noted. Perhaps I should do that."

"It's what Madam Age wants." Caretaker added. "She sees you as a powerful force who can combat the darker entitles at work. You're different than the other Creeds who've come before you."

"Ananchel told me you've dealt with Medieval yourself in times past."

"I did."

"What happened?"

"It was during the third Crusade. I was a member of the Knights Hospitaller. During the battle in Acre, Medieval appeared on the field and slaughtered all the Muslim forces of Saladin, giving way for us to achieve victory. But, that wasn't his desire. He attacked all of us and killed many. I fought against him with three of my brothers-in-arms. I alone survived the attack and sent Medieval on his way back into the spirit realm."

"You defeated him?"

"My skill set was enough to keep me alive. Medieval saw my integrity and grit as a badge of honor. He let me live."

"Will he do it again?"

"Probably not. It won't be the same this time."

"I have to ask. What is all of this about other Creeds?"

"You're one in many. During the Crusades, there was one. He stayed to himself and only appeared when there was a battle to be won. He was a mystery and still is."

Creed looked over near one of the headstones and saw a quickening shadow dash right before his eyes. Creed stood his guard as the Caretaker saw his stance.

"What is it?"

"We're not alone out here." Creed said. "Someone else is watching us. Closely."

From behind Creed, the shadow bolted like lightning, striking Creed and knocking him into the Caretaker. The two fell to the ground and Creed looked up, seeing the shadow figure molding into a physical form. Upon its body was the armor of a knight. 14th Century armor in detail. Covered in a black and worn-out tunic with no insignias or shields pertaining to any kingdom or country. He wielded a sword.

"Is that him?" Creed asked.

"No. That's not Medieval. But, he's dressed like it."

Caretaker stepped forward to face the entity with Creed's cloak surrounding the area. His shovel in hand.

"What's your name, spirit?" Caretaker asked.

"My name?" The spirit said with a hallowing voice.

"Yeah. You have a name. What is it?"

"My master calls me Middle Age."

"Middle Age?" Caretaker paused. "As in one from the period?"

"It is what I am."

"You don't belong here. Take your sword and walk on out of this cemetery."

"I cannot. For I have come under commands. To send you both elsewhere."

"Where's Medieval?" Creed asked.

"You'll see him soon. Right now, you must go there."

"Go where?"

"I'll show you."

Middle Age raised up his sword, striking the air, thus creating a rift between time and space. Caretaker looked on as did Creed. Middle Age turned toward them as the dark blue hue from the rift grew.

"Where does this go?" Caretaker asked.

"It goes where my master wants you to go."

"Alright, you smartass."

Middle Age took his sword and swiped the end of it against Caretaker's back, knocking him into the rift. Creed swooped over and grabbed the sword. Middle Age laughed before pushing creed into the rift himself. After entering the rift, Creed and Caretaker find themselves falling down within a portal. They collapse onto the grounds of somewhere else. Somewhere far from the cemetery. Creed stood up and looked around.

"Where are we?"

Caretaker stood on his feet and observed the surroundings. He knew.

"Ah shit."

"What?"

"I know where we are."

"How do you know?"

Caretaker pointed ahead of them. Creed looked out and saw bodies of knights on the ground. Blood covering their armor. Some wore the crests of the Knights Templar.

"We're in the past." Caretaker said.

"The past?"

"We're in the medieval times now."

"If I may ask, what year?"

"1202."

III

1202 AD

Creed and Caretaker walked over the field of bodies while hearing the clashing echoes of swords in the distance. With the sound of swords were screams. All of which were in a rage.

"We need to reach the battle." Caretaker said.

"Let me have a look."

Creed hovered himself into the air, passing over the trees and stone walls to see the battle before his eyes. What Creed saw was a battle of the Crusades. The Knights Templar were fighting against the Muslims. A gruesome sight to see. Creed wasn't bothered by the falling limbs and bodies. Blood covered the grounds.

"What do you see?" Caretaker asked.

"Templars. Muslims. This is a Crusades' battle."

Creed looked closer into the armies of men, finding Middle Age in the midst of the battle, killing both Templars and Muslims without being seen by the human eye.

"Middle Age is there!"

"Good. We need to get to him fast."

"Allow me."

Creed grabbed Caretaker by his arm and flew over the walls and into the middle of the battle. Quickly they were caught into the attacks of the Templars and Muslims. In the fighting, Creed fell a strange disturbance in the air. Something familiar to himself. What he was sensing wasn't Middle Age nor was it Medieval himself.

"What is it?" Caretaker asked, after impaling a Templar with his own sword.

"There's another Creed here."

"Ah. I know who you're talking about."

Caretaker looked out and saw him. Riding into battle on an armored horse was a knight. This knight's features were highly similar to Creed's own appearance. Only exceptions were the helmet and the armor. The knight jumped from his mount and crashed into the battlefield, fighting against the Muslims in such a quick succession. Creed watched him fight. Using familiar tactics of his own. Creed could even sense the Cryptic Zone's power upon him.

"He's a Creed."

"One of many." Caretaker said. "There are some things you've yet to learn."

During the Knightcreed's onslaught, another mysterious entity bolted out into the battle on a flaming horse. The flames were not the color of the average fire. These flames glowed with a bright white and blue. The rider himself was dressed in royal garbs covered with armor. His face appeared as a burning skull.

"A Chaser." Caretaker uttered.

"You're aware of them."

"Oh yes. I never suspected one to have been around during this era."

While the two fought in the field, Middle Age appeared before Creed and Caretaker. His sword in hand, ready for the fight.

"Why did you send us here?" Caretaker asked.

"I have my orders."

"I will ask once again. Where's Medieval?"

"He's here." Middle Age answered, moving to the side.

Walking up behind Middle Age was a figure, dressed in beaten and burnt armor. His face covered by the appearance of a skull. His footsteps made the sound of clashing metal. He stood at the height of Creed, yet was leaner.

"I am Medieval."

"I see you're still roaming around this era." Caretaker said. "Why?"

"Because it is where I thrive. Many souls have fallen to my blade. Yours should've been one of them."

"Turned out differently as I recall."

Medieval looked over toward Creed. He scoffed with a nod.

"You're him."

"Who am I?"

"The one they've sent to eliminate me."

"You know of it?"

"I'm a spirit. Time is only a means of travel to my kind."

"Then, you know why I'm on your trail."

"I do. Now, shall we begin?"

Medieval pulled out a shotgun from behind, aimed at Creed. The shot emitted a powerful blast, knocking both Creed and Caretaker back, but Creed felt the blow, causing a major wound on his chest. Caretaker rose up, seeing Creed holding his chest as the reddish-orange blood poured from it.

"Never in my existence have I ever saw the Cryptic-blood pour from one's body. It is something to behold."

IV

THERE'S NOTHING NEW

"Why use such a weapon during this age?" Caretaker asked. "Why not just run toward us with a sword?!"

"Because it is too simple. A weapon such as this is profound in this era. A rightful choice in war."

"I've had enough listening to him speak." Creed said.

"I'm not finished yet." Medieval replied, shooting toward Creed.

Creed moved himself out of the blast range with the strength he still wielded. Medieval sighed. Caretaker circled the enemy and from behind him appeared Middle Age, tripping the Caretaker to the ground. More of the Templar knights and Muslims ran into the foreground where they stood, covering Creed and Caretaker from their sights. Medieval commanded Middle Age to find them. While doing so, Medieval blasted all those who stood in his path, walking through the battle shooting both templars and Muslims. Caretaker carried Creed from the battlefield, laying him aside near a ravaged home. Caretaker saw the wound, it's still bleeding, not as much as before.

"You need to find a way to heal fast."

"I'm doing all I can. What weapon was that?"

"A shotgun."

"That was no simple shotgun. It took me down. Made me bleed. It has to be a weapon made by Adrambadon or someone in the same vain."

The trampling of a horse is heard near the home and came to a solid stop. Creed and Caretaker were awaiting to see who the rider could be and the door of the home opened. Caretaker saw him and Creed wondered with questions.

323

"Caretaker?" The rider said.

"Yes. I see you remember me."

"I do. Why does he have my likeness?"

"Why do you have mine?" Creed asked, staring at the Knight Creed.

"I see now. He's from another time. How far out?"

"From the future. Approximately eight-hundred and eighteen years."

"The Cryptic Lineage continues further I see. Well, no matter for the cause. He's wounded greatly."

"He just needs a moment to heal."

"I will handle it."

Knight Creed walked over and knelt in the presence of Creed. Placing his right hand upon Creed's chest and without a moment's notice, the wound was healed. Caretaker was astonished by the quickness of the process.

"I never knew you could heal others."

"It comes and goes. Mainly a cause for the battles."

Knightcreed helped Creed to his feet and the two gave a nod of exchange.

"Why are you both here in this era?"

"We were brought here by Middle Age. He's working with Medieval."

"You're saying what we're doing right now has no affect on the events of the future concerning Medieval?"

"They have affects. Just for a moment in time."

"You can't stay here any longer. The more you linger, the quicker you cause yourself to evaporate from the timeline."

"We don't know how to get back." Caretaker said.

"I will aid you. I have an ally who's out here that can transcend time and space. He'll be your way out of here."

"Where is he at the moment?"

"Battling the Muslims. He's Lord Klarson."

"Klarson?" Caretaker questioned. "I thought he was away when the battle took place."

"No. he's here and his fighting. With power that frightens those who don't believe."

Creed walked toward the door, passing by Caretaker and Knightcreed.

"Let's find him and get going."

"He takes after our kind." Knight Creed said.

"A little too much." Caretaker added.

Walking outside, seeing the battle continuing. Caretaker looked further, finding both Medieval and Middle Age. He pointed toward them, giving the notice to Creed and Knight Creed. Medieval continued blasting knights and Middle Age wandered around the dead bodies, checking their faces under the helmets.

"I see them." Knightcreed said, mounting his horse. "Follow my path and I will lead you to Lord Klarson."

"Will do." Creed replied.

Knightcreed rode off into the battlefield with Creed and Caretaker following. Right in the battle, Knight Creed took down several Muslims and Templar knights, giving an open pathway to Creed and Caretaker. While doing so, Middle Age gazed up from the ground over the dead bodies, seeing Creed and Caretaker. He pointed and let out a loud scream, giving the signal to Medieval, who saw them ahead.

"They're mine." Medieval spoke to himself.

Medieval ran with a mighty speed, bolting through the knights and Middle Age followed. Knight Creed led them up a hill, where they stood a small and sturdy temple. Walking out of the temple was Lord Klarson.

"The Chaser I saw." Creed said.

"Lord Klarson." Knight Creed said. "These two need your assistance."

"My assistance on what causes?"

"They need to return to their own time. They come from the future."

"The future? Yes. I see. It explains your doppelganger."

Klarson led them into the temple, where at the forefront was what looked to be a mirror. Nearly thirteen-feet in height and five-feet wide. Creed and Caretaker stood in front of the mirror as Klarson circled it. Knight Creed stood at the door, waiting for Medieval and Middle Age to arrive. Klarson whipped out a strange, sharp chain and he began to twirl it in the face of the mirror. The glass started to warp, forming a wormhole. Klarson's face turned into a skull, covered with sin fire. He pulled the chain back and pointed.

"Walk through and you shall return to your time."

Knight Creed looked out and saw Medieval and Middle Age rushing toward the temple. He grabbed his battle axe, telling Creed and Caretaker he and Klarson will hold them off. Caretaker nodded in a bid of farewell.

"Young one." Knight Creed said toward Creed. "Keep the faith. Never falter in the presence of your enemies."

"I will stand." Creed replied.

They stepped into the wormhole, hearing the clashing battle between Knight Creed and Klarson against Medieval and Middle Age. Medieval caught a slight glance at Creed entering the wormhole and screamed with anger.

"This is not over!"

Entering the wormhole, Creed and Caretaker are thrown back into their time period, right in the cemetery where they previously stood. Caretaker let out a sigh of relief.

"We're back."

"I see." Creed replied. "Although, something's off."

'What do you mean?"

"I can sense the Cryptic Zone. I sense Adrambadon. He's near."

DEATH CHASER—THE DEAL

I

<u>REPENTANCE IS NIGH</u>

It was a late night, elsewhere in a deserted landscape. Only the moon could be present in the midst of the barren grounds. The Death Chaser moved through the land, searching for his next target. A target which may indicate Demonticronto's apparent return. The Chaser did not utter a word.

In another location, John Clarkson continued his training with Widow by his side. He began teaching her the knowledge of the supernatural and the skills to fight against the demonic forces. The Chaser told John to instruct Widow in these ways to increase her faith and the chances for her survival in this world.

Between the physical and spiritual realms of existence, an entity emerged and stepped foot upon the earth. He was tall, dressed in black with dark-blue flashes of light emitting from his face. Only his eyes were as red as blood. Behind him stood three figures, shrouded in the shadows.

"We've arrived." The figure said. "Now, we find this Chaser and put him in his place."

"What of his allies?" Another figure asked.

"What about them? If they get in our way, we take them out. Simple."

"What if they do not?" Another figure questioned. "We leave them be?"

"Yes. We're only here for the Chaser. No one else."

"As you have spoken."

"That I have. Now, the three of you will travel to separate locations. I will give out the signal to bring the Chaser to each of you. Once, he is in your sights, eliminate him. If you fail, I hope the next one succeeds. We must take him out before Demonticronto makes his return."

"We will not fail."

"For your sakes. I hope not."

The three figures turned into mists and flowed above in the air, scattering themselves from Dieheart's presence. Dieheart smirked, holding out his arms with his hands wide open. He closed his eyes and exhaled.

"Soul of Retribution. There is a need that requires your aid. These locations are in need of your acquaintance. Go there. Do your work."

The Chaser continued moving through the desert and while on the move, he looked up, catching a bright flash of light. The light exploded and went into three separate paths. The Chaser knew of the light and the paths it made. He turned his focus from Demonticronto to the three paths and quickly made a right turn, heading toward the first path.

II
THE EARTH LIVETH

The Chaser had found himself after the traveling facing the Grand Canyon. He looked upon the structure of the area and saw a silhouette standing atop the Canyon. Even through the night sky, the Chaser keened his eyes and saw the form of the figure. He knew it wasn't human and stopped himself, pointing toward the figure.

"Whatever you proclaim yourself to be," The Chaser spoke. "Come down and face me."

The figure made its way to the ground to face the Chaser. As it stepped foot on the ground, the two entities shared a stare down. The Chaser could now see what the figure is and he nodded and pointed.

"You don't belong on this plane, demon."

"As a matter of fact, I don't. however, I was brought here in an urgent matter."

"Who sent you here?"

"A friend."

"The name of your friend?"

"You'll find out soon. If you can survive this battle."

"You threaten me?"

"It is my nature."

The Chaser stretched forth his hands and from them emerged the sinfire. The demon grinned, stepping back and raising his own arms, causing the ground to tremble. The Chaser kept his stance and his gaze focused.

"By the way, Chaser. I didn't tell you my name." The demon said. "I am Mineron, the Demon of the Earth."

"Never heard of you."

"Now you have."

Mineron raised up the dirt from the ground, forming it into a boulder. The dirt fell above the Chaser as he moved from the incoming attack. The Chaser rolled over the incoming boulder, turning toward Mineron and blasting him with the sinfire. Mineron brushed of the fire and smirked.

"I am made from the earth you see around you, Chaser." He taunted. "Fire cannot harm me!"

"So you believe." The Chaser replied. "Yet, you are not aware of how the things of the earth are made. What can change them and what can shape them. Yet, I am aware of such matters. This day, you will learn what happens to the earth when it feels the touch of brimstone."

Mineron levitated in the air above the Chaser with his arms stretched out and a large grin on his graveled face.

"Do your best!"

"I shall."

The Chaser twirled his hands and arms in a circle, conjuring the sinfire once more. He kept twirling as the circle grew in size and the flames brightened. Mineron crossed his arms and scoffed at the sight of the flaming circle. The chaser continued until the flames were in between himself and Mineron. The flames were the height of thirteen feet.

"What more is this?" Mineron asked. "What good does a jester trick do to stop me?"

"This is not a trick," The Chaser answered. "but a test. One you have failed."

"I'm ending this." Mineron dove down toward the Chaser.

"Yes, this is the end." The Chaser said, blasting the flaming circle toward Mineron.

Mineron flew directly in the circle and within mere seconds, his body was consumed by the flames. Mineron fell to the ground as the flames did not ceased and the circle started to close itself with Mineron in its grasp. Mineron struggled to get free, but the flames were like a tight band. Mineron couldn't stand up due to the circle as the Chaser walked over toward him, staring him down.

"Is this it?" Mineron asked. "What more must be done?"

"This is your end." The Chaser said. "You are done."

The Chaser waved his right hand and the flames consumed Mineron to the point his body became like magma, pouring from his eyes, ears, nose, and mouth. The Chaser saw Mineron's body melt and quickly freeze. At that point, the Chaser stomped Mineron's head into ashes and left his remains to burn in the sinfire. The Chaser left the Grand Canyon. While leaving, thunder cracked from above with a strange laughter following. The chaser looked up and felt the same energy that was within Mineron coming from the clouds above.

"Another one." The Chaser said.

III

STORMS OF THE AIR

While the Chaser sought after what was roaming in the skies above, John and Widow traveled into a small town. While tracking the source, Widow spotted a place where it read "Fortune Telling" above the doors. She stopped, pointing toward it as John gave a look.

"What about it?"

"We should go in there. See what they know."

"You already know that's not a wise move."

"How come? We need to find out if Demonti is returning soon. Perhaps, the fortune teller inside knows of it."

"There's no need for it. The Chaser will tell us everything when the time is near."

"What if it's hidden from him as well? Look, let's go in there, ask about Demonti, and see what we find. Afterwards, we'll leave and give our results to the Chaser."

John shook his head, looking back and forth between the building and Widow.

"This is on you if something goes wrong."

"I already know. I'll take my judgment justly."

They entered the building. Seeing its walls covered with gems and crystals. Near them in the front was a round table, carved with magical symbols relating to the elements of the earth. Widow approached the table, seeing the markings while John walked around the place, searching for someone. Anyone.

"Is anyone in here?" John asked. "We're at this table. Letting you know."

From the back walked out a young woman. Dressed in a violet dress from her chest to feet. She brushed back her black wavy hair as she approached John and Widow.

"I see visitors this night. I wasn't aware they'll be you."

"What do you mean?" John questioned.

"I knew you were coming here. You work alongside a Chaser."

"Yes." Widow said. "Yes, we do."

"Then, you are aware of why we're here."

"I am. You desire to find answers regarding Demonticronto's imminent return."

"Well, is he returning soon." John asked.

"Please, sit and I shall explain everything to you."

John sat at the table besides Widow while the young woman sat in front of them. She giggled.

"Forgive my manners, my name is Madame LoCasta."

"How long have you done this type of work?" John wondered. "You seem a bit young to be capable of this."

"I was born into this life. Grew up in the arts. Trust me, I am capable of accomplishing what to seek."

The Chaser moved into the skies through the fiery whirlwind and ceased himself in the air. Covered within the dark clouds and seeing quick flashes of lightning surrounding him. He could hear the mumblings of a voice.

"Show yourself, spirit."

A gust of wind blew toward the Chaser, not fazing him nor stumbling him. From there a small whirlwind appeared before him and formed into the image of a man. Yet, this form had the appearance of a man with uncertain features. Reptile-like eyes, long dark wavy and sharp hair. His teeth were like a tiger's and the nails on his fingers resembled claws. His skin was a pale blue. Yet, darker than the morning sky.

"Who are you?" The Chaser asked.

"I am Shinow. The Demon of the Air. Bringer of Storms."

"Who sent you?"

"You will know in good time."

"Your ally said the same before I ended him."

"There's only three of us and yet, you've managed to take one of us out? He didn't tell us you had such strength."

"Who is he?"

"The one who sent us."

"Enough talk, I'm going to finish you off for invading this realm."

"You can try. For one cannot catch the wind."

The Chaser scoffed and from his hands emerged the sinfire and with it he tossed it into the clouds surrounding himself and Shinow. Shinow summoned the wind, seeking to remove the fire, yet the fire was no kindled by Shinow's power. The Chaser bowed his head and a lightning bolt came from behind him, traveling through the clouds and striking the sin fire. Creating a vacuum of flames, burning the air within. Therefore, suffocating Shinow. Shinow raised his hands and rain started to fall from above. The rain was not enough to take out the flames as it had no affect.

"What is this?!" Shinow yelled. "My powers cannot contain the flames!"

"Because the flames burn all that has the residue of sin." The Chaser said. "You, demon of the air are consumed by sin. Therefore, you must burn."

Shinow yelled greatly as the sinfire consumed him. Burning him into nothing more than floating ashes of light. The Chaser sighed as he heard a distant voice higher than the clouds.

"The firmament."

Madame LoCasta sat still at the table while John and Widow waited patiently for an answer. Any answer. LoCasta opened her eyes and they were red as blood. Her pupils could not be seen and it frightened Widow, yet John was not afraid.

"I know you're not LoCasta. Who are you?"

"I am the one you seek." A deep voice said out of LoCasta's mouth with a grin.

"Demonti?" Widow said.

"You believe you can trace my actions. You sought after my patterns and it's led you here. To sit at the feet of a sorceress. What would the Chaser think of you now?"

"We're here on business. Not on some wicked adventure."

"Keep telling yourselves such lies. In time, we shall meet in the flesh. But for now, I wait until the time is appointed and I am called."

"We will stop you." John said. "When the time does come."

"We shall see. But, for now, I suggest you focus on the enemy at hand."

"Enemy?"

"Right at the door."

John turned around, hearing the front door open. He turned back to LoCasta, seeing her eyes have reverted to their natural state and Demonticronto was gone. John looked and saw who was approaching.

"Well, it seems I've just missed my chance to seek some answers."

"And you are?" John asked. "One of Demonti's dogs?"

"No. I am Dieheart. One who has worked with Demonticronto ever since the days began."

"Why are you here?" LoCasta asked. "Do you seek something of value?"

"I'm here to finally see the Chaser's allies. Fitting they'll be in a place like this. Unbeknownst to the Chaser himself."

"I suggest you watch yourself. He could show up here at any moment."

"I'm afraid not. I'm too wise to fall for the tricks of man. The Chaser is currently preoccupied with several of my own forces. Which leaves the two of you alone with me."

"We can handle ourselves."

"I'm sure you can. No need to prepare for a fight. I only came to see you as a warning. Remove yourself from this path or suffer much dire consequences."

"I think not." John said, stepping up to Dieheart. "We will live and die on this path. For The Chaser has shown us what must be done in these last days."

Dieheart nodded, grinning as he crested his chin.

"I see. Very well. When the time does arrive, I hope you're prepared for a quick death."

Dieheart turned and left LoCasta's place. She turned to John and Widow, sighing.

"Did you get all you came for?"

"That and a little more." John replied.

"Thank you." Widow said.

IV
THE SEAS OF THE FIRMAMENT

The Chaser went high into the atmosphere, reaching the second heaven. Looking out toward the sun and the moon across from one another, he listened closely once more, hearing the strange noises coming from higher above. Much higher than the stars around him.

"Is it possible?" The Chaser questioned to himself. "If it is such, this is not a matter of my own. But of the others."

From there, a voice echoed from above the Chaser, speaking in such language familiar to the demons he faced earlier. There, the Chaser knew he was dealing with another demon. However, this one was sitting above the firmament. The Chaser keened his flaming eyes, setting them clearly to focus. Upon focusing, he saw the demon in the waters above. Nearly camouflaged with the darkness.

"You do not belong up there, demon."

"This is the perfect place to settle this business. I'm sure the others won't be bothered by the battle."

"You have trespassed a place beyond your borders!"

The Chaser rushed himself into the seas above. Now covered by the waters and shrouded in the darkness. The demon was invisible to the Chaser's eyes, yet his flaming eyes did not evaporate. The Chaser swam through the waters, he couldn't even seethe second heaven beneath him, except for the piercing dim light near the top of the waters.

"Show yourself." The Chaser spoke.

Right in front of him, the demon morphed from the waters. Creating itself a body from the waters. The demon's appearance was very similar to Shinow, only for the hair to be flowing with water. The Chaser stopped himself, lifting his body upright to face the demon.

"Who are you?" The Chaser asked.

"My name is Flrange. This is my domain."

"Your domain? No demons are allowed to dwell in these parts."

"And you speak for the authority?"

"I speak for those who cannot speak. As they cannot speak such words."

"Go about your business or else I must deal with you swiftly."

"I have come to you to send you into the pit where you belong. With the others."

"You speak of Shinow and Mineron. I am aware of their defeat by your hand. The dealmaker told me of the events."

"Dealmaker?"

"We were sent here by a very powerful ally. To see if you were truly as Demonticronto and the others have said you to be."

"Who is this dealmaker of yours?"

"You'll only find out if you can defeat me."

"I was already set on doing such."

The Chaser grabbed Flrange by his watery coat, however, the water demon twirled himself around in the water, causing the Chaser to loosen his grip. Flrange speared the Chaser through the waters, deep until they impacted into the firmament itself. Not a dent. Flrange held the Chaser down with his foot on his throat and laughed.

"It appears your fire cannot conjure within the waters."

The Chaser's eyes quickly opened, only revealing the sinfire. Flrange stumbled as the Chaser shoved his foot from his throat and the Chaser grabbed Flrange by his neck and covered his face with his other hand.

"You've seemed to have forgotten where we are, demon. There are no boundaries here that you can undo."

The Chaser blasted Flrange with sinfire mixed with the waters and evaporated the demon into nothing but remnants of ash. The Chaser took a moment of refreshment before returning to the earth below. Once returning to the earth, the Chaser placed himself in the presence of John and Widow as they were already seeking his presence.

"Good you're here." John said.

"I felt your sense. I came as I could."

"We've discovered something." Widow said.

"Is it of Demonticronto?"

"It is."

Before John could tell the details, Dieheart appeared before them. Applauding with a great smile. Widow hid behind John as he stood next to the Chaser, who's eyes were piercing with fire. And embers brewing from his hands.

"You managed to do it. You took out the demons."

"I did." The Chaser added. "You must be the dealmaker the water spirit spoke of."

"I am. Allow me to introduce myself to you. I am Dieheart. From a realm not of this earth."

"I am aware. The darkness which consumes you is emitting from your very being."

"Of course. I've already introduced myself to John and Widow. When they were seeking answers from a teller."

The Chaser paused, turning to the two.

"You spoke with a fortune teller?"

"We needed a sure answer." Widow responded. "I thought it would be simple."

The Chaser turned to John, who stood quietly. The Chaser waved his hand before turning to Dieheart.

"The deal has been made, Soul of Retribution."

"What deal?"

"You will find out very soon."

Dieheart sunk into the earth with a laugh fading away. The Chaser looked back at John and Widow.

"We'll discuss this later. Right now, get yourselves some time. Mediate. Pray. Prepare yourself for what's ahead."

"What is ahead?" John asked.

"A greater fight."

TRAVIS VAIL, SPIRIT-SEEKER: LOST GIRLS AND FOUND

I

ANOTHER LOST GIRL

Travis Vail sat at his desk, looking over the cases which have been reported ever since the conflicts with Balthazar, the Sin Phantom, and Demonticronto. Vail remembered his encounters with the other supernatural forces. He chuckled under his breath memorizing their allegiance for the moment. He looked over as his cell phone began to vibrate.

"Who's calling?" Vail answered.

Vail listened and he listened closely. He nodded, taking out a pen and writing down the information. He nodded, ending the call. He looked at what he wrote and shook his head.

"Guess it's begun again."

He grabbed his gear, put on his coat and left. Sometime later, Vail arrived in the town where the call had come.

"Back in Chesterfield." Vail sighed. "Let's see what's happening here."

While in Chesterfield, Vail searched for the caller. The caller left an address for Vail to find. Which he traced, finding the address to be in the suburbs. A quiet neighborhood. Vail saw several children playing with each other in a field across the street. Others rode their bikes down the road. Confused, he found the address and approached the home's front door. Vail knocked. The door answered and Vail was surprised.

340

"Cooper Lawrence?" Vail said.

"Good to see you again, Mr. Vail."

"Wait, you're the one who called?"

"I am."

"But why? What's happened?"

"Come in and we'll explain everything."

"Certainly."

Inside the home, Cooper's wife, Janice saw Vail and she went to greet him. Sitting in the living room was Carrie. Vail saw her and she saw him.

"She's gotten older over the past few years, hasn't she?" Vail said.

"I'm not a child anymore." Carrie said.

"How old are you now? Fifteen? Sixteen?"

"I'm sixteen."

"You're not getting into any trouble, are you?"

"None of a major issue."

"Ah." Vail mumbled."

He turned back to her parents with a concerned, yet unworried look.

"Why did you call me?"

"Please come with us. We'll explain in private."

Vail nodded and followed Carrie's parents into Cooper's office. Once Vail had entered, Cooper closed the door as Vail sat down in front of the desk. Janice sat next to him while Cooper sat behind the desk. Vail was still confused, looking back and forth between Cooper and Janice.

"Why did you call me? I'm not understanding what's happening here."

"We called you because it's starting again." Janice said.

"What's starting again?"

"Carrie's been speaking to someone in her room."

"You're sure it's not just a friend of hers. Perhaps a lad she met at school?"

"No." Cooper said. "That was we thought. Until we overheard her say the name, Leta."

Vail sat back in the chair. Quiet within himself. Leta had returned? Vail was unsure of the possibility.

"Are you sure we're talking about the same Leta? The one who possessed your daughters all those years ago?"

"We're certain." Janice said. "We've never met any of Carrie's friend who have that name."

"You believe Leta is trying to continue what she started?"

"Yes. Why bother our daughter when she's done nothing wrong. She's a good kid."

"That's the thing, Cooper. Good children are often the targets for such spirits."

"So, will you do what you did before?" Janice questioned. "I'm positive it will cleanse her again."

"I will try. But I must be sure of all of this. Carrie's older now and the connection could be deeper than before. I cannot risk anything of importance. Carrie's life depends on it."

"Thank you." Janice replied.

"Please, do what you can." Cooper added.

"I will."

Vail left the home and went to the library, as per usual.

II

REMEMBERING THE ONE BEFORE

Travis Vail sat by himself in the library, reading up on the same files as before. He closed the books and pulled out his phone, dialing a number. On the other end was Raynard Brown. Vail had begun to tell him of Leta's possible return and the connection she has with Carrie Lawrence. Raynard refereed him to search the home's land once more to find anything unusual that may pertain toward the Lost Girl spirit.

"I will do that, Raynard. Just to be sure."

Vail hanged up and left the library, returning to the Lawrence home. While walking back to his car, he saw a homeless man sitting on the sidewalk beside the library. He was cloaked in a black hooded jacket from his shoulders to his knees. He walked with a hunch in his back and frail in his steps. Vail nodded toward him and the man stood up, approaching him. His hands were out and Vail grinned.

"I would give you something if I had anything. I'm sorry."

"Don't be sorry, Spirit-Seeker."

"Pardon?"

The man raised his head up, facing Vail. He stepped back, seeing the homeless man's face. He was old, very old. His long white beard was stretched outward and his eyes were near dim.

"How do you know who I am?" Vail questioned.

"I've been around for a very long time. I've seen those of your kind for many centuries do the work you're doing this day."

"Who are you?"

"I'm only a wanderer, Spirit-Seeker. I come and I go."

"A wanderer? From what part of the world?"

"A place far from here. Across the pond you could say."

"East lands, huh. I see. Well, I need to get going."

"As you shall. For I am aware of the task set before you. The Lost Girl has returned. Hasn't she? Attempting to bond with another host?"

"So I've been told. I'll stop her for good this time."

"I'm sure you will. But, take heed to these words. Her connection with the young girl isn't as simple as you would assume it to believed. For when a spirit goes out of one, it indeed returns much stronger and with friends of its own."

"I know the works. No need to repeat them to me."

"Of course. Now, you will see them in action. Take care, Spirit-Seeker."

Vail nodded, waving away as he turned to his car. He looked back and the man was gone.

"Every time."

III

THE STRANGE CASE OF LETA AND CARRIE

Vail returned to the Lawrence home, seeing Janice running out of the home toward him with Cooper behind.

"What's going on?" Vail asked.

"It's Carrie." Janice said. "There's something wrong with her."

'Wait here. I'll go look to her.'

Vail ran into the home, seeing Carrie standing in the living room completely still. Her hair moved smoothly as if the wind was within the home. Vail couldn't feel it as he approached her.

"Carrie, whatever she has on you, you must fight it."

Carrie did not move. Her hands twitched but could not bend. Her fingers were straightened. As if there was electricity holding them in place. Vail took another step forward and Carrie's head turned toward him in a quick rush. Her eyes were solid black, and she grinned. Vail sighed.

"You're not Carrie."

"I am not."

"Leta, release her from your control. Now."

"You believe this will end as it did before? I have learned much since our last encounter."

"I'm sure you have. Still bothering this young girl with your agendas for control."

"We share a bond. A bond that you broke."

"You don't belong here, spirit."

"Your words will not save Carrie this time. I have grown in such spiritual power since the last departure."

"You will leave Carrie and you will be gone for good."

"Make your move. Spirit-Seeker."

Vail reached into his pocket, taking out his book used in many of his cases. He began to recite a page and while doing such, Leta let out a great laugh. The laugh irritated Vail to the point where his reciting had ceased, and he could not utter the words. Vail immediately felt powerless, seeing Leta had truly grown in the spiritual arts. Peculiar for a spirit in Vail's words. Vail had no other options in his place. He paused himself, seeing the black eyes on Carrie and the laughter of Leta coming from her mouth.

"I know." Vail whispered. "I know what I have to do."

Vail placed the book into his jacket pocket, pointed toward Leta while walking back to the door.

"This is far from over."

"Where are you going?!"

"I have something in mind to get rid of you."

"You believe you can cast me away? After what I've just shown you?!"

"Not me. I know a guy and I'll be back with him on my side. And hers."

"I cannot let you leave."

"You will if you let Carrie have control of her body. When I return, then you can rise up and face me. Then, we'll see who will remain."

"Are you challenging me? Using this young girl as a tool for your works?"

"Truth be told, who's the tool in this story? It's not Carrie."

Vail walked back outside, seeing Cooper and Janice waiting in a slight panic mode. Janice ran up to him with tears in her eyes.

"Is she alright?!"

"Unfortunately, Leta has possession over your daughter."

"Aren't you going to do what you did the last time?"

"I tried. Didn't work."

"Then, what are you planning on doing, Mr. Vail?" Cooper asked.

"I know a guy who can help me with this case. Leta's become far stronger than the last time. I'll need some assistance with this one."

Vail walked to his car before turning back to the Lawrences.

"By the way, your daughter should be back to her senses. Leta would have left knowing what I'm planning on doing. Keep an eye on her until I return."

Vail left the Lawrence home. Traveling nearly afar off into the outskirts, stumbling upon an old building. Vail exited his car, approaching the building. The structure was pre-Civil War, yet with a mixture of medieval architecture. Vail nodded.

"This is the spot."

Vail walked up to the large double-doors and knocked. After a second knock, the doors open. Yet, Vail saw no one. He shrugged his shoulders and entered the building with the doors shutting behind him. The closing of the doors did not faze nor concern him. Vail continued walking forward, finding himself standing in a large room near a corridor.

"Hey, I know you're here." Vail said. "So, do us a favor and come on out."

Vail turned around, seeing a large window and hovering at the window was a silhouette of a figure, levitating in the air. Vail smirked, crossing his arms.

"I know who you are." Vail said.

The figure moved forward toward Vail, as he did not move himself. the figure came into the light and revealed itself to be Doctor Donald Fortune. Vail applauded.

"I knew this was your spot all along."

"One of many." Fortune said. "Why are you here, Travis Vail, Spirit-Seeker?"

"You're aware of my work?"

"I know everything that pertains to the mystic realms which surround our world."

"That's nice. Look, I need your help. It's a major concern."

"My help? Why?"

"There's a young girl. She's possessed by a spirit. A powerful spirit. I need your help in breaking the soul tie between them."

"Last I read, you call on the one who's words you read from your book. Didn't you at least try that?"

"I worked last time. Leta's grown more powerful since then."

"Leta." Fortune said. "The Lost Girl spirit."

"Yes. You've heard of her?"

"I've dealt when her kind before. Just not Leta herself."

"She's become stronger after I sent her away. I'm not sure how."

"You're telling me you were the one who sent her away those years ago?"

"I am. I was younger and much of a novice in those days. But, I did what needed to be done to save the girl."

"Now, Leta's retuned to the same girl and has an even stronger hold on her?"

"That's correct."

"I understand."

Fortune opened the doors of the building to the outside. Vail looked back and forth to the door and to Fortune.

"Aren't you going to tell me what to do? I need to break the soul tie between them."

"Yes, you do." Fortune replied. "However, I will not allow you to go alone."

"Why can't you just tell me what to do? I can deal with Leta myself."

"I need to see this Leta in person. Learn her motives. That way, I can prepare myself and my apprentice in case she returns again in the future."

"Your apprentice? There's no one else here."

"He's preoccupied on a task afar off. Now, are you ready to save this girl?"

"After you."

"I'll meet you there."

"Wait a second, fellow. You don't even know where she is."

"I'll follow your lead. You drove out here after all. You can drive back."

"Can't you just teleport us there. And the car?"

"I can. But, should I?"

"It would prove much faster and speed is what we'll need to get rid of Leta."

"Very true. Stand still."

"Ok. Why-"

IV

A STUBBORN SPIRIT ENTERS THE PIT

Within a sudden moment, Vail and Fortune were standing in front of the Lawrence home. Vail looked around, seeing the home and even his car. He turned to Fortune, who only nodded.

"How'd you do that?"

"The Orb of Quirinto." Fortune answered, showing the org attached to the amulet around his neck. Glowing with mystical energy.

"Where did you get it?"

"A long story not worth telling at the moment. We need to get Leta out of the girl."

"Agreed."

"I'm assuming she's inside." Fortune said.

"Let's go in then."

They approached the door of the home with Janice opening it as soon as she saw Vail. Cooper ran up behind her, confused about Fortune's appearance.

"Mr. Vail, who's the friend?"

"He's going to help me save your daughter."

"Who is he supposed to be?" Janice asked. "Some kind of magician."

"Sorcerer, madam."

"We assumed Vail could handle this on his own." Cooper mentioned. "Like the last time."

"This isn't like the last time." Vail replied. "Leta has a much stronger hold on Carrie. Doctor Fortune is here to aid me in setting your daughter free."

"Is your friend capable of this kind of work?"

"I've faced much more and far worse than a possession. I'm skilled enough."

Cooper nodded, allowing Fortune to enter the home. Upon entering, Fortune saw Carrie's body levitating above the living room floor. Vail entered, seeing the levitation.

"She's getting stronger."

"We have this under control." Fortune said. "I desire to speak with Leta."

Carrie's body moved around in the air as her head turned toward Fortune's gaze and her eyes were locked on. Still black. She grinned heavily, starting Carrie's parents.

"Vail, you've returned. And I see you didn't come alone."

"I did not."

Fortune stepped forward as a gust of wind rustled from Carrie's body, shoving him and Vail back. Fortune twirled his arms and the wind ceased. Vail noticed the tactic and shrugged his shoulders.

"That's convenient."

"Who are you?" Leta's voice asked.

"I am Doctor Donald Fortune. Supreme Enchanter of the mystical realm and I have been brought here to rid you of this young girl and of this material world."

"Supreme Enchanter? Another one?"

"She's familiar with your kind." Vail noticed. "Are you sure you can handle this, Fortune?"

"I am positive." Fortune clapped his hands together with the energy covering them. "Prepare to do your part in this, Spirit-Seeker."

"My part?"

"Do what you've done before. I will handle the rest."

Vail turned to Carrie's parents. Telling them to go outside and wait until the work is done. They agreed with tears in their eyes as the left the house. Vail turned his focus back toward Leta, while Fortune began levitating just a few feet off the ground. Leta had full control over Carrie's body, now posing it against Fortune. Vail slowly reached into his pocket, grabbing his book.

"Do you have what you need?" Fortune asked.

350

"I do."

"Then you're ready."

"I am."

Leta rushed toward Fortune as he stretched forth his arms, creating a barrier between himself and Leta. Vail was in the middle of the barrier with his book opened. Fortune looked toward him and nodded. Vail started to recite from the book the same words as before. Leta's focus was not on Vail, but on Fortune as she tried beating down the mystic barrier. She screamed with rage, punching the barrier. Fortune kept his demeanor. Focused and in control as Vail continued reading.

"Add one more to the speech." Fortune told Vail. "And speak it in something other than Latin."

"I got it." Vail replied. "*Tam qate alhabl alfidiya baynak wabaynaha alan!*"

Leta turned to Vail as he closed the book. Her eyes began to show the pupils as she struggled to hold herself and Carrie together. Her body was fighting between staying levitated and coming down to the floor. She glared toward Fortune as he could see Carrie's eyes starting to appear and Leta's power decreasing.

"You heard him, Lost Girl. The soul tie is broken. Leave. Now."

Fortune clapped his hands and the barrier collapsed as Leta let out a great scream. Carrie's body floated and fell to the floor, not before Vail could catch her. Fortune cleared the home of any residue of Leta's power. About thirty minutes later, Carrie's parents entered the home to find Carrie laying down in her room on the bed.

"Is she alright?" Janice asked.

"She's well." Vail said. "Leta is gone."

"Oh. Thank you. Thank you both."

Fortune nodded. Cooper approached the two and shook their hands. Thanking them for their help. Vail wanted to wait for Carrie to wake up and once she did, he spoke to her with Fortune standing by. Carrie told Vail that she was aware of everything that was happening. She stated she no longer feels the connection she shared with Leta. But, she told him that she could also see Leta's intentions. Her intentions were dire, and she was brought forth by a sorcerer who saw fit to distract Vail from some grander plan.

"Don't concern yourself with our affairs." Vail said. "We're just glad you're alright."

Afterwards, Vail said his goodbyes, hoping he doesn't have to return due to such similar events. Later, Vail spoke with Fortune about Carrie's words and he understood them greatly. Fortune warned Vail about an opposing adversary of his to which Vail stated he had no adversaries. Balthazar could be counted as one, but not a great adversary.

"I'm referring to anyone you met in your early years." Fortune said. "Someone who was very peculiar to your work. Like an opposite of the coin."

Vail thought, "There was one, however I haven't seen him since the investigation."

"I see. Meanwhile, you should keep an eye out. Just in case."

"One more thing." Vail said. "Why did you tell me not to speak the words in Latin?"

"Because you have to get outside of your box when confronting these matters. Spirits such as Leta keep memories, you know."

"Informative of you."

"Arabic was an interesting choice."

"It's the first one that came to mind."

"Good to hear. Just keep watch. All that Carrie told you, do not forget it."

"I will keep it all in mind. Thank you for the assistance, Doctor."

"It was a necessary duty."

Fortune warped the surroundings into a portal back to his true residence, the Citadel of Enchantment. Vail saw the large structure and how it was placed amongst the trees in a wilderness afar off. Vail smirked.

"That's where you reside."

"Indeed. I will be seeing you around, Travis Vail."

"Until next time."

"We'll see, Spirit-Seeker."

Fortune entered the portal and was gone. Vail took in the moment before entering his car and driving away, mediating on all that transpired. While on the road, Vail accepted the though in his heart and mind that Leta was gone. For good this time. To him, it was a great victory for the living.

THE DEVIL HUNTER: BLOODLUST GROUNDS

I

ANOTHER AMBUSH?

Once he returned to Washington D.C., Gabriel Abraham went about his business. His first duty was to track down Sierra the Succubus, whom had escaped in the woods during the battle with Hastur's demons. Abraham returned to the same forest as before, except without the assistance of Evan Wyatt or Andrea Coralline. He searched the area of the last encounter with Sierra and found nothing but dried bones of her victims. Abraham shook his head.

"Where could she be?"

Behind Abraham appeared seven shrouded figures. Cloaked in dark robes. Their faces were hidden by the hoods. Abraham turned toward them, pointing at their apparel and he scoffed loudly.

"You guys again? I thought the whole incident at the church was a clear message."

"We are not with the Cult." One of the shrouded ones said.

"Then enlighten me on who's your with. If you're with anyone to be mentioned."

"We want you to know our master knows of your works. He seeks to find you and to bring you in."

"Your master? I have to guess. It can't be Hastur because we already dealt with him. Is it Demonticronto? No? How about the Sin Phantom? Not him either. Well, you're have to do some talking with me to get my mind cleared."

"No need. Once our master gets an audience with you, he will clear your mind of all things you deeply desire. You will only desire his power and his will alone."

"And you said you're not with the Cult? Yet, you're talking the same message with me right now. They said about the same."

"Our master is very powerful."

"And your master has been around for centuries. It's no different than the others. Now, I will ask you simply to leave me be while I do my work. Otherwise, prepare yourselves for a fight."

The shrouded ones lunged toward Abraham with fangs. He saw the teeth immediately and slammed his hands into the ground. The earth quaked and opened beneath them, swallowing the shrouded ones. Before the last one was taken down into the pit, it glared at Abraham.

"Our master will find out what you've done and he will find you. Sooner than the sun can touch this city on the morning!"

The shrouded one fell into the pit and the hole was sealed. Silence covered the grounds and Abraham turned back to the bones. Still no sign of Sierra. Abraham brushed off his shoulders and entered his car, leaving the area to return to the Revelation Center.

II

HUNTINGS

Abraham enter the Center, finding Evan and Andrea scrambling in the library. Grabbing books which pertained to the recent events with Demonticronto. Evan and Andrea were somewhat jealous of Abraham's team-up with Travis Vail and the others. Abraham chuckled from their words and only waved his hands as he walked toward his office.

"There's something else going on. The reading can pause for a moment."

They entered his office as he grabbed a book from the shelf and opened it. On the pages were the same shrouded figures he encountered in the wilderness. He began telling them about their matching descriptions and how they proclaimed themselves not part of Hastur's Cult. Evan quickly assumed they were due to the similarities of appearance. Andrea was a little curious as to who they worship. If not Hastur, then who?

"I'm not sure." Abraham said. "But, one of them told me their master will find me before the sun rises. We only have about six hours till then."

"Well, what do you want us to do?" Evan asked. "Seal up the doors and windows?"

"This won't end up like last time. Whoever their master is, they talked well of him. So, I'm not expecting an ambush. Besides, they said he wishes to bring me into his group."

"Bring you in?" Andrea asked. "That would mean he's already aware of your existence and who you are."

"All I ask is that we be ready for his arrival. With only six hours till sunrise, he'll be here much sooner than we'll be expecting."

Evan crest his chin while looking at the images of the shrouded ones.

He pointed in the air and clapped his hands. Abraham and Andrea turned toward him in confusion. Abraham stared at him.

"Looking for some music to play?"

"No. I just thought of something. The words listed here, they describe these figures of having sharp fangs and using them to attack their victims. All of this sounds like they're some group of-"

"Vampires." Abraham replied. "I know. I saw the fangs myself before they went deep into the pit."

"Wait." Andrea paused. "First, we had to deal with some great demon. Then, you go off on an adventure with the Spirit-Seeker, then you have a team-up with a bunch of supernatural entities to fight against a demon stronger than Hastur. Now, you're telling us that vampires are around? Have been around?"

"You didn't know?" Abraham questioned.

"I just wasn't certain they existed."

"Much like werewolves, demons, ghosts, and superheroes, yeah. Vampires exist. In different forms as well. The movies don't usually get them correct most of the time."

"Well, Andrea." Evan said. "Now you know."

Andrea shook her head and left Abraham's office. Evan followed her out while Abraham grinned. He grabbed the book and looked at the images himself. Turning the pages, he began to learn a little of their master. An ancient entity. Their master made them into what they became. They live to worship and obey him only. Abraham was intrigued by this figure and graciously waited for the entity to show up at the Center. Abraham was not going anywhere nor was he planning on hiding.

In an abandoned ghost town. Deep underneath the town itself was the remnants of a medieval catacombs. The catacombs was damp, with tiny rivers of water flowing through and throughout. However, there was a heat coming from within the catacombs. A peculiar heat. Inside, there was a solid black coffin. Made of onyx and heated in a great temperature. The coffin's lid tilted and slid open. Out of the coffin came a hand, pale with white fingernails. The smell of sulfur irradiated from within the coffin as the figure stood up on the outside. Cloaked in all black. He raised his head up to the sky and sniffed.

"Ah." He uttered quietly. "Devilhunter."

III

MEET THE MASTER

With almost an hour till sunrise and still no sign of the shrouded ones' master. Evan waited in the lobby with a sword in hand. Abraham walked out of his office, seeing Evan with the sword and shook his head.

"Put that down. No need to hurt yourself before the enemy approaches."

Evan put down the sword, sitting it next to the wall near the bookshelf. Andrea entered the library, seeing Abraham standing with Evan. She closed the book in her hands.

"What did Evan do this time?"

"What?" Evan said.

"Nothing. He was just practicing his swordsmanship."

They laughed and the sound of the front door creaked into the library. They looked at one another and immediacy went to see who had entered. Evan stood up and before he left the library, he grabbed the sword. They entered the lobby and saw who had enter the Center. He was dressed in all black. A long robe with a cloak. Yet, no hood. His skin was pale and his beard was dark as a raven. His eyes were red as a fire.

"Well, this guy's not human." Andrea said.

"No kidding." Evan replied.

"I think I know who he is." Abraham said. "It all fits."

"Then, you know why I've come, Devilhunter."

"You're their master. They never told me your name."

"I am aware of what you have done to my followers. Sending them into such a pit where hey will have a hard time returning to the grounds of the earth. No matter. I will seek out new followers and they will worship me. With your help."

Abraham scoffed.

"I'm not helping a vampire achieve anything."

"I am not just a vampire. I am the Head of the Vampires."

"Yeah right." Andrea said. "So, you've been around before Dracula?"

"He is of another matter. I have led the vampire species throughout the eons of our time. I will continue to lead them until the end of all things is at hand."

"Well, the end isn't here yet." Abraham said. "So, here's the deal. You can leave this Center and go back to wherever you've came from. Or you can meet our end this day by my hands."

"And mine." Evan added. "I'm sorry, I just had to get involved."

"I have no desire to fight you, Devilhunter. I know of your works in this field. Your allegiance with the Spirit-Seeker and those others you've met on your quest against the great demon. Fighting you would serve no purpose in the higher affairs."

"Then, why have you come to my place? Last I was told by one of your worshippers that you seek to recruit me into your little cult."

"Only because of what you've accomplished in such a short time. You've built this Center to protect the lives of the innocents. Except for the one you lost some time ago. What if I told you she is still alive."

Abraham paused.

"What are you saying? She's still alive? Where?"

"I cannot give you more information unless you follow me."

The master extended his hand toward Abraham. Andrea and Evan yelled toward him to refuse and step back. Abraham was torn. He knew the Vampire was the enemy, but the thought of finding his lost student gave him such higher cause for his works. Abraham stepped forward and extended his hand toward the vampire. Andrea rushed and the master grabbed her by the throat. Evan raised his sword and swiped the vampire's back. It had no effect as the vampire knocked him across the lobby floor. Abraham held the vampire's hand and he laughed. Abraham smirked with his left hand behind his back, holding a silver dagger.

"I refuse." Abraham said, raising the dagger and stabbing the vampire in the chest.

The master stumbled as he pulled the dagger from his chest, burning his hand in the process. He tossed the dagger to the ground, holding his chest in burning pain. The vampire opened the front doors as he backed up, he looked up to the clouds and piercing through them was sunlight. He snarled.

"I could've given you such power, Devilhunter. Such drive. Such motivation. You could've seen your student again."

"If she is still alive, I'll find another way to save her. As for helping your kind, I refuse."

The Vampire transformed himself into a swarm of bats and left the Center. Abraham shut the doors and sighed. Evan stood up from the floor, grabbing the sword. Andrea approached him, telling him to put it down. Abraham stood quiet while Evan returned to the library.

"You're alright?" Andrea asked.

"I'll be fine."

"His words didn't sink deep, did they?"

"Not deep enough. But, I do wonder if my student is alive. In some other dimension or world. I must know if it is true. Get this burden off my chest."

"Then, what will you do?"

"I'll make a call. See what Vail knows."

"And what if he doesn't?"

"Guess I'll have to wait and see what comes next."

As they talked, a strange figure entered the library, cloaked in a mist of darkness, reached over to the shelves, stealing several books on the occult. The figure hears Evan's footsteps approaching and disappeared through a rift between the worlds.

THE MAN CALLED FABLE:
THE ART OF THE DEAL

I

LET'S HAVE A CHAT

Denise Kira stepped through the doors of the bar. The bar filled with all sorts of magical creatures. Inside, she glanced around at the trolls, satyrs, goblins, elves, and other kinds. She approached the bar as the bartender turned around to see her. Sitting her bag on the top of the bar.

"You're not one of us." The bartender said.

"I'm not. I've come to see someone."

"Someone? Like a lover or something?"

"More like an acutance."

"Ah. Why would they tell you to meet them here? Humans aren't usually visitors to such a place."

"His name is Fable. That's what I was told."

The bartender stopped what he was doing. Only to stare. Denise looked at him, waiting for a word to come out of his mouth.

"You mean to meet with him? The troublemaker?"

"Troublemaker? He helped me."

"Listen closely. Fable is a guy who comes and goes. He never stays. Unless there's a price willing to be paid."

"Must be a large sum." A voice said from around the bar.

They turned to see Fable, leaning against the bar with a smirk on his face. The bartender sighed. Denise smiled. Fable smiled back before looking at the bartender with a questionable face.

"Tell me, what have you told the woman?"

"Only that you're trouble. You'll always be trouble with the path you're on."

"Trouble can go a lot of ways. Good or bad. Best to take our chances."

"Hmm." The bartender turned and went about his business.

Fable nodded toward Denise.

"I see you came."

"Well, you told me to meet you here. Figured you would show up again."

"And I did. Although, not to drink and gamble as before. you wanted to talk, so we'll talk."

Denise agreed and the two went to a table near one of the windows at the back of the bar. Fable preferred such an area. Gives him a full view of the place and all who are inside can be seen by him. His eyes were focused just as his revolver was loaded. The bartender came to their table, setting down a mug. Fable grabbed the mug.

"Thanks."

"I'm doing it for the woman. Not for you."

"No offense taken." Fable grinned.

The bartender walked away as Fable took a drink from the mug. He sighed as Denise watched on.

"So, what did you want to talk about?"

"Um, what had happened in town. Between you and the other guy."

"Oh. You speak of Emblem. He's a troublesome lad. Never met him until that very moment."

"And what of the woman? The hooded one."

"Pandora. She's a nice girl. Although, she can be trouble at times. Drives me insane."

"Well, she visited me at my apartment."

"When?"

"Before I saw you on the streets with her and Emblem. She warned me not to be around you. Said you were trouble. Damnation would occur."

"Damnation? Ha. Pandora does have the soft spot for those words. I

363

wouldn't mind her sayings. She's an ancient individual."

"She told me the world has enough to deal with. Due to the risen heroes."

"Ah, those peeps. Listen, Denise, I've never encountered any of them. Do I wish to meet some? Perhaps one day. Until then, I do what I can for Manchester."

"There is something I would like to know."

"Shoot for it."

"Have you ever crossed over through the Rift?"

"I have. When I was a young lad."

"What is it like? The place?"

"Very… magical." Fable grinned.

"I'm sure it is. Are the colors brighter there than they are here?"

"Much brighter. If the general public saw what was beyond the Rift, they would believe they're in an alien's world."

"And those who live there?"

"Very magical. Trolls, elves, dwarves. All types of races."

"Do they get along?"

"It's more complicated to explain. But, they have their methods."

"I'm sorry to keep digging, but there must be a lot more."

"There is. And if I were to tell you, we would be in this bar for days. That is time we cannot toss away. Give it some time and eventually, you will come to know it all. Eventually."

"I see."

"Don't worry yourself. It will come. In time."

"I'm sure of it."

"Oh. By the way. You don't need to call me Fable. Let the blokes do that."

"Then, what shall I call you?"

"Kurt. Kurt Wesker."

"Very well. Kurt."

Denise smiled as Fable continued to drink.

In a far-off location within the Rift, Pandora stood before The

Hidden Four. Surrounded by fire, crystals sticking out the walls with various gemstones. Magic filled the place. It had a presence of its own. The Four aren't pleased with the previous actions of Fable when contending with Emblem. Pandora had sought out to reason for him before the Four, as they seek to pull him from the duty of the task.

"Fable is a skilled ally. When necessary."

"Necessary is not the focus on the task." One of the Four spoke. "We see that he should take these mattes urgently and complete them."

"I will send word to him about your concerns. I cannot change his mind."

"But, you can speak with him. See what it will take to get him on these matters. Quickly. Emblem is not far away. He is healing himself as we speak and he craves revenge."

"I can feel him." Pandora said. "Although, I shall be ready for the fight."

"And you will make sure Fable is ready as well."

"That I will." Pandora sighed before vanishing in a whiff of reddish smoke.

II

<u>NICE TO MEET YOU</u>

After the conversation in the bar, Denise and Fable returned to their homes. When Denise had arrived and turned on the lights, Pandora was standing before her. The presence of the hooded one startled Denise as she dropped her books and bag. She knelt to pick them up, however Pandora raised her hand and the objects lifted from the floor and onto the table near the kitchen. Denise nodded.

"I appreciate that."

"I must speak with you." Pandora said. "It is of urgent matters."

"You're not going to mute me again are you?"

"Only if you make such a loud sound."

"I won't. Why are you in my apartment? Again?"

"To speak to you, of course."

"Why me? I haven't done nothing wrong."

"You did not heed my warnings about Fable."

"He seems like a decent man."

"He is dangerous. The things that follow him only bring tragedy to those outside of the magic realm."

"He told me enough about the Rift and how it operates."

Pandora paused herself.

"What do you mean? he spoke more of the magic?"

"Yes. It was just him and I. nothing else. I asked some questions, he gave me answers."

"Where is he now?" Pandora asked.

"He said he was heading home."

"Very well. I will speak to him as soon as possible. For the meantime, anything he has told you, keep it to yourself. Do not speak of this to another human."

"And if I end up doing so?"

"Do not make me find you. Or anyone else from the magic realm."

Denise nodded with a slight pause.

"I see."

"I am positive we will meet again."

"I'm sure of it." Denise replied.

Pandora snapped her fingers and she vanished. Denise sighed.

Fable had returned to the Cheshire Plain. Sitting in his home peacefully. Until he moment a tremor occurred. He arose from his seat, his left-hand glowing with magical energy while his right hand is placed on his revolver. The shaking of the land increased, traveling toward Fable's home. He placed himself, ready to fight as the front door opened. Revealing the Hidden Four.

"Really?" Fable sighed. "Again?"

The Four entered the home as the door shut behind them. They surrounded Fable.

"What's going on here?"

"We are here to insure you of your duties."

"What duties?"

"Your duties to stopping Emblem."

"Yeah. Emblem. I remember the lad. Pandora and I faced him in town. We defeated him and he ran away."

"He did leave the area. Yes. However, he has retreated to heal himself and to grow stronger."

"So I've been told."

"When he does make his presence known, you must be there to eliminate him."

"I see. And what of Pandora? Will she be accompanying me on this quest?"

"Pandora will do what she is commanded to do."

Fable nodded with a slight scoff.

"I'm sure she will. By the way, where is she?"

"She is on matters which attend to the quest at hand."

"Ah. So, she's going about the realms. Back and forth."

"You must accompany her on this next task."

"What task? I've already said I'll help against Emblem."

"This concerns another. Another powerful force. You and Pandora will travel into the Rift. There, you will meet with Chernabog."

Fable coughed.

"Pardon. Chernabog?"

"Chernabog has some information concerning Emblem that will be valuable for you and Pandora to learn. See to it that you visit him. There is much to be done at such a short time."

"And we are supposed to trust him?"

"You will do what is necessary. That is all."

The Four turned from Fable and left his home in a collected fashion. Fable only took a sip of his drink and shook his head.

"Every time."

III

CHERNABOG

Fable had met up with Pandora at the Gate of the Rift. There, Pandora had told him of her meeting with Denise, to which Fable could only wondered of what reason. Pandora stated she told Denise to stay away from him and Fable disagreed. He understood her reasons, but he saw himself as no consequence or threat to Denise's life. Pandora shook her head hearing the words coming from Fable.

"Let's just speak to Chernabog and get this over with." Fable said.

"Finally." Pandora chuckled. "You're focus on important matters."

Fable scoffed at Pandora's words as they walked through the gate and into the Rift. Once through, they found themselves standing at the doorway to what seemed to be an abandoned shack. Pandora looked around the shack, seeing no entry points besides the front door. Fable pointed toward it as Pandora continued searching.

"We could just knock." Fable suggested.

"I'm not certain we should. Chernabog is one not to be easily missed."

"We won't miss him if we just knock."

Fable went ahead and knocked. There was no response. Fable knocked once again, still no answer. Fable sighed and knocked three times before kicking the door once.

"What was that for?" Pandora asked.

"To get a response. The knocks weren't doing good."

As they were speaking, the door creaked open with the sound of a whistling wind. The air pulled out with the door, causing Fable and Pandora to question where they stand. Within the doorway was only a long hall. Deep down into a path of darkness. Pandora took a step forward and a strange odor moved across her face. She frowned, shaking her head.

"What is it?" Fable wondered.

"The stench. Blood."

They proceeded to enter the shack. Walking down the hallway led them into a larger room. One that would seem impossible to dwell within a shack such as the one they saw on the outside. Fable realized it is all an illusion, just as many places within the Rift are. Sitting inside the room was a man, one who had the similitude of an elder. His long white and black beard flowed down to his chest. His long black hair sat over his shoulders. Above his head he wore a silver crown. His eyes were dark as the night, yet glowing as the red of fire. He was dressed in armor resembling the Middle Age.

"Is this him?" Fable asked, staring at him.

Pandora stood before him as his eyes raised up toward hers. He grinned.

"Chernabog. I am Pandora. This is Fable. We are here on urgent matters concerning Emblem."

"I know of you." Chernabog replied, standing up from the chair. "I am aware of all that has transpired."

"You do?" Fable said. "How?"

"I have my followers throughout the natural realm."

"Then, you know all there is about Emblem?"

"I do. You want him destroyed? Yes?"

"We want him stopped." Pandora stated.

"I just want him gone." Fable said. "Guy's becoming an annoyance."

"Hmm. Well, those hoods told you all there is to know. You came to me as was scheduled. Now, I must deliver to you what you've come for."

"And that is?" Pandora questioned.

"You will need me to help you defeat Emblem. But, I do not rise up and fight for a cause unless one of my own is finished."

"What are you on about?" Fable said. "What cause?"

"I will lend my power to the battle if the two of you eliminate an ally of Emblem and an enemy of mine."

"And who is this enemy?"

"He calls himself Dark Fright. A frightening figure to humanity. Appears as a human/bat hybrid. He is very skilled. Born in the Rift like many of us, but his power comes from a darker source. Shit, even darker than my own."

"Listen, we are not hear to do your errands." Pandora stated. "We are here to get your assistance."

"You will have my assistance when you take out Dark Fright." Chernabog replied calmly. "Now, do you want my help or not?"

Pandora grunted, staring at Chernabog while Fable stepped forward, with his hands clapped together.

"Panny, we need his help."

"Panny?" Chernabog noticed. "Is that what he calls you? And you allow it?"

"That is not my name and he knows it."

"He wants to agree. I agree."

"Look, we can go on out there, find this Fright fellow and take him out. That way, Chernabog here can help us defeat Emblem."

"I know, Fable. I know." Pandora shook herself. "Fine, we will confront Dark Fright. Then, you will aid us."

"I will. You have my word and my bond."

"Your word is received. Your bond is not."

Pandora turned away from Chernabog while Fable looked back at the Slavic god. Chernabog nodded and Fable walked away, following Pandora out of the shack.

Within the realm of the Rift, Emblem sat in a throne room made of gold and iron. In the throne's seat, Emblem sat still, his wounds from the fight with Fable and Pandora continue to heal as his body is made whole. Emblem let out a small breath as he heard footsteps entering the room.

"Who's here?"

"I am, my lord."

Emblem raised his head to see Dark Fright standing before him. The man/bat hybrid entity clothed in dark-clad armor with a helmet resembling medieval knights with two wings on each side. His armor appeared to look black, but in the sunlight of the Rift, it shined a violet hue. Dark Fright was on one knee before Emblem.

"Rise." Emblem said.

"I heard you needed my services."

"I do. There are two who seek to take me out. They wounded me a bit in our last encounter. I have summoned you to face them and eliminate them. By any means."

"May I ask who they are?"

"Pandora, the hooded woman and The Man Called Fable."

"Pandora is still doing the Cloaks' bidding?"

"She is and she has a human on her side. But, he's very keen of our world and the magic powers that exists. He's seen out world with his own eyes. Keep your eyes on him, he is a sneaky one. Clever in his tricks and powerful in the arts."

"I will complete this task, my lord." Fright bowed before leaving the throne room.

IV

<u>SEAL THE TAKE</u>

Fable and Pandora exited the Rift, returning to Manchester. Finding themselves at the front of the bar where Fable attends, they see a figure staring at them. Fable noticed the helmet and quickly pulled out his revolver and fired a shot. The figure dodged the round by disappearing in a flash of black smoke. Pandora noticed the sound, turning toward the smoke.

"What was that?" Fable asked.

"The one Chernabog told us to find."

The smoke gathered itself and formed Dark Fright in front of them. Fright groaned as he faced off with Fable and Pandora. Fable went for another shot, but Fright caught the round in his hand, crushing it into ash as it fell from his hand. Fable squinted.

"Damn."

"You know why we must take you down." Pandora said.

"You said the name Chernabog. That tells me all I must know."

"You are in our path against Emblem. I will not let that stand."

"You have no say in the matters!"

"Look." Fable gestured. "Can we just get this over with?"

"I agree with this one." Fright replied.

Pandora bolted toward Fright with energy blasts. Each one missing the mark as Fright transformed them into the black smoke. From there, Fable went ahead shooting more rounds toward Fright as he blocked the rounds from impact while fighting against Pandora's blasts. Fright speared Pandora to the ground and kicked Fable into the bar wall.

"Enough of this little play." Fright said, clapping his hands as bats emerged from the sky.

"Did he just summon bats?" Fable said. "Like real bats?"

Pandora looked up toward the swarm and rushed toward it, attacking the savage bats with her blasts. Meanwhile, Fable stood up and rushed toward Fright, trying to attack him with punches. Fright's speed was beyond average as he dodged every incoming blow. Fright ducked under the punch, grabbing Fable by the collar of his duster, slamming him into the concrete. Fright turned around, kicking Fable across the ground.

"Shit." Fable grunted. "This guy's strong."

"You are a nuisance, magician."

"I've been told."

Fright walked over to fable, snatching him up by the coat and tossing him into the nearby truck which was parked at the front of the bar. Fable struggled to get up as Pandora appeared from behind Fright, grabbing him by his head, tossing him across the street into the incoming traffic. Fright saw the scenery as an opportunity, rushing into the streets as the vehicles begin to cease and crash. Pandora ran into the street, shoving Fright out of the vehicles' path. Fright laughed.

"Knew you had a soft touch for humanity."

Fright head butted Pandora, backing her into the street as a car rammed her down the road. Fright nodded and walked through the traffic toward Fable at the bar. Fable was on his feet and he looked around for Pandora, not seeing her. He turned forward to see Fright approaching him. He continued firing more shots, but Fright walked through them as the rounds evaporated into smoke once again. Fable sighed.

"It's not enough,"

"You are right, magician. It is not enough."

Fright grabbed Fable by his throat, lifting him off his feet. Fright savored the moment, squeezing Fable's neck.

"I have something to tell you." Fable coughed.

"And that is?"

"You like fairies?"

"What?"

"Do you like fairies?"

"I will not partake in these foolish games!"

"You just have." Fable grinned, opening his hand as dozens of small fairies appeared.

The fairies swarmed al around Fright as he tried swiping them from his body. The fairies covered Fright in their dust, which shined with the sunlight. Fright yelled as the sunlight began piercing through his armor. Fable took notice and fired one more shot at Fright's helmet. The shot blew a hole through Fright's helmet and he fell to the ground. The fairies vanished into a small pocket of the Rift, which opened by Fable's hand. He sealed it as Pandora returned, holding her ribs.

"I see you came back."

"Don't. Do not joke now."

"If not now, when?"

Pandora walked over to Fright's body, seeing the round's entry spot on the helmet. However, she could sense Fright was not dead, just unconscious. Fable sighed as he approached her, looking down at Fright. Fable nodded.

"So, we've completed the task. We've defeated Dark Fright."

"Indeed you have." a voice said from behind them.

They turned to see Chernabog exiting the bar with a drink in his hand.

"You were in there the whole time?" Fable asked,

"Well, yes. I had to keep close eyes on you. Only to make sure you went through with the task. I now see you have."

Chernabog walked over toward them, gazing down at Fright's body. Chernabog grinned and waved his hand, causing fright to vanish. Pandora looked around for Fright, not seeing him. Fable was confused, extending his arms out.

"The hell just happened?"

"What did you do with him?" Pandora questioned. "Where is he?"

"He's right where I want him to be. No need for you or your hooded friends to worry about."

"So, you'll help us with Emblem?"

"You have my support." Chernabog replied, turning away. "You will see me again when the battle commences."

"How will we contact you?" Fable asked.

"You won't need to." Chernabog took a last gulp of the drink and disappeared in a dark portal, returning to his shack.

"Well, what do we do now?"

"Return to your home, Fable. I will contact you when the next objective is at hand."

"You or the Hidden Four?"

"I'll do the talking next time."

Sometime later, Fable returned to his home, speaking with Denise over the phone for some hours. Many hours later, a knock came from his door and he went and answered. It was Pandora, breathing heavily.

"What's wrong?"

"The books." Pandora said. "They've been stolen."

"What books?"

"The books. The grimoires of great power."

"Where are they now?"

"I do not know. But, you must find them. You're the only one who can."

"What about you?"

"I have some matters to attend to in the Rift. I will speak to you again soon."

Pandora left his home. Fable shut the door and sighed.

"Back at it again."

CINDERELLA: A HUNTSMAN IN LONDON

I

LONDON CALLING

The City of London have now heard the rumors of Cinderella throughout the area. Civilians arrived out of nowhere, claiming they have seen her at one time or another during the nights. Now, Stepmother Anne had sent out a notice to the city concerning Cinderella's threat to the people. She had hired a Huntsman to track down and find her before she makes a reappearance within the city.

While the city goes in a frenzy concerning the Sly Detective, a fellow woman from Germany arrived at the police headquarters in London. An officer approached her with caution.

"Ma'am." The officer said.

"I have a reason for being here."

"Your name?"

"Snow White."

Snow White later appeared to the people of London, proclaiming herself as a detective who's heard of the Cinderella sightings. Snow believed Cinderella is a product of the risen heroes throughout the world, something she distains. Now, she sees capturing Cinderella as an opportunity of stopping them one at a time.

During the scuffles of the public and the authorities, Cindy sat inside her home with her friend Charlotte, watching the news, seeing the outcry for her arrest. Charlotte shook her head.

"Can't believe they see you as a threat."

"It was bound to happen." Cindy said. "You help them and they want you dead."

"It must be a burden."

"Not exactly. I've done what I can to protect the innocent in this city. Not everyone will see my actions as beneficial."

"What you do is beneficial. To me. To all of us. The things you told me about what you had to do when fighting that demon guy, if these people heard that story, they would appreciate all you have done so far. You helped save the lives of everyone. Not just in London, but the world."

"You know these people don't believe in demons, right." Cindy scoffed.

"But, they seem to believe you exist. Without ever seeing you. Only going by the notions of some bystanders on street corners."

Cindy sighed, laying back on the couch.

"What of your stepmother and sisters?" Charlotte noted. "Have you heard from them about any of this?"

"I know they're behind it. They always are."

"Well, since you're friends with others in your field of expertise, perhaps you could call one of them to help you out with all this."

"I think they're busy enough with their own affairs."

Elsewhere, Stepmother Anne arrived at an office building not too far from Blackpool. She entered and inside the room stood a man. Tall, lean, wielding an axe. Anne paused when she saw him as the guards inside pointed her to the man.

"So, this is the guy." Anne said. "He has the appearance of a hunter."

"You sent word for my skill set." The man said. "I am here to accept your offer."

"This is good. Now, you received all the details to this task?"

"I read you wanted me to find Cinderella. Not sure why you would have me go and search for a fairy tale figure."

"She is not a fairy tale. Not in London anyway."

"Then, who is going around proclaiming themselves to be Cinderella?

And why do you wish them captured?"

"Because. She is my stepdaughter. Her actions have led her down this path and I cannot tolerate it any longer. She must be stopped. By any means. She's a capable fighter."

"A fighter? A young woman called Cinderella?"

"She's taken out armies of guards with her own hands. She was trained by a skilled fighter."

"I see. Very well, I will go to London and find your stepdaughter."

"Thank you for your aid in this cause."

II

SCOUTED

Later that night, Cinderella was out, scouting on the trail of her stepmother's criminal affairs. While on the search, the Huntsman was also out searching for Cinderella. After following the path she previously had taken, she returned to the warehouse where she saw her stepmother. There, she entered the building and immediately the alarms went off. Several armed guards rushed out from the doors, aiming their firearms toward her. Cinderella stood still, exhaling slowly.

"Nowhere to run, thief!"

"I'm not running anywhere." Cinderella replied.

"Don't shoot unless she moves first." Another armed man said.

"If I move first? Sure thing."

Cinderella slowly reached in her outer coat pocket as an armed one spotted her arms. He raised his weapon and she tossed out smoke bombs and quickly moved out of their sights as they began firing. She stood over them in the warehouse as the smoke cleared. The men moved with haste searching for her. Some spoke of her stepmother, saying she won't be happy with her reappearance.

Over at the main offices, Hale Prince spoke with Snow White concerning her disapproval of Cinderella's methods. Hale tried to reason with Snow about Cinderella's benefits to the city. Snow would not hear them. She stated Cinderella is a vigilante and must be removed from London in order to provide a safe and secure city for the people. Hale told

Snow he can find a way to get her to meet Cinderella and understand why she is good for the city. Snow disagreed once more and left the office. As she exited the building the Stepsisters, Angelica and Alexis entered the office, seeking to meet with Hale once more.

Cinderella sat still, watching the armed men search for her throughout the warehouse. They finished their third attempt at searching and she was nowhere in their sights. One of the armed men entered the room, telling the others Anne asked for them to stand down, as the Huntsman she called is on his way. Cinderella was confused. A Huntsman? Looking for her, she asked herself. She sighed and jumped down on the floor in front of the men, attacking them from all open corners. Taking them out as she had done before, she fled from the warehouse, running outside and when she stopped, she saw a figure staring at her, wielding an axe.

"Who are you supposed to be?" She asked.

"You must be this Cinderella I've been informed about." The figure said, walking into the lights of the streets.

"Ah." Cinderella replied. "You're the Huntsman I heard about."

"I've been brought here to eliminate you. It is my duty."

Cinderella stepped into a pose. Moving her coat back from her legs. Her fists out and her feet placed. The Huntsman scoffed, holding out the axe.

"You get the first hit." Cinderella said.

III

<u>DO YOU BELIEVE IN FAIRY TALES?</u>

Cinderella dodged the incoming attack by the Huntsman's axe, which slammed into the concrete of the road. Cindy ran behind him, jumping on his back and pummeling him in the kidneys and ribs. The Huntsman, grunting in pain, grabbed her by her leg and tossed her off.

"You're skilled." The Huntsman said. "Who taught you?"

"A good friend."

Cinderella kicked the Huntsman in the face, he stumbled as she grabbed for his axe. He pulled it away and tackled Cinderella into a nearby wall with his shoulder and swung the axe, colliding into the wall as Cindy ducked out of its path. The Huntsman pulled the axe, discovering it was stuck in between the wall. Cinderella noticed and tossed small daggers into the Huntsman's legs. He yelled, dropping down to his knees.

"Now, just hear me out."

"Why should I?" The Huntsman asked. "I know all there is to know."

"And what is that?"

"You're a criminal in this city. The people want you gone. The authorities are searching for you. That is why I was brought here. To find you and I have. The only thing left is to eliminate you or take you in."

"Well, I'm not being taken to the authorities. They don't know what's truly happening in this city."

"And you do?"

"Yes. The woman who hired you, my stepmother. She is the cause of the crimes in this city. Her men tried to kill me before. Didn't go as planned."

"Nonsense. She appeared to me as a kind woman. Only seeking to get you the help you need."

"No. she's the one who planned all of this. The only way this all stops is if she's eliminated. Her and my stepsisters. They are the cause."

Cinderella looked over to her left, hearing police sirens. The Huntsman sighed, holding onto his axe in the wall. He shook his head.

"If what you're saying is true, I will discover it for myself."

"How? You have two daggers in your legs. You can't walk."

"You are mistaken."

The Huntsman pulled the daggers from his legs and the wounds healed immediately. Cinderella startled as the Huntsman pulled his axe from the wall and stood up facing her.

"I have my ways as well."

The Huntsman looked at the daggers. Smelling the metal. He nodded.

"I will hold on to these. I'm intrigued as to what they're made of."

The sirens increased in volume, getting the Huntsman's attention. He looked over and Cinderella was gone. He scoffed, placing the daggers in his pocket as he walked away from the area just as the police cars drove by.

In a nearby area, Snow White followed the police to the warehouse. While making her way there on the sidewalk, Cinderella appeared before her from the shadows. White paused, aiming a taser toward her.

"You!" She yelled.

"I don't know you." Cinderella said.

"You're her. The Sly Detective they call you."

"Put down the taser."

"No. I've come to London to find you. Here you are. Now, I can take you in. justice will be served."

"Not today."

Cinderella kicked the taser from Snow's hand and punched her. Snow fell to the ground, holding her nose as she gazed the surroundings. Seeing Cinderella had disappeared.

IV

<u>ONE TO REMEMBER</u>

Anne arrived at the warehouse just as the police were going in and out speaking with the armed men. She passed them by as she saw the Huntsman standing guard with several of the men.

"What happened here?" She asked.

"Cinderella was here." The Huntsman replied.

"And where is she now? Did she escape?"

"She walked away.'

"Walked away! How could she have walked away?! You were supposed to take care of her!"

"I did what I could. But, you're wrong about her."

"Oh am I?"

"After our scuffle, we spoke. She told me all I needed to know."

"Did she? She told you about her criminal activities."

"No. I could sense it within her. Her true motives. They aren't set to cause chaos in this city. No. She wants to make London better than it was before she decided to put on the hat and coat. Cinderella is a true hero to this place. I understand she's your stepdaughter and you wish her dead."

"More than anything."

"And that is why I cannot help you. You're consumed with envy, covetousness, greed, and anger. Such impulses I cannot aid in my works."

The Huntsman turned and walked away, hearing Anne screaming words toward him concerning his work and Cinderella. The following day, Snow White had told Hale about her encounter with Cinderella, seeing the bruise on her face. Hale could not reason with Snow any longer. She desired to find Cinderella and to bring her in. The Huntsman had left London, after he was paid by Hale in the full price Anne had set for him. For Anne, she had traveled far from London to a small island near the Netherlands. There, she had a meeting with a woman, cloaked in all black, wearing a crystalline-gold crown. The meeting was simple, Anne wanted Cindy dead and the woman agreed to take the mission upon her own hands.

"You will do as the Huntsman should've done?" Anne asked. "Are you sure of it?"

"I'm a woman of my word. I take my missions seriously and I complete them at any cost."

Anne nodded with a dark grin.

"This is better. Much better."

"A Queen does as she desires."

HEAVEN HAS CALLED:
THE BOOKS OF THE HORRORS

I

<u>BEWARE MANY BOOKS</u>

Travis Vail, the Spirit-Seeker cracked open the door to an abandoned home during a late evening. A quiet one. The home was far from the standard suburbs of a city or town. Vail entered the home, seeing nothing but damaged furniture and torn walls. The floors creaked with every footstep he took. He walked through the rooms, going down the hallway toward what appeared to be the office area.

"There it is."

Vail entered the office and went straightforward to the portrait on the wall. The portrait was of a large field with two figures standing in the midst of follies. Vail pulled the portrait off the wall, finding a safe. Vail used his wits to find the code, unlocking the safe. Once he opened it, he saw the safe was empty.

"The hell?"

Vail searched through the office, not finding what he was truly searching for. He sighed.

"They're gone." Vail uttered to himself. "The books are gone."

Vail exited the home, while on the phone speaking with Dr. Galen Donovan concerning the books. Donovan told Vail the books should've been in the house for centuries after being left there by a powerful psychic. Vail suggested the books might've been taken and sold. However, Donovan had an alternative.

"Have you felt the strangeness in the air recently?"

"I have?" Vail replied. "You believe the books are responsible?"

"If they are, it would only imply they were stolen and are being used by some powerful forces."

"You think Balthazar may have them?"

"Not likely. To use the books properly, it would take more than one man to get them operating. It would need a team of many."

"I'll pay Abraham a visit. See what he knows. He has some of the books in his center."

Vail entered his car and drove from the premises. As he went further down the road, a silhouette of a figure stood at the window of the home. Watching the Spirit-Seeker drive away.

II

THE HORROR, THE HORROR

Gabriel Abraham walked through the Revelation Center while Andrea Coralline and Evan Wyatt sat at the desk, researching files pertaining to vampires. The front doors bolted open, snatching their attention and focus. Abraham turned around to see Vail entering the Center. Vail waved with a nod.

"I know you weren't expecting me, lads. But, this is of most importance."

"What's happened now?" Abraham asked.

"Some grimoires have been taken from a secret stash. That stash being an abandoned home that belonged to a long-time past psychic."

"Grimoires?" Evan said. "Are you sure they were such books?"

"I would know for certain. Anyway, we need to find these books and fast."

"Well, it's strange you've come and spoke of a similar action."

"What are you speaking of, Gabriel?"

"Grimoires here have been taken as well. After we dealt with the Vampire Lord, it appeared someone or something infiltrated the Center and took the books. Currently, we're not sure where they are or who has them."

Vail nodded.

"You know this isn't a coincidence. Someone has stolen the books from certain locations. Gathering them together. With those books together, they could cause a dire stray across the world. Everything could very well end as we know it."

"Maybe it was just a thief looking to get rich." Andrea noted. "I mean, that's what one of them would do."

"By any chance have you checked the library here in D.C.?" Vail asked Gabriel.

"No. perhaps, we can head there and see what we find."

"Noted. Then let's get going."

Vail and Abraham headed out to the library in downtown D.C. Once inside, they made way toward the New Age section of the library, Vail realized the people would place grimoires in such a spot. They found the section and began searching. Skimming through the books on the shelves from top to bottom, they found nothing. Vail sighed.

"This is not good."

"I know."

They stood talking about alternatives and behind approached a man. Well-dressed in suit and slacks. He was middle-aged and clean-shaven. Vail could smell the scent of cologne on him. Abraham was unsure who the man was, yet he was keenly aware of their reasons for being in the aisle.

"I see you are searching for something and yet have not found it."

"It happens at time." Vail said. "Good day to you."

"I wouldn't leave just yet Travis Vail." The man said.

Vail turned around slowly.

"How do you know my name?"

"We know you very well. As do you, Gabriel Abraham. My. My. I never thought the day would come where I would meet the infamous Spirit-Seeker and the renown Devilhunter at the same time. Let alone in a public place."

"Who are you?" Abraham asked.

"My name is not important. But who I am associated with is."

"What group are you with? The Cult? The Doctors? One of Demonticronto's followers?"

"I am with the *Mythologists*."

"The Mythologists?" Abraham replied. "Never heard of them."

"I have." Vail said. "Only heard of their name. never seen them or encountered them. But, today has ruled that out. This man claims to be with the Mythologists. So, why are you here?"

"I am here to tell the two of you there's no need in searching for the books. They're in good hands."

Vail stepped forward toward the Mythologist. Abraham prepared himself for the possible altercation. The Mythologist himself was very calm. No fear in his eyes.

"Where are the books?" Vail questioned.

"My master has them."

"Your master?"

"He has plans to use them to shape a better world."

"One man cannot harness the power of those books."

"He knows. That's why he has brought in an associate."

"Associate?" Abraham said. "Who else could manage that kind of power?"

"A greater kind. But, you'll know eventually."

The Mythologist walked away, he turned back toward them with a grin on his face.

"Best to prepare yourselves for what's ahead. The world is about to have a drastic turn of events."

The Mythologist had walked away, leaving Vail and Abraham mediating on plans and theories. Vail clapped his hands, getting the attention of the others in the library by accident. He waved them off.

"What's next?" Abraham said.

"We gather everyone." Vail replied. "We gather the team."

III

A GREATER KIND

Without haste, Vail and Abraham sent out word to gather the team together. With the aid of the Visitant Outlander and Dark Manhunter, they were able to teleport several of the members to the Revelation Center for the meeting. Vail and Abraham waited for the team to arrive and two bright flashes of light emitted within the lobby of the Center and out of the first flash came Outlander with Cinderella and the Ghost of England. The second flash walked out Manhunter with Creed, Death Chaser, and Papa Afterlife. Vail looked around as the light dimmed out.

"Where's the other lad?"

"Who?" Cinderella asked.

"The one with the white mark on his chest?"

"He has other matters to attend to." Afterlife said. "You have heard about the 'Steeler Incident' haven't you?"

"Not to my knowledge. No."

"Terror will be fine. We're enough for this task."

"Depends on who we're facing." Abraham noted. "Anyone have any clues?"

"Signs of the books have been felt throughout the universe. Both naturally and spiritually." Outlander stated. "Those who have them are gaining knowledge and power from them. Shaking the fabric of reality in total."

"I did hear about a stash somewhere in Manchester. "Cinderella said. "It was taken from some place."

"Then, you can lead us there." Vail said.

"I don't operate in Manchester, Trav. That's the other guy."

"What other guy?" Abraham asked.

"She's talking about the Fable bloke."

"Never heard of him."

"Few have." Cinderella replied. "Anyhow, that's where one stash was located."

"Ok. Anyone know of any other places?"

"Well, we only know two." Vail said. "Manchester and somewhere here in D.C."

"True."

"There is another place surging with energy." Manhunter spoke. "It's in a deep cemetery. Guarded by a restless spirit."

"Where is this cemetery?" Creed asked.

"Deep in Ireland."

"I see." Vail said. "Looks like we'll all be doing some traveling."

"How are we going to get to these places as quickly as possible?" Abraham wondered. "How will it be done. Not all of us can teleport."

Vail clapped his hands together with a smirk.

"I have the idea. We split up into teams. I'll led one over to the UK, find out about the books in Manchester while you, Gabriel, take a team and head on out to find out more about these Mythologists."

"It'll work. But, it still doesn't conclude the travel."

"I will aid Vail." Manhunter said.

"Then, I shall accompany Abraham's unit."

Vail nodded. "Then, it's settled."

"Now, who's going with who?" Abraham asked.

"Shaw and I will go with Vail." Cinderella said.

"I will accompany you as well." Death Chaser added.

"Fair point." Vail nodded.

"Creed and I will join Abraham and Outlander." Afterlife said.

"Everyone knows what they must do?" Vail said. "Good."

"I met a young man in London who had an encounter with the Mythologists." Outlander said.

"So, myself, Cindy, and Shaw will speak with him once we leave Manchester."

"I cannot allow that. the young man must see me. That way he will not be in fear."

Vail nodded.

"I understand."

Vail went and walked toward the door, stopping as everyone began heading out. Cinderella approached him, seeing something was on his mind.

"Those words." Vail uttered. "How could I have let them slip."

"What is it?"

"Me and Abraham met a fellow from the Mythologists. He told us they were working with someone outside of their group."

"Any chance you may know who it is?"

"I do now. The Mythologist said their helper was of a greater kind."

"A greater kind? I'm not getting what that means."

"It means Vernon Lance is working with them and that is trouble for all of us."

"The Satanist?"

"Yes. We need to find the books now."

IV

THE CON MAGE OF MANCHESTER

A portal opened in an alleyway in the city of Manchester with Vail, Cinderella, Shaw, Chaser, and Manhunter walking out. As the portal closed, they each looked at the location in which they stood.

"Recognize this spot?" Vail asked Cinderella.

"No. Should I?"

"Might as well see what's on the end of this alleyway." Vail replied.

They followed him through the alley, reaching the outer parts, seeing a bar just up ahead. Vail looked around, seeing the vehicles driving on the street, yet on one side of the road, construction was being done. Vail pointed toward it.

"What happened there?"

"Maybe a wreck." Cinderella replied.

"A wreck would not have caused that much damage." Shaw added. Something happened here and not long ago."

Death Chaser turned his focus toward the bar behind them. Sensing an energy coming from within. He pointed as Manhunter also was sensing the energy.

"The bar." Chaser said. "Something's inside."

Vail and Cinderella walked forward, facing the bar. Hey keened their senses. Cinderella knew there was something strange with the bar, while Vail shrugged his shoulders and walked.

"Let's go have ourselves a look-see."

Vail went ahead and entered the bar. Once inside, he saw the bar was filled with magical creatures. Vail spotted an orc near the back of the bar while there was a satyr sitting at the bar drinking whiskey. Cinderella looked around and was amazed. The Chaser entered with Manhunter following and the entire bar went from lively to dead silent. Vail raised his hands.

"Hello lads. Now, we're not from these parts. However, we have come for a purpose. Do any of you know of the Man Called Fable, the bloke who operates in this town?"

Everyone in the bar turned and gave each other looks. Quiet looks. But knowledgeable. The bartender stepped forward as Vail turned toward him.

"Yeah. We know of him."

"Mind you tell us where he might be? We need to speak with him."

The bartender pointed to the further section of the bar near the back. They looked and saw Fable himself sitting at a table, having a drink. Fable looked up toward them, grinned and held up his drink. Vail shook his head, thanking the bartender before approaching Fable's table. Vail and Cinderella stood in front facing Fable. Fable extended his hand at the chairs.

"You guys can sit."

Vail and Cinderella sat at the table while Shaw, Chaser, and Manhunter stood guard as there were several trolls who were glaring toward Fable.

"Listen, we've never met before." Vail said. "But something has happened which brings us to this moment."

"First off, my guy. Who are you people supposed to be?"

"I'm Travis Vail, Spirit-Seeker. She is Cinderella. While the others are-"

"Cinderella? Bullshit." Fable grinned. "She's not Cinderella. Can't be. Fairy tales don't exist."

"And yet you interact with a realm where such creatures are relative in fairy tales." Cinderella smiled.

"So, you're the one they've been searching for in London."

"I am and I would like it to remain quiet. Until this is all over."

"And what is all this?"

"Some powerful grimoires have been taken. Gathered to cause some major damage to the world. All of creation could suffer if those who have them succeed."

Fable took a drink and shook his head.

"She said something was gone."

"Who said what?" Cinderella asked.

"Oh. Pandora. She told me some books had been taken. I couldn't' find out where but she panicked over it slightly."

"So, what has this Pandora woman found out?"

"Nothing so far. But, the fact the two of you came here asking about grimoires leads me to believe this isn't just a Manchester-only situation."

"It's not."

"Fable, may I ask if you knew where the books were kept?"

"I have no clue. Never saw the books. Only heard of them being stored up in a place by Pandora and those Four fellas."

"What four fellows?" Vail asked.

"Doesn't matter. Look here, I will do what I can to help you guys out with this. By doing this, I'll be helping Pandora and she can stay off my back when it comes to matters like this. I can't take the stress."

Manhunter's cloak began flowing, getting the attention of everyone in the bar. Vail looked up toward him with concerned face.

"What is it?"

"Someone's coming." Manhunter said. "Someone powerful."

A flash of light emitted from the middle of the bar, startling the creatures inside and as the light faded, Vernon Lance stood in its place. Vail jumped from the table, ready for a fight. Cinderella followed and Fable stood up, his hand on the revolver. The Chaser's hands emitted with sinfire, and Shaw was prepared as his body was slowly glowing.

"Who's this guy?" Fable asked.

"Vernon Lance." Vail said. "A thorn in the sides of many."

"It is good to see you again once more, Spirit-Seeker."

"Why are you here?"

"To tell you and your friends something you should know."

"And what is that?"

"The grimoires you are searching for? They belong to me now. Their power already flows within me and soon all of the world will bow before me."

"Is he always like this?" Fable asked.

"Every day." Vail replied.

"What are we going to do?" Cinderella asked.

"You will do nothing." Lance told Cinderella. "Stay away from my work or suffer."

"Suffer what?" Chaser said.

"A greater fate worse than death."

"Meh." Fable said, raising up the revolver and firing a shot.

The round went straight through Lance's body, hitting the shelf at the bar. Vail knew it then. Fable stood confused. Cinderella stepped forward.

"He's not really here." Vail said.

"I know how to operate, Spirit-Seeker. You should've known by now."

Lance faded away from their sight. Vail grunted, pacing in anger.

"We have to find out where he is," Cinderella said. "It's the only way."

"And how are we going to track him down?" Vail asked. "His magic is too powerful now. I can't track him myself. Manhunter, Chaser. Can either of you track him?"

"He's shielded." Manhunter said. "Even from my own eyes and might."

"I cannot trace him." Chaser replied. "Something dark is over him. Hindering my power."

Vail walked toward the door as the others spoke of possible solutions. Fable was well involved. Fable told Cinderella he was no sorcerer and Vail clapped his hands together, returning to the team.

"That's it."

"What is?" Cinderella asked.

"A sorcerer."

"What about one?" Fable asked. "I'm not one."

"Not talking about you. I know one. He may help us."

"When did you meet a sorcerer?" Cinderella questioned.

"Very recently. He helped me with a favor to a family."

Cinderella nodded. "Then, where is this sorcerer?"

"We'll have to check the last place I met him."

"Then let's get going." Fable said. "I'm tagging along for this."

Elsewhere, Abraham's team walked through London during the night, standing outside of the library. Abraham looked around, seeing only civilians walking and going about their night.

"Where is he?" Abraham asked.

"Give me a moment." Outlander replied, extending his arms.

The ground became covered in mists. The civilians had vanished and the vehicles which were passing through were gone. Abraham looked around as did Afterlife and they were astonished by Outlander's feat of power. Creed stood quiet, looking past the mist and he saw someone approaching.

"There." Creed said.

Abraham looked out and saw someone coming toward them. Outlander stepped forward as he saw Jacob Wilson coming through the mist.

"You heard my call." Outlander said.

"I did. Why did you contact me?"

"Because my allies here need to know more about the Mythologists. They have taken something which does not belong to them. In turn, they could very well destroy all of creation if they are not stopped."

Jacob looked behind Outlander, seeing Abraham, Afterlife, and Creed.

"Who are they?"

"Those who you can trust."

"Jacob," Abraham said walking forward. "We just need to know what you know about them. Like the kind of places they meet up. Where do they operate out of? You know anything of them?"

"Primarily, they meet at all kinds of places. Restaurants, city halls, schools, stores. But, they mostly operate out of museums or libraries. That's where they keep their collections."

"Museums. Libraries. Ah, I should've known." Abraham replied. 'They've been sitting under our noses the whole time."

"At least you have your answer." Outlander said. "You did well, Jacob Wilson."

"We need to return to D.C." Abraham said.

"We cannot." Afterlife replied. "We have to reach the cemetery first. Find the books hidden there."

Abraham nodded. "You are correct. Let's get going. See you around, Mr. Wilson."

Jacob nodded as Outlander opened the portal for them to exit the area. As the portal closed, the surroundings returned to normal. Jacob looked around, seeing familiar events as before. He chuckled under his breath before walking away.

V

A SUPREME ENCHANTER
AND
A RESTORATION MAN

Vail led his team to the source of his information, following a path of peculiar magic within the air. Unseen by the natural eyes. With Manhunter and Chaser's assistance, Vail led them toward the Citadel of enchantment. Fable looked on at the structure.

"Where did this place come from?"

"It's been here." Vail said. "For a very long time."

"Do we knock or wait?" Cinderella asked.

"He'll know we're here." Vail replied.

"Who's he?" Fable wondered.

The doors of the Citadel opened and out of them came down Doctor Fortune, levitating down the stairs toward them as his cloak flowed with the wind. He saw Vail and nodded with a smile. Vail nodded back as Fortune measured the others. He looked at Chaser with a keen eye.

"A Soul of Retribution. Nice to meet one of you."

"You know of us?"

"I know of all of you. Robert Shaw, I am familiar with the events that made you what you are this day. Make no mistake, you will have your vengeance soon."

"I am honored of your words."

"I've heard of the stories across London of a sneaky individual. Famed by the fairy tales that proclaim your existence. Now, I stand before you, Cinderella."

"I'm not as detailed as the stories suggest." Cinderella grinned.

"I can very well see that." Fortune replied. "Manhunter, I know of your purpose and I know of your hatred to those of magic."

"Then, you know what I aspire to do."

"I do. However, we are not here to fight one another. Regardless of our paths. It seems Travis Vail has brought you all here for a reason. Vail, I would like the know that reason."

"I must guess you've felt a strangeness in the air. Reeking of some dark power?"

"I have. Me and my apprentice have been studying its paths. It's bouncing across the sky like I've never seen before."

"Because it's energy from powerful grimoires."

"What do these grimoires suggest?"

"Vernon Lance, a powerful priest in the Satanic field has them in his possession with the group calling themselves the Mythologists. I don't know what they're after, but I know why Lance is involved. He's seeking to become powerful. Much more powerful."

"What is your plan currently?" Fortune wondered.

"We don't have one exactly. The others are already heading to the cemetery to find the third stash of grimoires."

"So, Lance and the Mythologists have the first two stashes in their hands?"

"Correct." Vail said. "We need to know how to weaken the power that comes from them. By doing so, we'll weaken Lance and the Mythologists will cower in fear of what's to come."

"Books such as those should not be in the same place at the same time. Explains the darkness above the earth. The solution is simple. Separate them from each other."

"Wait." Cinderella said. "That's all? Just separate them?"

"Yes. How many grimoires are there?"

"Five from each stash." Vail replied. "Lance and company currently have ten."

"While the remaining five are in some cemetery." Fortune nodded. "Understood. I will help you find Lance and these Mythologists. You face them and scatter the books across the four corners of the earth. You do that, the task is done."

"Lance is too powerful for us to face head-on." Vail said. "we need some assistance."

"You're asking for my help in this endeavor?"

"You helped me with Carrie. I'm just asking, help with this. If Lance succeeds, all of creation could very well end. I know you cannot allow something as powerful as that to happen."

Fortune nodded, turning back toward the citadel.

"When the time comes, you will have me on your side." Fortune replied. "Right now, do what you must do."

Fortune entered the Citadel as the doors closed behind him. Fable threw his arms up, looking around the forest area behind them.

"So, that's it?" Fable asked. "He's not going to help out?"

"Fortune's a trustworthy guy." Vail said. "He'll help out. He already said it."

"We need to return to the others." Manhunter said. "Gather ourselves together and confront Vernon Lance and the Mythologists."

"Then let's return to D.C." Vail said.

Over in Ireland, Abraham's team arrived at the cemetery. A foggy and damp night. The cemetery had a presence of its own. A crawling sense tingled down their backs aside from Outlander and Creed. Abraham searched for the sight, but was unable to track it down. Outlander extended his right hand across the cemetery and one peculiar grave with an unnamed headstone shined like the sun.

"There it is." Outlander said.

They reached the grave, seeing it had appeared to have been dug up recently. Abraham sighed.

"No sign of the books."

"No." Creed said. "The books are here."

"How do you know?" Afterlife wondered.

"Because he has them." Creed pointed in front of them.

They looked out and a decomposed hand arose from the ground. The trembling feeling underneath them shook the cemetery and from the hand arose a head and a body. The figure stood above the ground, standing at the same height as Abraham and Afterlife. Dressed in rags of clothing, ripped pants, torn shoes. Its hair long and white. White as snow. Its eyes soulless, yet there is some form of life within them. Piercing through the veil. Creed's cloak spread widely, flowing with caution, Afterlife's hands became covered in smoke while Abraham steadied himself. Outlander stepped forward toward the figure.

"I know what they call you." Outlander said. "The Restoration Man."

"I cannot be killed." The Restoration Man said.

"True. we are not here to fight you. We seek the books. Where are they?"

"Why should I give them to you?"

"Because you do want to know what the second death feels like." Outlander replied. "Not yet anyway."

The Restoration Man paused himself. Stepping back behind the unnamed headstone. Creed noticed and rushed over, knocking the stone over to reveal the books.

"There." Creed said.

Abraham went over and grabbed the books. He nodded to the others. The Restoration Man stepped back as Outlander kept his eyes on him.

"You do well with those." Restoration Man said.

"We know what must be done." Outlander said. "Return to your service, fleshly spirit."

Outlander opened the portal and they returned to the Revelation Center where Vail and the others waited.

VI

A PRIEST IN THE BOOK

Vail stood inside the Center with the others just as Abraham returned with the books. Vail smirked.

"You found them."

"Yeah. What did you guys come up with and who's that?"

"I'm known as Fable. Some call me The Man Called Fable."

"Why is a stranger in this place?"

"He's here to help. Seriously. He's been tracking down the books himself."

"We have all that we need." Chaser said. "Now, let's find Vernon Lance and end this."

"That's a good idea." Vail said. "Only where do we find them?"

"At the library." Abraham said. "That's where they are."

"How are you certain of that?" Shaw questioned.

"Because it's what the young Wilson had given us." Outlander said. "He's familiar with their movements. He would know where they operate."

"And you rust the young one?" Manhunter asked. "So blindly?"

"It is not blindness, Manhunter. It is justice."

"Only when you're betrayed for a just cause."

"Now, there's no need to stir each other up." Vail said. "Save it for the fight ahead."

"We need to get the library now." Creed spoke. "End all of this."

"I agree with the darkly gruesome one." Fable said. "Let's find these guys, finish all of this so we can all return to our lives."

"He's right." Cinderella said. "I'm sure someone in London needs my help right now.:

"Eh, alright." Vail mumbled. "Let's get going. Teleporting again?"

"No other choice." Manhunter said.

The group teleported themselves into the library late in the night.

Upon their arrival, they found themselves facing off against strange shadow figures. Vail knew Lance has summoned them to keep the library guarded. Immediately the library became a place of war. Creed, Chaser, and Shaw took the fight to the shadow figures while Vail, Cinderella, Abraham, Afterlife, Fable went ahead as Outlander and Manhunter used their power to shroud the library from the public eyes. For when a civilian passed by the library, they only saw the emptiness within. The lights appeared off and the library seemed closed to their natural eyes.

"Where could they be?" Vail questioned.

"Downstairs." Abraham said. "I'm sure of it."

They went forward, finding themselves in what appeared to be an exceptionally large room. Large enough to be kept hidden from the public. Within the room were the Mythologists who were sitting in a circle, their heads were down with Lance standing before them.

"Your games end here, Lance." Vail yelled. "Give us the books."

"And why should I do such a thing when the plan is fully coming into motion?"

"Enough of your words." Fable said. "We're here for the books. Hand them over."

"Or what?" Lance grinned.

"You know what to do." Vail told the team.

They all rushed toward Lance without haste. Lance turned toward them as the Mythologists themselves did not move as Lance raised his hand toward them, stopping them in their tracks. He laughed as eh tossed them back to where they entered. Lance scoffed, returning to the books as they were opened.

"I'm not stopping here." Vail said, raising himself up.

"Keep coming, Spirit-Seeker. I will always knock you down. It is our fate."

"It is. But, it could use an extra hand." Vail said, stepping back.

Within the room streaked a bolt of lightning and from the lightning appeared Pandora alongside Doctor Fortune. Fable looked on, seeing Pandora. She turned toward him and nodded. Fable nodded back in respect as Fortune stared down Lance, seeing the Mythologists on the ground and the books ahead.

"This has come to an end, Priest." Fortune said.

"A Supreme Enchanter." Lance scoffed. "More power must I receive this night."

"Not likely."

Pandora whipped her hands around forming a magical bind, causing the Mythologists to rise from the ground and attack Lance. While she held her power upon them, Fortune quickly pulled the books toward him as Lance let out a loud yell. Vail saw what was happening and ran toward Lance, but Cinderella grabbed his arm.

"What are you doing, Cindy?"

"Now is not the time for your anger to get the better of you. Fortune has the books. We can go now."

"No. I cannot let Lance escape. Not this time."

Vail went to move ahead, and Cinderella kept her hold on him. Fortune appeared to him with the books in hand.

"We must go, Travis Vail. Pandora can only hold them for so long."

Vail looked out, string at Lance. Vernon saw him and smirked while fighting off the Mythologists. Vail sighed as they left the room through Fortune's wormhole. The Mythologists ceased their attack and fell to the floor. Lance looked around, seeing the books were gone as were his adversaries. He screamed as the floor beneath him opened and he went down into the darkness, only with his laughter to echo out into the open.

Afterwards, they gathered at the Center where Fortune spoke to Vail and Abraham, telling them the books must be scattered by only five of them across the earth. To keep them hidden from humanity and other forces which seek to do harm. Vail took three, Abraham took three, Fable took three, Outlander took three, and Manhunter took the remaining

406

three. They all went and scattered the books to various locations which will not be named. Only the ones who scattered the books will know the locations of the earth.

Returning to their own lives and operations a day later, Vail kept his ears and eyes open for Lance's return. Fable and Pandora returned to the Rift to meet with Chernabog concerning Emblem, Abraham went ahead with his studies with Andrea and Evan, Afterlife returned to educate the Yonderers, Creed kept his spiritual senses keened for Adrambadon's return as did Chaser with Demonticronto. Cinderella returned to London, finding a search warrant out for her arrest, Shaw had wandered throughout London and the spiritual plane alongside Outlander and Manhunter. The two figures hovered above the earth, looking down.

"Do you believe they'll manage to take on what's to come?" Outlander asked.

"In time, we will see what makes of them." Manhunter replied. "For I know we both are certain they will be ready when the war begins."

"As will we."

DOCTOR DARK: DARKNESS AND LIGHT

I

<u>THE FOOTSTEPS OF ONE MANY FEARS</u>

Standing in the realm of the Astral Dimension, Darkous looks upon Michael The Archangel. The two discuss with one another about the previous victory over Mazakala and how much they have to repair in order to avoid another event with his release in the near future.

"There is another command that has presented itself to you, Darkous." Michael said.

"What has been commanded of me?"

"After the events of your battle with Mazakala, there have been incidents occurring throughout the realms of the darkness and the light. We know that only you should be given this task to discover what is truly happening across the cosmos."

Darkous nodded.

"I will begin on this task as soon as possible."

Michael nodded and flew up in the air, exiting the Astral Dimensional realm of existence. Darkous prepared himself mentally for the task at his hand and exited the Astral Dimension, heading first to Earth.

On Earth, Carol Hunters, the supernatural reporter continues her studies of the occult, diving into more knowledge that she was aware of in her early beginnings of research. She later came upon a series of old documents from the museum that contained information that she recognized from the men within the museum who call themselves the Mythologists.

"I am curious as to what they are talking about." Carol said.

Carol continued studying and was tempted to contact Malach HaMavet for more details concerning the Mythologists, but decided on waiting to find more information before telling Malach about the circumstances in order to have herself prepared for what could possibly happen.

Darkous moved across the earth. Day and night. Going from country to country. He searches the ancient lands of old, finding nothing that would be tampering with the darkness and light powers. While going through the lands during nightfall, Darkous could feel a uncertain energy coming from the homes of people. Darkous stopped by at one person's home and entered in through the door, walking through it like a living vapor of mist.

"The energy here." Darkous said. "It is of another realm."

Darkous walked upstairs in the home, seeing the bedrooms of two children, a girl and a boy. Down the hall was the bedroom of their parents. Darkous could feel the energy surrounding them all, but the energy was strong on the little girl. He entered her room and walked toward her, seeing her fully asleep.

"What is happening amongst you, young one."

Darkous placed his right hand onto the little girl's head and instantly, he entered her dream. Within her dream was the little girl playing with friends in a yard. Her brother was seen walking amongst them. Darkous looked around, feeling the energy growing in strength.

He looked toward a tree and spotted a being staring at the young girl with piercing eyes.

"What are you?" Darkous said walking toward the being.

The entity glared at Darkous and vanished into the air with a swift blow of wind. Darkous looked around, not able to find the being and turned back to the young girl, still playing amongst her friends and brother. Darkous exited her dream and entered her brother's dream. The dream of the brother was different, involving a room covered in video games and action figures. The boy played with the figures along with the being from the girl's dream. Darkous approached the being.

"Tell me what you are."

The being turned to Darkous and smiled before vanishing. Darkous turned to the little boy and he stared at him.

"Where did my friend go?" The little boy asked.

"I don't think he was your friend, young one."

Darkous left the boy's dream and proceed to enter the parents' dream. Within their dream was a crowded interstate. They were in their car with their son and daughter in the back. Darkous walked through the street of the crowed roadway.

"So many stopped." Darkous said. "So many trapped."

Darkous could see the being once again standing in front of the road, causing the traffic jam. Darkous hovered up and flew toward the being. In great speed, Darkous tacked the being and rushed him into one of the cars.

"Tell me what you are now!" Darkous said.

"I'm what the little ones fear." The entity said. "I'm what their parents teach them of the night. I am what keeps them in line during the night."

"Your name." Darkous said. "Tell me your name, entity?"

"I'm the Bogeyman." He said with a smile on his face. Showing his decaying teeth.

Darkous released the Bogeyman as he vanished once again. Darkous exited the dream of the parents and left the home. After several hours going through the earth, Darkous discovered the Bogeyman had been traveling through the dreams of many. Tormenting them to the point of even killing in his running spree.

Darkous returned to the Astral Dimension and Beatrice is waiting on him. She sees the purpose in his eyes and can feel that something is taking place throughout the realms of the cosmos.

"I can sense some power going through the cosmos, Darkous."

"It's a power of torment and fear." Darkous said. "The Bogeyman is freely roaming the earth."

"The Bogeyman?" Beatrice said. "I thought he was killed during the early purge."

"Apparently not. He survived the purge and has made himself known once again. Now, I have to deal with him and the events taking place within the darkness and light."

"What do you have in mind concerning The Bogeyman?"

"I have to visit an old associate of ours."

"Who would that be exactly?"

"I'm going to the Patchlands."

Beatrice looked at Darkous as if he said something that made her feel ignorant of her place.

"You're not considering working with him again are you?" Beatrice said. "You know how cunning he can be toward us and those above."

"True. But, he knows the Bogeyman more than most would assume him to know. He could be of useful assistance."

Darkous prepared himself to head out for the Patchlands.

"Make sure you keep your awareness keen."

"I will. Surely."

Darkous hovered into the air, leaving the Astral Dimension as if he was a gust of wind during a thunderstorm.

411

II

PUMPKIN LANGUAGE

Entering the Patchlands during the brink of day, Darkous comes down from the sky, seen from the ground like a horde of bats or crows. Walking through the trails of the Patchlands was a figure that resembled a man but possessed a pumpkin for a head. Darkous stood on the ground walking towards the man.

"Mr. Pumpkinhead." Darkous said.

He turned and faced Darkous. His face showing a smile as he laid down his rake and approached the Keeper of the Cosmos.

"The Shrouded One makes himself known unto me in my own realm."

"I do and I come with a purpose of intent."

"Such as?"

"How much do you know of The Bogeyman?"

"I know much about him. His power, his hobbies, his lusts. I know much about him to tell dozens of stories with."

"I need to know all that you know."

"Why would you want to know all about The Bogeyman?"

"Because he's out there causing torment amongst the sleeping ones during the nightfall."

Mr. Pumpkinhead nodded.

"Ah. So, he has been released you're saying. I thought he was dead and gone."

"That is what we all assumed. But, we were wrong."

"I will help you, but it will involve you going in several directions to

412

find your answers."

"You're sending me on a puzzle quest?"

"In a matter of yes or no, I am."

"What will be in possession of these quests?"

"The answers you seek concerning The Bogeyman. Don't worry, you might have some fun in this. I know I would."

"Go back to your harvesting, Pumpkinhead. I will find what I need in your trails."

Darkous took his first step toward the first trail in searching for the knowledge of The Bogeyman. Mr. Pumpkinhead watched him walk forward and smirked.

"Wait till he sees what's in store for him. Ha!"

Back on Earth, Carol meets with Malach HaMavet inside of his cabin as she brought along her detailed and studies concerning the Mythologists. Malach looked at her findings, within the books she carried along the way and the papers of notes that she written.

"How long did it take you to study all of this?" Malach said.

"It took some time." Carol said. "I had nothing to do other than put my time into learning who those men are and what they're planning in the shadows."

"How are you feeling, exactly?"

"What do you mean?"

"I mean, how do you feel after seeing that horde in the streets a while back."

"Oh. It laid an effect on me that I probably will never have removed. But, it showed me there's more to this world than what we see with our own eyes."

"Trust me when I say this to you, what you seen is only a small drop in the sea to what is really out there."

Carol smiled as she laid her eyes back onto her findings.

On the Patchlands trail, Darkous walked through, looking around at the fields of plentiful harvest. He could see what appeared to be portals into parts of the earth. Within those portals were images of people

413

sleeping and The Bogeyman circling them around their bed, tormenting them in their sleep.

"He circles them. Why?"

As Darkous walked, a bolt of light flash in front of him. Halting his steps. Darkous walked through the light and swiftly wiped it away with his hand. He looked forward seeing two figures that appeared to be made of light.

"Who are you?" Darkous said.

"We were sent here to halt your findings on The Bogeyman." One figure said. "You cannot learn more about him."

"I will."

Darkous raised his hand and from it was released a small wave of energy that knocked the two figures on their back. They looked at Darkous with fear in their eyes.

"But, you cannot learn more. We promised him we would keep you away."

"Who is him?" Darkous said. "Tell me his name and I will deal with him."

"We will not speak his name." The other figure said. "He might destroy us from existence."

"His name. Now."

"We... we will not speak it."

Darkous stared at the two figures. No emotion on his face as his eyes are locked onto them and his pupils turning a dim blue.

"Very well."

Darkous raised his arms up toward the sky and above the two figures emerged a thick cloud of darkness. The two figures started firing blasts of light bolts toward the cloud. Having no effect except causing the cloud to grow in size, covering more ground.

"Please stop the cloud!"

"I will not." Darkous said. "You two have made your decision."

The cloud came down upon the two figures and swallowed them up. The faint sounds of their screams could be heard before silken came in. Darkous walked past the cloud and continued on forward down the trail.

"This is no matter of games."

Further down the trail way, Darkous finds himself surrounded by a group of shadow creatures. Darkous shook his head and released a small sigh. He looked at the shadow creatures.

"Do you know who you're surrounding?" Darkous said. "From the very realm you were birthed from, I rule."

"It doesn't matter now." One shadow creature said. "You're on our turf now."

"I see what I must do in order to make you understand."

Darkous released several shadow creatures of his own and they combated against the shadow creatures of the trail. Darkous stood by and watched the fighting commencing before him.

"Finish them off." Darkous said to his shadow creatures. "Send them on their way back home."

The shadow creatures of Darkous instantly killed the shadow creatures of the trail and they vanished into the air with a gust of wind. Darkous continued walking down the trail and spoke to himself.

"Something is not right. What has Pumpkinhead sent me on?"

After finishing the trail, Darkous returned to the Astral Dimension to take further looks across the cosmos in search of The Bogeyman. From behind him walked Beatrice. She looked at him as if he made some mistake. He glanced at her.

"I know what I did, Beatrice."

"You were taken for a fool by Pumpkinhead."

"I am aware of that. Though, the portal that showed the humans sleeping was no folly play. It was real and it confirms to me that The Bogeyman is still on earth. He hasn't left the earth because he cannot at this particular time."

"You think Pumpkinhead may know what Bogeyman needs to escape from being earthbound?"

"I think I do. You mind coming along with me?"

"With pleasure."

Mr. Pumpkinhead sat inside of his home on the Patchlands and the front door opened with a gust of wind. Pumpkinhead looked over toward the door and stood up, walking towards it to close it.

"Damn wind."

Pumpkinhead placed his hand on the door and closed it. He turned around and was stopped to see both Darkous and Beatrice standing inside of his home. He pointed at them while laughing.

"So, the wind that blew my door open. That was the both of you?"

"It was." Beatrice said.

"My, my. Don't you Astrals have amazing feats."

"We're not here to discuss feats, Pumpkinhead." Darkous said.

"Why are you both here? You again mostly."

"Don't take me for a fool." Darkous said. "You sent me on some folly trail surrounded with small diversions to keep me ignorant of the knowledge of The Bogeyman."

"Oh. You discovered what I was doing all along, huh. Funny."

"It is not something to laugh at." Beatrice said. "We need to know all there is about Bogeyman."

"Wouldn't it be best if you only left him alone. He's stuck on earth for holy's sake."

Darkous walked toward Pumpkinhead and snatched him by his throat, shoving him against the wall of his home.

"Give us what we came for or suffer a fate that is worse than a blinding light."

"Ok." Pumpkinhead said. "Alright, I'll give you what you want. Just let me back on the ground."

"Sure." Darkous said as he dropped Pumpkinhead onto his feet.

Pumpkinhead was crouched on the ground, catching his breath and gazing up at Darkous and Beatrice.

"Fair play." Pumpkinhead said. "Fair indeed."

"The knowledge!" Darkous said. "Speak it now."

"Sure. The reason why The Bogeyman is out and tormenting the humans is to find a way back to his plane of existence called the Dreamscape."

"The Dreamscape?" Beatrice said. "I thought that place was destroyed during the Purge."

"Apparently, my darling, it was not." Pumpkinhead said. "It was locked down to keep The Bogeyman from entering back into the realm. He derives his power and strength from that place."

"The Bogeyman is only trying to find his way back home?" Darkous said. "That is what you're telling me, Pumpkinhead?"

"That is what I'm telling you, Shrouded One. For right now, he is weak. Too weak to fight against those against him. But, if he finds his way back into the Dreamscape, he will be more powerful than he ever could be."

"We thank you for this information, Pumpkinhead." Darkous said. "We will meet again."

"Anytime, Astrals."

Darkous and Beatrice vanished into the thin air. Pumpkinhead sighed as he sat back down into his chair and continued to smoke his pipe.

III

MYTHOS TO EXPLORE

In her apartment, Carol read a newspaper that contain some information regarding a secret meeting between the men whom she knows as the Mythologists. The city is calling them the Bankers. They are scheduled to have a bank meeting amongst themselves and a few selected others during the day. Carol knows that there is more to the story and contacts Malach to aid her in discovering what is truly taking place at City Hall.

Carol traveled to the City Hall and saw the Mythologists sitting amongst each other. She proceeded to approach them, but one spotted her. Smoking his cigar, he looked at Carol and remembered her from their previous meeting before.

"I remember you, lady." He said.

"You... you do?"

"I do. Come over here and sit with us for a brief moment."

"Ok."

Carol sat down with the Mythologists. Shaken up a bit and hesitant to speak a word that might get her in trouble. She looked at what they were reading and it was an ancient grimoire. She pointed at it and the Mythologist looked and turned toward her.

"Do you know what that is?"

"I do not."

The Mythologist chuckled. He grabbed the grimoire and handed it to her. She grabbed the book and opened it, seeing it covered in spells and invocations. She looked at the Mythologist with uncertain ease.

"Is this a spell book?"

"It is. We found it amongst this old place. Makes you think how the politicians win their elections, huh."

"It does in a way. What do you guys intend on doing with it?"

"Ma'am, what we do with this book is none of your concern. But, I'll give you a little insight into what we have planned with it."

The Mythologist leaned toward her, his breath the smell of ash and smoke, covering the scent of his cologne.

"There's a certain figure that lurks in the dreams of Man. His power is beyond what average humans are aware of. We intend on bringing him here to aid us in our mission. To grant us entrance into his realm."

"Your mission?"

"Creating a new order of the world. Cleaning it up from its foul and awful stench of human selfishness and emotions. We have to do it because we're the only ones who can."

"How can you do it?"

"With this book, we will conjure up our figure. He will tell us of his realm and will aid us in entering the Third Heaven."

"The Third Heaven?"

"Yes. The highest of all the realms. The domain of the Eternal One."

"But, how could you do that? You do understand that you said the Eternal One."

"I did. There are powers that are at work that can do marvelous things for those who use it properly."

"So, that bank meeting that was in the newspaper, that was for show?"

"Of course, we had to come up with a diversion to keep the commoners away from knowing our real intent."

"Maybe they could help in some way."

"No ma'am, they cannot help us. They cannot help you and they certainly cannot help themselves. They are lost and they need order in guidance."

Carol looked at her watch, seeing the time. She stood up from the chair and the Mythologist grabbed her arm. Frightening her, he looked into her eyes.

"I will grant you an invite to our little get tighter this evening. If you desire to learn more."

Carol nodded with a faint smile.

"I would love to."

"Splendid."

"Will I have to ask for your name?"

"My name." The Mythologist said with a laugh. "We have no names. Only purpose."

Carol nodded.

"We will see you tonight, ma'am."

"Yes you will."

Carol left City Hall and contacted Malach on her phone.

"Malach, I have to speak with you and its very important that we do it immediately."

"Come by the cabin and we can discuss it all there." Malach said.

"Sure."

Carol hung up the phone and left in her car, going to Malach's cabin. Carol later made it to Malach's cabin. Malach, already sitting outside, sees her approach. He stood up and opened the front door as she walked toward him.

"How bad is it, Carol?" Malach said.

"I would pick worse over bad."

Both of them walk into the cabin and Malach closes the door. Inside, Carol sits down at his table and Malach sits alongside her.

"Tell me what you came here to speak."

"I met with the Mythologists."

"Again?"

"One spotted me and allowed me to sit with them for a moment. He told me of their meeting tonight."

"What of their meeting?"

"They had a book. It contained spells and invocations. He told me they're going to use it tonight to conjure up some being that inhabits the dreams of people. Said that he would grant them entrance into his realm and would help them enter the Third Heaven."

"Wait, wait, wait." Malach said standing up. "The Third Heaven?"

"That's what he told me."

"This isn't good. Even if they can't breach The Third Heaven, they'll still cause harm to the cosmos. We need more help."

"But, who's this being that inhabits dreams? I'm unaware right now."

"The Bogeyman." Malach said. "They're going to conjure him up."

"The Bogeyman's real?"

"Yes, he is and funny enough, my Master has been searching for him."

"You think he'll want to help us out with this?"

"If it concerns The Bogeyman, his realm, and The Third Heaven. I believe so."

Malach walked outside to the front. Carol watched him go as he closed the door. Outside, Malach stood still, his eyes closed. Though in his mind, he is contacting Darkous. Telling him of the recent news. From the sky comes down Darkous like a lightning bolt. His eyes intense. Malach opened his eyes and seen his Master before him.

"Master, You've come."

"I have. Let us enter inside and tell me more of this news you've spoken of."

Darkous and Malach enter the cabin and Carol sees Darkous for the first time. Frightened and excited at the same time, she stood up and faced him.

"Master, this woman is Carol Hunters. She's a supernatural reporter and has been aiding me on some information and I her."

"I recognize your features, Ms. Hunters." Darkous said.

"You do?"

"I know of you and how you wish to interview me."

"I… I didn't know."

"The interview can wait. I am here about what you said of The Bogeyman, his realm, and The Third Heaven. What of all this, Malach?"

"Carol knows of a secret society that calls themselves The Mythologists. They have in their possession a grimoire and are intending on using it to conjure Bogeyman and receive information as to enter his realm and The Third Heaven."

"This I will not allow." Darkous said. "Where is this group of theologians?"

"They're at the City Hall." Carol said. "They'll most likely be underneath the building for their meeting."

Darkous nodded.

"We will head there tonight. Confront these men and show them what true power is."

"Yes, Master."

Darkous walked out of the door and turned back to Malach and Carol.

"I will meet the two of you there."

"Yes, Master." Malach said. "We will be there."

Darkous flew up into the air and was gone.

The night fell upon the land and the moon glinted across the ground. Beneath the City Hall sat the Mythologists around a circular table and in the middle of the table laid the spell book. The lead Mythologist walked into the room and sat at the table.

"Gentlemen, we know why we're here this night and it is truly of great importance."

Outside of the City Hall walked Malach and Carol around the building toward the front doors. Malach had his sword prepared for battle as Carol noticed the door was being blocked by two men. She stopped Malach.

"What are you doing?"

"They granted me entrance into the meeting. Let me go in and when your Master arrives, you can enter then."

"I understand you. Be careful."

"I will."

Carol approached the two men. They stopped her from entering the doors.

"I was granted entrance to come to the meeting tonight."

"Let me check." The security guard said.

He contacted the Mythologists on the phone. He listened and put the phone away. He took several steps back and opened the door for Carol.

"You may enter."

"Thank you."

Carol entered City Hall and instantly could feel an energy going through the place. The energy was luring her downstairs to the meeting. She found the stairway and walked down to the floor. While walking down the stairs she could see the Mythologists at the circular table with the book in the middle. She walked toward the table and the Mythologists looked at her.

"Appears you've decided to come." The Mythologist said. "Wonderful."

"I couldn't miss something such as this."

"I can't agree with you more, ma'am."

She sat down at the table next to the Mythologist as he started to talk and go over the information that was given to them through the book.

"This book, lady and gentlemen, will grant us power beyond all belief of human reasoning. With this, we will possess true power."

Carol looked around for Malach, yet she didn't' see him. Outside, Malach killed the two security guards and entered City Hall. As he approached the stairwell, Darkous communicated with him through his mind.

"Wait." Darkous said. "Just wait."

"Yes, Master." Malach said. "I will wait on you."

The Mythologists opened the book and stopped on a page that referred to The Bogeyman. The Mythologist pointed at the spell and smiled to the others.

"This will give us power. I am thrilled for this."

He picked up the book and began to recite the spell. He spoke the spell in Latin. As he spoke, the lights began to flicker, he smiled.

"It is working!"

The lights flashed and the bulbs bursts above them. The Mythologists and Carol covered themselves from the falling glass. They looked around and could not see a thing. The room was in complete and thick darkness.

"What is going on in here?" The Mythologist said. "This isn't part of the ritual."

"No. It is not." said a voice within the darkness.

"Who is there?!" The Mythologist said. "Who is speaking to us all?!"

"You seem to be afraid."

"We fear what we do not understand because we know the power it possesses."

"Do you seek wisdom of the arts?"

"YES! WE SEEK WISDOM OF THE ARTS!." The Mythologists said altogether.

"Listen and listen good." said the voice.

"We are listening."

Within the thick darkness, they could feel an energy that was unknown to them, strange and uncomfortable, but their internal fear was becoming external.

"We're getting a little uneasy in this darkness."

"Do you fear it?"

"We do fear it. Because we do not fully understand its power."

"Why do you fear it?"

"We don't know who you are and why you've answered our request of appearance."

"The shadows are my domain. The darkness is where I dwell. Those who fear the darkness. Fear me."

The darkness faded away as the lights returned to its former state and atop the table in the middle of the Mythologists stood Darkous, staring at the lead Mythologist. Carol sat in awe of Darkous' feat as Malach entered the room with sword in hand. Darkous leaned in toward the lead Mythologist, seeing his fear.

"That is the wisdom you have received this night."

"Who the hell are you?!"

"I am Darkous, Keeper of the Cosmos and I am here to question you concerning your plots to conjure The Bogeyman, to enter the Dreamscape, and to make an attempt at entering The Third Heaven."

"Because we have to do so."

"Why would you even dare a feat that is impossible for humanity to partake?"

"Because humanity is lost to themselves. They have no guidance. No direction. They need it now or they will die amongst themselves in foolishness and ignorance."

Darkous stared at the lead Mythologist and kept his gaze toward him.

Searching the innermost parts of his heart and mind.

"You are not the true leader of this clan." Darkous said. "Where is your Master?"

"Our master?"

"You heard my words. Where is your Master?"

"Right there at the door."

Darkous turned and seen a man approaching them. Wearing a white cloak and his face hidden. He removed the hood and faced Darkous.

"Speak of your name, mortal."

"I am Dr. Geoff Hoff and this is my clan of Mythologists."

"Do you even understand what you are bargaining with, human. The feats that you have not even bared in your flesh?"

"That is why I sought out power and have discovered it."

"What do you mean?"

"I met a man, who possesses the powers of the dark arts. He aided me and gave me that spell book."

"Who is this man?"

"They call him Vernon Lance."

"Where is he?"

"He travels from church to church. Satanic churches and abandoned churches."

Darkous stepped down from the table and approached Hoff. He stood in front of him, towering over him in height. Hoff showed no fear in facing Darkous.

"What of this ritual to summon The Bogeyman, to enter the Dreamscape, and to break into The Third Heaven?"

"For you to know where The Bogeyman truly is located, you'll need to find a man they call the Spirit-Seeker. He will aid you in finding the answers you are seeking."

Darkous stared at Hoff and nodded before walking past him toward the door. Carol proceeds to follow him. Before exiting the room, Darkous turned back and looked at Hoff.

"Hoff. I give you this warning. If you ever make a breach into the cosmos, I will find you and show you what true power really is."

"I will look forward to it, Cosmos Keeper."

Darkous, Malach, and Carol left the room of the Mythologists, whom were frightened out of their seats. Hoff looked at them and shook his head.

"It seems there is more work to be done upon you gentlemen."

IV

DARKNESS SEEKS THE SPIRIT
<u>THAT SOUGHT IT</u>

Leaving a small coffee shop is the Spirit-Seeker, Travis Vail. Returning to his base of operations, covered in books containing knowledge of the supernatural and mystic arts. Vail sat down at his desk and started reading through a grimoire, which contained information of conjuring deities from their dominions. The book was taken in an earlier event.

"I've never dealt with this before."

While he took sips of his coffee and read through the book, he hears a knocking at the door. Vail looked over toward the door and stood up from his desk. He walked to the door believing it to be someone who's stopped at the wrong location and is preparing himself mentally to tell them to go somewhere else.

"Who could this be?" Vail said. "I hope you've found the right place and not wasting time."

Vail opened the door and was immediately stunned. For Vail was staring into the eyes of Darkous himself. Darkous stood still and quiet. His eyes were locked on Vail's own.

"Travis Vail, I presume."

"Yes." Vail said. "You've come to the right place."

"Appears I have."

Vail let Darkous enter his place and closed the door afterwards. Vail returned to his desk while Darkous took a small look at the place. Seeing the relics that Vail has collected during his occult cases. From an ancient Indian burial relic to a photo with the name *Leta* attached to it.

427

"You have been out there much haven't you."

"I go where I'm needed."

"Very well, Mr. Vail." Darkous said turning toward Vail. "I need something of you at this appointed time."

"What do you need from me?" Vail said. "Cast out some demons, remove some spirits from a location? What will my assistance require?"

"I need you to help me find Vernon Lance."

Vail paused for a moment.

"Vernon Lance? As in the satanic priest Lance?"

"Yes."

"So, he's popped back up again."

"He has something that I require. It is of great importance to my mission and cause."

"Do tell me of your mission and cause, Mr.?"

"Darkous, Keeper of the Cosmos. But, you can call me Doctor Dark if you would prefer."

"Fair enough." Vail said. "I can tell from your aura that you're not human."

"I am not. I am an Astral entity."

"An Astral entity? So, you're basically from the outer realms."

"I am. Will you aid me in finding Vernon Lance?"

"I will. But, it might take a while to find him."

"We don't have a while to take, Mr. Vail." Darkous said. "We must confront him and take what he has in his possession."

"I can see you're in a rush to find him."

Vail grabbed his black coat and walked toward the front door. He looked at Darkous.

"I might know a few places to look."

They walked outside toward Vail's 1970 black Impala. Vail entered the car and he looked at Darkous, who was only standing there, staring at Vail and looking at his car.

"You're not going to get in the car?"

"No."

"Thought you need me to locate Lance."

"I do. Go to the place and I will meet you there."

428

"How will you do that exactly?"

"Because I can."

Darkous vanished into the air. Vail shook his head as he started the Impala.

"I guess this comes with the revelations."

Vail drove from his base down the streets. After a while, Vail stops by an old abandoned home. The home was once used by Lance and some of his satanic followers as a small base of operations to keep their rituals a secret from the outside world. Vail exited the car and walked toward the home. A small gust of wind blew across Vail. He nodded and turned around, seeing Darkous standing behind him.

"You found me." Vail said. "I am impressed."

"He's not here." Darkous said.

"How can you tell?"

"I searched the home while you parked your vehicle."

"That fast, you say?"

"Indeed. The energy within the home has eroded away."

Vail shook his head, walking back to his car. Darkous looked at him after glancing at the abandoned home.

"The next two locations you know of, what are they?"

"Well, one is an old storage facility and the other is an abandoned church."

Darkous nodded. "Let me do a search on the two and I will come back with the information needed in finding Vernon Lance."

"Sure thing." Vail said. "Search away."

Darkous flew up into the night sky, disappearing in the darkness above. Vail sat by his car, looking at his watch and counting the time.

"Thought he would be faster than that."

Darkous came down from the sky, landing in front of Vail. Vail chuckled a bit and started applauding Darkous' entrance.

"My, my." Vail said. "That was only a couple of seconds."

"Vernon Lance is located at the abandoned church. His aura surrounds the place. Let us stop him."

"Sure thing. I take it you will meet me there."

"I will." Darkous said before flying in the darkness again.

429

Vail entered the Impala and drove away. Making the rounds to reach the abandoned church, he finds himself being surrounded by individuals wearing black and scarlet robes with purple attachments standing outside in the street near the church.

"His lads are out here." Vail said. "Walking about in the damn street."

Vail honked his horn and the hooded figures turned toward him. He looked and noticed their eyes were glowing a bright red as they slowly made their way toward him. Vail prepared himself for the possible fight to come.

"First one to make a move gets sent to the Lake!"

As the hooded figures made their way toward Vail, a large gust of wind blows them across the street into a yard. Vail looked forward and could see Darkous standing in the street. The hoods stood up and surrounded Darkous in the street. Vail exited his car and reached into his pocket, pulling out his book of rituals.

"I can take these guys, Dark." Vail said.

"I know you can." Darkous said. "But, your energy is required in use against Lance. I will deal with these reprobates immediately."

"I would like to see this." Vail said. "Show them your power."

Darkous raised up both his arms toward the night sky as the moon shined above them. Thunder began to crack from the sky and lightning started to flash. From the sky came down a small tornado, blowing only through the street, picking up the hooded figures and tossing them around the yards. Clearing the street of the hoods, Darkous turned to Vail.

"May we finish what we've come to do."

"Sure. After you, Dark."

Darkous and Vail walked toward the church's front doors and Darkous blew them open with a gust of wind. Inside the abandoned church sat Vernon Lance and around him were four of his followers, dressed in black and scarlet. Lance looked at Vail and Darkous, smiling. His long wavy hair glowing with the moonlight, wearing his black clothing and black trench coat.

"How are you still around?" Vail wondered.

"Travis Vail makes his presence known to me once again." Lance said.

"I am deeply flattered."

"Don't take it as a friendly visit, Lance." Vail said. "We're here on some important causes."

"I can tell by the way your friend blew the doors open."

"Vernon Lance, give to me what you have taken from a realm you do not understand."

Lance laughed as he stood up from his seat and started walking toward Darkous and Vail. He pointed at Darkous, looking at his dark violet and black apparel.

"I recognize you from somewhere." Lance said. "Have we encountered one another before in time past?"

"This is our first meeting, Vernon Lance." Darkous said. "I can sense the aura of evil around you. You have consumed its power and believe you cannot be stopped."

"I can't be stopped, Dark One. No one can stop me with the power that I possess from the ha-Satan."

"You believe he cares for you, don't you?" Darkous said. "I will tell you, he cares for no one but himself and enjoys seeing others suffer to his own mischievous acts."

"How would you know what he thinks and does?"

"Because, unlike you, who speaks to a statue with a goat's head and a woman's body, I have spoken to the ha-Satan face to face. Angel to Astral. You have no idea as to what exists and transpires throughout the cosmos of this universe. Your little worship here and there will continue to go forward until you are stopped permanently."

"Is that why Vail has brought you here? To kill me?"

"No. I have come to take from you what doesn't belong to you."

"Which is what?" Lance said, pulling a small pouch from his coat pocket.

"What is that?" Vail said.

"Sand." Darkous said. "Dream sand. It belongs to The Sandman in order to enter the dreams of those who sleep."

"Sandman, you say. This is getting more and more open by the minute."

"This was given to me in a sale." Lance said. "I don't intend on returning it to Sandman."

"You won't have to because I will."

Lance raised up his hand, shoving Vail against the wall. Darkous looked at the worshippers as they tried to attack him. One by one he grabbed them with a cloud of darkness and snapped their necks without the use of his hands. Lance noticed Darkous' power and giggled.

"When you said Astral, you were talking about yourself, huh?"

"I am." Darkous said. "What kind of spirit do you possess to wield such power?"

Lance showed a sinister grin.

"A greater kind."

Lance began reciting a spell, opening up a portal that released several demonic spirits to come out and they attacked Darkous. He fought back with the powers that he possesses while Vail got back to his feet. He glared at Lance.

"This is the kind of mess that you cause for the fun of it."

"I am a human with demonic intellect, Vail." Lance said. "Will you never understand that. I have true power in the palm of my hand. To do with as I please."

Vail looked around the church and noticed dozens of symbols that referred to portals across the world in different languages.

"You're using this place to conjure demons all across the world?"

"You're just now figuring that out. How slow has time made you, Spirit-Seeker."

Darkous defeated the demons and turned his attention toward Lance. He walked toward him. Lance tried to use his supernatural power against Darkous, but it has no effect on him.

"I know I can stop you, Dark One." Lance said. "I have the true power of darkness!"

"What do you know of darkness, mortal?" Darkous said. "You believe it to be of evil, yet, darkness was present before the light. I know all of this because I control the darkness and was commanded to keep it bound in its rightful place."

Darkous swooped over toward Lance and snatched away the pouch of sand from him. Lance looked and could see Darkous placing the pouch into his pocket.

"How dare you take something of such power away from one such as I." Lance said. "I possess demonic intellect! I am the kind of human that can change this world! A greater kind!"

"No." Darkous said. "You are not."

Darkous looked at Vail and nodded. "Send him to a prison somewhere. Do it quickly."

"I would love to." Vail said. "With great pleasure."

Vail opened up his book of rituals and turned the pages. While doing so, Lance began to recite a spell that started to suck the church up from the ground. A miniature earthquake was created as the wind started to blow like a hurricane and fires began to grow from the wooden floor.

"I got something for him." Vail said.

"Do it." Darkous said.

"Abba Pater, ex toto corde tuo et in virtute Spiritus Sancti , ut hoc mando tibi per gyrum dentium eius a daemonio in prisona ibi usque ad tempus statutum. Exite!"

Lance looked around and found himself being pulled into the ground by the spirits of Sheol. Lance screamed at Vail and Darkous with angry passion.

"This isn't the last of me, Vail! You hear me! I shall return!"

Lance was pulled and had vanished. The church and its location became silent as the wilderness. Vail looked around seeing no one inside but him and Darkous. He turned to Darkous and smiled.

"Looks like our work is done."

"It is." Darkous said. "I thank you for your support, Travis Vail."

"Anytime, Dark."

Darkous was preparing to leave, until Vail stopped him.

"I need to ask you of something."

"What do you want to ask?"

"All of this, Astrals, demons, gods, what more out there don't I know yet?"

"Travis Vail, I know you're new to all of this and I know the beginnings of your journey within the walls of paranormal investigation. It wasn't until you were visited by Kamagrauto that your whole world opened up. In time, you will see it was done for a much greater purpose. The team you've formed from the heavens. A purpose that will not only benefit those of the Spirit, but the future Kingdom to come as well."

"So, there's more of your kind out there? Astrals?"

"Yes."

"Any on the malevolent side of things?"

"There are. Some work for the forces of good. Others, the forces of evil. It's all for the balance of the universe."

They walked outside and Darkous looked up to the moon.

"I have to go, Travis Vail." Darkous said. "It was an honor to work alongside someone of your caliber."

"Whenever you require of my assistance, you know where to find me."

Darkous nodded as he disappeared. Vail returned to his Impala and drove away from the church that began to crumble apart.

Back in the Astral Dimension, Darkous looks at the pouch of sand. Analyzing it for the purpose of learning its power.

"With this, I shall find you, Bogeyman. I shall."

V

<u>OUTER SLEEP</u>

Searching for The Bogeyman's location, Darkous went through various attempts at finding him across the earth. He was nowhere to be found. Darkous later circled the earth's atmosphere to find him and he did not.

"He wouldn't take a break in the First Heaven. I know that to be true."

Darkous returned to his place in the Astral Dimension and studied the sand pouch. Beatrice appeared to him, seeing Darkous studying the pouch of sand.

"Is that dream sand?" Beatrice asked.

"It is." Darkous said. "It was earthbound."

"Last I knew, the Sandman wasn't walking about on the earth at this time."

"Because he's trapped inside the Dreamscape. The Bogeyman trapped him there to get out. This sand was in the possession of a Satan follower."

"Where's The ha-Satan now?"

"Going to and fro in the earth and walking upright in it as always."

"Can the sand give you a signal to finding Bogeyman?"

"No, it cannot. But, It can show me the entrance into the Dreamscape."

Darkous poured a tiny inch of the dream sand into the palm of his right hand and tossed it in the air above himself and Beatrice. The sand began to fall, but caught its own balance within the air. Flowing across the air by a cosmic current, the sand directed Darkous toward the entrance to the Dreamscape. Darkous looked and recognized the location the sand has chosen.

"The doorway is set within the Second Heaven."

"Are you sure about that?" Beatrice said. "I've never known there to be a door within the Second Heaven."

"I entered the doorway to Sheol through in the Second Heaven. Why not the doorway into the Dreamscape."

"Didn't seem to be a likely location is all I'm saying."

"I better be on my way to finding him. Contact me if something else comes up concerning the darkness and light issues."

Darkous left the Astral Dimension, traveling into the Second Heaven. Upon arriving in the Second Heaven, an archangel appears before him and stopped him in his tracks.

"Uriel." Darkous said. "What brings you to me?"

"Details concerning the matters of the darkness and the light."

"I was told about the issue by Michael. He gave me and advance notice."

"True. Though, you have been so concerned with the matters of The Bogeyman and he had diverted you from the real cause of concern."

"You mean to tell me that The Bogeyman is nothing more than a diversion set upon me? By who?"

"Who do you think, Darkous."

Darkous nodded.

"Should I let The Bogeyman be and Heaven will take care of him?"

"No. You have already made this your mission currently. After you have dealt with Bogeyman, you will receive a call and you will answer the call."

"Who will contact me afterwards?"

"You will know his voice."

Uriel disappeared before Darkous' eyes. He looked around for him and couldn't find Uriel. He set his attention toward the Dreamscape entrance and took some more of the dream sand and scattered it through the vacuum of outer space. The sand took some rounds and revealed the doorway to Darkous.

"There it is." Darkous said.

The doorway to the Dreamscape opened and Darkous could see the brightening colors pouring out as if it was a place of peace. Darkous made his way toward the door and could feel and aura surrounding him.

He entered the doorway and stepped on the grounds of the Dreamscape. Standing in front of him was The Bogeyman. Holding a set of blades ranging from a sword to a scythe. His eyes held a sense of torment within them as his stare could send a human into utter shock.

"You decided to appear to me without making a move?" Darkous said.

"You're in my realm now." The Bogeyman said. "Are you afraid of me, Shrouded One?"

"No. The thing is, after we have our battle, you will fear me."

"We will see about that."

VI

IN THE DREAM, WE SEE OUR CALLING

Darkous and Bogeyman engage in a battle of the powers of the realms. Darkous using various attacks against Bogeyman, whom used his sword and scythe to slash away at the darkness that Darkous would conjure up against him. Bogeyman laughed at Darkous.

"Your power isn't as strong within this realm. You're in my domain now!"

"You underestimate the power of an Astral entity." Darkous said. "We have more than what was given to us."

Darkous waved his hand to his side. Bogeyman was confused at the matter. Back on earth, Malach looked around his cabin and could feel and energy calling to him. He grabbed his sword and stepped outside and looked up, suddenly he disappeared from his home and appeared standing next to Darkous in the Dreamscape. Malach looked at Darkous, who turned to him and nodded.

"I need a little bit of your assistance on this one, Malach."

"Whatever you say, Master." Malach said. "So, this is The Bogeyman?"

"It is. In the flesh."

"Rather in the dream." Bogeyman said. "This will be fun for me, but tormenting for the two of you."

Darkous and Malach attacked Bogeyman at once. Ranging from side attacks to attacks from behind and front. Darkous fired a sphere of dark matter toward Bogeyman, knocking him back into the Dreamscape gates.

"What kind of place is this?" Malach said.

"They call it the Dreamscape." Darkous said. "This is Bogeyman's domain and the Sandman's."

"The Sandman is here?"

"I believe him to be. We'll have to release him from his prison."

The Bogeyman began conjuring illusions of himself and demons of the dreams to attack Darkous and Malach. Both using their abilities against the illusions to find Bogeyman within them. Darkous blew the illusions away with a gust of wind from his hands and grabbed Bogeyman by the head, slamming him into the ground of the Dreamscape, creating a sound resembled to a bell being rung.

Malach ,take this!" Darkous said giving Malach the pouch of sand.

"What am I supposed to do with this?"

"Use it to find the Sandman. He will help us trap Bogeyman back into his prison."

Malach looked around at the tall buildings within the Dreamscape and could see a castle ahead.

"Toss the sand into the air, Malach!" Darkous said. "The sand will lead you directly to the Sandman!"

"Yes, Master." Malach said throwing the sand into the air above the battle.

The sand rotated in the air, circling itself twice before moving across the sky, heading toward the castle. Malach ran after the sand, following its trail. Darkous and Bogeyman continued their battle with Darkous taking Bogeyman's sword and snapping it within his hands.

"Face me with your hands, dream demon."

Malach arrived at the castle, which the sand made a turn toward its lower doors connected to an underground area. Malach followed as the sand slid through the crack of the door. Malach used his sword to open the door. He continued to follow the sand until it stopped at a dark cell. Malach looked inside and seen a man sitting on the floor.

"Seems my sand has returned to me." The man said inside the cell.

"Are you the Sandman?" Malach said.

"I am. Thank you for bringing it to me."

"Me and my Master need your help right now."

"I am aware of the current circumstance. Lead the way, young one."

The cell doors busted open as the Sandman walked through. Malach stood quietly and stared at the Sandman.

"Lead, young one."

Malach led the Sandman to the outside where they could see Darkous and Bogeyman continuing their battle. Malach held his sword tightly, preparing to run into the battle, but Sandman placed his hand across Malach's chest.

"I need to assist my Master." Malach said.

"Do not run into the battle." Sandman said. "Let us deal with The Bogeyman."

Darkous slammed Bogeyman, but was kicked in the chest. He looked across the open area, seeing Sandman walking towards him and Bogeyman. Darkous released a wind of darkness, slamming Bogeyman back onto the ground.

"Keeper of the Cosmos." Sandman said. "I will finish this battle."

"By all means."

Darkous moved out of the way as the Sandman approached Bogeyman. Bogeyman, who stood up from the ground faced Sandman in the eyes. He released a small gesture of laughter.

"They set you free?!"

"They did and not I will place you in your eternal chamber."

Sandman tossed his sand toward Boegeyman, entering his eyes as he fell to the ground. The ground beneath his feet opened up, revealing a horde of shadow men as they grabbed Bogeyman by his limbs and dragged him into the ground. Bogeyman yelled for repentance.

"You will not be given repentance this day, dream demon." Darkous said. "Now, go into your prison in peace."

The ground closed itself with Bogeyman inside. The area was calm, Sandman turned toward Darkous and Malach.

"I thank you once more for releasing me from my prison."

"It was our duty to restore the balance of the Dreamscape." Darkous said.

As the Sandman spoke to them, Darkous glared up into the air. He could hear a voice calling to him. A voice only few can hear. Darkous listened and he recognized the voice he could hear. Malach looked at him and could feel there was a communication taking place.

"Master, what is it?" Malach said.

"I am needed." Darkous said. "My Master demands my presence."

Darkous returned Malach back onto earth at his home. Meanwhile, Darkous made his way toward the voice that called to him. The voice came from the Third Heaven.

DARKOUS OF THE ASTRALS SHALL RETURN.

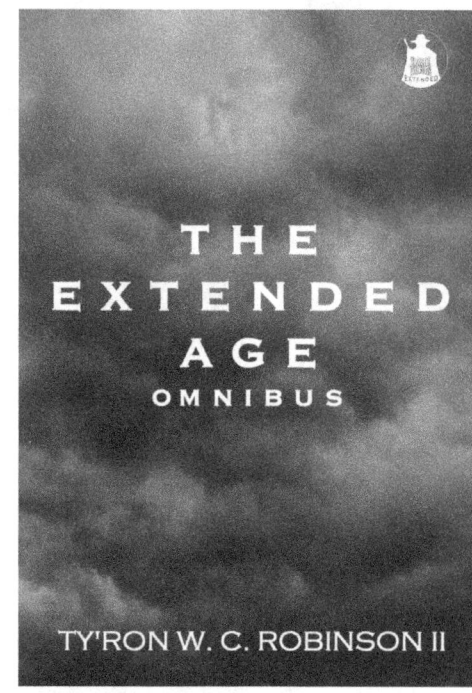

ABOUT THE AUTHOR

Ty'Ron W. C. Robinson II is the author of several works of fiction.
Including the *Dark Titan Universe Saga* series (*Dark Titan Knights,
The Resistance Protocol, Tales of the Scattered, Tales of the Numinous,
Day of Octagon*) and *The Haunted City Saga* series. Also of other books
(*Lost in Shadows, Hod, The Book of The Elect, Symbolum Venatores,
etc.*) and One-Shot short stories More information pertaining to the
author and stories can be found at darktitanentertainment.com.

FOLLOW THE AUTHOR
Twitter: @TyRonRobinsonII
Instagram: @tyronrobinsonii

FOLLOW DARK TITAN ENTERTAINMENT
Twitter: @DarkTitan_
Instagram: @darktitanentertainment
Facebook: @darktitanent
Pinterest: @darktitanentertainment

CPSIA information can be obtained
at www.ICGtesting.com
Printed in the USA
LVHW092028101220
673844LV00025B/794/J

9 781735 942964